Hat's Off to Chancey!

"As a dedicated bibliophile I sav ~ ...cey On Top,
obscene. Yes, a sexually exp ...tagonist with
█████████████████ * But : silky covers,
that sensual sojourn is wildly el ...he intricate,
multi-layered plot showcases a ...ıı, including seamless
poetic interludes from the come ...ume. The dazzling denouement
then ultimately ranks this literary ʋonbon among the finest novels ever. Sure,
the hero, Chancey Haste, is a two-timer, but so is the novel. It is one of those
rare works whose cunning moves arouse even as they satisfy. So once is not
enough. Full revelation begs the subtle master strokes be savored slowly, second
time through."—*New York Observer* review by American Civil Liberties Union
president, Nadine Strossen, from remarks to a disquistion into *Chancey On
Top* at the National Arts Club.

"Philosophically savvy, hilarious, whimsical—inspired."—Kirkus Reviews

---

"Stunning . . . ardent . . . strange and affecting. An unusual spin on a love
triangle—an exploration of moral quandaries and the passionate heights of
sensual love from leadership consultant John Wareham, whose writing is assured
throughout."—Publishers Weekly

"Hat's Off to Chancey! The greatest contemporary showcasing of the sonnet
form, in my humble opinion."—Charles Defanti, Prof. of Literature Kean University, author *The Wages of Expectation: the Biography of Edward Dahlberg.*

"Profound, profane, funny and unputdownable . . . eye-popping scenes and
insights. Chandler Haste himself is something new: a highly literate corporate
creature in hot pursuit of money, love and enlightenment—even as God, the
Devil and various sacred cows seem to be in pursuit of him. Beautifully written
and ultimately uplifting."— Prof. Eli Noam, Columbia Business School

---

"Those who find their wisdom in wild and witty packaging will love Chancey.
A beautifully written, deeply moving novel that chronicles a riveting psychological journey that sweeps the reader to a shattering catharsis. The end comes
all too quickly, but the characters live on."— Bernard Berkowitz, Ph.D. clincal
psychologist, co-author, *How To Be Your Own Best Friend*

"A magnificent yarn . . . funny and sexy . . . racy and contentious . . . literary and
erudite . . . ultimately profound and moving. Captures the inner conflicts of
conscience and provides authentic insights into attachments and transitions,
love and enlightenment, and the struggles so many upward-strivers
experience."—Harry Levinson Ph.D., clinical psychologist, author, *CEO:
Corporate Leadership in Action*, professor, Harvard Medical School

---

* Name intentionally suppressed above; important to the story and best discovered by the reader.

Chancey On Top

a novel

John Wareham, founder and chief of a leadership development firm, has authored several bestsellers, including *Secrets of a Corporate Headhunter* and *How to Break Out of Prison.* He has published widely, including articles and Op-Ed pieces in *The New York Times* and the *Financial Times.* In addition to his business interests he is founder and chairman of the Eagles Foundation, a non-profit corporation dedicated to developing leaders from the prison population and the socially disadvantaged.

On the Web
Authors Guild: *www.johnwareham.com*
Corporate Services: *www.wareham.org*
Pro Bono: *www.eaglesusa.org*

Chancey On Top

a novel

John Wareham

 Welcome Rain Publishers

1st Edition, Hardcover ,2003
Welcome Rain Publishers LLC, New York

2nd Edition, Soft Cover, 2005
Welcome Rain LLC, New York and London
Library of Congress CIP data available from the publisher.

Direct any inquiries to
www.chanceyontop.com

ISBN 1-56649-174-6

Printed by Hamilton Printers

2nd Edition:June 2005
1 3 5 7 9 10 8 6 4 2

Dedicated to Margaret

Salutations

Writing a novel brought me into contact with many intriguing people, not all of them fictional, whose encouragement inevitably proved more valuable than they realized, including, C.C. Lyon, Bernie Mindich, Geoff Loftus, Harry Ford, John McLean, Rob Rohr, Al Vogl, Jennifer Wynn, Kevin Roberts, Roger Donald, Ani Kavafian, Roger Steele, Ken Davidson, Noela Whitton, Roger Robinson, Chris Marlowe, Kenny Johnson, Danelle McCafferty, Ed Burlingame, Peter Isaac, Bill Manhire, Margaret Petersen, Eddie de Vere, Chris Hendry, Craig Rubano, Kati Holloway, Peter Cooper, Kristen Kirkland, Charles Defanti, John Weber, and Chuck Kim, and, of course, my wife Margaret and our four adult children, Anthony, Dean, Louise, and Jonathan.

Caveat

The literary middleman William Hall, the pair of patrician politicians in New York, the sexually audacious, diademed blonde in the United Kingdom, and Professor Brian Sutton-Smith of the University of Pennsylvania—whose concord is greatly appreciated—all at one time or another drew breath, though not always released it to form the words quoted. The name of a particular aircraft also inspired a *double entendre*, and this conceit, possibly purloined by savvy scriptwriters from an early *Chancey On Top* manuscript, apparently inspired two subsequent Hollywood movies. Otherwise, the characters herein dwell only inside the author's head, which is the only place they've ever lived, and the events chronicled happened in that same terrain and nowhere else. Any resemblance to any other event or person, living or dead, is therefore either entirely coincidental or a figment of the reader's imagination.

Chancey On Top

a novel

"Writers, professors, businessmen and lovers
are often absent-minded;
only the last two are dreaming
of the pleasures of conquest".

—Benjamin Franklin
Poor Richard's Almanac

Part One

Down Under Dreams

"Lust . . .
Savage, extreme, rude, cruel, not to trust;
Mad in pursuit, and in possession so;
Had, having, and in quest to have extreme;
A bliss in proof, and proved, a very woe;
Before, a joy proposed; behind, a dream."

—William Shakespeare
129th Sonnet

Prologue

THAT COULDN'T BE HER FACE.
Not in the rearview mirror.
Could it?

No. Just a fleeting fragment of memory. And he's probably hyped—his entire life's going to change in just a couple of hours, after all. So put her out of mind. The Connecticut-bound limo climbs onto the Triboro Bridge. Did she even exist? Wasn't she just an illusion?

He massages the ache in his malformed foot then peers into the mirror again. She's not there now, anyway. Just his favorite Manhattan vista. His eye travels south to north. That's right to left in the mirror. How does that work again? No one can explain it. Never mind.

Midafternoon sun bounces from the overwhelming Twin Towers. They seem almost to ascend, as the Tower of Babel never could, to heaven itself. Now comes the Empire State, the bejeweled Chrysler, Citibank's newfangled triangle. Is this the City of Oz, or what?

He hunkers into the gray velvet, closes his eyes. One of those persistent verses foxtrots into his brain:

> I'm a gung-ho
> ### CEO
> Taking care to never show
> Any care, concern or woe—

Hey, forget your dreamy doggerel, Chancey—something's happening. The air's suddenly warmer. He starts and stares through the Plexiglas sunroof. And that sky's infinitely brighter. He checks the mirror. And blinks. Hey! How did that happen? Sydney— gorgeous, gleaming, sun-filled, salty-aired *Sydney!* Dazzling water. Spinnakered yachts. Smoky tails atop funneled green ferries. The ivory-shelled Opera House—it's not quite complete, so this must be the seventies. And over there, in the cityscape, peering from a high-rise window, a young man's innocent, inquiring emerald eyes.

The eyes, in fact, that used to be his own . . .

1

Faces

J UST LOOK AT THAT GAGGLE OF gleaming yachts out
on the harbor over there, to the left of the Opera House, spin
nakers flying—

"Hey, Chancey!"

That honeyed voice at his back belongs to Ungerford Crawley.
"The Financial Review says the recovery's at hand, Chief."

Chief. Is that flattery or what?

"Nineteen seventy-three'll be a boomer, Chief."

Is it smarminess or suavity?

"We'll be Lazarus back from the dead, Chief."

Or maybe it's just ironic tweaking—never put that past him.

"I sure hope so, Crawley"—a gentle flick of the impediment
impels the green woolen-upholstered swivel chair to revolve—"we'll
go belly-up otherwise." He offers Crawley a smile, moves his weight
to his custom shoes, and draws himself to full five feet ten inches
accorded by his left foot, which is to say one and seven-eighths of
an inch higher than permitted by the right. He stands erect but the
gait's sometimes a little off. Big deal. He pats his blow-dried, sandy
hair, straightens his red tie, and taps the matching handkerchief in
his powder blue suit. "I mean, there's no money in headhunting
when no one's hiring, right?"

"Right as usual, Chief." Crawley's eyes dip. He seems never
to make eye contact. Not pupil to pupil anyway.

The tan carpet's soft beneath the aching foot. He strolls past
Crawley to the orange vinyl door and pushes it ajar. Three secretaries
are pounding at those new-fangled so-called automatic typewriters.
If only he could turn that cacophony into cash. He paces back to
the window. "Every advantage imaginable, Crawley, and we're sailing
like a wharf."

He spins, stoops, and plucks a thread from the carpet before Crawley's shapeless black shoes. They're a hangover from his kneeling days as an Anglican deacon. Or maybe he picked them up in a thrift shop. Quite a contrast with those poncey Elvis-flares on otherwise snug seersucker trousers. And there's that ghastly Ming-blue tie again. And the stuck-out jaw above it. Double occlusion, bottom teeth clenched over the top—makes for an uneven shave. He's losing the battle of the hair, too. Camouflages the bald spot with thatch dragged from one side then gums it down with hairspray. Who's he fooling? Hard to believe he's only thirty. But that's Crawley. Disguised to elude the Hound of Heaven. Afraid that God'll catch his eye and ask him where he's going with his life.

"We've got beautiful offices, Chancey."

"Maybe not for long. The rent's three months past due. And that goddamned printer's pressing. He called me an upstart, actually."

"You're an entrepreneur, Chancey. You'll turn the water into wine."

"Maybe so—this's a bamboo business. With the right people and even a modest market upturn, we could go from barren earth to jungle foliage in mere months. And when that happens we'll be looking for bigger pastures to play in."

"We'll expand the whole operation to the modern Mecca, Chancey—Manhattan." *Manhattan*—Crawley's big dream. "Then you'll really make everyone sit up and take notice."

Might the old man ever sit up and take notice? Chancey was never in the same league, according to that hypercompetitive curmudgeon. Then mind and money ran out. Now Chancey's footing the sanatorium tag—

"I've come for the money!"

That enraged voice is vibrating through the walls.

Crawley cracks the door and his face whitens. "He's crashed reception?"

"Who?"

"Old man Burnham. The printer. He's come for his money."

"We can't cough up thirty thousand dollars at half past two on a Friday afternoon. Or anytime soon."

"We'll talk him down."

"Even a ten-dollar check would bounce."

"Are you sure of that?"

"The salaries cleared—with nothing to spare—only yesterday."

"Grace under pressure, Chancey. We'll negotiate something. He'll create a scene otherwise. You okay there, Chief?"

I've a mouthful of numbers,
A mindful of dares,
A brainful of Valium,
A soulful of cares—

"Yeah, just thinking. We'll pay the devil his due, in full, as promised. But he'll have to wait, even for partial payment. It'll be months before he can get anything."

"We'll have to at least see him though, Chancey. And when we're face to face, you'll know exactly what to say."

AUCKLAND, NEW ZEALAND

HA FUCKING HA. MR. FULLER FYFE. RAINMAKER OF GODZONE, that's what this polished brass desk plaque says. It was awarded to him by Chancey—who flew all the way over from Sydney to this very Auckland office to make the presentation. Won and awarded and there it sits. Trouble is there's a subtle subscript: *What have you done for me lately?* In this business, you're only as good as your last placement.

And there's a typically hazy, sticky Auckland sky outside that modest window. It's an okay climate but inevitably balmier than ideal. A couple of skyscrapers are rising down by the harbor. They say that one of them might exceed twenty floors. Big deal. Auckland's a big city with a backwater feel—no wonder he so often feels like an eagle in a canary cage. Maybe that's why he's putting on weight. Oh, Christ, just twenty-fucking-seven years old and already approaching middle age. *De-press-ing.* See that degree certificate on the wall behind the desk? Well, that's *his. He* completed it. Okay, so it wasn't medicine or law. And his grades were rotten. And it took forever. But who cares? The certificate's on the wall. *On the fucking wall.* And recruiting's becoming a profession, too. If you're a professional it's a profession. Chancey says that. Easy for Bigfoot to say. The little Rumpelstiltskin's got people spinning gold for him.

Decent, hardworking people with degrees. Who was the prick who said that people only got into recruiting after failing at all else? Very funny, oh yeah, sure, very funny. Ha fucking ha. Okay, so they call him—and him alone—the Rainmaker of Godzone for very good reason. Never forget that. What they don't appreciate, however—neither Chancey nor that Crawley sidekick of his in their glitzy Sydney offices raking in all the shekels—is the *mountain* of spadework that precedes the actual *consulting* side of things.

Okay, then, time to ease himself into the prison of this black vinyl swivel chair, lock his feet under this tidy teak desk, and contemplate the double-broadsheet recruitment pages of the *New Zealand Herald*. There's *gold* in those columns. You just have to know how to extract it.

He grabs the scissors and clips out six advertisements—six beseeching supplications, surely—and tapes each to an index card. A quick perusal of the phone book reveals the matching telephone numbers. His heart's racing. He's ready for battle. Well, almost. He reaches beyond the elegant silver flask in his desk drawer, grabs his dog-eared copy of *How to Sell Anything to Anybody*, and turns to his favorite page:

> Selling is a numbers game. The more calls you make, the more success you'll enjoy. Bless every rejection. For, according to the law of averages, every rebuff brings you closer to ultimate success.

How very true, how utterly profound.

> Listen to me my friend: Wherever you are in the world, whatever your stage in life and whatever your educational accomplishments—or seeming lack thereof—it all begins with the first call! So MAKE THAT CALL—I DARE YOU!

Hey, you're talking to the Rainmaker of Godzone, mister. So let's accept that dare, stuff you back in your drawer, and take a closer look at the cry for help attached to this particular index card:

Dynamic Cost Accountant
Generous salary + superannuation plan +
car allowance & subsidized executive cafeteria lunches

Immediate opening for a dynamic qualified
accountant to join the executive team in newly
renovated, air-conditioned headquarters. Must be 28
to 32 years of age with three years costing experience.
Demands stable married man. Applications strictly
in writing to:
Mr. Bruce McGillicuddy, Managing Director
Tru-Hold Septic Tank and Pump Company
11451 Mangere Road, South Auckland

Holy shit! Doesn't this McGillicuddy, whoever he is, know
that cost accountants are as scarce as unsullied altar boys? And
someone in this age range? Give me a fucking break. They'll never
find anyone to traipse out to that forlorn, swampland airport. Not
even for an elephantine kickback on hare pie. Somebody should
tell him. So grab the phone and wind the dial. "May I speak to
Bruce McGillicuddy?"

"Whom may I say is calling?" Snotty bitch.

"Fuller Fyfe. I'm calling on a sensitive personal matter."

"One moment, Mister Fyfe."

"Bruce McGillicuddy." Bruce's voice is a touch testy. Apparently
the old memory needs a little jogging.

"Hi, Bruce. Fuller Fyfe, with Chandler Haste and Company.
We met at the Management Institute."

"We did?"

"As I recall."

"My secretary said the call was personal."

"She did? Oh, yes. But no. Not *personal*—personnel. Perso*nnel.*
I spend my time talking to movers and shakers like yourself, Bruce,
and, as you can imagine, I hear heaps of hush-hush stuff. I heard
on the grapevine, for instance, that Tru-Hold's into succession
planning—"

"You heard that?"

"Got it on the QT that you might need a top financial wallah."

"We handle our own recruiting."

"Sure, Bruce. I only called because I have an on-file, go-getting,
twenty-nine-year-old accountant who happens to live in your neck
of the woods."

"He does?"

"Sure. We've checked his references and run our tests on him, too. He came up trumps. Stable and married, too."

"Does he have costing experience?"

"Three and a half years."

"What's his name?"

"Ethically I can't release personal information without candidate permission. But you'd like to see him, I take it."

"Too right—but at what sort of fee?"

"Nothing unless he joins. And a refund if he's gone within four months. Can't do better than that. I'll chase him up for you right now."

He cradles the phone and gazes out the window. A bus thunders down Queen Street. Ah, if only such a bright-eyed young fellow actually existed. How easy life might be. But, hey—what's *this*? Aha!

SYDNEY

ASK YOURSELF A QUESTION, CHANCEY. Can courtesy calm the heart of an angry creditor? Can it buy a little time? Crawley's long on tact so let him to the talking.

"Glad you could drop by, Mister Burnham."

The red-haired, pasty-faced, pot-bellied printer shuns the extended hand. "We need our money." One incisor's missing. The voice is nasal and phlegm-laden.

"Of course, Mr. Burnham," says Crawley. "We'll be delighted to work something out."

"I'm through talkin'. You've had your chance. You're a hundred and fifty days past due. I need my money *now*."

Money . . .

> I've a go-getter suit
> with a catch-your-eye tie
> and a real-leather briefcase
> with nothing inside.

Rationality might win the day, so jump in, Chancey. "We always pay, Mister Burnham. We never haggle. But I have to confess that right now we're in a cash crunch—"

"With my knackers in the vise!" The bloodshot eyes blaze.

Crawley clears his throat as if about to address an elder statesman. "I suggest we pay one-quarter of your account immediately and the balance in equal installments over the next three months."

"Never!"

"It's the best we can do right now, wouldn't you say, Mister. Haste?"

Where in the name of the holy sages will Crawley find such money? "If you say so, Mister. Crawley."

Burnham softens. "I could maybe take ten thousand. Right now. Right this minute. And the balance in thirty days."

"What about eighty-five hundred now, Mister Burnham," says Crawley, "and the balance in two equal monthly installments?"

The old man' nods unhappily. Crawley glides from the room. Where the hell's he gone? Burnham's sullenly mute. How long can this awkward silence last?

> Fate's a puppeteer
> And money's his string
> And the dangling profiteer
> Is a slave and not a king

"Eight thousand five hundred dollars, Mr. Burnham." Crawley's back—and poking a company check under Burnham's nose. The beady eyes focus on the numbers. They exchange nods and Crawley stuffs the appeasing piece of paper into a manilla envelope. Burnham snatches it with a freckled fist.

"And you'll have more for me in thirty days?"

Crawley bestows his variation of the Cheshire grin: his eyelids close, his head bobs, and his lips widen but fail to reveal his teeth. Burnham, inferring an affirmative response, assents to the supposed settlement by grunting and jutting his jaw—then strutting out the door.

"He's heading for the bank, Crawley—it'll bounce."

"Too late for today. He'll have to wait'll after the weekend. And Monday's a holiday. So, Tuesday at the earliest."

"Then it'll bounce."

"It'll take a week to get into the system."

"*Then* it'll bounce."

"And so it should." Crawley smiles. "It has no signature."

"No signature?"

"He didn't notice. My thumb got in the way. When it comes back, we'll apologize for the oversight. We'll send a courier to pick up the check. It'll get lost. We'll stall for a week or two then mail it back to him. But it'll get lost again."

"We could string this out for some time."

"And something good'll happen meantime."

"Maybe. I'll hop a plane and make a one-day stopover to scare up some luck in Godzone."

"*Godzone.*" Crawley glances down his nose. "*New Zealand.* God's. Own. Country. Just sixteen hundred miles across the Tasman Ocean. Habitat of the tongue-tied, out-doors crazed Kiwi." He smiles. "Just remember when you get off the plane to set your watch back thirty years."

"We're making money over there. Some anyway. If only we could pull it out. But that's currency control." Crawley's eyes follow him as he drifts to the window. "But we can at least pluck Fyfe." He pivots on the good heel. "And I hear he's aching to be plucked."

2

Godzoners

WHAT AN ABSOLUTELY TERRIBLE SHAME. What a grave adversity. What a cause for tribulation. What a tragedy. What a *disappointment*. But wouldn't you just know it. That imaginary twenty-nine-year-old go-getting cost accountant—that prized but ever-fucking-mythical unicorn—just *happened* to take a job with another imaginary client. And just this morning, too. Oh, shit! *Who'd* have believed it? Who in-fucking-deed? Poor old Bruce McGillicuddy, that's who. But—but, but, but—there's a silver lining to every cloud. Tru-Hold's still got a job to fill. So, once again, the Rainmaker of Godzone is coming to their rescue.

A quick riffle through this bunch of cards in the pine box inherited from his failed predecessor should do the trick. Yes indeed. Now. Right *here*. A *real* prospect for Tru-Hold. But *DBB?* The fellow's been judged a *DeadBeat Bookkeeper?* That's probably very unfair. He turns the dog-eared card in his hand. Fifty-four. String of jobs. Laid off for putting his hand in the till.

Got to be objective, though, alcohol was the root of that problem. The fellow subsequently gave serious thought to going on the wagon. People can come to see the light. Got to be prepared to give them a second chance. What's the point of being an HR professional otherwise? So then, this reformed fucker—this, ah, seasoned, senior accounting professional—really could put a bit of ginger into the septic tanks. With a bit of finesse, the Rainmaker of Godzone could land a quick fee and meet the target to qualify for bonus. Ha fucking ha. Everybody wins.

He tugs at his lower desk drawer, bypasses the flask, retrieves the current issue of *Playboy,* slides it into the folded *Herald,* and heads for the lavatory.

"HEY, CHANCEY!" That outstretched paw of Fuller's is unsullied and pink. "You'd have taken us completely by surprise if that quirky Brit from *Management* magazine hadn't called."

They survey the bustling bistro and savor the suffusing scent of beef stroganoff.

"Henry Haverford? I'm having a drink with him tonight."

"He's the *Honorable* Henry Haverford, Chancey. In line for a peerage if he ever gets back to England." He grins. Something's coming. "And I hear he's got a luscious convent-school daughter he likes to show off."

"He has?"

"Yeah, a brilliant scholarship student—completed a fistful of university credits while still in high school. And has lovely long legs that go all the way up to her gray matter."

Fuller has a prurient streak and a nose for other people's business. Just as well he never became a gynecologist.

"Really."

"I hear she's maybe only seventeen."

"Seventeen?"

"I gather she was heaving against a flimsy school uniform mere weeks ago and sporting shiny braces inside perfectly puckered lips." The broad grin is a tad more impish than lascivious. "Unless, of course, her honorable father had the orifice laced with razor wire to repel the local lads."

"I'm on target, Chancey." Fuller demolishes the remains of his stroganoff and drops his fork to his plate. "Just need to close out one certainty."

Incense and the ping of cymbals waft through the air. There's a ragtag band of Hare Krishnas bouncing past the open door. But stay focused on Fuller.

"What about this DUI problem of yours, Fuller?"

"Oh, shit, Chancey. I was taking migraine medication. It fucked up the breathalyzer." The chanting's receding. "They ripped out my shoelaces and belt and tossed me in the slammer." A waiter ducks under his chin to remove the empty plate. "I had to hold up my own pants. Can you believe it? Me!"

He motions for a crème caramel.

"What happens now?

"The judge'll throw the book at me. Same thing happened last year."

Here's the opening. Drop it softly. "There's a way out, Fuller."

"There is?"

"Yes. I got a legal opinion. The judge can do absolutely nothing if you relocate to Sydney."

Fuller's pupils dilate. He's intrigued. "Really, Chancey?"

"You'd just have to officially immigrate before the trial date. Then lay low for a year or two."

"I could make a lot of money for you in Sydney, Chancey."

"For the two of us, Fuller. How do you think you'd get along with Crawley?"

"Don't know much about him."

"I hired him out of the church when no one else would. A two-way street. No one'd join me then, either."

The waiter slides the crème caramel under Fuller's nose. "I heard he lives with some other male refugee from the church."

"Who cares? He's a savvy, hard worker. Whenever we need business he comes up trumps."

"I heard he has big ambitions."

Fuller excavates a pile of custard with his spoon and elevates it to his jaw.

"Crawley got his dreams from his failed-actress mother. She scripted him to reform the world."

"Hence the stint with the church?" Fuller gulps the pudding then savors the caramel upon his tongue.

"I guess so. But now he hankers to serve in the cathedral called America. Or to write a life-altering novel."

"I'm sure I could work with him, Chancey. Just say the word."

"I'll talk to Crawley when I get back, then call you. Meantime I'm going to try to land some trans-Tasman business. After that it's on to Henry Haverford, who might just help us extract a burst of publicity somewhere."

"Maybe you could extract a burst of something from the long-legged schoolgirl, too."

HE RESTS THE IMPEDIMENT upon the polished-brass foot rail of the boisterous, tiny, humid, smoke-filled Press Bar of the Queens Ferry Hotel. The fading Roman numerals on the graying face of the phony antique clock amid the upturned, teated liquor bottles put the time at a couple of minutes past six. He checks his tie in the mirror. Sharp shade of orange. Contrasts nicely with the maroon shirt. Complements the lime suit perfectly.

He drops his focus to the weary calendar affixed by a stick pin beneath a once glossy color shot of the Franz Joseph Glacier. Yet another Godzone natural wonder. Lovely hotel up there, too. Jill's keen to make that trek. Bring the kids, maybe.

"Hey! Chancey!" Henry Haverford, balding, beaming, presses into the sweaty throng. Is *that* the daughter? Bouncing along behind him there. Very nice. Henry's outstretched hand is soft. His smile's a happy cluster of clean but yellowing, crooked teeth. "How absolutely wonderful to see you, Chancey!" The accent's Oxford. The suit's rumpled charcoal, the shirt white, the collar frayed but starched, the tie a lifeless regimental; the burnished but broken-down black shoes are well heeled. "Allow me to introduce my daughter, Elan." Hey, what a lovely, winsome smile. "Watch out now, Elan, for this is Chandler Haste, the celebrated headhunter, and, at just thirty-two years old as I recall, something of a biz whiz.*"* He chuckles. "Eh! Chancey! Eh!"

Striking, indeed. Light perfume. Radiant complexion. Shining cinnamon hair cascading to the small of her back. About his height, say five-eight. Trim body sheathed to just above the knee in a neat if tired forest-green lamb's wool. Full sail. Long, lithe legs. Scuffed black pumps. Might the dress be a hand-me-down? Maybe. And those jade hair clips seem plastic. No matter. Just look at that face: large, inviting, deep-set, slate-gray eyes and a perfectly proportioned Roman nose. If she inherited her father's uneven teeth you'd never know it. What a gorgeous, full-mouthed smile. That Kiwi orthodontist's earned every cent of his fee. She's a stunning blend of innocence, warmth, vulnerability, sensuousness, and mystery. She's an amalgam of Botticelli and Norman Lindsay. Whatever, however, whenever, did God manage to misplant such an exotic flower into Godzone soil?

"Chancey's disguising himself as an Aussie executive these days," says Henry to Elan. "They love their shiny suits and cocky colors. But beneath the plumage, he's still one hundred and ten percent Kiwi."

"Perhaps, but I'm thinking of opening an office in New York." Henry seems impressed. Elan's smile is merely enigmatic. "Maybe London, also."

She offers long, slim fingers. They're soft and supple, too. "Ambition could surely not be made of sterner stuff." The voice, though bereft of accent, is subtly laced with class.

"You're quoting Shakespeare to me?"

"Oh, Mister. Haste—a colonial who knows his *Julius Caesar*? How can that be?" A drop of adrenaline flickers in his spine. Is this stunning teenage Brit attempting to mock him? Well, at least he's caught her interest. "As I remember that line belonged to Mark Antony."

She beams. She's poised beyond her years. "Forgive my joshing, Mr. Haste." Josheen—she confects a lovely almost Irish lilt. Where'd she pick that up? "And you're right—the play *was* Caesar, but the line was delivered by Mark Antony."

"Over Caesar's corpse, as I recall."

"With great irony, too. Who, after all, could be more ambitious than a Roman emperor?" She grins. "Not that I imagine you to be dying, Mr. Haste." *Dyeen*—that lilt again. She certainly seems to know her subject. So Fuller was right, brains and beauty both.

Henry smooths his short-back-and-sides. "You'll have a Bass ale won't you, Chancey?"

"Sure. But let me get the drinks. Bass all around, right?"

The barman whisks up three glistening, foam-capped mugs.

"To peripatetic people wherever they gather," says Henry. Amid background laughter they touch mugs, and glance across the foam. As Elan tilts her glass to those decidedly vulnerable lips an overhead spotlight gently bathes her face.

God she's lovely. The complexion's luminous. Where does that kind of magnetism come from? If, as they say, the eyes are windows to the soul, then she's been blessed on that level, too. And her innocence to her many charms merely enhances them

"You look a little lost, Chancey. Planning your next bold business move, no doubt. Always thinking, planning, scheming. Note the vacant stare of the wild-eyed whiz, Elan. That's what it takes to break into the big time. But don't let it go to your head, Chancey. Remember Wilde's quip: 'To fall in love with oneself is the beginning of a lifelong romance.'"

"He also said that they do not sin who sin for love," says Elan.

"Did he, darling? Did he indeed? Well, look where it got him."

"You've done well, Henry."

"I've just bumbled around the world in a string of magazine jobs."

"Daddy fought in the Battle of Britain."

"Yes, darling. Navigated bombers and got out alive." He pauses. "Not everyone was so lucky. As a postwar sop the government sent me to Oxford. I studied literature, which was, of course, hopeless for the pocketbook. That's how I finished up in Godzone. Cost of living's cheap. I'm in line for a peerage back home, but the family's broke. Meantime, I've had four children to raise."

"So you take the Pope's teachings seriously—"

"Indeed." He raises his palms and his eyebrows. "God's will, Chancey. We've got to give God room to work. Elan's the baby of the family, you know—she might never've been born if we'd not been good Catholics. But, hey"—he smiles—"let me get a last round."

Henry bumbles backward into the sweaty throng.

Just look at those sparkling eyes. Has she turned up the wattage, or not? A burst of exhilaration floods his gut. Is it the Bass? The excitement of jet travel? Friday euphoria? Maybe there's a full moon. Maybe he needs someone so beguilingly versed and radiantly unaffected to realize that he exists. He should emulate Ulysses, block his ears with wax and strap himself to the mast. But there's no control. He reaches out and gently touches her fingers.

"Wilde also said," he whispers, "that a kiss can ruin a person's life."

"Wilde, too, Mister Haste—watch it!" Her wide-eyed grin's a half tease. "Wilde's the patron saint of sensitive sinners." She gingerly removes her fingers. "He'll lead you astray don't you know." Her perfume mingles with the sweet-and-bitter scent of Bass.

Henry's back all too quickly. They down the Bass as the din around them rises.

"Conversation's impossible in these surroundings, Chancey," says Henry. "I've booked for dinner in a little bistro. Maybe you'd care to join us?"

They burst out into Queen Street, Auckland's wide main thoroughfare. The air's warm, and a thank-god-it's-Friday atmosphere lights streets. The bars are full, the crowds cheery. All around, Kiwis are anesthetizing themselves with alcohol, and looking forward to their weekend sports. The threesome strolls to Henry's car, a tiny, tidy, well-worn Morris.

"You sit in the front and talk to me, Chancey," says Henry. "And you, Elan, you sit quietly in the back." The leather on the bucket seats is soft, but a fresh set of springs might be in order. The engine's loath to respond to the ignition, but finally does. Henry unleashes the ailing clutch and the vehicle staggers out into the traffic.

"Maybe I'll record your thoughts for publication," says Elan.

"Only if Chancey agrees. Be warned, Chancey. Elan has a magpie's eye for literary material, and the memory of an elephant." The Morris rattles through Auckland's red-light district. "Bear in mind, Elan, that Chancey's first dream was to be a poet. Eh, Chancey?"

"I almost won a school prize once."

"Not many competitors in Godzone, I imagine." Henry chuckles.

Her radiant eyes have appeared in the rearview mirror.

"No money, either, Henry."

Oncoming headlights refract from her shining face.

"So I'm dedicating my talent to recruitment advertising."

He's aching to reach back behind Henry's bucket seat and touch that pliant hand of hers, again. But why? She's no lovelier than Jill. Is it budding lust—"savage, rude, cruel, not to trust." Who said that? The swan of Avon, surely—who doubtless succumbed to the feeling."

"You're very quiet there, Chancey."

"I was contemplating temptation."

Henry grins. "An irresistible force at work on a movable body?"

Elan pipes up. "Wilde said he could—"

"Resist everything except temptation, Miss Haverford?"

"Yes, right!"

"Wilde was too clever for his own good," says Henry, drawing shakily into the curb, then jamming on the brake. "He wisecracked that the only way to resist temptation is to yield to it, but failed to forsee that giving in to temptation might lead to his incarceration. I mean, *that's* the moral—right, Chancey?"

"Or maybe he found something too good to miss no matter what the price."

The flimsy legs on the tiny dining table wobble on the sawdust floor, causing the red candle to flicker upon their faces.

"I turned fifty just last week," says Henry, draining his glass and reaching for the thick carafe.

Fifty. Will Chancey ever be fifty? Will he innocently parade such a darling daughter before a too-admiring family friend? He flicks her a glance. She's sitting between them. Her smile's enigmatic. He glances into a decaying mirror behind Henry's head. "I'm not intending to grow any older, Henry."

Henry aligns the battered cutlery upon the chipped white plate and pushes away the remains of the bouillabaisse. "You'd enter a Dorian Graylike pact with the devil, would you, Chancey? In exchange for your soul, your portrait ages but you don't. It won't work. Life always catches up with us. Today's plum is tomorrow's prune." His laugh uncurtains a chorus of black-fillinged teeth, and the rickety cane chair beneath him creaks.

Elan's voice comes out of a shadow. "Ram Dass says we must live in the now, Mister Haste."

Henry's bemused. "Elan's suddenly enamored of Eastern religions and Persian poets." He drains his glass.

"Just out of the convent and already she's questioning her Christian indoctrination?"

She laughs for them both. "It's the words and ideas I like. I'm not sure we need religion at all."

Words and ideas. She's into philosophy, too. He smiles into those charcoal pits. "You might be right. I'm still recovering from the priests who messed with my childhood head. So now I focus on business—the people business."

Her face glows in the candlelight. Her fingers are on the red-checkered cloth. Can't touch them there.

The bill arrives. It's very modest. Henry insists on paying.

"We'll drop you to your hotel, Chancey."

They head for the door and bundle back into the Morris. Henry cranks it into gear. There's no traffic this time. They rumble along. Henry's focused on the road. Only the stuttering engine attempts to converse. Passing streetlights paint shadows upon her face in the rearview mirror. The hotel's rapidly approaching. Unless he speaks up she'll be gone forever.

"You seem like a thinker, Elan. Maybe you could set me on the straight and narrow."

It's Henry who responds. "God's got you fretting, Chancey?"

"Not really. I just wondered what the brightest new minds are thinking."

Her smile's in the mirror. It's rather engaging. Maybe the attraction's mutual. "They say the best way to know God is to love many things."

"No time. I'm flying back to Sydney in the morning."

"The bird's on the wing?" She smiles. "Then we'll just have to meet again in some other life."

Henry grinds the Morris to a halt.

"We'll gather again in this one, surely."

Her eyes flicker. " 'And if not this parting were well made' "— she beams a bright grin. "That's the Roman soldier's farewell, you know, from *Julius Caesar*. Good-byes can be tragic, so we should never retreat without an appropriate send-off."

"On that proper note, then, I guess I can take my leave." He cracks the door, steps out onto the road, and glances back. "Thanks for everything, Henry." He presses the door closed. "Especially for the opportunity to meet this charming daughter of yours." He steals a good-bye snapshot of her smile.

Henry waves, then slams the stumbling engine into gear and pitches out into the road. The Morris emits a fog of blue exhaust as Henry navigates her over the horizon.

Catch up in some other life? He jumps backward onto the pavement and kicks the sawdust from his platform shoe. The problem with resisting temptation, of course, is that a second chance might never appear . . .

The ping of a cymbal shimmers in his eardrum and a barefooted, shaven-headed figure steps out of the shadows. It's the leader, surely, of that bunch of Hare Krishnas who boogied through the town at lunchtime. The fellow looks almost genielike in those pantaloons. Best set him straight immediately.

"Proselytizing will be pointless, my friend, I'm a fellow headhunter."

The response is measured. "Enlightenment will come, ultimately, nonetheless."

"And you'll be the channel?"

"Perhaps." A yellow streetlight falls upon the shaven pate. "For now I'm merely reproaching your covetousness."

"You're jumping to conclusions. That girl was merely the daughter of a friend. She's straight out of a convent, almost an angel, I imagine."

"Then fear for your soul." Mr. Krishna claps the tiny cymbals, flourishes them momentarily above his head, then drops them into his pocket.

"I'm not sure I believe in souls."

The waistband on the pantaloons expands as the fellow inhales. "Many Western males deny their souls." The breath is curiously pepperminted. "They suppress the spirit then wonder why their lives are numb." He offers a confiding smile. "Perhaps it will help if I confess that until my enlightenment I procured bodies rather than souls."

"You, uh, pimped?"

The hands rush to the heart. "I was in another incarnation and saw procurement as an honest living. I believed that if all parties derived pleasure I was merely promoting happiness."

"Then you saw the light and became a messenger?"

"In many ways my role is unchanged. I listen to sinners. I bring love to the broken-hearted. And I effect conversions."

"Perhaps you could share your best line for making a placement."

"I could suggest"—he pauses—"that being who we are is the key to becoming better than we are"—now comes a half smile—"but first we must realize that the person we think we are is typically an impostor and a stranger."

"All body and no soul?"

"Body and soul are not two substances but one. They are man becoming aware of himself in two different ways."

"If that's true, a lusty glance is merely a function of the soul."

"Perhaps more than you realize, for the events of life are deliberate tests of character specially devised for spiritual advance." Mr. Krishna brings his palms to his chest and forms a little steeple. "Mind is to soul as wave is to ocean, and passion in the soul makes fools of the wise."

The trouble with street genies is that they waffle.

"Can you be a tad more specific?"

"Abstinence is the path."

"Is there a middle way?"

"Temperance is troublesome."

"Maybe so, but if people love each other where's the problem wth a little excess?"

"Passion perverts the imagination, and what passes as love can be many things, including promiscuity, licentiousness, and possessiveness"—the torso moves back into the shadows, but the pale face hangs in the air like a mask—"whereas true love is as innately spiritual as the journey that reveals it. Only by such love can the soul find ultimate realization and peace."

"And that's the lesson for the day?"

"The message for the evening"—the cymbals ping again—"is that no woman ever falls in love with a man"—now the mask, too, fades into the bottle of night—"unless she has a better opinion of him than he deserves."

TRANSTASMAN AIRSPACE

THROBBING ENGINES DRAW HIM across cumulus cushions.
Fly away home, Chancey. Back you go, back. You really are happily
married, so heed the genie's advice and leave that lovely girl for the
rascals of Godzone. Yes. Put her out of mind. Yes. Obliterate that
haunting image. Yes. And silence that siren voice, too. Yes, of course.
But first, before you commit that ultimate act of guilty repentance,
why not catch her in the blue goo that oozes from this bleeding
Biro? Indeed. Enshroud all memory of her on airline notepaper,
then roll it all into a ball and toss it down into a murky tomb
beyond the tentacles of memory—

> You touched a place in me
> You fixed a space in me
> You left a face in me
> —You

She did more than that—

> You struck a spark in me
> Lit up the dark in me
> Left a raw mark in me
> —You

She set the animal prowling—

> You kissed the frog in me
> Unleashed the dog in me
> Goosed the agog in me
> —You

But she's just a tease, surely—

> But who would endeavor
> love?
> Once and forever love?
> Whithersoever love?
> —You?

No!
A smile
 in the afterglow
Where did it ever go
Who will I never know?
                    —You

SYDNEY

IS THAT BESUITED, BRIEFCASE-SWINGING reflection really him? Yes—a version, anyway, sprightly but askew, a mix of two parts Chandler Haste and one part Chancey. And, hey, who's that standing within his image and waving brightly? Not Elan, that's for sure. No, those two neatly school-uniformed kids are his own—nine-year-old Blake, and seven-year-old Angie. And right behind them, a hand on each shoulder, big, wide smile on her face, stands Jill. She loves those kids—and Chancey, too.

Open sesame! A rude burst of air-conditioning chills his face as the door slides wide, and he strides into the arrival lounge. Angie squeals and rushes forward. But his eyes are on Jill. She's five feet two and 115 strong, square, lean pounds. Her high, wide cheekbones frame large blue eyes, a chiseled nose, a sensuous mouth—though she denies that—and even, pearl-white teeth. She's insouciant, as ever, in red cotton slacks, black silk blouse, red canvas shoes, and red-scarfed hair. The whole effect is complemented by a touch of eye shadow, a hint of lipstick, and traces of subtle perfume. She looks altogether too young to be the mother of these kids. He plunges in and tugs her to him. Angie's wrapped around his hips. Jill's peck is slightly coy. She's often a touch demure when he returns from a business trip. The smile's warm as ever, though. "Welcome home, lover-boy. We missed you."

Lover-boy. She likes to tweak him. Sardonic, that's the word for her lover-boy shtick. Unless her intuitions are on the prowl.

"Yeah, we missed you, Dad." Angie swings on one foot, lithe and slim. She's got her mother's huge eyes. He swings her up and pecks her on the cheek. "No need to miss me now." Blake needs a burst of attention, too. "And you, demon. How've you been?" No answer. Blake just stares off into the throng of arriving passengers. He's going through a surly stage. Jill's got her eye on him, though. She'll straighten him out.

"WHAT A PLACE TO COME HOME TO." He slips through the ranch-slider doors of the beige-bricked, double-decked, waterfront duplex. Jill didn't hear him. Maybe just as well since he's still a touch infatuated with the memory of that beguiling Brit. "That Opera House really does seem close enough to touch, Jilly." She still doesn't hear him.

A warm, sweet scent, laced with salt and diesel, catches in his nostrils. It's coming from Neutral Bay wharf, a hundred or so yards beyond that cluster of rubied camellia trees. The ferry kicks up water, gathers speed, and plows toward the city skyscrapers. It's fun to be home, but, gosh, it might also be great to be plowing back to the Queens Ferry. But, no, it was just a momentary fancy. A momentary *fantasy*, actually. So get real.

He steps back inside. They're just renting but that doesn't matter. When they had to sell the other house to pay the bills. Jill said she didn't care—nor did she seem to, either. This's more fun. Anyway, he'll make it all back and buy another house. Maybe even buy—or lease—a yacht.

Now there's a thought—and a thousand more to ponder in the hefty original oil painting that sits so nicely on that cedar wall. You can see anything you want in an abstract. Even that beguiling face.

No, Elan'd not disappoint. The mere memory of her guns a burst of adrenaline. Yet why? They met only once and nothing happened.

Jill certainly got value when she discovered this place. That convict-hewn, clinker-brick fireplace is an authentic status symbol. And there's Jill and Chancey, imprisoned in a monochrome mantel photo, astride his gleaming Triumph motorcycle. They look like kids. Hell, they *were* kids. She's on the pillion, jacketed and bejeaned, arms around him. He, in corduroys and brown leather jacket, is balancing everything with his left foot. They went everywhere, did everything, on that machine. Everything.

And there's Jill's reflection in the mantel mirror. She's in the bedroom, sorting out his gear. She's working at the nuts and bolts of marriage. So should he.

The white wool plucks at his bad foot as he steps past the velvet-upholstered Scandinavian couch into the bedroom, and strides past Jill into the ivory-tiled, en-suite bathroom.

She catches his eye in the bathroom mirror. "Good trip, lover-boy?"

There's that Jillian irony again. "Grueling." He straightens his trousers, saunters to the bedroom, grabs her hand, and leads her into the living room. "But what'd you do while I was away, Jilly?"

"Missed you. But the kids kept me company—didn't you?" Blake, in his blue shorts and gray safari shirt, says nothing. Angie, in blue cotton dress and basketball sneakers nods sheepishly. "Blake got into a spot of trouble."

"Trouble?"

"Smashed a window. Got sent to the headmaster."

"What do you say about this, Blake?"

"Nothing left to say."

"You're a shifty rebel, Blake." Blake's staring at the floor. "And I guess it's not the first time you've attracted attention." He grabs the reluctant radical by the shoulders and spins him around. "He'll be okay, Jill. Just spreading his wings."

"Angie's got something to tell her dad."

"Got A's on my essays!"

"Hey, bravo! You're not just pretty, you're an academic, too." Angie beams. Blake's slipped away. He's always got some secret somewhere.

Condensation sparkles on the glass of Bass that Jill's slipped into his outstretched hand. She slips into her wicker chair and raises a glass of chilled white. Harbor lights are blinking.

"Did you meet anyone interesting?"

"Not really. I had lunch with Fuller Fyfe and dinner with Henry Haverford. Might have to go back soon, though. I could have something bubbling." Bubbling and smiling and lilting and saying clever things.

"Can't you deal with it by phone? The kids really miss you."

"Yes, it's a drag, I know." He catches her wide blue eyes. She looks so soft, smells so good, sits so gracefully, cooks so well, looks out for him so solicitously, and is such fun in bed. Who'd guess her psyche's forged of solid steel? "How're your silent friends?"

"Those kids are not just silent, Chancey. They're autistic. And they're like family. It'd be easier if they weren't. They block me out. It's depressing. Rejection's a new experience." She smiles "But the Haste and Company donation was good for morale."

"Five hundred dollars won't buy much—but the check cleared, right?"

"A couple of weeks ago." Her eyes widen. "Should it not've?"

"Just got low there for a day or two. But the tide's turned."

She smiles. "So you think you might get lucky, then?" She raises her glass impishly.

"I'd drink to that, Jilly."

In the dream he's riding on the rear seat of a tandem bicycle, escorting a georgeous teenage girl. He impulsively reaches forward to fondle her breasts. He's shocked to discover that she's clutching a loaded revolver.

3

Destinies

MAYBE THAT SHIMMERING HARBOR could double as a Rorschach inkblot. For, see, there, just beyond the ripples of northerly breeze in the water, that's Elan's profile, surely. Something about the way the light caught her: the promising eyes, the laughing smile, the inviting lips. Well, there she goes, her image vanquished by a passing cloud. He strides to his desk and studies this month's check for the old man's nursing home. Will it bounce? Will they push him onto the street? There's a thought. Crawley says trust in God. So let it go—

"Maybe Fyfe's heaven-sent." Crawley's crept in. "God knows you can't carry everything on your own shoulders."

"Trouble is, Fuller milks his clients. He'd be more effective if he knew when to ease up."

"Why doesn't he, Chancey?"

"He's money-and-status-hungry. His father was a failed social climber. Never quite got off his knees—owned a trouser bar and always had his thumb and a tape measure tickling someone's testicles. He desperately wanted Fuller to become a doctor."

"A healer." Crawley nods. "What does the father do now?"

"Depends upon one's religious perspective. He rolled his secondhand Bentley and killed himself." Crawley's eyelids flutter. "Fuller was in his teens. The car was on the never-never and the bank repossessed it."

"So Fuller's driven by the spur of poverty?"

"And status. Never got into med school."

"If only we could instill your ethical framework into Fuller."

"He's unmanageable from this distance."

"Let's pluck him from Godzone before the judge puts him away."

"You're right! Let's get him on the phone *now*." He dials and Crawley purrs, delighted to have inspired a little action. "Just pray he doesn't screw up over here, Crawley." He swings on his good heel. "Hey there! Fuller! Said I'd get back to you—"

"Hey! Chancey!"

"I'm talking with Crawley. The consensus is that your brush with the law might've been inspired."

"Divine intervention? Really?" The voice is hushed.

"Destiny's written all over it, Fuller! A happy outcome for you. A big bonus for the Aussies. And great for the firm."

"You want me before the end of the month?"

"The sooner the better. We'll put you up at the Travelodge till you find an apartment."

Fullerian pause. "I was hoping to stay at the, uh, Wentworth."

"The *Wentworth*? That's a big number."

"I want to make you rich, Chancey. A harborside suite'd impress my subconscious. I'd pick up big-ticket business right away. None of this purchasing-officer shit."

"A harbor suite? Hell, Fuller, you'll break the bank before you reach the office."

"Break the bank!" The voice quavers. "We're not financially secure?"

"A figure of speech, Fuller. We're as solid as anyone. Crawley'll handle the details. Here, talk to him."

Crawley fondles the phone. "We'll do the right thing by you every step of the way, Fuller." He's giving a pastoral performance. "Yes, yes of course, *everyone's* looking forward to working with you. You're a *legend* around here. Yes—a really *lovely* suite." He cradles the handset.

"That's Fuller for you, Crawley. Not even in the country and already begging for a golden hello."

"But as you say, Chancey, that's the stuff of the sales star: needy, greedy, and charming." Crawley looks at his watch, then, ever the thespian, sets himself for a dramatic exit. His back's suddenly stiff as a ramrod. His eyes are resolutely fixed on some vacant inner space. He glides towards the door as if borne by roller casters. He stops in the frame, glances out, then back. "Your other potential eager beaver's pacing in reception, Chancey."

"I have an appointment? Let me see, now." He fingers the leather-bound, gilt-monogrammed *London Times* desk calendar. Wrong country, but, hell, it looks nice. "Oh, yes. Richard Brittle." He grins. "Or is it Brittle Dick?"

"ETHICS ARE CENTRAL TO MY PERSONALITY." Richard Brittle's crisp, twenty-eight-year-old voice carries a faintly whiny north of England accent.

The face is fresh and earnest—but no one would ever mistake it for Elan's. Steel-rimmed, squared-lensed spectacles. Short-back-and-sides haircut. Gray suit, white shirt, black shoes. Is that a private-school tie? Probably.

"I inherited my high principles from my father," Brittle continues. "He was from England. In the army. Retired as captain. We arrived here twenty years ago when I was eight. I'm the only child, which didn't do me any harm. I excelled at Cranbrook then got my MBA at Sydney University, topping the class."

Topping the class, my, my . . .

> I've a head for business
> and communication skills
> You can trust my judgment
> to cure your ills—

"First in the class. That's a wonderful achievement."

"Well not actually *top*." He's momentarily abashed. "But *in* the top. I got all A's. That got me into a big-chain retailing program. But it wasn't really me."

"You like the idea of recruiting?"

"On a recent trip home to England I saw that it was a real growth industry." Brittle pauses. "People say it's going to be like printing your own money." He smiles uncomfortably. He clearly hadn't quite meant to let that slip. "Of course if I'm to be working as a recruiter, I'd need to feel I was working within a highly principled organization." He tugs at his tie. "My fiancee, Bronwyn, feels the same way. We'll be moving to the North Shore. We have our eye on a place in Saint Ives."

"Saint Ives—that might cost a pretty penny."

"We'll start out with the smallest house among the best people."

No, that bespectacled face would never be mistaken for her face. But it might well inspire a clean-cut client's confidence.

"I never much understood about ethics."

Brittle blinks. "Haste and Company hasn't committed its ethical creed to paper?"

"My father used to say that people who hang their ethical creeds probably need to."

"We need to know what we believe."

"One day I'll know what I believe. Meantime I just want to be able to come back and look every candidate and every client in the eye and know I did the right thing. If I can manage that I figure I'm as good as the next guy."

"That has the virtue of pragmatism."

"So we have a deal then?"

"You have better than a deal, you have the word of Richard Brittle."

The words inspire, yet the grip's surprisingly flaccid.

> Never recruit
> An empty suit

BRITTLE TRAILS NO SCENT, but Crawley divines his exit nonetheless, and pokes his head inside the door. "Brittle's on board, then, Chief?"

"You seem surprised."

"Wasn't too sure he's our type."

"Ambitious, money-hungry, status-driven—that's not our type?"

"He seems green and priggish."

"Let's see what he can do."

"By their fruits ye shall know them."

Beyond the window a gleaming plane spurts a tail of fumes onto the bright blue sky. Catch up in some other life? Leave that vulnerable girl to the hairy-legged, rugby-mad rascals of Godzone?

That's the right and proper way to go, of course. But there'd be no harm in talking to her. Conversation's just words, right?

"Meantime, Crawley, I've got to hop over to Godzone."

"You really should. The founder's feet make the best manure— ah, no, what I mean to say there, Chancey, is that, uh, when the cat's away the mice will play." Those fumes are fading in the sky. "So let them know not when the master of the house cometh."

4

Couples

"IT'S ME, CHANCEY HASTE. We met three weeks ago."
Silence. He's pacing the tiny Auckland boardroom. "I'm
over to talk to a client." He catches sight of himself in
the mirror. "And to you, too, of course." His breath creates a film
of condensation on the phone. "You agreed we'd be friends."

"I changed my mind when we exchanged tragic good-byes."
Her voice is gently mocking. It was a mistake to call her.

"Well, then"—he pauses—"I guess it's farewell."

"Farewell?—sounds very Elizabethan."

"I was in mind of a line from a poem."

"Really?" She's saying *show me*.

So give it a shot. "Yeah—'Farewell, thou art too dear for my
possessing.'"

"Hey, that's from the sonnets, right?"

"As I recall. Care to chat about it over dinner?"

"I don't think so. I mean, tragic good-byes really do trump
everything."

"I shouldn't have pressed, I'm sorry—it's just that I've one
night in town, and I'm alone."

She pauses. "My pursuer sounds a truly tempting tongue."

"Now, there's a nice line—whose is *that*?"

"I made it up. I might use it in a sonnet of my own—just
need eleven more lines."

"I thought a sonnet had fourteen lines."

"I was testing you. Yeah. Three quatrains and a kicker."

"A kicker?"

"Yeah, the last two lines are the kicker. They sum it all up."

"And spell out an ironic moral."

"So"—she pauses—"you do know about poetry then."

"A little. I know what I like."

She pauses. "I guess I could maybe keep you company."

"In the Great Northern at seven?"

"I'll do it." She's gone.

SHE ARRIVES IN THE SAME green lamb's-wool sheath. The carburetor that controls his heart gives it a burst. The tortoiseshell clips in her hair are imitation. She's wearing a hint of eye shadow, and a touch of lipstick. A neat black vinyl bag hangs from her shoulder.

They peer into the cream-walled dining room. A hefty chandelier lights up a dozen or so murmuring guests sitting upon white cane chairs at pink tables. In the corner of the room sits a large cage, the home of two huge parrots, one green, one orange.

"A table for two, sir?"

"Please."

A white-jacketed waiter seats them alongside the parakeets. "We're recommending the fresh broiled snapper with sweet new-season potatoes."

"Sound okay to you, Elan? Yes—then we'll have that for two, and a carafe of the house white wine, thanks, waiter."

Elan's quiet but one of the parrots is cackling softly.

The waiter returns, pours the wine, then departs.

"I'm not sure I should be here, Chancey."

He raises and tips his glass. "No point quibbling with the gods."

"Quibbling with the gods?" *Quibbleen.* Her eyes are wide, mocking. She sips the Chardonnay.

"They wanted us to meet. They know there're chords in us that need to be struck by other people." He reaches for her hand. "Especially by a Kiwi girl who quotes Wilde." Her fingers are soft and pliant. "And does it with an almost Irish lilt. Where'd you pick that up?"

"I don't really know. And I'm English, by the way." The soft light refracts in her cinnamon hair. "Well, maybe. I've lived all over, including spells in Capetown and Toronto."

She unslips her hand as the waiter returns with the snapper. He gently sets the two plates down. It's nicely presented, with lemon on the fish, parsley and butter on the new potatoes. As the waiter disappears, they spread their starched white napkins, then reach for the antique cutlery.

"Your literary interests seem as eclectic as your domains."

"I guess I love most things. Wilde and Donne. Thomas Mann and Herman Hesse. And the Beatles, of course—Maxwell's silver hammer and all that."

She's forgotten her reticence.

"Anyone else?"

"The Stones and Jerry Garcia. And the Bee Gees. And Mahler. A friend also recently turned me onto Schopenhauer."

"What'd she write?"

"Don't try to con me. *He* says most people are zombies."

"Zombies?"

"Eleanor Rigbys who wake up too late—if ever."

"But Shakespeare's your first love?"

"A close friend, anyway. I'm studying him for my B.Lit. I've already learned"—she gives him a soft stare—"that 'love's like a child that longs for everything it can come by.'" She smiles. "Duke of Milan, *Two Gentlemen of Verona.*"

A subtle remonstrance, surely. On the bright side, she's not noticed that while they've been finishing their second carafe, the other diners have been quietly departing. Everything closes too quickly in Godzone.

"You think I'm a child who longs for everything I can come by?"

"What I think, Mister Haste"—she sets down her fork and glances about her—"is that we're almost the last couple in the room."

"Hey, you're right—you've proved Einstein's theory of relativity."

She smiles. "I'll bite, Chancey—how?"

He reaches forward and touches her fingers. "By demonstrating that time accelerates when you're having fun."

She pauses and sighs. "Look. I have a confession." She smiles. "I agreed to come because you're the only Godzone male I know with a taste for poetry. And all that outdoors stuff they go on about here sometimes leaves me feeling, uh—"

"Lonely?"

"Hey, you know the feeling. Well, don't get me wrong. I'm not just a pseudy Brit. I just happen—"

He wraps her hand in his. "To love poetry."

"Yes. I brought my copy of Will's sonnets along, by the way."

"Will?"

"Shakespeare—since he's a friend, I sometimes call him Will."

"So show me your favorites." He pauses. "But not here— they're about to close for the night."

"I really should go."

"But first you'll show me Will's sonnets, right?" He stands. She's dubious. "There's somewhere we can talk?"

"I know the perfect place."

THE PERFECT PLACE? Well, unfortunately this tiny, musty, dimly lit bedroom doesn't quite qualify. It's hard to believe the Great Northern's still one of Godzone's best hotels—no wonder tourists bitch, these are the seventies, after all. They perch on a badly sprung single bed jammed against faded wallpaper. Black hands on a yellowing, plastic bedside clock put the time at a quarter to eleven. A wall radio emits a tinny sound.

She unzips a vinyl pouch, extracts a dog-eared paperback, and smiles. "I've several favorite sonnets, Chancey"—she riffles the pages—"but here's something you might like. Listen, now: 'Poor soul, the center of my sinful earth' "—she's a tad diffident, but that lilting voice is no stranger to recitation—" 'rebuked by these rebel powers that thee array.' "

"So what's he saying?"

"That his sexuality is rebelling against his soul."

"And there's a message here for me?"

"Will's not into messages. He's just observing the tug of war between the flesh and"—she stops and cocks an ear. "Hey, Chancey, turn it up!" She reaches across him. Her body's warm, her breath sweet. " It's the Beatles."

"I was enjoying the poem."

"So was I till Sergeant Pepper told the band to play." They fall back on the faded green candlewick bedcover. "*Do ya neeeeed—any—body ... The Beatles are so great, Chancey.*" She sings along. "*Ya need some-body to love.*" His arm involuntarily enfolds her. "*Do ya waaaant—any—body—*" He pecks her cheek. "*Ya want some-body to love.*"

Is she just a Roman Catholic virgin seeking unrequited pleasure and empathetic vibes? Perhaps his deformity's evoked maternal affection.

Well, look at that. She's nodded off. Maybe she drank a touch more than she should've. He sets his head back on the pillow and closes his eyes.

> *He's in the box for his first confession. The priest slides the grate open and harrumphs. Forgive me father for I have sinned ... Well, not really—an infant can't sin. He's done nothing. Nothing. Another harrumph. He wants to know what the hell you're up to right now Chancey. "Nothing, Father, nothing. This sleeping princess and I are fully clothed. See for yourself. It's all about concepts and conversation." But the priest's deaf. He just harrumphs again.*

She's stirring. "Two A.M. I have to go. They'll be peeved if I don't show." She rises, then arches, catlike, in the mirror, plucks a thread from her shoulder, smooths an eyebrow, and draws a plastic comb through her hair. She drops the comb into her satchel on the bedside table, slings it across her shoulder, and smiles. "You stay here, Chancey. There's a cab rank right outside. I'll be okay."

He stands, stretches, and pecks her cheek. "My plane leaves late tomorrow."

"I can't see you again, Chancey."

"Never?"

"Not in the morning, anyway."

"Noon?"

"Albert Park. By the fountain. One o'clock."

"I'll see you to a cab."

"Best not. I'll understand."

And so she's gone. Until tomorrow. Maybe.

He's back in the confessional. This time he can see the priest. It's Jill. She's wearing a tight black blouse. "There's no need to forgive me Jill, I've done nothing wrong. I've committed no sins." She unbuttons the blouse and exposes her breasts. He reaches out to touch them but the grate's in the way. "Oh, for Christ's sake, Chancey," she exclaims, rebuttoning the blouse, "don't try to con me, too."

IT'S WISER TO FOCUS ON REALITY THAN DREAMS. And the truth of the moment is that Elan's made good on her commitment, for there she stands, waving to him from the fountain, in a faded, yellow cotton dress and matching canvas shoes. Cumulus clouds float in the clear blue sky. The steamy air enhances the rich scent of the newly mown grass. He reaches for her extended hand and catches his breath. Her breasts are against his shirt. The sun that warms his back floods her face. His lips brush her perfumed cheek. "I wasn't sure you'd come."

"Yet here I am."

They saunter through the lush green slopes of the manicured but near-to-empty park, then settle under the shade of a wide oak. He leans against the knobby trunk. She huddles to his chest. Leafy branches filter the sunlight. Her skirt has ridden above her knees, revealing her lovely long slim legs. She nuzzles her ear to his chest.

"Can you hear my heart?"

"Sounds like Sergeant Pepper, Chancey."

"None of this is happening."

"Everything is happening and nothing is happening." Clouds race over Manurewa Harbor. A zephyr breeze carries the scent of daffodils . . .

Four years old, bare-chested, spread-eagled in a backyard deciphering cumulus clouds in a brilliant blue sky. His mother—slim, young, sweet, sad—stirs blood red laundry in a fired copper cauldron. He jumps and runs to her. Am I suntanned yet?

She's nuzzling his ear. "Yeah, lonely, Chancey. I mean on one plane Godzone is spectacular. Yet the very splendor of those wide-open spaces can also leave me feeling, kind of, well—"

"Isolated?"

"Yeah, isolated—and maybe alienated and rejected, too. Poetry eases those feelings. Trouble is, it can stoke them, too. I mean the plays and poems I love are all from another time and place and therefore utterly irrelevant. Most Godzoners are too taken with the skies and beaches, sun and surf, hills and ranges to notice."

"Or care?"

They amble hand in hand, down from the park, back along the warmly yielding tarmac of the empty downtown streets, to the Great Northern.

She turns to him. "I won't come inside. You'll have to check out PDQ."

"So, we really have run out of time."

"Maybe just as well." She half-laughs and swings back on her heels, her soft hands clutching his for balance.

"And maybe not. But, hey—Sydney's just two hours away."

"Not a good idea, Chancey."

"You'd shun a friendship?"

"Friendship? *Go-onnnn.*"

He rocks her forward off her heels and kisses her gently. "We'll meet again."

She nudges him, then draws away and springs a half step down the street. "And, if not, why then at least this parting were well made."

Sydney

"HEY, WELCOME HOME, TROUBADOUR." Jill's peeking over the top of her sparkling Chardonnay. The table's set with napkins, wine, and candles. "Your favorite, Chancey. Fresh snapper. And new potatoes."

Oh, no—a replay of dinner with Elan. Or a trick of the imagination? Maybe there was no Elan. Or maybe Jill's clairvoyant and has set an elaborate trap. But nothing happened. So just put that Godzone virgin out of mind.

"Missed you, baby."

"Missed you, too, Chancey." She kisses him lightly on the lips. The big blue eyes are bright and warm, and the smile's as innocent as ever. "I sometimes think I should've gotten beyond missing you, by now."

"What does that mean, Jilly?"

"Well, we met when I was seventeen."

"With photo cutouts of ballet dancers on your bedroom walls."

"And visions of becoming a dancer."

"Maybe you should've gone after it, Jilly."

"And missed out on marrying you?" She half smiles. "No, you were always the one with the head full of dreams. I wanted whatever you wanted."

"I've got go-getters working with me in Sydney now. They'll wind it up. But Godzone's still crucial."

"Really?"

"Afraid I'm going to have to invest time there." She's studying his eyes. "I mean, I know it's hard on you." He saunters to the ranch-sliders. "But there's no other way, really."

There's his reflection in the window. And a head floating on his shoulder. Elan's.

Jill's arm wraps itself warmly around his chest. "See something out there, Chancey?" Her perfume's sweet but her voice is sweeter.

He spins, wraps his arms around her, and kisses her cheek. "Passing ferries. Lights on the water. And a stunning reflection of the beautiful girl I married."

She really is beautiful, too. You've got to keep that in mind.

In the dream he strolls at evening along a secluded country road. A sultry yet vulnerable teenage girl sits by a break in a hedge. They have delicious sex in the bushes. He abandons her and strides off—then glances back. She's still sitting in the hedge. He memorizes the place. Next time he passes he'll tupple her again.

5

Set-Ups

FIVE MINUTES PAST ELEVEN by the clock on sun-filled Customhouse Quay. Should he call her or not? No. Yes. No. Yes. He presses the phone to his ear and dials.

"Back so quickly, Chancey!" She sounds surprised.

"It's a business trip, but maybe we could meet."

"I don't think so, Chancey."

"I don't see why we can't at least meet. Talk a little. Maybe have a drink."

"Sounds like the entry to a slippery slope."

"A tiny spritzer wouldn't send you down the primrose path, surely."

"I'm flattered. But it's not a good idea."

"I'm sorry. I found a lovely quote. I think it's from one of those Elizabethan poets you fancy. I was hoping you might identify the author for me."

She pauses. "What was the line?"

"I don't remember precisely. But I have it on a scrap of paper in my travel bag. I could retrieve it in time for a cup of coffee after work."

Another pause. "I could maybe manage fifteen minutes. At six o'clock."

"In the Peninsula coffee lounge."

He hangs up the phone and studies the impediment. Compared to her he's a clumsy, waifish schoolboy. Look, he shouldn't be doing this, right? Yes, right—but some irresistible inner force is arguing otherwise. He feels the sun disappear behind a cloud. Sydney's a couple of thousand miles beyond that horizon. And lagging by two hours. And what's happening there? Someone's got to fund this junket.

SYDNEY

FIVE TO NINE, and, yes this really is Fuller Fyfe, the radically recharged rainmaker. He's the one who's striding through this glitziest of office suites upon the fortieth level of the high-faluting Australia Square office tower. Okay, so his private oak-paneled office is a touch compact, but no matter—just feast the old peepers on that glistening Opera House. It's a vista that always arrests the eye and is ever reluctant to let go. He'll be dealing with a whole new totally upmarket class of top wallahs in these swanky surroundings—

"Harrumph."

That grunt's a tap on the shoulder. Christ— his nine o'clock candidate's already in the room. He turns—

Shhheeee—iiii—tttt! What the fuck is *this?* Is it a giant, gray, nauseating, about-to-sour blancmange? No. An eerie creature-from-the-deep out of an old horror movie? No. In fact, it is a bloated, fried-egg-eyed, staring, sniffing, wheezing, sweating—*quadriplegic.* And it's encased in a gleaming, cagelike, black-leathered, battery-driven, silver-spoked, rubber-wheeled chair. But show no surprise.

"Delighted to meet you, Mister, uh, Ballast." Tiny pupils peer up at him from darkly circled eyes. "*Really* delighted." That scent might be bicycle oil. The hands are grimy, the nails black. Perhaps he greases his own contraption. The quad grunts a greeting. The breath's stale. Well, not to worry. Just slip into the swivel chair and mop the brow with this lovely white handkerchief. "Yes. I really mean that. At Haste and Company we see every executive candidate as a *person.* Any eventual fee is the mere by-product of a caring, personal service." His stomach rumbles. Still queasy from last night's prospecting. Shouldn't have downed that last Sambuca.

The quad's face is basset-houndish. He can't be bad as he looks. What does the bio say: purchasing officer; forty-four; gloriously unemployed after lasting nearly two years with an air-conditioning company that went belly-up—the only bright spot in a redundancy-punctuated career. On the upside, though, the demand for dead-end purchasing officers exceeds supply. And the fucker'll probably take a below-market salary. Could be good money for quick work. He'd rather handle someone more salubrious, but the bills cry out to be paid. And some things about this fellow pique one's natural curiosity.

"You'll see from the certificate behind me, Mister Ballast"—gentle doctor-style throat clearing—"that I'm *degreed.*"

The quadly pupils dart to the red seal within the black frame. "Call me Bob."

"It's in the human sciences, Bob. I'm a professional. Just like a doctor."

"Yes, yes, of course."

"So our conversation'll remain confidential."

"Yes. Yes, of course."

Now the quadly lamps are peering downwards. Perhaps he's caught sight of— and envies—these elegant new Church wing tips. But stay on track.

"My job calls for me to come to an understanding of your motivations, your skill set, your whole set of circumstances."

"Yes. Yes, of course."

"I couldn't help but notice, Bob, that you suffer a partial disability."

"Yes. Yes, of course. Result of a car accident ten years ago."

"But I see you've gone from strength to strength, Bob. Married seven years. And now you and your good lady have two young children. Bravo!" Let that sink in. Empathetic doctor mode. "I mean, well, I imagine congratulations are in order, Bob." Little smile. "I mean these two wonderful children are *your* children. Your *biological* children?"

"Yes. Yes, of course. They're our children. Not adopted."

"Ah, yes, bravo indeed." The mind boggles. Shrink mode is surely called for. He applies the 180 degree swivel and lines up the quad's reflection in the window. "In my role as confidential adviser, I need to know you *intimately.*"

"You do?"

"Indeed. And, I mean, it's unusual—wonderful, a great achievement, perhaps—to have pulled it off." Velvet voice. "I imagine that the little lady and you continue to enjoy an intimate life together, Bob."

"We get along about as well as most people."

"I mean where there's a will there's a way, I imagine."

"My wife's a very willing person."

"So she can initiate wherever initiative is required." Now. Go for it now. A gentle touch of his wing tip to the floor effects a reapplication of the 180-degree swivel. He revolves ever so slowly and locks onto the quadriplegic's eyes. Softly. "And, I'm sure she has many ways to bring your, uh, manhood to, uh, readiness."

"Oh. Oh, yes." The thick lips bobble. "Life'd be impossible without Alice."

"Ah yes, of course, *Alice*—Alice Ballast. But with her *all* things are possible."

"Just about all."

"Your, uh, lovemaking's only marginally restricted, Bob?"

"Alice can do pretty well anything."

"But I imagine the, uh, logistics, they must get a little, uh, tricky."

The quad's eyes are suddenly alight. "She gets on top if that's what you're driving at."

"Yes, of course. Alice assumes the upper posting. Naturally. And the actual, uh, pleasure itself, the, uh, delectation—that's not, uh, circumscribed, is it, Bob?"

"Not a bit." The fucker's smirking. "In fact, I bet I'm getting more than most people."

"I think I see what you're getting at, Bob. Compensatory rewards, right? Given your other, uh, disabilities, the nether regions reap compensatory gratifications—yes?"

The smirk widens pridefully. "I am indeed hypersensitive in those regions, Fuller." The fried-egg eyes momentarily bulge. "There are other pleasures, too."

Oh, shit, Fuller gets the picture: it's a near full frontal of Alice Ballast toppled back upon her ample haunches working the quad's shaft. Humping and heaving, jumping and jiggling, firing and perspiring.

"Visual pleasures, Bob?"

The lips twitch. "Visual, oral, anal, you name it."

Oh, Christ, the quad's feasting upon more of absolutely everything than Fuller—and gloating about it, too. It's all so obscene and depressing.

"This is very inspiring, Bob." Gentle throat clearing and nurturing smile. "And very helpful, too."

"It'll help you find me a job?"

"Oh, yes. Indeed. For my diagnosis is that you're an overachiever, someone who warms to a challenge, and a stable, loving family man, too." And now to business mode. "So let's just turn to the question of salary—which I see you left blank on the form." Expectant eyebrow lift but no response. Soften the voice. "So, how much were you actually earning in your last job, Bob?"

The fucker's tight-lipped. Sever eye contact but maintain silence. The break will come.

And it does.

"Isn't that an unnecessarily personal question, Mr. Fyfe?"

So, the fucker's suddenly stalling. Afraid to 'fess up to a lousy paycheck, no doubt.

"Personal? Well, I suppose it could seem so, Bob. But to set up an effective marketing plan I really need to know. I mean, that's the ultimate purpose of this kind of professional, in-depth interview."

"Do you really need to pry into those intimate aspects of an executive's life?"

"Only if I'm to help you get back on your feet, Bob."

The quad slowly softens. The teeth drop to the vest pocket, pluck a grubby envelope, and drop it beneath Fuller's nose.

"Didn't mean to seem to be intrusive, Bob."

The envelope smells a little musty. The tax return is dog-eared, and, as predicted, shows a decidedly below-market income. So at least one tightfisted employer's going to snap at this bait.

"The prognosis couldn't be better, Bob. We're gonna get you back on track, pronto, gonna find you a fulfilling role within a dynamic, enlightened, growth company." The quad nods. "And, as it happens, precisely such a client is calling for a tight-fisted purchasing officer right now."

"I'm an acquisitions executive."

"And that's *precisely* what they're looking for. A *seasoned* acquisitions executive to become a *key* member of the *senior* management team. Someone to help them go on making great strides."

"Making great strides?"

"Actually Bob, they're in the security-alarm business."

"I was thinking of something blue-chip."

"It's the *freedom* business, Bob. In fact, that's the name of the firm, *Freedom Unlimited.* They're making Australia a safer place. The world, too—they won an export award. So let's not cut off any options before your first meeting with the dynamic CEO, Hank Van Epenheusen. You can look at the job and polish your presentation. And, of course, if you hit it off, I'll get him to make you a written offer that you can either accept or use to get a humongous leg up on something else. But I think you're just gonna love working with Freedom in Blacktown."

"Blacktown! That's a two-hour commute."

"Distance's nothing on modern highways, Bob. And I see you still drive and that someone's knackered a vehicle together for you."

"Blacktown's a prison suburb."

"It's true enough there's a very historic prison out that way, Bob. But the place's developing quickly, too. Another Kentucky Fried Chicken outlet went in there just the other day."

"I dunno, really— "

"That's because you don't know Freedom. It's all your choice, Bob. But in my professional opinion, the chemistry'll be perfect, and you'll be on your way to earning a fortune."

"I could maybe look—"

"Smart choice, Bob. So let's get you taking one step at a time. If you'll just get yourself home and wait by the phone, I'll have some news to knock your socks off."

AUCKLAND

FOURTEEN MINUTES PAST SIX by the Peninsula bedside clock. Will the wish to identify a line of poetry really impel her to share a cup of coffee? Adrenaline racing, he pulls on his gold-buttoned, double-breasted royal-blue blazer, checks his bearing in the mirror, then glances over the boxlike room. The blandness is redeemed by a harbor view and a Rimu-framed print of a fern above the king-sized bed. The inner demon tunes the radio to soft music and adjusts the lights next to the bed and over the coffee table.

SYDNEY

QUARTER PAST FUCKING FOUR! Where *does* the day go? "I'm Fuller Fyfe"—he leans into the phone like a fortune teller into a crystal ball—"senior recruiter with Chandler Haste and Company." Diagnostic mode. Polished and professional. "Our professional duty requires us to vet every candidate we recommend. We're considering a fellow who used to work for you, Bob Ballast."

"The quadriplegic?"

"I believe Bob does suffer an impairment."

"Whattaya wanna know?"

"Well, since you raise the question of his impairment, did it hinder his job performance?"

"Bob's job was to get on the phone and talk to suppliers. That was no problem."

"How was his work?"

"Did he tell you we fired him?"

"He mentioned being rendered redundant—"

"We canned him. He had an attitude problem."

"What sort of problem?"

"He's surly and stubborn. A pain in the arse."

"Aha. A personality clash?"

"He clashed with everyone."

"What were his strengths?"

"Some people might say he worked very hard."

"That's a very real strength—"

"Unfortunately he never got anything done."

"He needed focus?"

"He could never see the wood for the trees. Poked his nose into other people's business and pissed everyone off. He got the office in an uproar."

"So if you were to reemploy him, it would be in, uh, another role—"

"Look, *nobody* would be better than Bob Ballast. But if we were forced to reemploy him, we'd stuff him in a back room and leave him there to rot."

"You've been incredibly helpful."

"No problem, mate. Just warn any client to waste no time making Bob Ballast a job offer."

Incredibly helpful, indeed. He casts an eye over his notes as he reaches for the phone.

AUCKLAND

"SO HERE I AM THEN, CHANCEY." Butterflies flutter in his groin. "Couldn't resist your offer to share an anonymous line." Elan's sheathed in a short black dress draped with a necklace of red plastic baubles.

"I'm glad you succumbed." Her cheek tastes of perfume. He nudges her toward raucous laughter in the main bar.

"I thought it was coffee."

"We just missed out. I had to order two white wines in the bar instead. See, the barman's setting them up right now."

"Oh, yes, I see a barman." She eases into the barstool. "And I think I might just sense a setup, too."

"Fate's a kind of setup." He raises his glass in a mock toast. "That might be what you're feeling."

She follows his lead but inflects a mild reproof, "To Elizabethan poets, Chancey." She sets the glass back onto the polished timber bench and smiles her half-mocking smile. "So what's the line that's got you puzzled?"

He fishes a scrap of paper from his breast pocket—"Here it is: 'Whoever loved that loved not at first sight?'"

She pauses. "Well, it *sounds* like Shakespeare." She mouths the words, counting the syllables on her fingers. "It's iambic pentameter— ten beats to the line—that's his signature." She pauses. "But the actual author of that line, Mister Haste, if I recall correctly, was his passionate contemporary, Christopher Marlowe"—she breaks into a semi triumphant smile—"who used it to great effect in *Hero and Leander*"—she eyes him a touch suspiciously—"as I'm sure you very well recall."

"In fact, that is something I really did not know. I just happened to catch the line somewhere."

"I think you're teasing me with tantalizing lies, Chancey."

"Lies—what lies?"

"Tantalizing lies." She fingers the stem of the glass. "They come at the end of the second line of my sonnet."

"You've finished it already?"

"No, just two lines."

"Can I hear them."

She smiles a touch self-consciously. " 'My pursuer sounds a truly tempting tongue, And teases me with tantalizing lies.' "

"Do you have anyone in mind?"

"Do you know any liars?"

"If I was a liar, I'd say no."

"If you were a liar that'd be your destiny." She clutches the riding hem of her skirt. "Destiny's about character, Chancey. And the hidden flaws within our strengths."

"Hey, so serious and profound—tantalizing, too. We really must finish this discussion over dinner."

Sydney

"AH, HANK—GLAD I GOT TO YOU before you left for the day. About your search for an acquisitions executive—"

"It's an entry-level purchasing officer I'm needing, Fuller." There's a familiar blend of concern and irritation in Hank Van Epenheusen's thick Dutch voice. He's heard that sound before. "It's a go-nowhere job. A dead-end. A blind alley. A year's experience'd be more than adequate."

"Of course, Hank. A prudent, no-nonsense purchasing officer. No one high-falutin'. Someone solid, dependable. Not too ambitious. Yeah, I have the spec clearly in mind. No worries."

"But did you find me anyone?"

"Yes, no, and maybe."

"Yes, no, and maybe—whatever does that mean?"

"I found one really *outstanding* fellow, Hank." Pause. Inflection of deep sadness: "But I frankly doubt you'd be interested."

"Whyever not?"

"Let's not bother about that. Let's cut to the chase. Let's talk about the two other candidates whom I know you actually will be interested in."

"Two others?"

"Yes, two. One of them is very pricey. Pricey and fond of himself. The other is in your range. Lives close by, too. But I'm afraid he might be unstable."

"Pricey? Unstable? What about the first one? The one you said was outstanding?"

"Yes, well he *is* outstanding. I mean that's something we *know*. Ran him through our tests. I *personally* subjected him to an *in-depth* interview. I probed every area of his life: motivations, skill set, management style, acumen—the whole ball of wax. He's a standout all right. Unfortunately you just wouldn't like him—"

"Wouldn't *like* him? You're not suggesting I'm prejudiced?"

"*Prejudice* is too strong a word."

"I can get on with any worker. Any real worker."

"So you want me to fill you in on this fellow?"

"Yes, of course."

"Well, he's a stable forty-three-year-old with a doting wife and two kids. They live in French's Forest."

"That's a helluva commute."

"But *loves* Blacktown. His wife's dead keen to relocate there, too."

"What experience does he have?"

"A *ton* of it, Hank. Came up the hard way. Ran the gamut of office duties, then got promoted to purchasing."

"What'd his boss say about him?"

"I've got the notes right here. Let's see now—said he was a *very* hard worker—enjoys immersing himself in the detail that others find mundane—a sharing person—goes out of his way to involve his colleagues—"

"Did you ask if they'd reemploy?"

"I did indeed." Conspiratorial chuckle. "And they were *very* emphatic. They said nobody would be better than Bob Ballast. Absolutely nobody! And, get this now: *urge your client to waste no time in making Bob Ballast an offer of employment.*" Silence. Say nothing. Nothing. Nothing. Slow segue—now: "*Pret-ty* damned positive, I'd say."

Long pause.

"He really does sound good, Fuller." The irritation's gone. The voice is infinitely softer. "So what's the problem?"

"Well, Hank, I have to level with you. A lot of Aussie employers can be intolerant of people who are, well, uh, different."

"Oh, Christ, you don't have to tell that to me. I'm a Dutchman. I can't begin to tell you how much discrimination I've suffered from some of these intolerant, ill-bred, know-nothing Aussie bigots. So send Bob Ballast out here, pronto. I don't care who or what he is. Just as long as he's not a Paki or an Abo. Anything else I can handle."

"If only all my clients were so enlightened, Hank. But no worries on the race issue. No, Bob Ballast's a highly motivated man of European extraction—the Caucasian variety. The problem's merely a physical disability."

"Hell, that's nothing, Fuller. Not if it doesn't affect his performance."

"Not at all, Hank. I probed that point most vigilantly. I'll get him to you right away."

"Sure. And what's his problem by the way? Bad hand? Bad leg? What?"

"It's nothing. Not really. A car accident left him a, uh, well, I think the precise term is, uh, *quadriplegic*."

"A *quadriplegic*?!"

"That's the full extent of the problem. No other difficulties at all. None whatsoever. He's an extremely hard worker. And he has absolutely no emotional shortcomings."

"A *quadriplegic*?"

"Yes, Hank, an intensely energetic, highly motivated disabled man whose home environment is supportive, whose job commitment is tightly focused, and whose mind is razor-keen. In fact, both my in-depth interview and our tests indicate that Bob Ballast's motivations and mind have actually been *enhanced* by his tragic disability."

"*Enhanced*? Huh. How does that work?"

"Something like the idiot savant. All his drive's channeled into one activity."

"So he really could be outstanding?"

"He really is—you'll see. Being a quadriplegic confers innumerable benefits. Especially to someone working alongside an enlightened and compassionate leader like yourself."

Rainmaking's all about empathy and timing. He cradles the phone. Now, if he can just catch up with that oversexed quad. Probably at home right now greasing his contraption. Or maybe Alice's doing it for him.

AUCKLAND

ELAN GRINS. "I hear there's a baby in every one of those vinegared oysters you're shucking, Mister Haste."

Her face is bathed in candlelight. A phalanx of business executives schmooze. A trio of guitar, bass, and drums softly renders "By the Time I Get to Phoenix." They touch glasses.

"So what's all this running-around-the-world stuff, Chancey?"

"I'm just getting out of the blocks."

"But what's the *race*? Who's competing? What's the prize?" She sips her Chablis.

"King-of-the-Hill."

"You're already king of a hill."

"*A* hill is not *the* hill. Life's about being all you can be. Frog and the puddle. All that."

"We've got to be who we are, Chancey. And become what we can be—the nuns were always telling us that. I want to do something with my life. I want to learn all about literature, the best ideas most beautifully expressed. Maybe I'll become a teacher. One day I might even become a poet. Meantime, I need to be a woman. I'll fall in love in a daring way. Then I'll marry and have children. Nothing's more important than children."

"Especially if you're programmed Catholic. Next you'll be falling for some aristocratic Brit."

SYDNEY

ANSWER YOU FUCKER, ANSWER. And he does.

"Great news from Hank Van Epenheusen and FU, Bob—"

"Eff you?"

"No, no. Not Eff you—FU: Freedom Unlimited. They're busting to meet you."

"Alice says Blacktown's too far away."

"And I appreciate the concern, Bob. But what you have to be clear on is that this's a great chance to hone your presentation skills."

"Maybe."

"And to get them to make you an offer. It's a small world, Bob. The chief of the next company you interview might just be one of Hank van Epenheusen's friends. They get to talking at the club. The conversation turns to your candidacy. You don't want Hank to say, 'We looked at Bob Ballast—but didn't offer him anything.' No. No. No. You don't want that."

"I don't?"

"Never, Bob, never. How much better when Hank says, 'Oh, Yes! Bob Ballast! What a *wonderful* fellow. Came out to FU and impressed us immensely. We offered him a key job, but to our eternal regret we just couldn't attract him. Damned shame.'"

Long pause. Don't break it. And here he comes—

"How do I get them to offer me the job, Fuller?"

"Just be your own warm, natural self, Bob. Don't complain or criticize. Show a real interest. Ask what you'll be doing after five years with them. Let them see you're a sticker."

"That mightn't be easy. I've had a lot of jobs."

"Best fudge on a few of those, Bob. I'll give you a new résumé to memorize."

"Isn't that, uh, dishonest?"

"Not when you're being marketed by a professional, working to a strict code of ethics."

"You sure?"

"A career history should reflect true personality. And at least three of your past jobs've fallen through because of simple bad luck. Best omit them so as not to confuse."

"What if Van Epenheusen checks up?"

"I'll be handling that, Bob. As long as I know the full story, nothing else matters." Rise, ever so slowly. Now perch, ever so professionally upon the edge of the desk. "No need for you to be bothered with these professional details, Bob. Just make the same dazzling impression on Hank that you've already made on me."

"What if he wants to talk salary?"

"Don't talk numbers. Just prospects. Leave the rest to me. I'll be dedicating all my professional negotiation skills to your best interests, Bob. I'll get the best package for you, no worries."

AUCKLAND

MANTOVANI GREETS THE OPENING DOOR. Elan slips to the bedroom window. He trails the wake of her soft scent. A half moon flickers on the harbor. A ferry glides toward the quay. The downy nape of her neck tenses beneath his lips. Her cinnamon hair shines. Her mouth is gentle.

"Hey—we came for the view." She embraces him. "You're an okay guy, Chancey. I feel safe." She smiles. "Yet nothing's right at all."

She bounces to the bed, perches, and flicks off her pumps. He tosses his jacket over a chair, kicks off his own shoes, and joins her. Her hem rides to her thighs as she pulls a pillow to her head. She's breathing quickly.

"I shouldn't be here, Chancey, but I can stay till two. Mother'll be peeved if I mess up my dress, though. I just got it back from the cleaners."

She eases the sheath over her head and stands in the moonlight. White bra, yellow panties, suspendered stockings, and a sensuous, olive stomach. She seems oblivious to his gaze. Might there be a problem in following her lead? Maybe not. He tosses his socks, shirt, and trousers onto the bedside chair. Everything but the briefs. The sheets are fresh, clean. She nuzzles his neck. Is there such a thing as an avuncular nuzzle?

"What's with the foot, Chancey?"

"You noticed. Nothing really. A gift from the gods."

"Oh, Chancey, don't mock yourself. Does it bother you?"

"Might've helped actually."

"Richard the Thirdish?"

"As I recall, King Richard was a villain—"

"He was his own man, or so he claimed. Unfortunately, he made a silly invocation, 'Since the heavens have shaped my body so, let hell make crooked my mind to answer it.'"

"I see my problem as more of a cross than a devilish pact."

Her soft fingers run nimbly across his temple. "Wow—a Messiah." The voice is mocking, but the embrace is soothing and warm. "I guess that makes me Mary Magdalene."

His mother stands at the front door and gazes out to sea. A three-funneled ship billows smoke into the still, blue sky. Soldiers coming home, she says. Your uncle got his jaw blown away. The scent of daffodils rises from the garden. His tiny fingers tug at her cotton floral-print dress.

"Two A.M., I have to go, Chancey." She slips from the bed.

So nothing happened. Well, thank God for that. Moonlight's silhouetting her willowy frame. She adjusts her bra and stockings, then slides into her sheath. She props one hand against the wall and steps into her red pumps. Then she smiles and reaches for her shoulder bag. "Did you ever read the sonnet about the angel in hell?"

"If I did I've forgotten."

She extracts her paperback and flicks through the pages. "Listen up now." Her voice becomes an earnest whisper. " 'To win me soon to hell, my female evil tempteth my better angel from my side, and would corrupt my saint to be a devil.' "

"I think I get the drift."

"He's saying what the nuns liked to say, that the body's in battle with the spirit."

"A recurring theme—but who wins? Does the angel ever get to go to hell?"

"Will's conclusion, I gather"—she returns the paperback to her bag—"is that mere mortals get to experience everything"—she pauses—"at some stage in their lives." She zips the bag shut. "But I really must go, Chancey."

"I'll see you to a cab."

"That might not be discreet." Her lips brush his. She glides to the door, holds it ajar, and glances back. "I like you, Chancey." A shadow engulfs her. The lock snaps. She's gone.

Her scent lingers. He wanders to the window and gazes out. Temptation, that's the message. So maybe they're both being tempted to put the angel into hell. But is it—and was it—worth risking what he has with Jill? Would it be a mistake—a sin? Not if it happens in another country. Somebody said that. It's a famous line from somewhere. Jill might cuff him if he dared utter it. Crawley'd understand, though. And let's not lose sight of the fact that nothing happened. Nothing more than the sharing of a few lines of poetry with an aficionado of the same. So why worry? But if everything's kosher why does he feel so depressed? Get some sleep, Chancey. It'll all be nothing in the light of day.

Elan comes to him wearing a blood red nightdress. They embrace passionately, and her kisses come hot and heavy. She presses his hand into her crotch. She's got a thick, sensuous, silky tail down there, and she's urging him to stroke it. And now she's writhing and moaning. The angel has entered hell. Now he's writhing and moaning, too.

SYDNEY

"MMMM!" Fuller savors the aroma of fresh-brewed coffee and studies the offered delicate, orange-rimmed, saucered cup. "Real china, too, Chancey." He's perched on the edge of the low backed guest sofa.

"Glad you like it. Crawley set it all up. He said ritual nourishes the spirit—gets people thinking on a higher plane."

"So he's still a deacon at heart, Chancey."

"He's still into the rituals, anyway."

Fuller sets the saucer back onto the table, splashing his coffee. "Mind if I grab one of those lovely chocolate macaroons?" He slides one onto the side of his saucer. Then, with extreme delicacy, his fat pinkie pointing toward Chancey's eye, he raises the cup to his lips. His eyes meet Chancey's. "So, I had a feedback session with Brittle."

Feedback . . .

I'm a high-performance player
on a tip-top team
where things aren't always
quite as they seem—

"How'd it go?"

Fuller shifts to sharing mode. "Well, I said, 'How's it going, Richard?' And *he* said, 'Pretty good.' And I said 'Smiling and dialing?' Well, you wanna know what he said? He said he was developing a *game plan*! So I said, 'Huh?' And he said his father taught him that the key to success is *methodology*." He raises his eyebrows and gulps.

"The rubber's got to hit the road sometime."

"That's *exactly* what I told him, Chancey." He grabs the macaroon from the saucer and chomps down greedily. "I said success in this business comes from smiling and dialing."

"Did he get it?"

"Didn't seem to. So I spelled it out. Said you've gotta get on the fucking *phone*. Get people out on *interview*. Put bums on chairs."

"What'd he say?"

"Said he's developing a *mission statement*! I just looked straight at him. I said, '*Place the buggers*! That's the fucking mission.'" The cup's shaking in his hand. "Into the right jobs, of course. I mean that goes without saying."

"Absolutely. How did he respond?"

"Said he'd done some *research*. Said he was *quantifying placeability*."

"Meaning what?"

"Says we've been doing unethical things."

"We have?"

"He says we're showing *prejudice*. I said, 'How can that be when I'm working with a quad right now?' Well, he commended me for that, of course." He's pointing with the uneaten half of the biscuit. "But then he said—get this—'But, you know, we haven't placed any *Pakistanis*. Or *Abos*.'" He sets the cup and saucer onto the tray.

"There's a reason for that, of course."

"And I fucking told it to him. 'No shit,' I said." He's waving the biscuit. " 'Well, what *you* need to realize,' I said, 'is that there's a *ton* of prejudice against those darkies. So why make things hard for ourselves?' But then he said—and get this now—he said that we have a *moral duty* to be in the *vanguard of change*. Holy shit! *Then*, with hardly a pause, he added that we're not placing enough fucking *females*, either." The remains of the biscuit, propelled by pudgy fingers, disappear into his eager jaws.

"Well, idealism's great, but did you try to temper it with reality?"

"Too right!" His gullet's expanding with the biscuit's descent. " 'Moon madness,' I said. 'They don't stick—and when they quit we have to refund our fees.' He said that's not an enlightened attitude. So *I* said, 'Go to it. Slip as many onto chairs as you can. *But* just make sure you turn a dollar while you're at it. And make sure they stick. Pakis and Abos, too. And the best of British luck.'" He notices the chocolate stuck to his fingers.

"What'd he say?"

"Said that since I'd mentioned the word *British*, we weren't placing enough of *them*, either." He dusts his fingertips together.

"Brits?"

"Right, well, Poms, actually. Well, I told him straight off. I said, 'Look, your father was undoubtedly top-drawer.'" He drops his voice. "Which may not be true, of course, but for counseling purposes I saw no harm in a tiny, white lie." The chocolate's sticking to both hands.

"Sometimes we have to protect people's feelings."

"Then I gave it to him." He's sucking his fingers. " 'The Poms who wander in here are whiners with chips on their shoulders a mile high,' I said. 'They're jumped-up shop-stewards who screwed up in Pommieland'—*back home*, as the buggers say—'and they come out here just to screw up the unions.' " He extracts a handkerchief, swabs his fingers, then glances back. "He said we should be placing *real* managers. People like his fucking father."

"How did you handle that?"

"Told him straight up." The handkerchief hovers over his lips like a mop. "I told him the ones *we* see have usually just stepped off the boat." He's painted a chocolate mustache on his lip. "They're just lookin' for a fast buck to tide them over. We spin our wheels to get them good jobs—then a month later they quit for something better. And the few who don't quit are mostly ingrates who suck up to some gullible CEO—who stupidly stuffs them into personnel. And then the little scumbags never give us any business."

"So the whole session was a reality check for Richard." That mustache's a real distraction.

"I hope so." Here comes the swab again. "Told him to get on the phone and place a few fuckers. And the more the merrier." He clears the mustache. " 'Or,' I said, *'burn the fucking shoe leather.*

Get out of the office, chase down corporate clients in their own lairs and pitch them for honest-to-God assignments.' " His bullfrog chest inflates. "Which is, by the way, precisely how I came to land Hank Van Epenheusen at FU."

"You going to place anyone there, Fuller?"

"Got a certainty—the quad. I'm working with him very closely."

"And he's good at what he does, so it'll be a happy marriage, right?"

"You know me, Chancey. I'm a sucker for the underdog, so my heart went out to him immediately. He's got a couple of problems but Van Epenheusen's got some too. As we all have, of course. But I got on the phone and spoke to his former boss. As a professional I could do no less. The fellow was very frank. My considered opinion is that I've uncovered everything." His pudgy hand hovers over his heart. "And that I have an ethical duty to place him in a job befitting his talents."

"Well done, Fuller. You're more than just a rainmaker—you're a real professional, too."

Fuller's eyes dip. "It all comes to something in the end, doesn't it, Chancey?"

"If we keep at it." A shadow crosses the sun. He strolls to the window. There goes that plane again. He spins. "I mean, Crawley's right. We've got to feed the spirit. But we've got to keep an eye on the ball, too. So I'm just going to make a quick hop to Godzone. Make sure they share our fixation for focus."

6

Placements

HENRY'S PHONE VOICE IS SOLICITOUS. "Heard on the grapevine you might be in town for Anzac Day." He pauses. "That's tomorrow, Saturday, the twenty-fifth of April."

"Of course. Anzac Day, memorial day of the Australian and New Zealand Army Corps ever since that disastrous nineteen fifteen Gallipolli landing."

"I'll be marching in the dawn parade, Chancey. Care to breakfast with me following remembrance?"

"I'm not sure I'm up to observing a day in which so many Down Under soldiers were sacrificed for nothing."

"Those boys, and they mostly were boys, too, Chancey, mere virgins in tunics, died fighting for the Empire. It was all a terrible blunder by the British High Command. Ten thousand soldiers shot and bayoneted to pieces upon an unknown, unprotected beach. Never had a chance. And all volunteers, too." He pauses. "But all the more reason to remember the blood those valiant Anzacs shed, Chancey."

"Well, thanks for the offer, Henry, but I'm just not sure it's my thing. Maybe you'd join me for a drink tonight at the Peninsula instead?"

"Half past five?"

"I'll look forward to it."

"Did Jillian make the trip?"

Jillian. Does he suspect something?

"Alas, no. Short notice and all that."

"Pity. But since you're alone we might have you home for dinner."

"I couldn't intrude." And had best stay clear.

"We'd be delighted"—he's sensed nothing—"but let's play it by ear."

He dials. Then abruptly cradles the handset. His windowed reflection catches his eye. Look a little guilty, there, Chancey. Quit while you're ahead. The reflection merely smiles and redials.

"You got home okay?"

"I did."

She sounds hurried. Maybe someone's in the background.

"I'm meeting your father for a drink tonight. He mentioned dinner later."

"Can't make it." She pauses. "But maybe we could all get together at tomorrow's parade." She laughs and clicks off.

The reflection's a voyeur. If the image in the window is reversed, that is to say, if his left eye is really looking at his right eye, then why isn't he also upside down? It cradles the phone and stands. But of course the left eye is looking at the left eye. It just seems like the right eye. She'll be there. With those lovely gray eyes. Mirrors of the soul and all that.

SYDNEY

"BOB BALLAST DIDN'T SEEM INTERESTED IN FU—"

"He's *bustin'* for the job, Hank. He's just a canny purchasing officer who plays his cards close to the chest."

"I think he's looking for more."

"For sure he's thinking long term. For now he just wants his foot in the door. An offer'll lose you nothing, Hank. There's no fee till he starts. And a refund if he's not on the job after four months."

"I suppose we could do worse than try him out."

"I'll structure a win-win for both parties, Hank."

AUCKLAND

HE PERCHES ON A CHROMIUM-STUMPED STOOL at the Peninsula's fake-marble bar, rests his impediment upon the foot rail, and studies the mirror that backdrops the barman. The hands of the embedded fluorescent clock put the time at half past five. To the left of the clock is the static reflection of the main door. To the right of the clock is the reflection of a harbor glimpse. Late afternoon sun and ferry fumes. Same scene as last time. He closes his eyes. What was that line again: "Whoever loved that loved not at first sight?" The same might be said of lust—

"Rest easy, Chancey."

A quick glance to the mirror confirms what he already knows: that's Henry's comradely arm upon his shoulder. He's in an old-soldier mood, no doubt.

"Hey, Henry! What can I get you to drink?"

"I'll bid the week good-bye with a Watney's. Let me get it, though." He motions to the bartender. "I'm having a guest along. And, hey, speak of the devil . . ."

Elan's headless, legless torso enters the mirror. The breasts heave against the white blouse. Such flimsy buttons. He swivels on the toadstool seat. She's silhouetted against the windows. The blouse is neatly tucked into an above-the-knee black skirt.

"You remember Chancey—"

"Of course." Her extended hand is soft, her half smile a tease. "The biz whiz."

"A glass of white while we think about that, sweetheart?" She nods. "Now, tell us darling, how were your classes?"

"Not too demanding. *Hamlet.*"

"Raising a family will be demanding enough, when the time comes. Meantime, Mister Haste might think about recruiting you a Mister Right." He glances to Chancey with mock seriousness. "Can't rely on serendipity to produce the ideal husband." He salutes the fading autumn light. "For most people, courtship is nothing more than a game of pin the tail on the donkey." He chortles and sips, then smiles donnishly. "But the wise know how to improve their chances. First, of course, a spouse should be *British.* The Americans speak English and are mostly white, so it's easy to think they're like us." He points his fingers to his pectorals. "Whereas they're really *foreigners.*" The upturned parental digit pokes the air. "No different, really, from the Poles, Greeks, Russians, whatever. So our children should never marry Americans. The men are weak and spoiled, the women pushy and aggressive."

"Elan won't need to look so far ashore. Some local rascal'll snap her up."

"Our daughters should never marry colonials, either. Kiwis are mostly rough diamonds. And the Aussies are convicts and warrant officers."

"Who does that leave us?"

"Well-bred English gentlemen—that's who our daughters should marry." He nods in Elan's direction. She's bemused. "Right, Elan?"

"Was it ever in doubt, Father?" She's heard all this before.

"And our sons?"

"Not English girls, Chancey. Never. The well-bred ones are spoiled, and the rest are prisoners of the class system. No, our sons should marry Kiwi girls. They're sensitive and nurturing, yet savvy and upwardly mobile." He beams. "Just like your Jillian, actually."

"So Elan'll be off to England to find a husband."

"I'll take an Englishman as husband and an Italian as lover."

"You can think about that when you graduate, darling. But there's more to marriage than lovemaking. Right, Chancey?"

"I've not been married long enough to know."

The sun's disappeared. Lights glisten on the water. Elan looks to Henry. "I've arranged to see my friend Beryl for dinner. I might even stay in town with her for the weekend."

Henry checks his chromium watch. "I'll need an early night if I'm to attend the dawn parade." He jumps up. "Shall I deliver you to Beryl, darling?"

"She's meeting me at seven."

"Well, then, I'll leave you two to finish your drinks."

"And I'll make sure this charming girl catches up with her friend."

"Don't forget, Elan; Mister Haste's in the people business. He can match you with a Mister Right."

"Or a Mister Close-Enough," she calls. But he's gone.

SYDNEY

"WONDERFUL NEWS, BOB! Hank's bustin' to hire you!"

"I'm not sure the job's for me."

"It's not a *job*, Bob. It's a *career*. You'll be creating a safer world. It's got your name written all over it."

"How much?"

"Gotta think in terms of *opportunity*, Bob—"

"Alice says money's important—"

"And she's right. And the money *is* good. But we're not *just* talking money. We're talking life. Happiness. Security. Advancement. *Fulfillment.*"

"How much?"

"He said he'd *start* you—start you, remember—on what you were earning in your last job."

"I need more. I never got a raise in that hell-hole."

"I didn't want to point that out, Bob. But I bumped him up for you."

"You did?"

"After six months he'll pay an extra ten percent, and—get this—*retroactive to day one!*"

"It's an improvement, I suppose."

"It's a *humongous* jump, Bob! And it's *guaranteed.* And that's *only the beginning!*"

"They'll pay more?"

"Of course! Hank Van Epenheusen's lavish with his top wallahs. Just have to make the team first."

"I suppose I could give it a shot."

"Hey, congratulations!"

"Congratulations?"

"You've seen the challenge and you've seized it, Bob. That takes *courage.* Hank said he picked you for a man with a mountain of savvy and ton of inner steel. How right he was. Now, let's see, you can start Monday, right?"

Auckland

"I COULD SEE MY FRIEND if I wanted to, Chancey."

She's a touch abashed. Or coy, maybe. But don't go jumping to conclusions.

"But you haven't arranged to, not yet, anyway, right?"

"Well, no, but I could."

His heart races. She's got the evening free. Maybe even the weekend. "Under the circumstances, I'm sure your father'd insist that you join me for dinner."

"You're really sure?"

"He'd say it was only polite."

They finish the wine but not the meal. The trio renders "Wichita Lineman."

"Did I show you the view from my room?"

"I remember it well."

"This is an entirely different room."

"With a different view?"

"Of course. One's whole perspective is changed."

"Sounds like Scientology."

The lights are soft. That's Donovan's "Mellow Yellow" wafting from the radio. Elan saunters to the window. "I can stay until the morning, but—"

He takes her hand. "Don't worry, nothing'll happen."

" 'If all the world were love and young, and truth in every shepherd's tongue.' " She smiles. "I believe you, Chancey. Nothing'll happen. We'll just talk poetry."

"Sure. Ever read 'Kubla Khan'? "

"The nuns taught it."

"I hear it's a description of the female genitalia—and copulation."

"Go *onnn*!"

"Really. Gives the lines a whole new meaning—'the deep romantic chasm which slanted down the green hill athwart a cedarn cover'—and so on."

"The chasm and the cover? Oh, hell, Chancey—that's definitely not what the nuns teach."

"Can't complete one's education in a convent."

"So, are you the demon lover, Chancey? The one with the flashing eyes and floating hair? The one who fed on honeydew and drank the milk of paradise?"

The buttons on the blouse are as flimsy as they seem. And the zipper on the skirt's just as yielding. Suspenders and a rush of musky warmth. Olive skin. Hooks and eyelets. Full, sweet, vulnerable lips. A swelling nipple. Moonlight upon skin. Silken stockings that float like butterflies to daisies.

She slips between the sheets. He settles alongside her in his undershorts. Her mouth is sweet. The breasts heave. Her quim's a flower to the sun. She arches. He doesn't want to press to have her.

Do I dare and do I dare? She cares and doesn't care. His lips to the petals, his tongue to the pip. Do I dare disturb the universe? The garden bright with sinuous rills. "Chancey. Chancey." The rich, fresh scent. "Chancey. Chancey. Chancey." Her torso tightens. He wraps her in his arms and holds her gently. Her heart pounds. He nuzzles her neck.

"Sorry, Chancey." She wraps her legs around his. They lie still.

"Doesn't bother me."

"You're an impartial observer?"

"An observer, but not impartial."

"A voyeur?"

"If your body were to pulse, your breasts to tighten and dance, your face were to shine like a van Gogh, well, it'd be discourteous to look the other way."

They sleep fitfully. He slips from the bed and half closes the blinds. As he slides back her slender arms enfold him. Her breath is fast, her mouth velvet, her nipples tight, her tongue sweet. "Chancey, Chancey, Chancey." The petals are wide, the pip inflamed. Her warm, perfumed neck offers no sanctuary. She wraps him in a vicelike grip and gasps. She softly yields and sheaths him tight. So sweet so warm, so dark the night. The two-backed beast seems content, for the moment, anyway, mostly to observe. She moans and cramps. There's no stopping the flood. No delay. No way. So this is the way the world ends. She arches and moans again. Then lies as still as death itself—

> *He kneels beneath the life-sized timber crucifix and stares at Christ's spiked feet. It's his turn to kiss the big toe of the foremost foot, then wipe it clean for the next supplicant. Saliva and friction have discolored both toes. Ghastly technicolor stations of the cross adorn the walls.*

Her head's turned, her hair spread out across the pillow like a sunrise. A crimson blot upon the linen sends his head spinning. The bloodstained sands of Anzac Cove? Not really. Yet something undoable's been done. She'll never be the Friday ingenue again. He offers his back to the window. Later will be soon enough to face

the light. The air's warm. One sheet is cover enough. He draws to
her but does not touch her. He closes his eyes—

> *You need discipline. His father leads him to the bedroom.
> His stomach forms into a knot. The whip whines through
> the air—*

A sharp crack resounds in his ears. He slips from the bed and
tweaks the venetian blind. A phalanx of ghostly, bemedaled, gray-
haired men are assembled at the downtown Anzac cenotaph to lay
their wreaths. An honor guard's presenting arms. Bayonets flash.
Gun butts crack. Heels click. Old soldiers salute. Is Henry there?
Who can tell? They all look like Henry in this faint dawn light. A
lamenting bugle sounds "The Last Post." He jams the window
tightly closed, then tugs the cord to cut the light. His mouth's furry—
the aftertaste of Chardonnay and honeydew. He slides alongside
her. She arches sensuously, and the sheet slips slowly. The nipples
are inflamed. The flower's aching for the bee. This time the beast
runs to the rhythms of the universe. This time the froth's slower to
rise. She draws him to the hilt, closes tightly, arches intensely. Her
tongue's a sensuous invader, her thighs a jungle trap, her nails a
tattooist's needles.

Steam floats from the bathroom. She's struggling with the
shower. "You okay there, girl?"

She cracks the door and peeps out, wide-eyed. "I checked
myself in the mirror, Chancey." The white hotel bathrobe highlights
her olive skin.

"Mirrors are magic."

"How come?"

"We can never see ourselves in them."

"What do we see?"

"A topsy-turvy world. Everyone going the wrong way. I'm
figuring it out." He grins, "What'd you think you saw?"

"I still look the same, Chancey." The voice's a husky whisper.
"A wave of something, passion, I guess, came over me." A hot
vapor curtain continues to rise behind her. "It was like a fierce wind
roaring high up in the bare branches of trees." She smiles. "I suppose
it's just lust. But it was awful and holy, like thunder and lightning

and wind." A dark expression suddenly descends upon her face. "I look the same, but I'm not the same. I'm a counterfeit." A touch of guilt singes his stomach. Might she weep? "I've tossed a part of me, the sweetest, nicest part of me, into a running stream, and it's being carried to the deepest ocean." She's a beguiling mix of irreverence and intensity. "It's lost forever, Chancey." A wan smile returns. "But it was my choice. So I thwarted destiny—right?"

"They say we meet it on the road we take to avoid it."

"So we might slip it by embracing it?"

"Sounds like a good idea."

Perched upon the guilty bed, he eavesdrops on the conversation between the steaming showerhead and her olive epidermis. Such a lovely, cleansing dialogue. But, hey—he grabs the phone. Might just catch Crawley in the office.

"So, Ungerford, hard at work?"

"I'm the original industrious virgin, Chancey. Trimming my wick. But you'd not be calling on Anzac Day unless you were diligent, too."

"Maybe not. Everything under control?"

"Yes and no. Burnham issued a summons. Our lawyer told him he's wasting his time. Explained we're flat-out chasing business. Promised he'll be the first cab off the rank when the money comes in."

"What'd Burnham say?"

"Left the summons in place. It's not all bad. Gives us time to breathe." He pauses. "There's a lot of wailing and gnashing of teeth on other fronts, too."

"You've got some trouble there?"

"You want the short answer?"

Trouble . . .

Some head for the can
When the ice hits the fan
But never the mover and shaker
He turns to the problem
And woos that hobgoblin
He knows to never forsake her

7

Stickies

SYDNEY

*S*HHHEEEE—IIII—ITTT! It's the quad on the line! He's gonna quit within the four-month guarantee period.

"I'm unhappy, Fuller!"

It is! It's him! The quad's coming unglued. So check the date—the *exact* date—of Bob Ballast's commencement with FU.

"Unhappy, Bob?" Doctor mode. "Hmmm. Want to talk about it?"

And here it is. The fucker's been there less than three months. If he spits the dummy within the next five weeks, Van Epenheusen'll scream for a refund.

"The job's just not me."

And the rainmaker's bonus will evaporate.

"Not quite you, eh, Bob? Hmmm. Not quite you."

"Van Epenheusen's a tyrant."

"I see. Hmmm. Yes. A chemistry problem."

"He's a nightmare. Last week he concocted a humongous list of things for me to do. He's taken to breathing down my neck. Literally. I think he wants my skin."

"Clarity, Bob. He likes clarity. I'm sure it's nothing personal."

"I'm not happy. I'm gonna quit on Friday."

Oh, shit!

"Let's get together first, Bob. Bat the issues around."

"I'm just going to tell him to stick it!"

"In a storm, you need to keep one hand for the boat, and one for yourself."

"I was never a sailor."

Don't doubt it. No sea legs. No fucking legs *at all*.

"Never let go of what you're holding on to, until you're holding on to something else, Bob."

"There's nothing here to grab."

I'll find you a new job, Bob. But you have to hold on to FU meantime."

"For how long?"

"Another five weeks'll do it, Bob."

"Sounds very precise."

"Well, I mean, about a month or two."

"Can't hang on that long." The voice drops. "And there're things about Freedom you need to know."

"Like what?"

"Like I can't say right now."

"So drop by and we'll talk."

Dear God, let me get a crack at him in the flesh.

"After five?"

"Not a problem for a friend, Bob."

JILL SNAPS OUT THE LIGHT. Her warm body's at his back. She wraps an arm around him, then touches her lips to his ear.

"I don't mean to destroy the moment, Chancey, but we've got a problem."

He pulls the sheet about him and closes his eyes. Elan's image flickers in the back of his mind like a continuous feature film.

"With what?"

Elan's face comes up in full color, luminous as ever. She beams and beckons.

Jill's breath is on his neck.

"I'm worried about Angie."

Elan unbuttons her blouse.

"What's the problem?"

And cups her silky breasts.

"Angie gets down on herself."

Elan's navel delights the tongue.

"Well, it might be nothing."

The flower is sweet.

"And she works too hard."

The buds are ripe.

"And she's so demanding of attention."

Elan's thighs tighten on his ears.

"Something's worrying me, Chancey."

He pulses within the twin planets.

"I don't quite know what."

The mouth is velvet.

"Don't worry, Jilly."

"But I do worry, Chancey. I worry too much—and you don't worry enough."

"Don't fret, Jilly. Worrying never helps."

"Yeah, Chancey. You're probably right." Jill pauses, lost in thought, then spoons herself to him.

THE QUADRIPLEGIC'S EYES ARE WIDE. "FU isn't in the freedom business at all!"

"They're not?"

"They fabricate alarms and locks. But that's not where the profits are. They're assembling land mines—"

"Land mines? Hey! *There's* a growth industry. Wow! You sure?"

"I crept through the files. Dug it all out." He leans forward in his contraption. "That's how they got the export awards. They supply weapons to terrorists."

"That's an exciting business."

"FU's mission is blowing people's legs off!"

"One man's terrorist's another man's freedom fighter, Bob. And FU's looking out for us Aussies, right? Do we care if Arabs or darkies blow each other to bits? I mean, ethically, our duty's *not* to care." Clergy mode. "Our moral duty, irrespective of race, color, creed, or even sexual orientation, is to supply the highest bidder." Economist. "Free enterprise's all about not undermining the system so long as everything's legal."

"Oh, it's legal enough. But FU's blowing legs off, too—"

"Not *Aussie* legs, Bob." Statesman mode. "FU's *safeguarding* Australia. *And* building the economy. *And* paying taxes to educate our kids. I mean *we* haven't just stepped down from the trees. Look, Bob"—stare the fucker down—"my moral concern is with *you.*" Don't even blink. "If you were my own brother I'd still say"—soft purr—"don't let go of what you're holding on to 'til you're holding on to something else."

"That's easy for you to say."

He's one of those close-minded minions who can't hear good advice.

"Not at all. It's *hard* for me to say. I'm a trained HR professional, so I know you're hurting. But this's not a time to quit." Pause. "It's a time to *dig in.*" Still skeptical. Only the romance card left to play. Here goes. "It's a time to consider your *loved ones*, Bob. Alice and the kids. Your own flesh and blood."

"What about them?"

"Quit now and you'll put their lives at risk. One wrong move and finding another job could become"—deep breath, long pause—"impossible." Head-drop to sternum. Sad, slow, three-second side-to-side shake. Raise the orbs, square the jaw, stare right into the bugger's eyes. "God only knows what Alice might end up having to do to make ends meet." Deep sorrowful sigh.

Silence. Utter silence.

The jackpot—he's hit the jackpot!

"What else've you got for me?"

"You place me in an ethical dilemma, Bob."

"An ethical dilemma?"

"Ethics are intrinsic to the HR profession, Bob. It'd be a huge feather in my cap to place an achiever like you again. I could grease the way for you, too. I could explain the chemistry problem at Freedom."

"You've a client in mind?"

Pushy, pushy—God, he's pushy.

"I have *two* clients in mind. Both paying more money."

"When can I meet them?"

Has he no shame?

"Ethics, Bob, ethics. I need to do right by you. Find you a perfect fit. Advance your career. Safeguard Alice and the kids. But I also need to do right by FU. You see"— conspiratorial staredown—"Hank always planned to promote you after four months."

"Four months?"

"Special plans are in the works."

"I never knew."

"Hank's not a carrot dangler. He wanted to see you perform first."

"Plans—what plans?"

"I'm not at liberty to say. Hank doesn't like his right hand to know what his left hand's doing. But a nod's as good as a wink, right? So, hang in there for another couple of months. *Then*, if you're not thrilled and amazed by what happens, I'll whip you straight across the street to one of these other clients." Fuller pauses. "*But*— meantime—*just sit tight*. Have I made myself clear, Bob? Can you see where your best interests lie?"

"AH, MR. HASTE, HOW CAN I HELP?" The narrow-eyed travel agent extends his moist palm. The stale breath is beer-tinged. The shirt's losing the struggle with the belly. A touch of yellow stains the crotch.

"I need to book a weekend in Queenstown."

The beady eyes sneak a peek at the impediment. "Lovely time to hop the Tasman. Takin' anyone along?"

"Sort of. My wife might just join me later. And, by chance, a Kiwi friend has asked me to make some bookings, too."

"Be traveling with yer wife or yer friend?"

"My wife's plans are still unsettled. I'll fly to Auckland, pick up my friend. Then on to Queenstown. Leave the return reservations open."

Stubby fingers start to write a ticket. "Just need yer friend's name."

"Well, she's not the actual friend. She's the, uh, daughter."

"A minor?"

"No, no—she's, uh, eighteen."

"Eighteen."

"Or so."

"And the name?"

"Haverford. E. Haverford."

"I'll need the full first name."

"Elan."

"*Elan*. Hmmm. Lovely name." He smiles broadly. "You're gonna Fokker, of course."

"I'm going to what?"

"*Fokker.* You're gonna *Fokker.* You'll not have much choice. You'll have to Fokker. Fokker-Friendship. It's the name of a plane. Twin props. Rattles a bit. Krauts make it." He winks. "Lots of vibration in the seats. I hear some of these Kiwi girls can really get off on that." He smiles. "Anyhow, it's the only way to get from Auckland to Christchurch that day." He pauses. "Then you've gotta take a DC Douglas." He winks again, then clears his throat and swallows his phlegm. "What about Queenstown accommodations?"

"Two rooms. A double and a single."

"I can pull you a special deal on a *very* romantic, out-of-the-way spot overlooking the Remarkables." He smiles. "And we'll put yer friend's daughter in an adjoining room so she won't come to any harm." He stands. "Leave it all to me. I presume I shouldn't send the tickets to yer office?"

"I'll collect them."

"Of course. Can't have a getaway if everyone knows yer fokking whereabouts."

THAT DOUBLE-GLAZED Sydney office window's warm to the touch, Chancey. And the time's just one minute to three by the distant clock. The harbor's brilliant, windswept. The business elite with money and time to burn has gathered. Their yachts jockey like floating serpents for position on the starting line. Bright white clouds scuttle overhead. A strong northerly wind whips the sails. Be great to be out there and show all that to Elan—

"You'll have to have a word with him, Chief." Crawley, trouser flares flying, is pacing the floor. "His sales skills are mediocre at best."

"Brittle?" He offers Crawley a soothing smile. "You're talking about Brittle Dick?"

"I also sat in on one of his client visits." Crawley's got that unbelieving headshake down to a fine art. "He's just not got the warmth."

"He seems eager. What's his style?"

"Scoutmaster. Tries to bore them into submission. It's not a problem with candidates. He can ferret them out if he has a job to peddle. But his client-gathering skills are inferior."

"He burns the leather?"

Crawley adjusts the ungainly knot on his shocking-pink tie.

"He gets out to see prospects, but he never converts. Talks up his MBA, then fiddles with his glasses and goes on about his principles. He quotes from the ethical creed he prepared himself. Carries it in his briefcase."

"But clients aren't persuaded?"

"His pitch plays against him. When he goes on about *not* poaching from *his* clients, he creates the impression someone else here would."

"And would we?"

"You wouldn't. I wouldn't either. Be self-defeating. I suppose some others might be tempted—"

"They'd poach from a client?"

"Who knows what people might do to meet the monthly bills? The spirit can be as weak as the flesh sometimes."

"So Brittle peeves his prospects? How does he rationalize this?"

"Says he's a long-term operator. Says they'll come back later."

"I suppose they might."

"Maybe. But meantime his figures are rotten." Crawley shifts gears. "The tide's turning in our favor, Chancey. But we can't afford to lose momentum. A word from you could make all the difference. You're a brilliant and inspiring teacher. You could dangle the carrots of expansion and promotion."

"I'm flat-out fixing up Godzone. But I'll definitely buttonhole him." He slowly turns on his good foot. "Meantime— meantime why don't we"— he addresses his remarks to the window— "might it not be possible to—" He spins and studies Crawley. Must do something about that dreadful tie. "Why not send Fyfe along with him on a few presentations? Brittle could do his professorial turn and Fuller could close the deal."

"Wait a minute, now!" Crawley whirls in a circle. "You might just've had another of those brilliant insights of yours, Chief." He twirls again—then smiles. "Yes—*balance* them. Brittle *and* Fyfe. Get some synergy going. Keep them both focused, both on the straight and narrow."

He strolls to that warm window. The yachts are on a reach, heading to the lighthouse. Now, there's an allusion she'd love.

"I have to confess the insight's not entirely my own." Crawley's attentively silent. "Got the idea from my Roman Catholic upbringing." He turns. "You know why nuns go around in pairs?" Crawley shakes his head. "So one nun can make sure the other nun gets none."

Crawley's head bounces like a jack-in-the-box. "Brilliant, Chancey! That's simply brilliant." He's still nodding. "A dazzling unconscious application of folklore wisdom. What a gift. Yes, indeed. When we get to New York, we're really going to knock 'em dead." He gyrates out the door without looking back.

That warm window's bewitching. The boats are on their way back from the lighthouse, spinnakers flying beneath the deepest of blue skies. Blue skies. Why does he associate Elan with blue skies?

8

Kleptomaniacs

BURSTS OF CLOUD stream past the throbbing window. Verdant farmland shimmers. Azure waves wash the coast. Twin props drag them southward.

"You're fidgeting, Chancey." Elan's wearing the lightest of makeup. The navy sheath's ridden above her knees.

"I'm jumpy. Godzone's too tiny. Queenstown's too popular." He glances over his shoulder. Might be a touch conspicuous in his two-tone tan shoes, flared gray flannels, white polo neck shirt, and silver-buttoned, double-breasted, blue knit blazer. He slides the identifying clubfoot, as best he can, under the seat in front. At least the conversation won't carry over the jabbering propellers. He buries his head in a newspaper long on racing form and rugby but short on everything else. She drops a leaf of bond paper under his nose, then slides her hand into his. She's warm and sultry. Four lines this time. Ten to come, no doubt—

> My pursuer sounds a truly tempting tongue
> And teases me with tantalizing lies;
> I merely smile and let myself succumb,
> Thus feigning innocence of subtleties.

Her red earring tastes of perfume. "A very nice first quatrain— and truthful, too. *Feigning's* such a lovely word. Did you ever succumb, by the way, to the view of the Southern Alps from the private rooms?"

Her smile's impish. "The small rooms in the rear?"

"They say the perspective's breathtaking."

"Maybe I could stretch my legs."

She saunters back. Follow her, but not too closely. He presses through the folding door she's left ajar. He slides the lock. They're crushed together face to face. Her skirt rides to her thighs. He unbuttons the blouse. She jiggles braless beneath the cool air vent. The nipples are inflamed, the pupils dilated, the face flushed, the mouth parted, the lips moist. Time is of the essence. Her tongue is sweet, her breasts sensuous. The blouse falls to her waist. A film of perspiration forms on her torso. The engines roar. The floor vibrates. The walls rattle. The beast writhes like a demented cobra. He's lost in space . . .

> *He kneels upon a wooden floor in a classroom of seven-year-olds. A catatonic brother leads the murmuring of Hail Marys and the tallying of plastic rosary beads. Midday sun strikes a depressing wall-mounted Virgin and Child. Stolen money from his father's cash register burns in his pocket. He feels guilty, empty, remorseful. The brother fixes him with a half-open eye—*

Her face's still flushed as she drops her voice to a whisper. "I'll go first." She reaches over his shoulder and slides the folding door. Lights flutter. She slips past. He tugs on his zipper of his pants and turns—to find himself gazing directly into the beady eyes of a somber, nerdy, dark-haired, forty-something Roman Catholic priest. He reflexively grabs the door and slams it shut. The lights flicker on again. Oh, shit—the buggers are everywhere. But that full-bladdered friar doesn't know what happened. Not for sure. And who cares if he does? Who's he going to tell—the Pope?

He hoists the zipper, then washes his hands. The wall signage is reversed in the basin mirror. He turns and gently slides the door ajar. The condemning eyes fix upon his face. The little devil's been waiting.

"Your turn for a little heavenly relief, Father?"

His Holiness is not amused.

SYDNEY

JILL SOUNDS DISTRACTED. "We have to talk, Chancey."

"About?" He presses his back to the airport phone booth.

"About Blake! Oh, shit, Chancey—haven't you been listening?"

"Yeah, I'm listening. Bit of crackle on the line. Just run it by me again."

"*Shoplifting*, Chancey. The store outside the school. They *caught* him."

"Most kids steal."

"They've suspended him. Next time they'll *expel* him."

"Really?"

"That's what they said!"

"Not good. You want me to have a word with him?"

"He didn't need to steal, Chancey." She pauses. "Kleptomania's a cry for help."

"He's got everything he needs—"

"Except a father. He needs *attention*—and you never give him any."

"I give him a lot."

"He doesn't think so. Wake up, Chancey. You're missing out. You're sleepwalking. Childhood's brief." There's a quaver in her voice. "These kids will be gone before you know it." She clicks off.

> I've a top-drawer wife
> In a harbor-view home
> Two mortgaged kids
> And a lover on the phone

CHRISTCHURCH TO QUEENSTOWN

A SURGE OF SEMIPARENTAL responsibility infects the Chancian conscience as Elan clasps his hand and they join the half dozen assorted sight-seeing couples striding across the Christchurch tarmac. They jam into a refitted twin-prop DC3 that might've carried cargo in World War II. She takes the window seat. He's next to her. The plane struggles shakily upward and the cabin chills. They level out and the engine din eases. The snowcapped peaks of the Southern Alps push upward through a carpet of cloud. An apparently free-floating descent seems quickly to follow. The Remarkables emerge through the clouds. They look like an enormous sundae for the gods; white sugar peaks, chocolate shoulders, lush green base fronting to a glistening, crystal-clear lake. Then comes a sprinkling of tiny chalets and houses, all bathed in a setting sun. The plane flutters, hovers like a seagull, then skates gently to rest upon the tiny Queenstown airstrip. They step out onto warm tarmac. The clean air smells of wildflowers.

MOUNTAINVIEW MOTEL. The sign's shocking-pink neon—and it blinks. MOUNTAINVIEW MOTEL. The building's a shabby-stuccoed bungalow. MOUNTAINVIEW MOTEL.

A porky, weathered witch slides the register across the counter, sticks her head into their space, and peers at the impediment.

He blurts the words in an all-too-shrill pitch: "Separate rooms!" He drops his voice an octave. "My wife'll be joining us later so *I'll* need a double."

The witch eyes Elan. "Best we can do is twins," she says, not without satisfaction.

"My wife'll be very disappointed."

"You won't find anything better at this hour."

He signs the register and pushes it to Elan.

"We'd like to get a drink."

"Outta luck. We've no liquor license, and all the pubs closed at six."

"There must be something open."

She points a grimy finger to a tired antique clock. "Nearly nine. Outta luck." She peers to Elan. "Anyway, yer friend's gotta be overage."

TIME FOR ONE PHONE CALL, CHANCEY. Might just catch Crawley in the office.

He jams himself into a tight booth and presses the clumsy, black MountainView phone to his ear.

"Hey, Chancey!" It's Brittle. Honing his ethical creed, no doubt. "Crawley's gone. I'm catching up on some paperwork. Glad you called, though." He defaults to earnest mode. "Fuller says you're serious about a New York office."

"I'm definitely working that way."

"You'll need a first-rate manager here then, Chancey."

"I certainly will."

"I'm a real manager, Chancey. Not just a salesman." The line crackles. "You might think I'm a little too, uh, *straight*."

"Straightness has no gradations, Richard."

"Right. And I'm a tough nut. I don't just do the right thing. I get results, too. I'd attract the right kind of person."

A dig at Fuller? Probably. Or Crawley? Perhaps.

"Everyone knows you're a great guy, Richard. I've got to satisfy someone of your caliber. You're definitely in line for King-of-the-Sydney-Hill when New York opens up."

"I don't mean to press, Chancey. I just have to be up front."

"Is there any other way to be?"

ELAN'S CONTEMPLATING her sagging single bed. There's a wardrobe, a dresser, no window, and a small bathroom across the hall. A corner door adjoins his quarters. They stroll through. The sheetrocked walls are gray, the floor linoleumed. A faded aerial photo of Queenstown hangs between the faded, flowered-linened twin beds. Opposite stands a Formica-topped bench and sink.

He checks the cupboard: electric toaster, crockery, battered cutlery. An overbright pumpkin light hangs overhead. "Pretty swish, eh?"

"Yeah, but look at that." She turns to his near-black picture window. "Sun's long gone, but you can almost make out the Remarkables."

She wraps an arm around him. "One should always have something remarkable to look forward to." She grins. "Oscar said that, you know. Or something like it."

CRACK! THE SLIDING HATCH FIRES like a shotgun as the witch's hands thrust it skyward. Bony fingers propel a battered metal breakfast tray onto the Formica top. A shriek pierces the cold air. "Eightta-clock! Breakfast. Get it before it goes cold!" The crone disappears. The hatch crashes back down.

"I hadn't imagined breakfast would be served in the room. Yet here it is. Two of everything."

She peeps from the covers. "Pretty swish."

"Best tuck in quick, the air in this room could chill just about anything." He struggles out of bed, crosses the icy hall to the communal toilet. His tug upon the dangling chain discharges a torrent of icy water that splashes his feet.

"Not bad," says Elan when he returns. "Bacon and eggs, tea and toast." She pours the steaming tea into thick white mugs and passes him one. As he reaches out they're suddenly aware of the surreal, overpowering, snowcapped Remarkables in the picture window.

"Looks like the lid of a giant chocolate box."

"They're awesome. God's been spying."

They gulp breakfast. Elan springs back into bed. He jumps in next to her. Her face shines in the reflected light of the Remarkables. He closes his eyes and lowers his head to her lips.

Crack!

Oh, hell, not again.

"Finished yer breakfast, then?"

"Ah, not quite," he replies.

"Stickit-back-when-yer-through."

The hatch crashes closed. He tosses back the bedcovers. "Come on, girl—we're checking out!"

"That's impossible. Where—"

"Somewhere. Anywhere." He springs from the bed and pulls on his trousers.

"Really?" She cracks a smile. "Hey, good one, Chancey. Time to move it. *Eh, boy, eh,* as the locals say." She jumps up and pulls on her jeans. She catches him peeking in the dresser mirror. She raises the nightdress, cups her blue-veined, strawberry-nippled breasts, and purses her lips. "Bad boy, Chancey!" she scolds. "Bad, bad boy!"

She pulls her black, crewnecked, lamb's-wool jersey over her head and brings it down like a stage curtain. She perches on the bed and tugs on her tan riding boots. She applies lipstick and a trace of perfume.

She tosses a faded denim jacket over the jersey, grins, and bumps her hips. " 'Lord won't ya buy me a Mercedes-Benz . . .' " She warbles the words slowly, slipping in a couple of choo-choos. "Janis Joplin, Chancey—did you ever hear of Janis Joplin?" The jacket's open. Her nipples stab the lamb's-wool sweater. " 'My friends all drive Rovers, I must make amends . . .' " Arms akimbo, hips and thighs rocking, she belts out the last line, " 'So, Lord won't ya buy me, a Mercedes Benz.' "

ONCE MORE INTO THE MOUNTAINVIEW PHONE. Crawley's out chasing business. Fuller wants to talk. The voice is plaintive. "Is it all leading somewhere, Chancey?"

The meaning of life. He wants to know the meaning of life.

"Of course. Just got to keep on working at it."

The sigh is lugubrious.

"Got something in mind, Fuller?"

"I sometimes feel I'm getting nowhere. Just moving bodies around. Putting bums on chairs. Ya-know-what-I-mean?"

"Here's the thing, Fuller." This had better be good. "Lawyers handle conveyancing. *Bo-or-ring*. Or divorce. *De-pressing*. Bankers refuse loans or give them to people who don't need them. *Frus-trat-ing*. Dentists deal with rotten teeth, doctors mostly treat hypochondriacs, and, in the end, undertakers put us all into coffins. *We're* the lucky ones, Fuller. We're *professional HR men*. We meet people at the crossroads of their lives. We point them in the right direction and make their dreams come true. We make a difference. We change the world." Silence on the line. "*That's* where it's all leading, Fuller—right?"

"Yeah. Well. I dunno, Chancey. I need something to perk me up."

"A double espresso for the soul??"

"I was thinking of promotion."

Money, status, more of absolutely everything—that's what he wants.

"You're doing a great job, Fuller. We're turning the corner and establishing a war chest. You and Brittle have transformed yourselves into a great team. You've got some real synergy going. So promotion is at hand. I'll get us going in New York. Crawley'll join me. Then you'll be in line for King-of-the-Sydney-Hill."

"What about Brittle?"

"Too early to say."

The sigh, though heartfelt, is a touch less melancholy than the last. "I just don't get the respect I should, Chancey. I need a better title, at least."

"Like?"

"Maybe Manager Executive Selection, Sydney. Whattaya say, Chancey?"

"Well. Sure. Why not?" *Crack!* The witch's back. "Got a likely prospect here, Fuller. Got to race. Catch up with you next week."

He clunks the chunky MountainView phone back into its clumsy cradle and stares at nothing. Meaning of life? Money? Respect? Status? Power? Beautiful women? What *is* it all about? Maybe he's the one who needs the guru. A sage to say, "One moment, young man—is any of this leading in the right direction?"

But he's racing somewhere, surely.

To other worlds.

And they, frankly, are racing—very quickly now—to him.

9

Pursuers

ELAN'S FINGERNAILS BITE INTO HIS PALM. The wind compresses the color from her face as the jet boat rips to full speed. Tears run from her eyes. Her hair streams backward. That racing-gloved daredevil at the wheel seems barely out of his teens. The other half dozen sightseers are frozen with panic. They plane through mere inches of shallow water kicking up curtains of foam. Razor-sharp overhanging cliffs whistle perilously close to their eyes. They lurch into plunging rapids. Ice-cold water hits their faces. Is this a thrill-seeker heaven, or what? And all too suddenly—and none too quickly—the gut-churning ride is over.

And, now, a change of pace as the noon ski lift draws them into the sky. The window table at the Coronet Peak restaurant seems almost to float above the shimmering lake, two thousand feet below, at the foot of the Remarkables.

He raises a glass of white wine and sunlight.

"To the gods who brought us to their mountains."

"And the MountainView Motel?"

"We need the lows to appreciate the highs."

He peppers his oysters, stabs one with his fork, dips it in vinegar, and raises it to his lips.

"Looks good, Chancey."

"It is good. It's great. Want to share?" He quaffs the oyster and slides three of the remaining dozen onto her plate. She spears one, dips it in vinegar, and raises it.

"Damned right! Is good, eh boy?"

A burst of sunlight hits her face. Time freezes. Chardonnay and oysters. Elan smiling, joking, laughing. The sun-filled lake beneath their feet seems incredibly tiny, as if viewed through the wrong end of a pair of binoculars.

"Long way to fall, baby."

She studies the drop. "There's another world beneath that looking-glass lake, Chancey."

"A world of elves and gnomes and magic dragons?"

"A world of souls and dreams and unlived lives." She's suddenly lost in the world of imagination. "It's a whole other dimension. It's the universe that all the streams run into. It's EBC's timeless realm."

"EBC?"

"Elan Before Chancey, the girl I used to be. She's happily ensconced in that peace-filled place where our deepest longings are fulfilled."

"What more could a girl want?"

"On that side of the glass, nothing." She tips her goblet. "On this side, altogether too much."

JILL'S VOICE CRACKLES ON THE LINE. "I'm worried about Angie."

His reply echoes in his ear. "Sorry, Jill, didn't quite catch that."

"I'm worried about Angie." She sounds far off. She worries too much.

"What's the problem?"

"She works too hard."

"Angie?"

"Yes, she drives herself. She frets."

"What can I do?"

"She's looking for attention."

"She gets a lot of attention."

"*I* give her attention. It's not enough. She wants *your* attention, Chancey."

"I give her time—as much as I can. I'm hectically busy."

"You're always chasing a dollar somewhere, Chancey. But you need to give her time."

"Quality time?"

"Real time, Chancey."

"I'll be back soon, Tuesday or so. Let's go over it then."

QUEENSTOWN TO MOUNT COOK

"YOU OKAY BACK THERE, MISTER HASTE?" The solicitous voice belongs to the pilot of the twin-engined six-seater Cessna. Discount the sincerity of the inquiry, however, for the fellow's navigational eyes are fixated upon Elan.

"Everything's just fine, thanks."

In fact the cabin reeks of high-octane petrol. Fortunately, he and Elan are tucked away by the rear exit. The smell's probably worse up front. But, holy shit—who's that clambering aboard? A mop of red hair atop a sunburned pumpkin head. Oh, Christ—it's that dreadful printer, Burnham! He's hunkering into the seat next to the pilot. And now he swivels the pumpkin backward to address the floral-frocked, blue-rinsed matron in the seat immediately behind.

"You all right, luv?" She's his wife, no doubt. She nods and grunts—more of a quack, actually. Burnham tosses a vacant glance to the back row and grins. "We're Aussies!" he gurgles.

Show him no more than half an eye. Hide all else behind the blue rinse.

"We've been catchin' the sights on a package tour," says Burnham, this time to Elan.

Elan smiles and Burnham swells. He studies her closely, then grins.

"Now, I'll bet *I* know what *you're* doin'!" The grin widens, exposing the missing incisor. "*You're* stoppin' in Franz Joseph!"

Elan involuntarily nods.

Keep Blue-Rinse between you and those pumpkin eyes, Chancey.

Burnham licks his lips and bobbles his head. "Honeymooners, eh? Am I right?"

Elan blushes and pockets her hands.

Blue-Rinse cackles and half-turns.

Burnham grins to Elan. "No worries, darlin'." He proffers the Aussie thumbs-up salute with a wink. "Your secret's safe with us. We're not stoppin'. Just connecting back to Sydney."

"Everyone okay?" All eyes snap to the Kiwi captain. "All strapped in, right?" He hits the ignition and the propellers kick.

As the plane flutters down the tiny runway, stutters into the air, and dog-paddles to just above the snowcapped mountains, it's the image of Burnham that commands the mind. Is Pumpkin-Head a messenger? Is his presence an omen? Is the Almighty telling Chancey to bring the focus back to work? No, don't be absurd, there's no deeper meaning to Burnham. Mishaps are the stuff of life. Doubly so, perhaps, when one dares to live according to the strictures of the heart. Or is that strictures-of-the-heart idea just another rationalization for doing the wrong thing while descending into the depths of everlasting hell? Oh, *please*, there's no such place as hell. Maybe Burnham's some kind of authority figure. Authority.

The old man always had an opinion on everything. Politics, law, religion, ethics, business—there was no way to get a word in. He could talk the leg off an iron pot, so maybe he figured he could perform a similar trick for his son's clubfoot. Might have been wiser to attempt to soothe the mangled footprints in the heart. Well, there's no way that conversation's ever going to happen, right?

Hey!—the tires screech and the cabin bounces. They've touched down.

The rattling Cessna taxis to a beaten army-green Range Rover. Burnham turns to Elan, shoots his right thumb into the air, and nods.

"Enjoy yerself, darlin'!" The pumpkin eyes search for the bridegroom. "Both of youse—God bless both of youse." The loved one nods approvingly.

Keep the head down, Chancey, pretend not to hear. Focus on exiting this tiny, confining rear door. Elan follows and grabs his hand. The pilot loads their two travel bags into the Rover. They step to the vehicle. He glances backward. A mistake. Burnham's bloodshot eyes, framed in the Cessna window, bore into the impediment. Then up to his face. Then to Elan, then back again. Stern-faced, he mutters something to Blue-Rinse. Now she's gaping, too.

Mount Cook
"LIKE THE ROOM, CHANCEY?"

Clean white walls. Natural Rimu trim. Fauna watercolors. And a king-sized double bed overlooking a private garden of natural ferns. "Yeah, it's more like what I had in mind."

"I don't think I want to know what goes on in your mind, Chancey."

"I was thinking you'd like the view from the bed."

"Of the ferns?"

"Maybe." He falls backward onto the forgiving mattress and gazes up at a tiny skylight. "There's also a daring glimpse of Franz Joseph from right here."

She springs onto the bed and, standing, gazes upward. "Hey, there really is! I can have a choice of views." She drops to Chancey's side. "I can peek at the mountain." She smiles. "Or we can find a way to study the ferns. You're a devil, Chancey."

"Don't blame me, it's a Wildean idea."

"He was gay, Chancey."

"No, no—nothing sexual."

She smiles impishly. "I was referring to his wisdom. He said we're all lying in the gutter—"

" 'But some of us are looking at the stars.' Bravo, Chancey."

"It was Oscar's idea."

"Ahead of his time, as usual." She jumps up, saunters to the writing desk, and picks up a brochure. "Hey, Chancey." Her voice drops. "They have a chapel."

"I'm sure they have a Gideon Bible, too."

She smiles. "A chapel on a mountain." She flips the pages. "And a seven A.M. service." She glances to him. "Could be fun."

"I'm trying to give it up. Just depresses me."

"It's a whole other dimension, Chancey. The spirit, you know?"

"Yeah, kind of. I went to a Rosicrucian meeting once. With Jill—" Oh, hell—why'd he say that? Looking for a smart reply. He should never've mentioned Jill. Not to Elan.

"We never talk about Jill."

"I know."

"I think about her, Chancey."

"I try not to."

"You love her, don't you, Chancey?" She glances away. "I shouldn't have asked." Then back at him, with a wan smile. "I can deal with it, Chancey."

"WE MIGHT BE ON THE MEND, CHANCEY!"

"Things are looking good?"

"Much better. *Much* better. I guess you're thinking about the parable of the talents, these days."

Crawley loves a little artifice. He inherited it from his failed-actress mother, no doubt. Elan's soaping herself—there, back over his shoulder—in a steam-filled shower.

"Yeah. Sort of. Among other things."

"Nothing's covered that shall not be revealed, Chancey—ah, no—what I'm saying is, there'll be no need to hide your light under a bushel."

"I guess not."

"The natives are getting restless."

"Who?

"Fyfe, Brittle. The rest of them. They're looking for raw meat, Chancey."

"Where're they going to get it?"

"*We* have to come up with it, Chancey."

"Where are *we* going to get it?"

"He either fears his fate too much—"

"Huh?"

"Or his desserts are small—"

"Whatever are you saying, Crawley?"

"That puts it not unto the touch—"

"You've lost me."

"To win or lose it all."

Can you believe it? The bugger just hung up.

HE ADJUSTS HIS TIE AND GLANCES over the dining room. A fireplace crackles in the corner, and there's a spotlit fern garden beyond the French doors. The tables are very properly set with starched white linen, real silver, and glowing candelabras. The dozen or so well-dressed guests momentarily mute their murmurings as they glance first to Elan and then to him. He recognizes no one. Thank goodness for that. And now the would-be voyeurs refocus back into their own conversations.

"The wine register, sir."

The laminated list's in gothic type. "We'll try the Grange."

"The Grange Hermitage. Oh—an excellent choice, sir. Even at the price." He disappears.

"Holy shit, Chancey—must've cost a bundle for him to say that." The short, white, lamb's-wool sheath highlights her tan.

"No, the price's very reasonable. It's the top-of-the-line Aussie red. A secret blend of rich earthy grapes, aged in oaken casks."

She glances toward the softly flaming log fire, then turns her eyes back to him. "Anything special about the fucking bottle itself?"

Fucking. She rarely swears, but when she does, she confects it with that same lovely lilt. So now the word is fuckeen. Very erotic.

"Gem green. It could make a lovely bedside lamp."

"Maybe a jeweler could fashion it into cuff links."

"You might prefer a brooch."

The waiter reappears, uncorks the bottle, wipes the lip, and pours a mouthful into Chancey's glass. He passes the glass to Elan.

"You taste it."

She raises the glass, studies the color, sips—and smiles. The tannin glistens in her perfect teeth. He touches his good foot to her unstockinged leg.

"Yes! And yes I said yes." She nods to the startled waiter. "Yes, I will, yes."

He dims the lights and sets the quarter-full Grange bottle on the bedside table. She tugs at his blazer and tie. Her tongue tastes of Shiraz. She kicks off her pumps and loses the dress. She spins, braless. He stands behind her. Her breasts press sensuously into his palm. He glances into the dressing-table mirror. Her eyes are closed, her skin flushed. Her neck is warm, sweet. And now she's naked. He leans forward on the dressing table. Her hair cascades across her breasts. Her nipples are cherries. Which is right and which is left? Who cares? She's warm and tight. She draws away, unbuttons his shirt, then falls back upon the bed. He sets a pillow beneath her. He reaches for the Grange and tilts the scarlet to the triangle. Shiraz never tasted better.

Face to face now, lost in time. Now, she contracts, now she pulls him down, now she closes like a vise, now her whole being draws his essence from him, cleansing all his sins and sending him spinning . . .

*He sets the seething fur-ball on the faded wooden seat of the
outside dunny and raises the hatchet. The yellow eyes burn.
The cat springs, clawing, hissing, pissing, crazy. Then it
bolts through a gap in the door. He puts on his innocent
face and ducks back into the house. She's ironing. She says
nothing, then looks at him oddly. "You been trying to kill
the cat?"*

SYDNEY

"BIGFOOT MUST BE PICKING UP stray pussy in Godzone."

"Judge not, Fuller."

"Goes there all the time."

"On business—we have business there."

"Weekends at the Peninsula, Ungerford. Trips all over the place."

"Chancey's attracted some nice trans-Tasman business for us, you have to admit that."

"Well, yeah, but he's as distracted as buggery when he gets back. Been goin' on I don't know how long, now."

"Maybe you're envious. Maybe you'd like to rush around like a tycoon, too."

"I'd settle for some stray pussy—"

"If you could find it."

"There's a ton of it around. You just need credit cards."

MOUNT COOK

HE REACHES OUT, BUT ELAN'S NOT THERE. Just an empty indentation in the bed. He rolls into that furrow and basks in her scent. Where is she? Five to seven by the bedside clock. He listens. She's gone. He knows where. He springs into the shower, then out of it just about as quickly. He tosses on his clothes, runs a comb through his hair, and strides to the chapel.

He eschews the holy water—they say it's holy, anyway—and stands in back of the tiny, white-walled chapel. Five small Rimu pews sit upon a bare, polished Kauri floor. One sun-filled, vertical, narrow slit of a window drops a stream of diffused white light onto a boxlike, white-linened altar. Elan and half a dozen others are at the rail. A green-and-gold-robed priest raises the chalice, then the wafer. He begins from the left. His right. She's third in line. She takes the silver paten in her left hand and slips it beneath her chin. Now the priest holds the wafer aloft, as if to effect a coronation. She tilts her head backward, and the cinnamon hair cascades toward the small of her back. Nimble fingers set the wafer to dissolving upon her tongue.

What's she thinking? Does he know her at all? She's taking communion, so she must've been to confession, too. How does she reconcile any of this? She's so much fun on one level, yet so perplexing on another. She must often be at odds yet she rarely shows it. Is she hypocritical? We're all a bit that way. But she's too young and too pure to be bogus. So what is she? A mystery, that's what.

And what about him? Does he think about any of this, this, this—*ambiguity*. This double-dealing. That's too harsh a judgment, surely. No one's getting hurt. It's costing money, though. And time. But be truthful, Chancey. You just don't think about any of that. Some delightful mental gremlin blocks it. Bravo! And thanks, Mr. Gremlin. And *encore!* Do it again! And again. And do it now. Abruptly interrupt these ruminations in this godforsaken mountain chapel. Cut the puppet strings that hold him rocking upon this Kauri floor, from the bad foot to the good foot, and back again. So, Elan's visiting an ethereal space that he can't enter—and doesn't want to. But she'll be back. And he'll be waiting. But not here. He slips through the Rimu door. A pair of footsteps—they sound like hooves, actually—tap at his heels. He holds the door and glances backward . . . into the beady eyes of that very same nerdy priest—the one who caught them fokking.

The voice is rigid Irish. It strives for empathy but is as humorless as the eyes. "Are ye troubled, son?"

"Not really, no. Not at all, in fact."

"God chooses mysterious ways to bring us to him."

"So I hear."

"The Almighty's calling ye."

"Can I quote you on that?"

His Holiness jerks a thumb over his shoulder. "Do ye know that lassie?"

"She's a friend."

His Holiness moves to full-pontificater mode.

"The devil inspires lust to divert the parties from prayer."

"How does that actually work, Father?"

Why call the phony "Father"?

"Sex annihilates identity. Lust without love is the realm of animals."

"That mightn't be all bad."

"In the climax of the sexual act, we forget ourselves. That's commonly thought to be one of its recommendations. But we forget God, too."

"Maybe that's what God wants."

"That's *not* what God wants. Not at *all*. The world's full of sin. It's everywhere. The space given to sex in contemporary culture—in films, plays, novels—is an avowal of evil."

"And a disavowal of God?"

"Precisely. And God's real. And he's callin' ye, *now*, right at this very moment. And he's called *me* to liaise." His open-pored nose is suddenly in Chancey's face. "He wants me to inform ye that eroticism often arrives late at its own banquet. He wants ye to realize that affection between two people across an otherwise unbridgeable barrier of age or status can quickly degenerate into lust."

"Are you saying that God has given it a lot of thought and doesn't want my friend and me to copulate?"

His Holiness draws back, then blinks and sucks. Purple rises in his cheeks. But he presses right on.

"Lust's more abstract than logic." He's a programmed dummy. "Lust seeks for some purely sexual, hence purely imaginary, conjunction of an impossible maleness with an impossible femaleness." He sucks a deep breath. "What this means is that in your blind sinning, you're merely chasing after illusions."

"If you say so, Father."

"Ye were baptized Roman Catholic—"

"Who told you that?"

His Holiness nods triumphantly.

"An inspired guess." He pauses—then begins to hit his stride. He's Fyfe in pursuit of a placement. "You're in rebellion! The devil's fighting for your eternal soul!"

"Look, Father Whoever-You-Are, I'm not beholden to any religion. So neither you, nor the Pope, nor any gods or devils have any hold over me."

"Ye *say* that. But God'll not be denied. He's brought ye into me presence." He half smiles. "Twice now." He drops his voice to a whisper. "Are ye married?"

"Who's asking?"

"*God's* asking!" The eyes bore into Chancey's. "And is your wife Catholic?"

No way to control the involuntary head shake. The inquisitor pounces.

"So! You're Catholic and your wife's Protestant. But this beautiful young lassie out here, *she's* Catholic." He rolls his eyes. "You're in the deepest of deep peril, son. You're sinning, and since you're a Catholic ye *know* that you're sinning so you've no excuses." He pauses. "But what ye don't know, son, is that you're missing out. Ye think that by sinning ye can calm a troubled heart."

The cranium above the clerical collar pivots side to side. Plop a clown's hat on that swiveling curate head, and it would fit right into a battery of openmouthed, red-cheeked carnival dummies swallowing Ping-Pong balls.

"But you're just messing up. Not just your own life but the lives of others, too. To calm your troubled heart ye have to come to Christ. Ye have to repent. Ye have to be forgiven. Ye have to make a sincere act of contrition." He's paused for breath, but it wouldn't take a clairvoyant to know that the vicious little Vaticanator's going to go for the close. And here it comes. "Make your life right, son. *Now,* do it *right* now. Come to confession *now.* I'll make time to hear your sins right now—"

> *When he looks into one mirror he can see the lacerations to his back in another. Some are red and some are blue. And some have bled in the night. He pulls on the school uniform. It covers the wounds but sticks to the worst of them. His father delivers Chancey to the iron school gates, then drives away. Marist rituals, dense black catechisms, holy waters, signs, rosaries, Eucharists, wafers, holy waters. No. He turns on his good heel and heads for the downtown slot machines—*

At last, there's the sound of her footsteps inside the chapel. He glances to his watch.

"Hey, thanks for the offer. But I have to help a friend climb a mountain. No kidding." Even merely one step away from his orbit feels so much better. "Maybe we'll meet in the hereafter."

The purple cheeks puff. "We already did, son,"—the cranium bobs—"we already did." The humorless eyes make a last attempt to fix onto Chancey's. "And as ye rush from God's offer of salvation to the devil's temptation to sin, remember this." The eyes blaze. "To despise legitimate authority, no matter in whom it is invested, is unlawful; 'tis rebellion against God's will." A clean, pink, Fulleresque finger points to the ceiling. "Pope Leo the Thirteenth said that, ye know."

The door swishes open. Elan's gliding through it. One hand's clutching a red-ribboned prayer missal, the other's reaching for him. Her fingers are infinitely more flexible than this fellow's mind.

"Hey, I'm sure he did, Father. And it's a lovely line, too. Maybe I'll use it sometime."

The freshly squeezed orange juice is slightly tart to the tongue.

"Ever think you might have a problem with priests, Chancey?" Her smile's a blend of reproof and humor. "I mean, maybe you're confusing the world of the spirit with priests and churches—"

"And smells and bells?"

"Oh, Chancey! The spiritual side to life is unrelated to religious dogma."

"So why carry a prayer missal?"

She smiles ironically and sets her sparkling glass back onto the bright white linen.

"Hey—I'm flattered!" She drops her voice. "But you're not really jealous of a prayerbook are you? No, you're just befuddled because I left you dangling and accompanied that text to a mountainside service." Her eyes have captured his. "I guess you fret about how I can be in your bed one minute and dipping into my missal the next. Hey—I have that right, don't I?" She draws a deep breath. "I do it to discover who I am. And who I am when I'm with you, which is something else again. I say that fate's tempting me for my ultimate good. I might be kidding myself, but I say that physicality—fucking—is just the icing on the cake of intimacy—"

"Now there's a lovely word, *fuckeen.*"

"Oh, Chanccy, don't mock. Intimacy's what poetry's all about. It helps us tap—and share—the spirit." She pauses and plucks a piece of hotel letterhead from her missal. "I finished my sonnet this morning. See what you make of it." Her bronze blue handwriting's neat and sharp:

> My suitor sounds a truly tempting tongue
> And teases me with tantalizing lies.
> I merely smile and let myself succumb,
> Thus feigning innocence of subtleties.

"I've graduated from pursuer to suitor?"

"Not necessarily—just sounds better."

> But subtle ties will bind his heart to mine,
> And truths untold will overpower my woes,
> His chancing eyes for me alone will shine;
> I'll have no need of otherworldly beaux.

"I have chancing eyes?"

"The world behind your eyes is always seeking something, Chancey."

> He'll never flinch or leave me in disgrace,
> Nor come to me without a tender show,
> He'll always know he won by perspicace,
> Seducing me with derring-dainty prose.

"*Perspicace?* Wherever do you find these antique words?"

"They come in a special gene reserved for well-bred Brits."

"Is it all saying that I'm too clever by half?"

"Check the kicker."

"Of course, the ironic couplet—the catch."

"The moral, Chancey."

> In love then, poets are constantly gracious,

Yet all their stratagems quite mendacious.

"Hey—does it mean we're both liars?"

"It means whatever we want. Poets can define their own souls, make their own rules and take their own meanings. That's the beauty of poets and poetry."

The schoolgirlish, Sunday-white blouse swells as she cups her hands behind her head. It's an optical illusion, of course, but that light-filled window beyond her shoulder seems almost to create a halo around her cinnamon hair.

"But you know, Chancey, sometimes a prayer book's even better than a book of poems. Every creed needs a few icons and incantations. I figure the Catholic rituals and relics are as good as any. And I say that since I was born into that faith then maybe that's what fate had in mind, and so I choose to go with it."

Her intensity's beguiling. She might also be making more sense than that wretched representative from the Vatican. But is she just another confused Catholic dedicating her intellect to unsustainable beliefs? Maybe. But if so, God, she looks beautiful doing it. He lays his palm across her tan knuckles.

"Maybe you're right, Elan. Trouble is your fiery friend failed the first test."

"The first test?"

"Yeah. The first test of a good religion's whether you can joke about it."

THE DILAPIDATED YELLOW BUS levels out and lurches toward a pile of boulders. The driver jams on the brakes, tossing fourteen eclectic climbers forward in their shabby seats. The craggy, bestubbled, beshorted, khakied, sixty-something Kiwi guide springs to his hobnailed boots and grabs a once-chromium-plated pole behind the driver. "You were probably wonderin' why the bus doesn't have shock absorbers." His breath smells of nicotine. "Well, we just wanted to put you in the mood for what lies ahead." He chortles. "Actually, if you've got the right gear, the two-mile hike to the Franz Joseph Glacier surface isn't too bad. Now, stay together and follow me."

"Have we got the right gear, Chancey?" She's pirouetting. Blue denim jacket, polo-neck sweater, jeans, and dilapidated, lace-up, hobnailed boots.

"Love those hired moccasins."

"And you look like a muscular Christian in your Irish woolen sweater, Chancey. But how're your boots?"

"Don't know. They're not a pair. Different sizes. But they'll get me to the glacier."

"And home again?"

"Thomas Wolfe said—"

"Yeah, I know."

"For some of you this trek might seem tougher than you'd expected," says the guide. "But we're only a hundred yards from the glacier surface. We need to take this next hop carefully, though. There's a potentially nasty drop to negotiate—two hundred or so feet straight down. If you go that way, try to land in the stream down there. See? It's twinkling at you." He leads them to the ravine's edge. They study the drop in silence. "If you're in any doubt," he continues, "just batten down here, and we'll pick you up on the way back. I'm leaving this thermos of tea and some tasty sandwiches."

He strides six paces to a clearing. "Now, for those going on, the only way to cross is to hop from here"—he springs to a large level rock just six feet away—"to here." Silence. "Then, gather yourself, take a bit of a run, and spring from here"—he's jumping again— "to here." He makes the leap look easy. Then he smiles. "And I'll be ready to grab your hand in case you fall." The eyes are decidedly empathetic. "You going to be okay for this, mate?"

"Call me Chancey. But, yes, it'll be a piece of cake, Captain. If it weren't for that daunting drop, nobody'd give it a thought."

Elan's inching forward. A glint in the stream catches in her eye. "Why not just stay here and sip tea, Chancey?"

A hush falls. They're the focus of the group's attention. "Just what we need," he whispers, "sympathy."

"Do you care what people think?"

He surveys the chasm. Is it widening? Is that glinting stream receding? A breeze hits his cheek. That sun's suddenly brighter. The climbers are silent. And he's suddenly outside himself, spectator to his own predicament. The odd shoes have rendered him lopsided. The gammy foot's become a monstrous clump. What was it his father used to say? "The lion takes its fierceness from your fear. You have to face down the lion of your fears." Ah, yes, time to face the paternal lion. A last glance to Elan. "The undiscovered country calls!" She's watching wide-eyed. His boots scrape upon the rocks as he propels his twisted body into the air and suddenly seems to float—Happy now, old man?—and land. The knot in his stomach's disappeared. "No problem, Elan, see." The second hurdle's wider than the first. He coils and springs. And lands again. Gnarled fingers tighten like a steel trap around his wrist and pin him to the rock. Steel-blue eyes fix upon his. "Nice going, mate." The breath from within the three-day beard is tinged with nicotine. "And on the way home you get a second chance to enter that bourn from whence no traveler returns."

The hot mug of tea warms the fingers, and the thick brew seems to soothe both the nerves and the impediment.

Elan's eyes meet his. "I'm glad we did this, Chancey—really glad." Her voice's a whisper. "I mean, it's a special week for us, you know."

"As is every moment, surely."

"Oh, Chancey—Anzac Day falls next Tuesday." She pauses. "It'll be our anniversary."

Anniversary? He met her only yesterday, surely.

"You look a tad confused, Chancey. We met earlier at the Queens Ferry, but Anzac Day's our day—remember?"

He's been entranced and she's been counting.

"Of course—but isn't that a melancholy day to choose for a personal anniversary?"

She's been a mesmerist's spinning concentric circle—but who's the hypnotist?

"There was no choice, the day chose us"—she smiles— "and, anyway, melancholy has its charms."

A shadow falls across her face, as a nondescript Kiwi trekker steps into their space with a question already falling from his lips: "Do I know you, mate?"

"Doubt it, my friend, I'm over from Aussie."

"Aussie, eh. Hey, whattaya know?" The eyes dart to the impediment. "Didn't I see your photo in the papers?"

"You must be thinking of someone else, mate."

The guide coughs, the inquisitor steps away, and the group falls to rapt attention. "The glacier's been here for a thousand or so years . . ." And on he goes.

"See, Chancey, glaciers have anniversaries, too."

The lilt in her voice, the self-mocking humor, the winsome smile. Maybe His Holiness was right. Yet how can anything that feels this good be bad?

> A breeze can be fair
> And a squall can be foul
> And the storm a testing teacher
> But keep a sharp eye on
> The dicey horizon
> For unseen conditions can beachya.

Hey, listen to your intuitions, Chancey. There's a mess right ahead . . .

10

Hexes

"FULLER'S *BECOME* THE FATTED CALF, Chancey." Spittle's bobbling in the corners of Crawley's mouth. "He's put on more than thirty pounds."

"Thirty pounds—maybe he should go off his liquid diet."

Crawley sniffs. "Booze's not a problem in this town."

"Paying for it is. He's whining for more money, but showing symptoms of call reluctance."

Crawley glances down his nose. "Fyfe is a tad slower to pick up the phone these days. But he and Brittle are working well as a team—as you predicted, of course. And I imagine Fuller's happy with his new title?"

"Manager Executive Selection, Sydney. He should be happy, he chose it. Trouble is, Brittle's taken to using the acronym: MESS. Fuller was hoping for a mantra and got a hex instead. He doesn't like to be ribbed. He vanishes from his office."

"Onanism."

"No wonder he's running out of steam."

"Brittle might be, too."

"He is?"

"He said he'd like a word with you."

"A serious word, no doubt. Maybe it's you he needs to talk to. Maybe he needs to get a confession off his chest."

"Brittle's not the kind to acknowledge his own sins, Chancey." They stroll to Brittle's office. "I imagine he just wants to eyeball der Führer."

"If I'm not out in ten minutes come and save me."

Crawley vanishes as Brittle cracks the door.

"Oh! Chancey. Hi." He pauses. "I'd have come to your office."

"No worries, Dick. The mountain can come to Mohammed, see." A silver-framed desk photo displays a studio portrait of the

Loved One, Bronwyn. It's a head-and-shoulders shot but she clearly wears the pants.

"If you don't mind, Chancey"—he perks upon his swivel chair— "I prefer *Richard*."

"No problem, Richard. Sorry."

The harbor's sparkling behind Brittle's shoulder. Is that an Admiral's Cupper out there? Nice spinnaker anyway.

"So what's on your mind, Richard?"

Brittle fingers the row of Biros in the pocket of his shirt.

"I'm concerned."

"About?"

"Principles—and Mr. Fyfe." His voice is almost soporific . . .

> There may be other worlds,
> (You said there were)
> Yet, trapped in empty rooms,
> I mouth to strangers . . .

"So, I gather you've a problem with Fuller."

Brittles voice assumes his trademark whine. "Yes. And with serious ethical issues." The glint in Brittle's spectacles is almost hypnotic . . .

> Aliens, upon whose shoulders
> you sit, smile, beckon, and dance . . .

"First, Chancey, we're working on contingency." He spits the word as if it were urine. "We don't get paid unless and until, as Fuller puts it, we put bums on chairs. Hence the temptation"—his lips purse—"to engage in unethical practices."

"Such as?"

"Fuller'll do literally anything to make a placement."

"He's certainly a rainmaker."

"He does things we should never countenance."

"Like?"

"He invents scenarios. Rehearses untrue stories. Jerks people around like puppets. Promises the world. I've been amazed at his excesses. And his gall."

"Not to excuse him, but he did help effect the turnaround."

"That's an expedient view, Chancey, if I might say so. As leader you must surely provide moral direction . . ."

> There may be other worlds
> (I think there are)
> But I can see no door
> Out of this one . . .

"Ah, yes, of course, Richard, moral direction. Crawley quotes some Kraut, Brecht, I think, who says grub first, ethics later. I guess the moral is that nobody can provide any kind of leadership without some business to lead."

"I topped the MBA ethics class, Chancey." His fingers drum the desk. Very neat, might even be manicured. "We should observe Kant's categorical imperative."

"What's that?"

"A bedrock principle. Says that when we engage in a practice, we endorse it for all mankind."

"An upmarket Golden Rule?"

"Kind of, but much deeper."

"A lot of competitors are out to cut our throats, Richard. Should we slit theirs first?"

"In fact, Chancey, that's exactly what'll happen. But it'll happen to us. Fuller's past misdeeds will come back to haunt us. I mean, what about that quadriplegic?"

"So, the shifty Dutchman got irked when he couldn't get his fee back. Well, that's not good, of course. But the hiring decision was his, and he knew the terms of the contract so he had four months to watch the fellow perform." He smiles. "But if I'm being honest I have to admit that I was grateful to hang on to that money and pay some bills. And Fuller's impaired candidate wasn't totally ethical, either."

"Right!" Brittle produces the parental digit. "He was terrible. We should've had nothing to do with him—not under any circumstances." The lips are pursed and thin. "But that's my point. Fuller was working on eat-what-you-kill contingency, so he simply had to make the placement in order to survive." He's wagging the feisty finger. "We should collect *retainers*. And progress payments."

"That'd be very nice. But we'd never've established ourselves on that basis. Personnel people cover their asses by giving that work to big-name firms. But we overpowered those toffy-nosed phonics." Brittle blanches. "Those, ah, colleagues. And, you know what? They're ethically suspect, too. Because they've been paid up front, they can afford to push empty suits onto their unsuspecting clients, then rush onto the next sucker."

Brittle's cheeks puff like a frog's. "Principled people *always* behave decently." Now he's trying to extract a smile. "I joined because this is a growth industry. Some people don't always meet my standards, but I'm reasonably comfortable with your perspective."

"Thanks, Richard." Better to stand on a bad foot than spend a moment longer in this purgatory. "It's nice to know we both take these things seriously."

THAT SAND'S HOT ON HIS BACK, even through the beach towel. Getting back to Jill after a week with Elan is like escaping a pressure cooker. That sun beats into his eyes. He should feel rotten, and maybe limp, too, but he doesn't. Waves thunder in the distance. Jumping from one country, one bed, and one woman in the morning, to another of each in the afternoon is exhilarating, actually. A touch of salty sea breeze hits his bare chest and legs. Maybe it's like owning both an apartment in the city and a house in the country.

"Hey, stud!" Jill's perfume's in his nose. She's kneeling before him. "Open your eyes and get a taste of this." The chuckle's in those big blue eyes, too.

"Aha, a drumstick—thanks." The chiseled face beneath that red bandanna's almost as mysterious as all those years ago when she was just seventeen. "Looks good, Jilly." Having kids just added poise. She pushes him a yellow canvas backrest. "Mmm, great sauce, too."

"Have some salad, Chancey." She sets her own backrest alongside his.

"Hey, this dressing's great."

She grins. "I hired a fancy Frenchman to whip it up."

Not so. Jilly's always a knockout chef. The kids should be enjoying this, too. "What's happened to Blake and Angie?"

"Angie's under a tree catching up on her Homer. Blake gulped his lunch, waxed his surfboard, and headed for the horizon." She eases into the backrest. Her toenails are fresh red. "He's out there now, see." The gold ring on her finger's glinting in the sun.

He shades his eyes with his hand to shield the glow from ochroid sand and sparkling water, then scans the horizon. "He's a long way out."

"He's between the lifesaving flags, Chancey. Lifeguards are watching and so am I. But, yeah, it's kind of dangerous. That's why he goes. He's a sucker for excitement and doesn't want to miss out on the big wave."

"I guess he'll ride it back in a hurry."

"Or fall off."

"Maybe you should've told him not to go."

"Then he'd just get secretive and surly, Chancey."

"You sure all this child psychology stuff you're learning works at his age?"

"A child's got to learn from his own mistakes. At some point, the only way for that to happen is to let him go." She glances toward the horizon. "But I'm watching more closely than he knows. One day he'll wake up and realize that I gave him a priceless gift—all the license he needs to grow up. It's tough to watch him right now, but with luck he'll thank me later." She shrugs her shoulders. "For a rebel like Blake—or a maverick like you, Chancey—if you really love him, is there really any other choice?"

"I guess you could've written your own psych books, Jilly."

"Proof'll be in the pudding, Chancey." She keeps her eye fixed on the horizon.

She looks great in that red bikini. Those breasts are a pert, firm, appetizing thirty-two-B.

Her oiled fingers smooth his nose. "You have enough sunburn lotion, Chancey?"

"I'm all oiled up."

She grins and her face glows. "We've not been doing enough of this, Chancey." Her skin's still virtually unlined.

"This?"

She works hard to keep that milky-white stomach so flat.

Her fingers dance upon his hand. "Going out as a family. Having fun."

"Yeah, I know. I'll get Godzone under control, and we'll do it more often."

Her voice is suddenly a gentle whisper in his ear. "Do you want to fuck then, lover-boy?"

"Hey, what'd you say, Jilly?"

Her grin is impish. "I said, let's go off somewhere and draw close."

"You really want to?"

"You always used to be looking for an excuse to get me off into the woods."

"I was so young."

"Saturday and Sunday, as I recall." She's not as tall Elan, but just as lithe. And her complexion's milky.

"I'd do it, Jilly. But where?"

"Back over there. Behind those dunes. We'll stick up the umbrella. No one'll see."

The lifeguard's irritated, Popeye-like voice breaks the spell. "I don't know what the parents are thinkin' about."

Jill springs to her feet, adjusts her bikini, stands on tiptoe, and glances over the dune to the water. "It sounds as if Blake caught his wave," she says.

She strides across the dunes to the water. "*I'm* his parent," she says. She sticks both hands on her hips. "What's your problem?"

The surly bronze guardian lowers his binoculars and glances to Jill. "*You're* the mother?" The lips pucker. "That kid's out too far for anybody's good."

"Maybe," says Jill. "But he's on his way back in a hurry, now."

"And if that wave breaks, lady, he could be up shit's creek."

Blake, crouched and keeping the racing-striped lime-green board to the leading edge of the foam, rides the wave. A funnel of fury chases his heels. "If that board pops, the kid'll not know what's hit him."

"He's coming fast, Jilly." Her shoulder's tense beneath his hand.

"Too fast for a kid that age," says Popeye.

Blake surges ahead of all danger.

"He's out of harm's way now," says Jill.

"She's right. He's with everyone else now."

"And he can see us," says Jill.

Blake waves, then pops the board with great panache and disappears beneath the water.

"Flaming little showboater," says Popeye. He eyes the impediment. "Probably trying to impress the old man."

Jill smiles and reaches for his hand. "Aren't we all."

Those eyes of hers. So big. And sooooo blue.

In the dream he captures an exotic pearly-white fish from the ocean. He drops it into a bowl with a beautiful domestic goldfish. Will they savage each other? The goldfish'll surely lose. But pearly-white won't survive domesticity, either. They nudge each other playfully, and kiss. He wants what he can't have: both of them under one roof.

"JUST WAIT'LL WE GET TO NEW YORK, CHANCEY!" Dreams resonate in Crawley's voice. "We'll really knock them dead!"

"*We'll* knock 'em dead?"

"Of course."

"Why do I get the feeling you're rushing me to New York?"

"Because business is either going forward or going back. We survived the crash, and we turned the financial corner, Chancey. And now the future beckons. And, if I may be entirely frank, I have to confess that I'm truly excited at the prospect of the level of success someone of your talents would realize in New York. You really could fulfill all of your incredible potential there."

"Why're you so keen on New York, Ungerford?"

Crawley produces a fresh handkerchief, dabs his spittle, and glances directly into the Chancian chin. "New York's a state of mind, Chancey, a place to realize dreams. Oh, sure, Australia lives up to its reputation as the lucky country. And Sydney's doubly blessed. Lovely weather. Fantastic wines. Gorgeous women. Minimal poverty. All that." He gazes to the window. "But it's not the big

time, Chancey. It's not a soul-stirrer. And the Aussie thinking—not
to mention the bigotry, racism, and sexism—is still rooted in the
fifties. America's actually resolving these problems. Prejudice is not
only unconstitutional—it's un-American, too." Sunshine's bouncing
into his face. He looks older these days. And that's precisely because
he is older. "Even here, of course, America's redemptive ideology
and images—on paper, television, movies—raises local
consciousness." His eyes are shining. "But, mostly, when we try to
embrace that vision from this distance, it's as if we're merely"—he
purses his lips disdainfully—"masturbating."

He's suddenly seized a fix on the Chancian eyes. Christ—
Crawley never makes eye contact. Those eyes are blue and wide
and deep. They still burn with fire and idealism. He's another person
again when he looks you in the eye. Why wouldn't he always?

"Tell me, Chancey, why accept an illusion when you could be
making love to the flesh-and-blood reality?"

Crawley glides to the door, opens it, and glances back. "You're
a Shakespearean scholar, Chancey. Shakespeare knew the value of
timing." He's summoning the cadence of a Charles Laughton—no,
that's Fuller. Of an Olivier. "He said, 'There's a tide in the affairs of
men, which, taken at the flood, leads on to fortune.'" Dramatic
pause. " 'Omitted all the voyage of their days is bound in shallows
and in miseries.' " One hand on the door, one foot beyond it. "Let's
not miss the tide, Chancey." He blinks and evaporates. How does
he do that?

Shakespeare. Crawley's spouting Shakespeare—just like his
mother. Fact is, in this hemisphere, Crawley's an odd man out. Why
won't her ghost let him write his life-altering novel in Sydney? He
could win a local prize, become an Aussie intellectual. Too lonely?
He probably wants to hide out among New York's weirdos and
misfits.

Hey, look at that lovely harbor. Multicolored spinnakers are
breaking out as those yachts round the lighthouse. Now they're
surfing back, the wind behind them. Who'd really, when you get
right down to it, when you toss out the baloney you have to pitch
to inspire a team—and maybe catch a bit of press—who'd really
want to leave all this? Sunshine. Watersports. Waterfront home.

Doting wife. Settled kids. And Elan just a hop across the Tasman. The yachts bear down on Pinchgut . . .

That quote of Crawley's was from Julius Caesar. He mouths the lines—

> There's a tide in the affairs of men,
> Which, taken at the flood, leads on to fortune—

Go now and win fortune?

> Omitted, all the voyage of their days,
> Is bound in shallows and in miseries—

Or wait and repent? Surprised Crawley didn't finish the lines.

> On such a full sea are we now afloat,
> And we must take the current when it serves—
> Or lose our ventures.

So, go! Now. Soon. This time, next year, sometime, never. Maybe. Perhaps. Make up your goddammed mind— But who was the character who uttered those lines? They played very nicely in the film, remember. And it's coming back. It was that silken voiced Pom—*James Mason*. Who played—*Brutus*. Brutus! The classic noble nitwit. The dopey idealist tricked by a ruthless sidekick into overreaching. And in the end they both wound up impaled on their own swords. So those inspiring lines became a curse.

Not really. There is, after all, such a thing as the human spirit. And if you really do want to make people sit up and take notice, you have to take a few risks.

But first things first.

ROTORUA

ELAN WRINKLES HER NOSE. "What *is* that smell, Chancey?"

The tomato-red Mini-Minor races through the steam that rises from tarmac cracks in Rotorua's main drag.

"It's the sweet scent of sulfur, baby." He jams the window shut. "The whole town is going to explode one day."

She winds up the volume on the radio and jives with the Beatles. A fiery sun sinks over the barren plain, and a full moon's already rising. The clock says time's running short, so jam the pedal to the floor.

"Where're we heading, Chancey?"

"To Wai-o-tapu, a wonderland bathed in solitude. Difficult to reach and too dangerous for casual sightseers." A suddenly arid, burned-brown countryside races by the window. "It closes at seven. I have to stop to make one phone call. But if we're late no one'll be any the wiser if we jump the fence." Gravel-road dust billows in the mirror.

FULLER'S SIGH WHINES DOWN THE PHONE WIRE. "Does it all come to something in the end?"

"Something worrying you?"

"I'm racing around, Chancey. But I never seem to get ahead, personally, ya-know-what-I-mean. I need to pull down big bucks. I need to live comfortably. So I need to be a real manager. Like you and Crawley."

"What about London? It's a natural after New York. You'd love the Brits, and they'd love your style. And your class. And your way with language. You'd have them eating out of your hand from the get-go. You'd pull down those big bucks in London, Fuller. You'd live real high on the hog there."

Fuller's breath quickens. "Shit, Chancey!" He's agog. "You're a fucking dynamo!"

"I do my best. Right now I'm stuck in Godzone—"

"Again?"

"Yes. It's a drag. But I've got some big things cooking. All confidential, of course, but something's going to break."

WAIOTAPU

"IT'S ANOTHER PLANET, CHANCEY."

A yellow bulb moon's burning above the eerily barren hill. And two hundred feet beneath Elan's saffron legs, surrounded by half a dozen multicolored pools, sits that sizzling sulfur lake.

He produces half a bottle of Shiraz from his pocket and extracts the protruding cork. "It's called the Artist's Palette." He sips from the bottle, then passes it to her. "You can see why." Bubbles burst from the pools, emitting sickly sweet fumes.

She sips. "A feast for the senses, eh?"

He takes her hand. "This way, baby. A hundred yards. All downhill."

A stream of clear, blood-warm water falls fifteen feet into a natural, white-sulfurized swimming hole. "It's a rock star's backyard pool, Chancey—but can we swim?"

"No problem. The depth varies. Maoris say it's only for the gods, that trespassing mortals come to sticky ends. My take is that the gods brought us here, so they want us to swim."

"And a full moon trumps all other spells."

They toss their clothing in a heap and wade in, chest high. She floats on her back, eyes closed. Her hair, mahogany in the moonlight, drifts like a halo. Her breasts peep through bubbling water. "You look like a golden Maori god yourself."

The moon falls behind a cloud. The light fades from her face. That milky water's almost as silken as her skin. Her lips taste of Shiraz, her breasts of sulfur. Her legs encircle him. Let the gods be envious if they wish.

SYDNEY

CRAWLEY AFFECTS HIS FINEST NONCHALANT POSE—a bizarre blend of Cary Grant and Fred Astaire—in the sun-filled office doorway, nursing his cup of fresh-brewed coffee. He raises his eyebrows and chortles. "Brittle certainly hasn't figured out what makes you tick, Chief."

"What's he saying now?"

Crawley saunters inside, presses the door closed, and perches on the edge of a guest chair. "You always said that when the recovery manifested, we'd be in the catbird seat. And you were right. Your investment in space, people, equipment, and image really is paying off in this market. We're handling triple the volume with the same overhead. Brittle says you've created a cash cow."

"And Brittle's whining about this?"

Crawley steeples, his fingers, wisemanlike. "In a way, yes. He's a little puritanical."

"But what's the problem?"

"Conspicuous consumption." Crawley half smiles. "He's uncomfortable that you seem to have invested the profits in a yacht."

"Oh, Christ—I merely leased the thing."

"It's all conspicuous consumption to Brittle. He believes that as leader your duty is to pursue the vision of accelerated corporate growth. He needs to feel that things are happening." He offers his droll smile. "Brittle's something of a Boy Scout seeking a leader, you know."

That sun's a touch bright in Crawley's face, highlighting a couple of spots he's missed shaving. There, a quick adjustment to the venetian blind within the double-paned window has improved the view. "He wants a guru?"

"He needs to feel he's doing something big and clean."

"Tell him to go wash an elephant."

"Exactly, Chancey." Contemplative pause. "Unfortunately, his intolerance for ambiguity is infecting the troops."

"He's wetting the communal blanket?"

Crawley grins. "I bumped into him in the men's room." He pauses. "He'd just finished peeing and was giving his member a final shake when he raised the prospect of a New York office."

"We'll open in New York, Crawley, we really will. At Rockefeller Plaza. We'll do it. I've just been so hectically busy in Godzone."

"Of course." Crawley offers the polite nod of an upper-crust auctioneer. "A very real distraction. I made it as clear as anyone could, Chancey."

"Made what clear?"

"Your commitment to New York." A long pause from Crawley. "Brittle said he'd heard it all before."

"He didn't believe you?"

"He stuffed his percy back in his pants and tugged on his zipper. Then he said, 'I guess it's on the five-year-plan.' Then he laughed and scratched his arse."

"Laughed and scratched his arse. Did he, indeed? What'd you say?"

"I told him the truth."

"You did?"

"Yes, I did. 'You just watch,' I said. 'Chandler Haste's an authentic leader. He always walks the talk.'"

"Did that shut the devil up?"

"Sort of."

Who gives two shits what that little Boy Scout thinks? Say, is that the sun playing tricks—or is it her reflection? In the window, see . . . no . . . on the water . . . maybe. Way over there. No, it's just a spinnaker flogging. They'll never control it now—have to cut it loose. He glances at the calendar. Tomorrow and tomorrow and tomorrow. She'll be in town tomorrow. Really. This petty pace, indeed. She's never been *here* before—and never said why she's coming. Unless she's intending to stay on until Anzac Day—their second anniversary in her eyes—but that's almost a week away, yet.

11

Trysts

SYDNEY

HE SUCKS THE DIESEL-LADEN SALT AIR that kicks from the propeller burst, propels himself into the air with his good foot, and jumps the swirling water onto the departing 6:34 a.m. ferry. A couple of passengers wince as his thick heel crashes onto the hardwood deck. He hustles to the outside upper deck. The wind braces his face and hands. Dazzling November sunshine bounces off the deep blue brine. The ferry cuts a foamy swath to Kirribilli. Elan's in town. Go ferry, go!

"My, my, Mister Haste"—Elan touches a finger to her lips, nods over her bathrobed shoulder, then speaks for the benefit of a stranger—"you really are the early bird." He glances past her into a sun-filled, boxlike room that smells of hair spray, instant coffee, and soggy white toast. A twenty-something female friend in a too-tight, overcleavaged, candy-red dress clunks an aerosol can onto a vanity table.

His breath catches Elan's ear, but his words are for her friend. "I guessed you'd be in town only briefly and thought you'd want to go sight-seeing. Best thing seemed to be to catch up on the way to work." Her fingers are as supple as ever.

She pulls away, drawing him into the room. "I don't think you've met Beryl. We're traveling together." A slim, painted, sharp-featured, auburn-haired Beryl takes in Chancey's purple business suit, glances to the tan riding boots that hide his clubfoot, then flutters her freshly painted red fingernails.

Chancey turns to Elan. "Your father asked Jill and me to look after you. We're hoping you'll join us for the Squadron's Friday twilight race. There'll be wind in your face and salty air to savor."

Elan raises her eyebrows. "You're sure that's okay?"

"It'll be delight. And there's a barbecue after. Come to the office first. Four o'clock. We'll catch a cab back." He glances to Beryl. "You're very welcome, too."

She teeters on ankle-strapped red high heels, gulps her coffee, and shakes her head. "Outta the question." She sets the lipstick-rimmed cup back on the table. "Gotta rush. Things to do."

She wobbles to the door and flings it open with a flourish that accidentally propels her red purse out onto the corridor floor. He semigallantly retrieves the glossy vinyl pouch and passes it to her.

As she takes it from him, she subtly latches onto his wrist and draws her face to his. "You're playing with fire." The voice is a whisper. "I'm not making any judgments. You just need to know." She turns, and her heels *rat-a-tat* down the hall. Silence.

Elan gathers the white bathrobe about her and pirouettes on tiptoe.

"What're you thinking, Chancey?"

He gathers her in his arms. "Of you, who else?"

She smiles, then pulls away.

"It feels funny to be on your turf, Chancey. Kind of scary, actually—illicit, I guess." Her voice drops. "Where's Jill?"

"In bed when I left. I'm breakfasting with a client. It might take up the whole morning." He smiles. "Then I'm lunching with Brittle Dick."

She laughs. "Not *the* Brittle Dick?"

"If there's such a one he's it. I'm meeting him at the Squadron. It's just around the corner. I'll hoof it." He paces to the window. Jill's just around that corner across the cove. Elan's eyes are on him as he turns. "When did you get in?"

"Late last night. We're only here till Sunday." She pauses. "Then on to, ah . . . on to, ah . . . London, actually."

He turns. "To London?"

He arrives home from school. The furniture's gone, curtains, too. She stands at the door, lost in thought, depressed. "What's happening?" She eyes him oddly. "You know what's happening." She's right. His five-year-old heart knows. She and his father are splitting—

"London? You're going to London?"

"I always said I'd do it when I graduated, Chancey."

"Yeah, but I never believed you."

"I believed when you said you'd go to New York."

"That was in another lifetime." He runs one hand through his hair. "Oh, shit! Whatever happened to the time?"

"It'll be our second anniversary next week, Chancey."

"I hadn't forgotten. I thought you might have been staying on for it, but I guess that's not to be." He takes her by both arms. "How long're you going for?"

She looks away. "Don't know, Chancey. My parents are pressing me to stay for at least a year, maybe two. They've people they want to look up. They say it'll be good for me."

"Two *years!*"

"That's what *they* want. It'll be less, of course."

"Or maybe more. Looking for Mister Right. The Honorable Mister Right. Lord Right." He sighs. "And I'm still here. You sure you believed I'd go to New York?" Her mouth is winsome, her lips full. "You must've known I could never leave you to the rascals of Godzone."

"I believed you. Kind of. But we've got to dream, Chancey. Dreams are what make life bearable."

"Who said that?

"Not Buddha. He wasn't too hot on desire."

"Are you sure about that? I mean, did you ever meet him?"

"No. Nor any of those Maori gods either. If I met any of them I'd kill them. You have to kill the Buddha to grow up; it's a key principle of Buddhism. Comes somewhere down the eightfold path."

"You're going to quit on me but not kill me?"

She grabs his lapels. Her body's soft and warm. "How're you doing Chancey? Really?"

She's poised, womanly.

"Pretty good. I mightn't survive your departure for London, but I outlasted the recession."

"Sydney lifestyle catching up with you?"

"Well, yeah. Hops, wines, steak—"

"Maybe you need something more in your life."

"Like what?"

"Maybe you could open another office."

"Maybe I could just go on jumping the Tasman and anesthetizing myself with you."

"I won't be there, Chancey."

"You won't be there. You won't be here. You won't be anywhere."

"I'll be where I always am—thinking of you." She wanders to the window. The sun's in her face. "One day I'll write a sonnet about *Thinkingofyou*—it's a specific place you know, a proper name with one word, four syllables, and no hyphens." She turns, lost in thought. She's coming from another place. "I know it so well that I could draw a three-dimensional map of the melancholy town of Thinkingofyou from mere memory. I could color it in, too. I know the hues of the dawn and the windows it burns as it rises. I know the hills and valleys, the trees and seasons, the brooks and streams. I know the steeples and the spires and the sticky-tarred, water-towered roofs. I know the pastel facades of the houses and homes and the shops and the bars and all the good-night places. I know the dusk that settles in the corners of the cobblestone streets. I know the shimmering lake upon which the golden moon rises, and the black clouds into which it inevitably disappears, leaving me alone to my reveries, dreams, and remembrances." She steps, ever so softly, into his space. "Maybe it's a geography lesson I should never've signed up for, Chancey." She smiles that winsome smile. "But what the hell, I know all about this moment, too—and I know we should live in the now whenever we can." Her lips flicker on his. "And we're both right here right now."

A rush of warm air rustles the curtains. Her bare shoulders are silk beneath his fingers. Playing with fire? Such melodrama. Beryl doesn't understand Elan at all. Or maybe envy comes in many guises. He catches the reflection of his hands in the Hopperesque wardrobe mirror. His whitening nails harvest her soft shoulders. Her hair dances like a wave on the sea.

Home to England. She never used the phrase. Thank God for that. One has to realize, however, that for denizens of the far-flung

Empire, most especially the elitist young ladies, the return trek to England is both a rite of passage and a finishing process whereby they polish their patinas and elevate their elocutions. Home itself is something else, of course. It's a state of heart and mind, an affinity not a place. But perhaps she'll bond with the English—the *Een-gleesh*. Perhaps she'll succumb to some titled Tory. No—block that thought. She'll visit the queen at Buckingham Palace, no doubt. All the lords and ladies will come out to welcome her, and they'll all get along famously—*famously*. It will all be so super—*sup-ah*. Chancey, meanwhile, will be back here in the colonies, bereft of her presence, tending to the ache in his heart and the chip on his shoulder. But how to keep her out of mind? Already, his head feels leaden. Already there's a tainting taste of melancholy settling in his mouth. But relax. For her it's just a coming-of-age thing. So she will return. He'll see it happen, surely.

"IF I HAD A TELESCOPE I COULD SEE YOU, JILLY. I'm on the public phone at Kirribilli. On my way to meet Brittle."

"I'm looking at our wedding photo, Chancey. We seemed so young."

"We *were* young."

"My gown was ivory."

"An adroit selection."

"My eyes're puffed and teary."

"Our wedding certainly pissed your Masonic father."

"And the groom a brainwashed Roman Catholic."

"With a clubfoot—"

"Oh, Chancey! You do go on about that foot. Nobody gives a damn. Really." Long pause. "So what's happening?"

"I got a message that one of the Haverford girls is passing through town."

"Which one?"

"The youngest."

"The sunny one who wins all hearts?"

"You should know, Jilly—you're a youngest child yourself."

"She's brainy and pretty both, too, right?"

"So they say. It really doesn't much matter because she's on her way to England. To meet some toffy boyfriend, no doubt. I promised Henry we'd take her sailing with us on the harbor."

"Tonight?"

"The twilight race. Then maybe the barbecue. I'm bringing Fuller along, too. A little bit of team-building won't go amiss."

"Sure, and I'll bring the kids for the same reason, Granddad."

HE SLIPS INSIDE THE THICK overhanging camellias and slides the special silver key into the snap-lock of the tall, timber gate. He likes this special members' perquisite. Hardly anyone enters this way. They mostly glide their Porsches and Mercedes right into the private members' car park, or maybe roll up in a cab. It's nice to have a key to yet another secret garden. He eyes the lush pink camellias, then strolls up the narrow, winding path. He props himself against a jacaranda and catches a whiff of purple petals. And just look at that magnificent, whitewashed colonial clubhouse. Right next to the governor general's mansion, see, over there in the distance. Built from local, turn-of-the-century timbers. And beyond the manicured lawns that roll to the water's edge, a hundred or so yachts dot the bay and bobble upon their moorings.

And there's Brittle—raking his hooves over the bristled straw mat at the lacquered oak door. Black-shoed, gray-suited, and gray-faced. A line of silver Biros in his breast pocket. He adjusts his steel-rimmed spectacles, checks his watch, then peers into the midday sun that bounces from Careening Cove.

It's time to slip the camouflage of the jacaranda. "Hey, Richard!"

Brittle shows surprise and his terrier teeth. "Very mercurial, Chancey."

"You think so?"

The flaccid Brittle handshake as the eyes absorb the harbor.

"Most people arrive by car."

"The plebes come by cab."

"Not too many plebes in this place. Too high-faluting."

He turns to follow Brittle's gaze. The yachts swing at anchor in the cove. A zephyr whistles through the shrouds, setting off the ping of wire upon aluminum. He turns back to Brittle.

"And what do you make of these?"

Brittle's eyes follow his to the pair of waist-high naval guns that guard the clubhouse entrance. "Don't know, Chancey. Remnants from a convict past?"

"Something like that. Hey, let's get inside and grab a bite. Glad we could make it early. I'm going to try to make the one-thirty ferry. I need to get back to town and sit in on a session with this hotshot HR guru from Chicago. Apparently some people are discomforted by the delight he takes in revealing the darker side of human nature."

Brittle studies the blue Squadron monogram within the rim of his now-empty plate. "You did well to get into this club," he says. "They tell me it's the best smorgasbord in town."

A cackling seagull swoops into Careening Cove. Brittle leans back in his aluminum shell chair to sight it. Sunlight filters onto his upturned face through the yellow-and-white-striped umbrella perched to shade their linened outdoor table.

A white-jacketed waiter sets before them two steaming espressos in delicate white cups.

"So, what's on your mind, Richard?"

Brittle adjusts his gleaming row of silver Biros. "I'm concerned." He folds his linen napkin into a neat square.

"About?"

"Principles." He pauses. "And Mister Fyfe."

Best appease this bee in Brittle's bonnet.

> Building a business
> Is jumping through hoops
> And keeping top players
> Keyed in to the loops—

"Ah, yes, Richard. I'll have another word to him. I'll press it home that his past behaviors are unnecessary and counterproductive."

Brittle sets his glasses to a perfect horizontal. "We've no further use for Fuller. He's irredeemable. He's totally amoral. I sometimes think he might even be a psychopath." Brittle's lips are thin. "We should fire him." Chancey's in the lenses again. Bluish tinge, bizarre wide face. "He's served a purpose. I'd personally never've employed him, of course. But if you're serious about building the right culture, you should examine your conscience, Chancey." The image slides from the lenses as Brittle reaches for the napkin.

"I promised Fuller a stint in London. He's hanging on for that."

Brittle's glancing at his watch.

"Well, just so long as he's not around to mess up any office that I run." He dabs his mouth. "I need to be up front on these things."

"Probably the good influence of your father."

It's a relief to stand, stretch, study the harbor, and savor the salt air. There's the one-thirty ferry emerging from Neutral Bay. It's kicking up a bright white wake as it plows toward them. He presses his chair back into the table.

"If we hustle we'll make that ferry, Richard. It's a lovely ride. And the Oracle awaits."

"EEE-MOT-ION-AL RE-TARD-EES!" The seventy-six year-old shaman delivers the words with caustic delight. "Such so-called *executives*, are, in fact"—he pounds the podium—*"ee-mot-ion-al re-tard-ees."* He casts a sunken eye over the awed, upturned faces of the Antipodean audience gathered to pierce the innermost mysteries of executive behavior. "They're ee-mot-ion-al *cripples,* and they systematically recruit underlings an inch or two ee-mot-ion-ally shorter than *themselves."* The audience remains guiltily silent. "And *those* cre-tins in turn do *likewise!"* The thunderous voice now drops to comic sadness. "Soon their entire organizations are nothing more than—*cringing congresses crawling with emotional pygmies."*

Dr. Jim T. McCracken might just be Gandalf. The oratorical flourishes emanate from a handsome silver-maned head atop a cruelly polio-shrunken trunk. When not propped by a podium, the frail frame is supported upon a shaky pair of crutches or a wheelchair. Is he an actor or an intellectual? A performer or a practitioner? A sage or a sham?

And here comes the answer. The guru's perceptions, showcased in *Harvard Business Review* reprints, are being distributed to the wide-eyed seminar delegates. So, the Ph.D. really was earned in Freud's Vienna. The messenger is authentic, the advice weighty. The sharp mind might be fading, but he's clearly forgotten more about executive horseflesh than Chancey's so far learned.

A mealymouthed sales manager asks the old man a tacky question about personal ethics; more of an affront than an inquiry, actually. Doc contemplates the garbled query. "*Well,* what I think you might be *trying* to ask," he drawls, "is: Did I ever sell a customer something that was not in *his* best interests to buy? Is *that* what you're asking? Is that what y'all would like to know?"

The questioner stumbles, embarrassed to have his tortuous query restated so succinctly. "Ah, yeah. I guess so."

Doc gazes over the upturned faces. "*Well,* the answer is"—he pounds the table—"*Yes!*" His eyes blaze mischievously. "I've done that!" His expression turns to sadness. "But it was in the depression. And I was *hungry.* And when you're hungry you do things you wouldn't when you're not."

Such candor is inspiring. Doc could be very helpful. So why not buttonhole him during the coffee break?

"I'm Chancey Haste, Doc. I'm in the HR business too." The Oracular eyes widen. "And soon I'll be expanding to the States."

The Oracle beams. That's a hell of a smile. The outer world disappears. The eyes shine, the teeth flash. He extends his hand and undivided attention.

"*Well,* is *that* right? *Wow*—is *that* right?" The hand is surprisingly soft, almost fragile. The guru's eyes bore into his. "*Well,* when you get there"— he supports himself on Chancey's palm— "look me up. Be *de-light-ed* to help in any way I can."

ELAN, IN HER SAILING OUTFIT—loose purple pantsuit and sneakers—might seem a touch out of place in the Haste and Company offices. Fuller was rubbernecking, that's for sure. She slips to his window. "Some scene, Chancey."

He gently closes his door and saunters to her side. "I always thought so."

"I'm not sure it was a good idea for me to come to your office."

"Maybe not, but I needed you to see what I see."

"So, now I've seen your harbor view and glitzy offices, Chancey." Her eyes catch his. "But I kind of think you're looking for more."

"Like—"

She glances back over the harbor again. "Something beyond the horizon."

"A yellow brick road?"

She turns. The dark eyes sparkle. "Yes. I think you're precisely the kind of guy who believes in wizards and yellow brick roads, Chancey."

She must be right. Otherwise, why not let it all go and ask her to marry? Just look at her: beautiful, radiant, vibrant—and here right now. And in the twinkling of an eye, she'll be lost to the toffy-nosed lads of London. But would she have you, Chancey? Really?

"I guess I also want, and don't want, the world to know that the incredibly beautiful Elan finds me attractive."

She smiles. "When the gods want to make us mad, they grant our wishes, Chancey."

He runs his hand through his sandy hair. "Come on, let's go sailing."

A COMMODIOUS MOTOR CRUISER—what the Aussies call a stink-potter—crosses their bow casting a spray of salt, a pall of petrol, and a nasty, rolling wake that sends *Scaramouche* rocking and rolling. Fuller cups one hand to his mouth to address the passing potbellied skipper. His other paw displays an inverted central digit. "*Fuck you very much!*" he cries.

Elan and Jill glance nervously in the direction of the helm. These odd-sized Docksiders don't make for an ideal balancing act. So brace the Squadron-shirted back and hold on tight to this sturdy chromium wheel.

"Half past five, Chancey." Fuller, beshorted, T-shirted, looks up from his racing watch. They glance toward the orange starting boat. A puff of smoke, followed by the thump of a gun, signals the ten-minute warning. With a bright but fading blue sky overhead and the scent of gunpowder hanging in the air, thirty yachts circle one another looking for a strong start. The air's warm. A fading twelve-knot breeze drifts across the harbor. Fuller gazes skyward. "Sun'll be up for a couple of hours yet."

Jill's hunkered in the rear of the cockpit wearing horn-rimmed sunglasses, jeans, royal-blue T-shirt, and Docksiders. Elan's next to her. Angie, still in her school uniform, is up next to the mast where she can come to no harm. Blake, in shorts, T-shirt, and Docksiders, is next to her. Time for action.

"Here we go, Fuller—*Coming about!*" The wheel's a sleek animal spinning in his palm. The giant white genoa foresail points to the wind, loses all air, and flogs. Blake jumps forward to ease it across the deck as Fuller grinds the screeching winch.

Magic-lantern images of Sydney pass before their eyes: the massive, overpowering bridge itself; the burnished Opera House that floats above the water like a giant butterfly; Pinchgut prison, the turret-stoned hellhole for recalcitrant convicts that rises like the devil himself from a jagged, water-lapped rock in the center of the harbor; the glistening Manhattanized skyline whose glass-and-concrete phalluses proclaim triumph over criminal origins; the green and white ferries, darting back and forth like giant fireflies.

The genoa slowly flogs and refills. Fuller tosses the sheet around the winch, then furiously winds. He glances twenty feet upward. Elan's eyes follow his. A pair of three-inch woolen threads tagged to the leading edge of both sides of the sail are fluttering.

"They're telltales," says Fuller. "Gotta get 'em streaming evenly. Then we'll know we're pushing this sucker to the max."

They brace as *Scaramouche* tilts, then glides, as do thirty other yachts—red, white, blue, green, ruby, whatever—all heading for the same narrow starting line, all kicking back gusts of wind, dollops of foam, waves of palpable excitement, and a wall of sound.

"Gonna be a real squeeze here," says Fuller. He glances to his watch. "Nearly time, Chancey!"

Yachts are lunging from every direction. They seem close enough to touch. There must be a couple of hundred ecstatic sailors of all stripes—old and young, dandies and deadbeats, chauvinists and charlatans, weathered and fresh, bloated and wiry, agitated and earnest, bosses and underlings, fathers and sons, mothers and daughters, wives and lovers—all yelling, or so it seems, to be heard over the wind and the foam and the gnashing of gear.

"Up! Up! Up!" they cry. "Room! Room! Room!" they demand. "Give us some fucking room!"

Fuller, face flushed, breathing heavily, counts the seconds to the final gun.

"Three. Two. One." A puff of smoke and—Boom! *"Go Chancey! Go!"*

They thunder across the line and set to a reach across the harbor. The wind's on their portside cheeks.

Jill passes up a Toohey's six-pack. "Only for the afterguard." She nods to Blake and Angie. "Cokes for you guys." Blake stares sullenly.

The aluminum cans hiss and the sticky scent of hops bursts free to seduce the salty air. Fuller elevates his golden cylinder to the sky. It'll be okay to follow his lead and offer a toast.

"To good friends."

"Where're we heading, Chancey?" Elan sounds and looks a little dazed.

"Toward the harbor entrance. Locals call it the Gap. Our mark's that far-off lighthouse."

She flicks him a grin. "To the lighthouse!" She stands, straightens her pantsuit, and gazes up at the mast. "Lovely boat."

Fuller jumps right in. "Got a great set of sails, too. Three spinnakers and a cheater."

"What's a cheater, Chancey?" asks Jill. Her face is deadpan, but might the remark reflect wit or intuition—or a wily blend of both?

"An Australian," says Fuller.

Best play it straight. "A cheater's a sail that catches the air that would otherwise pass under the spinnaker. A Kiwi sailmaker first tossed one up in a race against the Aussies."

"Beat the pants off them," says Fuller, gulping his Toohey's. "They called a protest and screamed bloody murder. Aussies whine like buggery whenever they're beaten by their country-cousin Kiwis."

"Sydney must be a great place to race," says Elan.

"Yeah, and everyone who's anyone belongs to the Squadron." Fuller makes the point with some delight. "No boat niggers. Just the best people. It's an elegant scene. Very gracious. As you'll soon enough see."

Salt spray dashes their faces as *Scaramouche* follows the flurry of boats that rounds the lighthouse amid shouting, flapping, and screeching of gear. Now the wind's behind them.

"Keep your eyes skinned," says Fuller. "There's a shoal we've gotta clear before we caper around Shark Island." He grins at Elan. "Discount the scary name. It's just a tiny picnic island."

They set a reach. *Scaramouche* glides alongside half a dozen other yachts. Their sails shake and puff. Their transoms kick back foam.

So many scents and sights enhance the fantasy of Elan. It's amazing she's out here, yet there she actually is, crouching on the upside of the cockpit, arms wrapped around the lower safety line. Reflections from the water flutter upon her defenseless face. The wispy purple top struggles to contain a cleavage drawn forward by the tilt of the boat. The fleeting glance. The vulnerable smile. And Jill beside her. She's got her eye on Blake and Angie. Well, half an eye on them and half an eye on him. That's what wives and mothers do. And of the two of them, Elan and Jill, who looks the loveliest? Answer that, O mirror on the wall. What a question. They're both so beautiful. So why, really, does any man, even a clubfooted colonial, feel the need for two such comely companions? And, why, for that matter, are there clouds in the sky? And why is the sea blue? And why does the wind bring tears to the eye—

"Watch out for this bugger beside you!" cries Fuller.

Thank God for the warning. *Destiny*, a battered, gray-hulled racer, is altogether too close. And, shit! Who's that on the wheel? Shit oh shit! Surely not! But, yes, he'd know that angry, sunburned, pasty face anywhere, even beneath a faded yellow terry-toweling hat. But what's the worry? Burnham got paid in full, without even going to court. Could've chiseled him but, as promised, paid every nickel.

Burnham's bloodshot eyes are popping. He's discovered a new triangle. His eyes flit from corner to corner. Elan, Jill, Chancey. Round and round they go. Elan, Jill, Chancey. Blue-Rinse suddenly appears beside him. Her eyes are on stalks, too.

"He wants to cut inside us before the wind dies behind the island," says Fuller. *Scaramouche* tilts to an even keel. *Destiny* looms even larger. "Now the bugger's poaching our wind, Chancey."

Angie looks up from her spot by the mast. "Destiny's ruthless, Dad!" She's been listening all along.

"The only way for some people to get what they want is to steal from others," says Jill.

He offers a half smile. "The wind belongs to everyone." He glances backward. *Destiny's* sails collapse.

"That know-nothing sailed too close to the island," says Fuller. "He lost every bit of puff and shot his bolt completely."

"He never read his *Ulysses*, Dad!" Angie smiles. "The island sirens tempted him."

"What should he've done, Angie?"

"Blocked his ears with wax and strapped himself to the mast."

Indeed, he should've.

A breeze hits the backs of their necks. *Scaramouche* tilts and accelerates. The telltales stream.

"We're outta here!" Fuller jumps to the transom, cups a hand to his mouth, and assails the Burnham's receding faces with a raucous mocking verse:

> *"We didn't stall and wouldn't linger*
> *So we're givin' Destinee—"*

He hoists and pumps the inverted central digit—

> *"The finggerrrr!"*

"Tempting fate, Mr. Fyfe?" says Elan.

"Not a problem, luv." Fuller's teeth flash. "The bugger'll never catch us now. He's history. And, he's just a tagalong, anyway."

"A tagalong?"

Fuller points a stubby finger at Burnham's flaccid masthead burgee. "That's not the Squadron flag. The twilight race's open to all local clubs. He's just Middle Harbor riffraff."

Fuller struts them up the Squadron lawn. Salty air carries the scent of camellias, jacarandas, freesias, diesel, and now, smoky barbecuing T-bone steaks. Attractive families mix with hard-muscled crewmen and their sloe-eyed female companions. The beer's flowing. An equal number of revelers are also into the house wine. Twilight has arrived. The Opera House, bridge, and city lights burn in the dusk, reflect in the water, and hover in the sky.

"This claret's great, Chancey," says Fuller. "I tested it for you already." He produces a tray with five glasses of Cabernet and a full carafe. The fifth's for Crawley. He's just arrived, upbeat and breathless in his twee-est thrift-shop casuals: black church trousers, long-sleeved yellow Viyella shirt, desert boots, and a quirky black beret. Time for another toast. Jill, Elan, Crawley, and Fuller watch closely. Best play it straight.

"To good times and good friends."

"See, Chancey, you really did turn the water into wine."

"Fuller deserves a lot of the credit for that."

Fuller drains his glass and swells. "Did my best, you guys." He refills and turns to Elan. "And what does Henry Haverford's daughter think of Sydney?"

"She only got here today," says Jill.

"But what I've seen I like."

Fuller guzzles, then smiles. "What'd ya see this morning?"

Best cut Fuller off quickly. "Hey, the barbecue's going fast. Let's not miss out."

They set their glasses on a round wrought-iron table, assemble in a semicircle overlooking the harbor, and juggle paper plates laden with steaks and salads. Reflected moonlight hits their faces. Elan, Fuller, and Crawley are on his left flank. Jill's on his right. Blake and Angie are off alone somewhere, talking to newfound friends, maybe.

Fuller downs yet another glass of red, reaches for a refill, and turns to Elan. "Sydney lovely enough for you?"

She glances to the full moon on the harbor. "It's a magical place, Mister Fyfe."

Crawley fixes on her bosom. "The city's beautiful." The Crawley half smile. "Just a shame about the people." A little wider, this time. "Just ribbing. I imagine people are the same everywhere. Perhaps."

"The Aussies were handpicked by England's finest judges,"
chortles Fuller.

"It's who you meet," says Jill.

"Yeah," says Fuller. "And some of the nicest people hang out
just around the corner on Cockatoo Island." There goes yet another
glass of fine Squadron claret. No wonder he's staggering. "You'll
make sure she takes in Cockatoo Island won't you, Chancey?"

Elan seems to sense where Fuller's conversation might be going
and offers him an innocent smile.

"Alas, no time for sight-seeing. I'm flying to London early in
the morning." She glances back to the harbor. Jill sets an eye for
Blake and Angie.

"Hey! *You!*"

Oh, shit! Not that gurgly voice again. Ignore it.

"Yes, you—you little upstart!" Burnham crashes right into the
middle of their circle. His red hair's crimson in the moonlight. His
clinging white shirt glows neon yellow, highlighting the button on
his potbelly. His ham fists are clenched. The image of Chandler
Haste in a Squadron shirt is clearly inflaming this hapless bull. The
bloodshot eyes glare angrily. "Your crewman gave my missus the
finger!" Spittle flies and the pasty face is livid. "I demand an
apology!"

"Get outta here, you lowlife," says Fuller. "We don't know
any Middle Harbor riffraff."

Burnham's gaze swings slowly. To Crawley. To Elan. To Jill.
Elan again. Then back. "We've met all right, mate." He smirks. "I'd
never forget a cheatin' cretin."

"Don't you dare speak to my husband like that." Jill spits the
words and glares at Burnham as if she might actually cuff him.

Fuller springs forward. Belly to belly he glowers into the
bloodshot eyes. He pokes Burnham's chest with his stiff and stubby
forefinger. "We sailed by the fuckin' rules, mate—so you just mind
your fuckin' language."

Burnham scowls right back, then shoves Fuller backward.
"Get your fuckin' hands offa me!" He suddenly flashes recognition.
"Hey! Hey! *You're* the one who gave my missus the finger!" He
spins toward Crawley. "And *you're* the fucker who gave me a bum
check!" And here he comes again. "And as for you, you little cheat."

His eyes dart to Elan, then Jill, then angrily back. "You think you're so smart with your gaudy offices, your showy boat, and your flashy pieces of pussy." He turns to Jill and smirks. "But what *you* need to know, luv, is that—"

Fuller's fist flashes into Burnham's solar-plexus. Burnham gasps hungrily for air. He staggers backward, arms and legs flailing, and collapses on the lawn.

Oh, Christ, a gaggle of rubberneckers are gawking. Crawley's slipped into the background. Elan's disappeared. Fuller, fists still up, is swaying wildly.

"That buffoon won't call your wife names again, Chancey."

Burnham sucks, moans, and kicks the air.

"Is he okay?" says Jill.

Fuller crouches to inspect—then emits a stream of vomit that descends like raspberry topping onto the moon-washed sundae of Burnham's belly.

Jill surveys the wreckage. "Not truly a scene to share with sensitive, upper-class young ladies, Chancey—I rather doubt we'll be seeing Elan again."

"Best pack it in for the night, Jilly."

"Where's Miss Haverford?" asks Crawley.

"Skipped back to her hotel, I imagine."

Fuller's crouching and retching.

"I'll get him out of here," says Crawley.

"I'll grab the kids and a cab, Chancey."

"Fine, you run ahead. I'll check the moorings on the boat and then follow you."

He strides toward the marina—then doubles back. Where is she? There—alone beside the clubhouse guns, discreetly waving to him. He checks the impulse to run to her. She couldn't have selected a more strategic meeting place. No one uses the front door so late in the evening. Shadows from an overhanging palm tree offer camouflage, yet she still has a clear view of the harbor. She reclines against one of the guns. The moon strikes her. Her lips are full, her eyes deeper than the harbor behind her. The purple pantsuit's inviting.

"Is destiny catching up with us, Chancey?"

"Fuller stopped it cold. Then introduced Burnham to Herb and Ralph."

"Herb and Ralph?"

"Sailing euphemisms. The names mimic the sound of throwing-up."

"What the poets call onomatopoeia?"

"Something like that."

"So he puked." She laughs. "On *Destiny*!"

"On *Destiny*'s skipper, actually. And in so doing bought us some time."

She spins in his arms and braces herself on the cold-metal gun. Her skin is warm. They gaze at the shimmering harbor. He sights two moons, one on the water, one in the sky. The cunt is velvet, the breasts silken, the tongue a Bluff oyster. Might his seed hit that yellow orb? The one in the sky—

She'll be back. It's just a coming-of-age thing. She'll come back.

"Tomorrow, Chancey?"

"There'll be a tomorrow?"

"My plane leaves at six."

"Last call?"

She cracks a smile. "I'm not dying, for Chrissake, Chancey—only visiting London—and I'll be back."

"Maybe I'll take a lover's leap in the meantime." He squeezes her hand. "Call you in the morning."

"Yes, call me, Chancey." A cloud drifts across the moon, darkening her face. "There are things I need to say."

12

Chasms

*I*N THE DREAM HE'S MAKING LOVE *to Elan on the sands
of a cliff-backed beach. She's on top, wearing only an unbuttoned army
tunic, leaning back, nipples pointing to the moon. He blinks. She guffaws
rudely. He opens his eyes. It's not her. Now he's ass-fucking Fuller from whose
gaping mouth dollar bills spurt. The money turns to vomit and seeps into the
sand. A rising sun burns into Chancey's eyes—*

Don't raise those lids. Head's too thick, mouth too furry.
Squadron red can do that. No matter. A small enough price to
celebrate the realization of a fantasy. Hey, yes, Elan! She actually
sailed with him on Sydney harbor, then rode the guns. Oh, hell, the
guns! So maybe the furry taste is honeydew. And what about
Burnham? Did Jill suspect anything? No need for guessing, for
here comes the answer.

She pushes into the room. He glances through near-closed
eyelids. She's carrying a breakfast tray. He puts his knuckles to his
eyes. She suspects nothing. He props himself on an elbow.

"Hey, Jilly—smells good!"

"Don't get too excited." She's smiling. "It's only a couple of
boiled eggs." She lays the tray beside him.

"Looks good, too." Silver coffee pot and condiments. Two
brown eggs, both opened. Hot buttered toast alongside a thick
dab of marmalade on a floral plate. Linen napkin within a silver
ring. "You certainly know how to keep a man happy."

"Sometimes, maybe."

She's wearing her best blue jeans, ivory silk blouse, and black
canvas shoes with platform soles—clothes for going somewhere.
She'd loiter if she were suspicious—wouldn't she?

"When it comes to keeping husbands happy, you're the world
champion, Jilly." Control this guilty hyperbole. "You should be giving
lessons in the subject to young women." Tone it down—way down.

"Maybe you'd like to be off with some young thing yourself, Chancey." She strides to the sliding veranda doors, throws them wide, and gazes towards the sunbathed Opera House. Warm, salty, camellia-scented air surges inside. She glances to him. "Gallivanting to the other side of the world with Elan, maybe."

Dodge that gaze. His eyes dart to the dresser and alight upon their wedding photo. No, no, not that. They move to the mirror. Oh, Christ, his face looks so vacuous. So shifty. Relax. She's merely fishing.

"How could a man in his right mind ever leave you, Jilly?" He hates the sound of his own voice sometimes. "The world's greatest wife and mother."

"Cut the baloney, Chancey." She perches on the bed and touches his hand. "I just do what I can for the good of the team." She smiles. "I guess I also have an interest in your soul."

"I'm not sure I believe in souls."

"But you said we were soul mates, remember?" She pauses. "You wouldn't lie to me, would you?"

Play it steady. "Why would I ever do that?"

"Why would anybody? Because the truth can hurt, I guess." She pauses. "Because we married so young. I mean, I never got to see the world before settling down, Chancey. And . . ."

"And . . ."

"And I guess you never got to sow any wild oats."

"You said to think twice about marrying you, Jilly—but I didn't need to, we were in love."

"I said don't just be a nice guy."

"Me? A nice guy? Never. I married you because you were beautiful, on every level. And because I loved you."

It was true and still is. She's just as lovely as Elan. But you're dancing on hot coals here, Chancey.

"I know you love me, Chancey." She offers a half smile. "I'm just not sure you love me enough. But stifle any wild declarations, and just think about it. Who's Burnham, by the way?"

"Just a printer we slow-paid."

"But you did pay him?"

"Of course. He just got huffy because Crawley stalled him with a kited check. Then Fuller gave him the finger." He smiles. "That's what really set him off."

A car horn's calling.

"The kids are getting restless, Chancey. I have to get them to this play rehearsal." She pecks him softly on the cheek. "Got to run." She paces from the room, then pokes her head back. "Fuller chucked up again." She laughs. "In the cab. Crawley helped the driver clean it up." He blinks. She's gone. The front door snaps shut. The Alfa purrs into distance. Only the scent of her perfume remains.

He rolls onto her side of the bed, grabs the phone, and dials. "I'm on the loose. I'll pick you up. We'll grab a bite of brunch—" A peripheral shadow appears in the doorway. Oh, shit! No! She's back. Torrents of adrenaline assail his gut. How'd she slip back in like that? But this's no time to panic. He nods to Jill and holds his voice steady in the mouthpiece.

"Just, give me an hour or so." He gingerly slides a finger across the phone switch and cuts Elan out of the conversation— Jill didn't notice the maneuver, thank God for that—and keeps right on talking: "*Okay, Fuller?* No problem, Fuller. None at all. It's the least I can do, given all you went through last night for me, Fuller. See you real soon then, Fuller." He cradles the phone and casts her a smile.

She's not smiling, though. "You're going to have *another* breakfast, Chancey?" She's irked.

"I felt a moral obligation to check on Fuller's condition."

"A moral obligation, Chancey?" She half laughs. "To Fuller? You'd make time for brunch with Fuller, but you're too knocked out to see your own children rehearse a play?"

She looks suspicious. Has she twigged to Elan? Is that why she slipped back? Thank God that conversation with Elan was brief, coded almost.

"Let me 'fess up, Jilly." She's waiting and watching. "My motives were not entirely pure." What to say, what to say? "Fuller's the rainmaker, you see." Okay so far. "He's got a big-time prospect to see on Monday morning." Getting better. "So I thought I'd sneak in the chance to run him through his pitch." She's still eyeing him oddly. "I guess I'm just a workaholic, Jilly." He offers a wan smile. "Overcompensating for this silly hoof." A low blow but the only way out.

Her face softens. Her suspicions, if they existed, seem to wane.

"I rushed out without my pocketbook and left the car running in the street. This time I really do have to run."

And, indeed, there she goes. Too close a call for comfort. Best to hear whatever it is that Elan has to say and then pack her off to London before Jilly's intuitions catch up with everything.

You're a cad, a rogue and a rascal, Mr. Haste. Don't listen to this fellow in the shaving mirror. You like to imagine that you're a square shooter, but you know you're doing the wrong thing. Maybe—well, yes, if you insist—it might well be wrong, but so is life. You don't really want to try to make the argument that you're a victim do you? Well, no, there's a better explanation, a clarification that reconciles everything to everyone's delight. And would you care to share that so-called clarification Mr. Haste? Sure—what's happening is happening because it is happening and because that's the way that humans are and because the moment is all there is and because the fleeting moment will fleet—and because of *Carpe Diem* and Die.

"NICE JAG, CHANCEY." Elan's jaunty, arms akimbo. Her hair's pinned with red plastic clips. She's wearing a front-buttoned sleeveless white cotton dress. He's in jeans, sailing shirt, and casual white custom shoes. He stashes her three scruffy suitcases into the car.

"Yeah, a blast from the past. Classic nineteen sixty-four. Original white paint, too."

She peers inside. "Real red leather. Mahogany dash. All the fucking trimmings."

Quarter to eleven by the dashboard clock. He winds onto the Cahill Expressway, then glances over at her. "So when does that wretched plane leave, again?"

"Six. I have to be at the airport by four."

They sweep over the bridge, past the Opera House and the botanical gardens and on into the eastern-suburb bays.

"Pretty posh, Chancey."

"When Sydney was settled, the convicts were incarcerated beyond the far side of the harbor in the grimy, overheated western suburbs. Officers, on the other hand, set themselves up just inside the Gap, here in the eastern suburbs—so they got the harbor views and sea breezes. And so it is today. Western suburbs for the proles, eastern for the plutocrats."

"And the aristocrats?"

"Never left England. Closest thing to an Aussie aristocrat's a white collar criminal."

"Where do *they* live?"

"In waterfront mansions."

She steps from the Jag, stretches, and gazes down the narrow street. "Great little beach."

"Yeah, Watson's Bay."

Dazzling sun bounces from crystal water and bleached sand. They cap their hands to their eyes. He turns and points back to the hill.

"See that hill a couple of hundred yards back there?" She gazes upward. "Shields the beach from the open ocean. You can see the Gap from the top of it. There's a fantastic view from a hideaway setting. Maybe you can share what you need to say up there later." Fishing boats are unloading at the jetty. The warm air's redolent with the scent of fish, shells, and salt. "The bay itself is tricky to get to, but pretty damned popular. Especially on the weekends. People come by road, ferry, yacht, and motor cruiser."

She eyes the throng of Sunday revelers. Most are wearing little more than cutoff shorts—stubbies—T-shirts, terry-towel hats, rubber thongs, and sunglasses. Most of the women sport skimpy bikinis.

"At least it's not too formal."

"That's for sure. Nude bathing's de rigueur around the corner. Gays, mainly."

"Crowd's getting noisy," she says.

"Alcohol might have something to do with that." A radio blares the Bee Gees. *Ah—Ah—Ah—how can you me-e-e-end a bro-o-o-ken heart?* The sky's tapestried with cumulus. *How can a loser ever win?*

Way in the distance, rising like a surreal kingdom of Oz are the Sydney skyscrapers. *How can you stop the sun from shining*—beyond them the western-suburbs smog—*And let me love again.* He takes her hand.

"We can eat at Doyle's and look back at the city, or we can seize a takeout lunch and a bottle of wine, sit alone up on hill, and look back at the Gap. What's your poison?"

"To be alone with you, Chancey."

They select a punnet of fresh-cooked prawns, a cup of seafood sauce, and two buttered rolls from a curbside vendor. The hotel liquor shop clerk sells them a bottle of Perrier, and an iced, half-uncorked Chablis, then tosses in a couple of plastic wineglasses.

"Do you realize the time, sir?"

Whose ominous voice is that?

"Hey, you nut!" The clerk glances to the back of the store. "I've told you before not to wander in here bothering my customers."

They turn to face a foreboding pair of dark-ringed eyes. The wise course would be silence, but the question begs a response. "The name's Chancey. Are you asking whether I *know* the time, or whether I *realize* the time?"

"Don't waste your breath," says the clerk, "he's a tramp and a fanatic."

The tramp draws back and gathers his tatty outer garment, a stagey cloak, no less. If he's trying to cut an unsocial, otherworldly figure he's succeeding. "Time's a storm in which we are lost," he says, setting a skinny hand to an unshaven chin.

"Lost?" says Elan, softly. "Then how might we be found?"

The dark eyes study her. "The only light upon the future is faith. The light of faith can wake us and guide us."

Oh, no, he really is a zealot. "Are you saying that I and my faithful female friend here are asleep?"

"Love is a potion—both you and your, uh, rapture, are drugged."

"How might we waken?" asks Elan.

"Too late, my child, too late."

Hey, *there's* a quick response to a tricky question.

"I imagine you've used that line before, comrade, but here's a dollar for your trouble, anyway."

"An inch of gold cannot buy an inch of time."

"You don't want my dollar? Well, no matter. But, listen, if we really are asleep, how would we know?"

"To see what you look like asleep, sir, stand in front of a mirror with your eyes closed." The fellow struts toward the door.

Elan calls after him. "What would a person see if he woke from such a sleep?"

The tramp glares and points a bony finger. "He would realize that the curtain that conceals the future"—he taps his heart—"is knitted by the hands of mercy." One last toss of that stagey cloak and he disappears.

"Well! What do you make of all that, Chancey?"

"A dour old devil, that's for sure. A down-and-out character actor, I guess. Or maybe that clownish mountain priest has fallen upon hard times."

They grab a blanket and pillow from the backseat of the car, trek to the top of the hill, and catch their breath. The deep blue ocean rolls in remorselessly, all the way from the horizon. Hands to their eyes, they swivel, slowly. Waves surge through the canyons, kicking foam against the towering layers of the Gap.

"Stout Cortez should've caught this scene, Chancey."

A gentle breeze puffs her cinnamon hair, presses the cotton dress to her thighs, and sends her perfume to him.

He spreads the blanket under a secluded cluster of jacarandas. Playful distant voices sound. He uncorks the wine. She lays the prawns, sauce, and bread rolls on the white wrapper. He pours the wine, then leans back against a jacaranda and raises his glass.

"To the Gap in our lives."

"Everybody needs a little space, Chancey."

It's a coming-of-age thing, no doubt about it. He sets the glass back on the blanket.

"Now, let me direct your attention to the prawns, a subject in which I imagine well-bred British girls are entirely innocent. First thing is, *don't* just throw away the heads. There's more flavor in them than in the flesh."

"No kidding—so how do we get to it?"

"Just pull off the head. Stick the gory end in your mouth. Like so. Suck and savor whatever comes out—then toss what's left back into the pile of shells and legs."

She grabs and dissects a prawn. "All looks pretty primordial to me."

"The best things usually are."

She bites on the prawn and sucks. "Hey, Chancey—you're right. It's deep-sea nectar. Food too fine for angels." She laughs. "That's Henry Taylor, circa seventeenth century." She holds up her hands. "How do I get this goo off my fingers?"

"Wash up with Perrier."

The wine disappears as easily as the prawns. She stretches out across the blanket. The shade of a jacaranda falls across her torso. "I'm starting another sonnet for you, Chancey. It's about you and me and time running out. Here, see—" The sun refracts from bronze-blue lines on cream bond paper:

> My paramour belongs in other places,
> He trims his words to suit a distant peal,
> And marks the dipping sun beyond my graces,
> And flees from me as shadows prick his heel.

"A nice beginning, but it's you who's running away, not me."

"Running away, Chancey? No." She wraps her arms around her knees and rocks forward, elflike. "I need to confess"—her voice is earnest, childlike even—"that I'm confused. Confused and conflicted. I pretend everything's great, but sometimes I feel so bad. I say to myself that what we have together is special. I say that other people's rules don't apply. I really believe that, too. My life, my rules, I say. It's a badge of honor for me that we've never said we love each other. The words are redundant. We don't need the chill of analysis. We don't want to exit the best side of the looking glass. But you know all that anyway, don't you? So you also know that I could never leave you, even if I knew that I really should— which I do not know, and would never attempt to believe, even if I could."

She stops suddenly, breathes deeply, then reclines, gingerly stretching those lovely limbs. "The other thing you need to realize,

Chancey"—she smiles that sweetest smile—"is that in mere minutes I'm scheduled to take my leave of this perpetually revolving, ceaselessly giddifying, eternally upside-down hemisphere."

Will he miss this tang of Chardonnay upon her lips? Can memory house the thrill of unslipped buttons? The tingle of so many touches? The taste of petals? The subtle pleasures of the green glass phial? "Some far-sighted adman," she whispers, "a Frenchman no doubt"—she arches gingerly—"surely calculated"— the phial glides—"the shape to serve," she sighs, "precisely such a purpose." She smiles with lidded eyes.

"It's a secret garden, Chancey. Go gently. Make it last."

Ah, yes. Make it last. Make it last forever. Center it in the cerebellum, engrave it on the gray matter, enmesh it in the mind. He retrieves the phial from the garden, and himself from the quim. With an advance guard already winning the battle to burst free, he tests the enigmatic portal. She draws him into her and pleasures herself, slowly at first, then faster, faster, flushing crimson.

So, will he miss the tang of Chardonnay? Will melancholic memory capture the abandon of the two-backed beast—convulsed, moaning, releasing . . .

She buttons the dress, gathers her poem, and slips it into a pocket. She glances at him, then away.

"Don't sweat it, Chancey. I'll come back and be your mistress." The sun hits her face. A few lines but still so very, very lovely. "It's a noble role, Chancey. Princes and potentates have mistresses. So do generals, commanders, philosophers, and artists. No point messing everyone up. I mean, is there?" She glances beyond him, strolls to a boulder, plucks a wild red blossom from a crevice and holds it up. "What do you know, Chancey, an impatiens? Could have been named after you." She drops the stem between her still-inflamed breasts.

A cloud captures the sun.

"Hey listen, Chancey." A cool, soft breeze rustles the jacarandas. "So, there it is"—she takes his hand and holds on tightly— "the inaudible and noiseless foot of time." Her gray eyes brim. "It's caught up with us."

13

Valedictions

S HE'S GONE BUT SHE'S NOT. She's with him waking,
walking, working, sleeping—

> As I was going up the stair
> I met a girl who wasn't there,
> I missed her in the elevator,
> Couldn't quit her, couldn't fete her.

She's in every city and conveyance—

> In Sydney town I took the lift,
> She wasn't there, and wouldn't shift;
> I jump a windy cable car
> And there again, she never are.

Every accommodation and carriage—

> They send my dinner by dumbwaiter,
> I never get to tête-à-tête her,
> And when I catch a Melbourne tram,
> She's not there, she never am.

No call. No letter. No show. No hope—

> She's gone for sure, there's no soiree,
> The mood that is the mind's valet
> Abhorring inner disarray
> Has blocked the door to her entrée.

Face up to it, Chancey—

> She wasn't there again today
> With quick riposte and repartee;
> She's made her fateful getaway,
> Well, so the intuitions say.

But she'll be back. Of course, she will. She will. She will.

IT'S HER HANDWRITING!

Ink. Bronze-blue.

He weighs the envelope in his hand. Good news or bad? Why does he always fear the worst? A childhood carryover. Silly when you think about it. Return address? An Earls Court Hotel. He holds the envelope to his ear. Silence. He slits it and removes the creamy, watermarked paper. He touches it to his nose. The faintest scent. Of what? Perfume? Of something far, far away . . .

> Dear Chancey,
>
> I suppose it's a paradox that my Roman Catholic upbringing inspired me to promise to be your lifelong mistress. My commitment was to meet that covenant with passion and panache. But I'm just a pretender, a dizzy dissembler, a fantasy-fanatic, a solipsistic looking-glass gazer. Too many tears. Too many depressions. Too many guilty feelings. I don't mean to excuse myself, but here's my inevitable last goodbye and valediction—Poet's are permitted lies, there'd be no poets otherwise.
>
> Elan

His head spins. And spins. He rereads it. *Poets are permitted lies?* Perhaps the entire letter's a lie. *There'd be no poets otherwise?* His head reels anew. He grabs the envelope and checks the date. Mailed ten days ago. He checks the calendar. She left two months before that. Screw the calendar. They say there's no such thing as time. That everything happens at once. Maybe so. Didn't he meet her only yesterday? A welcome distraction, delight, and affinity. If only she'd stayed that way. Time in a bottle. Now she's off. Undoubtedly with some well-bred Brit. But she's also claimed permanent brain cells in this Down Under head. Indeed. Permanent? Is this ache going to be permanent? So replace her. Find another distraction. But what? Or who? (Should that be whom?) He stands, props himself at the window, and gazes out. Gray skies. And rain. How can that be? This is Sydney for Chrissakes. So what'll he do? What *will* he do? He returns to the desk to watch the ink slide from the Biro—

I will swallow strong pills
To conquer love's ills
And rid you at last from my thoughts
You will pass from my brain
And that tortured membrane
Will suffer no further onslaughts

Does such a pill exist? If so—

You'll vanish in exile,
And so will your sweet smile,
Your lilt, and your sparkling eyes;
You will surely depart
From my mind, soul, and heart
All trace of your face exorcized

Trouble is, he's been addicted for too long. Withdrawal will be
agony—

The doctor attending
Will say it's all ending
And be utterly certain it will
Meantime he'll be urging
Mind-altering purging
And say to keep on with the pills

He tucks the poem into the letter he wrote her. Maybe they'll
forward it and maybe they won't—and maybe he'll never know.
He wanders back to the window and studies the harbor. No one's
out there today. This time she really is gone. A silver bullet grazes a
cloud. It's a passenger plane and it's leaving a tail. But where's it
going? Somewhere. And where's he going? Nowhere.

IT IS EASIER, PERHAPS, FOR A MAN TO HAVE A SON
than for a son to have a father. Maybe a boy wants something
altogether too special from his father—something that can't be given,
something that has to be seized. Maybe fathers and sons are natural
enemies and each is happier and more secure in keeping it that way.
Now that the old man really has become an old man, maybe it was
a mistake to come visiting him in this sickly scented sanatorium,

where he's dying in that bed. How the mighty have fallen. And don't they both know it. Jill says kids need to feel a father behind them, solid as a mountain. Unfortunately, this particular mountain only ever wanted to be looked up to. To win his approval was impossible, for other people's successes pricked the bubble of his vanity. Yet something in every son needs to win a father's approval—and go on doing so. At some point, however, the game is not so much to win approval as to get even. To level the board he tilted. Ah, yes, here lies the man who cheated his son at more than checkers—and would probably do so now if he could; the man who sought the last word—and the first word, and every in-between word—in every so-called chat; the fellow who, in frustration at his own inadequacies, raised his fist and . . . Jill says to give it up and let him go in peace. Well, it's not time for that just yet. The gypsies say you have to dig deep to bury your father. That day will come, but right now the old man's still watching, hoping for Chandler Haste to fall. Oh, yes, he is. But no such luck. There are mountains for your clubfooted son to scale—and one way or another, you'll feel it happen, oh, yes, you will.

THE SQUADRON BAND STRIKES a medley from *Midnight Cowboy*. There's a lot to be said for sailing increasingly larger yachts around Sydney harbor. Who said that? Does it matter? A white-shoed, barrel-bellied Aussie croons. *Say good-bye to all my sorrow.* He surveys the beery, sunburned revelers in rented tuxedos. *I'll be heading back tomorrow.* He catches her reflection in the wide window. Or is she on the other side of the window looking in? In which case the image is not reversed. Ghostly yachts drift at anchor behind her. *I'll be on my wayyyyyy.* Her reflection's suddenly gone. Or maybe that little priest was right and everything was just an illusion. Maybe it was never really there at all. And if it was, well, it probably wasn't her anyway. And if it wasn't her then the image was reversed. But she's gone, better face it. *I think the Lord must live in New York City.*

NEW YORK FREEWAY

HIS EYES SNAP OPEN AND HE SITS BOLT UP-RIGHT. Hey, relax, Chancey, you're back in the present, back on the New England freeway, back in the limousine's gray velvet seat—you've been dreaming, that's all.

Well, not so much dreaming as peering into life's rearview mirror. Your reveries were doubtless sparked by yesterday's out-of-the-blue phone call from Henry Haverford. On a solo sojourn through Manhattan, he said—so might it be possible to meet over a quick and comradely pint of ale? Well, years have passed, so why not? And tonight's the night.

But stay focused, Chancey, for here, right ahead of you now, comes the future. See, there, over the driver's shoulder, in the center of the highway. Oncoming stripes are hurtling toward the limousine bonnet like gold bricks. An optical illusion, of course, for those nuggets of gleaming, ochroid pigment are both lifeless and stationary—you, in fact, are rolling over them. But maybe they're portents. Maybe you really are riding the yellow brick road.

And, hey, let's not forget, today's a *very* special day.

Success, money, power, all the traffic's going your way. Your whole world's going to change within this very hour. Oh, yes—and there'll be no looking back then.

Part Two

Star-Spangled Realities

"My past and not my future
lies before me."

—Oscar Wilde

14

Monday Bridges

DUCK?! SHOULD HE DUCK? They seem almost to be racing into those oncoming overhead flashing lights that alternately proclaim the date, time, and temperature. *BLLLINK!* MON 16 APR 83 *FLLLASH!* 03.46 PM *BLLLINK!* TEMP 65° WHOOSHHH—Gone!

In New York for five years now. Five years—it's been both a time warp and a transforming phenomenon. Take Crawley, for example, perching in his velvet seat there, nose buried in the *Wall Street Journal*. He's out of those flares. Strictly Brooks Brothers these days. Nothing fits but maybe that's the look. Less hair than ever, of course, and a wider pate to cross, just takes more glue.

The driver spins the limousine off the New England Thruway. Overhanging oaks, just beginning to show their leaves, offer some shade. They wind past stately Greenwich mansions. Crawley's wide-eyed.

"See, Chancey, a rich man *can* pass through the eye of a needle." He's excited. "It really is the big time! For us, too. Top-drawer retainer work. That bread upon the waters is returning. The investment in Rockefeller Center offices, the phone calls and fighting to see top people, the lavish entertaining Jill put on for all those key prospects, it's all about to pay off."

"Yeah. A high-profile client like Horst Everness would spin us into another league. He's as savvy and particular as investment bankers get. If we can just juggle all the pieces well enough to make him happy, and keep him happy, there'll be no looking back." His mirrored image pats the incipient silver in its temples. "So let's not screw anything up." He glances to his freshly glossed, jet-black wing tips. A long way from two-tone tan. And lime suits—ugh. How could he ever've been so vulgar? The limo glides past blossoming magnolias into the Greenwich Sailing Club marina, then gently comes to rest.

"Very snooty, Chancey." Crawley's impressed. "Simple, but snooty."

Ah, that Greenwich air is so fresh. What a relief to stretch the legs. He fluffs the white silk handkerchief in his lightweight, worsted, charcoal, pin-striped suit, then turns and points to Greenwich cove.

"See—out there on the water, Crawley, that sixty-five-foot racer-cruiser swinging on the mooring, the blue one with the red stripe, and the name on the transom, *Piranha*—it's Everness's toy. He's got everything in it. And I mean everything. Cocktail cabinet, microwave oven, huge double bed with black silk sheets. He goes after what he fancies and likes to get it."

Crawley stares, wide-eyed. "Has he taken you for a spin around the cove?"

"He's suggested it. Wants Jill to come, too, of course. Rumor has it he's a pussy chaser. But that's probably just gossip. I imagine he's very discreet."

"You seem a touch harried, Chancey. Are you going somewhere later?"

Crawley misses nothing.

"Just checking my watch. Nothing important. A blast from the past. Henry Haverford called. He's passing through town—"

"Haverford? Not the Honorable Henry Haverford?"

Crawley's voice shows surprise. But not his face. Other than to touch his nose he reveals nothing.

"Yeah, on his lonesome, too. And jetting out in the morning. We'll be back in Manhattan in time for me to buy him a drink. Might never sight him again."

Another nose touch. Never underestimate Crawley's antennae. "Hey, Crawley—there's our man. Over there, see, standing in the doorway." Crawley sets his jaw. Softly now, "Ready for some fancy tap dancing are we, Ungerford?"

> When bringing in the client
> It is best to seem compliant
> For it's not by chance they call him Mr. Big
> Sure, be self-reliant
> In the toppling of the giant
> Just never act like you're the biggest wig

Everness waves his fresh pink hand over the blue inland water lapping the marina. Traces of a European accent lace his speech. "That's my boat, the big blue sloop, see it there, the sun's just hitting it now, Mister Crawley."

Crawley's eye dutifully follows Everness's prideful, foremost finger, politely settles on the gently swaying hull, then moves beyond it to the established mansions within the surrounding hills that'll soon enough be lush. For now, the setting sun highlights emerging springtime buds.

"I was just telling Ungerford all about *Piranha,* Horst. The finest yacht in an achiever's marina. I'm told there's a greater density of strivers here in Greenwich than anywhere in the world."

"A truly impressive yacht, Mister Everness," says Crawley. "And a very charming club, too." His big eyes take in the array of sailing flags that grace the whitewashed pine room. Subtle lighting glistens in the golden grain of the tiny timber bar. "Beautifully understated."

"Well, thank you. It's perhaps not as celebrated as Chancey's New York Yacht Club, of course, where first we met. You and that absolutely *gorgeous* wife of yours, Chancey. So charming. So intelligent." So many porcelain-capped teeth in that wide smile. "How *is* the lovely Jillian, by the way?"

"As sweet as ever, Horst. Said to send you her regards."

> I've a head full of dreams
> And I'm upwardly inclined
> As overt an overreacher
> As the devil ever dined.

Fresh tulips adorn the table. The sun'll set in about an hour. Boats sway at anchor in the cove. They sip the last of the white wine from crystal glasses. Horst pushes away the remnants of his lobster salad. "It might help in your search for a compatible CEO to know the special culture of Swedish Cruise Lines, of which, as you know, I'm not only investment banker, but also part owner and chairman of the board." He's suddenly all business. "First, SCL is *the* deluxe cruise line." Crawley eyes the banker's paisley pocket handkerchief. He's listening intently, nodding approvingly. "By that

I mean the most expensive." The banker pauses. "We have only one boat. It's small—relatively—but beautifully appointed. SCL passengers have been the richest people in the world." He leans into the candlelight. "Secondly"—the voice drops—"Jews have always been excluded."

Crawley confers the Cheshire nod. "Official policy, Horst?"

"Not written. Merely understood. As a matter of business necessity, you appreciate. Our market evolved as non-Jewish. Rich Jews wanted to be on the boat, of course. They wanted to be seen to mix with our regular clients."

"How did you handle that?"

"When they tried to register, we took their names but told them the boat was full. One week before sailing, if we didn't have a full complement of passengers, we offered them cabins on the lower decks."

"So you'll want us to recruit a very sensitive president," says Crawley. "Someone who'll appreciate your special market positioning."

"Of course. But perhaps not in the way you think." He taps the pink forefinger to the silver temple. "SCL *used* to make a fortune. But that was in the days when rich WASPs were always sailing back and forth to Europe. Now, in the new jet age, there simply aren't enough of them to fill a boat. That's how I came to acquire SCL so cheaply."

"So you're looking for a marketing strategist," says Crawley. "A turnaround artist."

"We'd *like* to keep our ethnic *mix*." Everness smiles at the ineptness of the word *mix*. "But our market is anyone who can afford the tariff. We *say* we're looking for a chief executive. But what we really need is a star salesman. Someone who knows the travel industry inside and out. Someone who can manipulate travel agents. Someone who can bring us rich, warm bodies of any hue. Someone who can charm rich old dowagers out of their pants—and, of course, have them coming back for more, with their tongues dragging." The teeth flash. "Now, the question is—can you find us such a person?" He raises his palm like a traffic cop. "And, of course, summer cruises must be sold urgently, so we need this person *yesterday*—as I'm sure you understand. Can you help me?"

Time for some soothing words. "Finding people who think they can run a cruise line would be very easy, Horst. But finding an authentic achiever to effect a turnaround in a falling market is never easy. But, yes, we can do it. And we're used to working under pressure. You can count on us to bring home the bacon. And, with a touch of luck, very quickly, too."

THEY GLIDE BACK ACROSS THE TRIBORO. The sun's gone—but there's the fountain of Manhattan lights. The Twin Towers, altogether too tall and too flashy, yet perfectly symbolizing the New World capital, which is doubtless why Everness makes his downtown office there. The Empire State's spotlit in red, white, and blue. Other landmarks gleam in gold, purple, green, and ivory. It's still a wonderland to Crawley. "Look! Chancey! *There*—six sixty-six—the Sign of the Beast!" He's right, of course. Such neon digits really do blaze. "Six. Six. Six. They call it the top of the sixes, Chancey. It's just up the street from us on Fifth Avenue, you know."

"I guess if there really is a devil he knows the value of publicizing a prime location."

Crawley's suddenly serious. His voice's somber, his brow a little furrowed. "Are we comfortable with Everness and his assignment, Chancey?"

Reflected light, intermittently broken by shadows from vertical steel cables, bounces off the chastising clerical eyes.

"Absolutely! It's a plum job. Fill it and everyone'll notice. Clients'll roll in the door. We'll never worry about the rent again."

"But his prejudice seems right out of Dante."

"Come *on*. That prejudice is what New York is all about. They don't call it the melting pot for nothing. We're agents within a cauldron that simultaneously contains and dissolves prejudice. I mean that's why we're here, right? The prior owners of SCL might have something on their consciences, but we're not discriminating. Neither is Everness. He's a just a pragmatist." He pauses. "Our yardstick's competence."

"So was Eichmann's—"

"Oh, Christ, Crawley, we're the good guys. We'll be taking the company in the right direction." Explaining reality to failed priests can get exhausting. "And it might not even be a time-eater." He looks a little happier. "He said he wants someone yesterday. We already have a bunch of travel-industry hotshots on file. And one of them, as I seem very clearly to recall, might be right up Everness's alley."

"You mean Jesse Green?"

"Yes—so get him back into the office and extract every last detail of his life. Then I'll run everything past Doc—and maybe set about negotiating the placement with Everness."

MANHATTAN

"CHANCEY! HOW SPLENDID YOU LOOK with your new corporate haircut." Henry's mellifluously Oxfordian accent resonates within the marble foyer of the New York Yacht Club. The epauletted black doorman nods politely. Henry's grip is as soldierly as ever. "And what a setting." His wide eyes take in the foyer, then the tiny vestibule just beyond it. "My word, Chancey. Is that really the Holy Grail over there?"

They climb two steps and move to the tiny, windowless space. Henry eyes the glistening silver trophy.

"The America's Cup, indeed! O happy and holy sight! Mounted on a pedestal. Entombed in a thick, bullet proof glass case. And spotlit, by Jove." He steps back and surveys the pedestal base. "Bolted to the floor, too, I hear. They certainly don't mean to lose it, Chancey."

"If so, it's to be replaced with the head of the defending skipper. That's the talk. Some say it's not just talk, either."

They wander to the adjoining mahogany-lined bar. "What can I get you, Henry?"

Henry eyes the long, gleaming counter, the green baize card tables, the several twosomes playing backgammon, then smiles.

"Is a Bass Ale possible?"

"This isn't the Queens Ferry, but I'm sure they'll find you a Bass."

"Ah, yes, the Queens Ferry—so long ago. My word. Anything else you miss about Godzone?"

Godzone, the Queens Ferry, Fokker Friendships, and Queenstown.

"A dozen natural Bluff oysters might be nice."

The white-coated Irish bartender produces two iced bottles of Bass and pours them into glass mugs. Henry's eyes are smiling over the froth.

"To your continued peripatetic prosperity, Chancey." They laugh and gulp. "Long way from Down Under. You must be just about the only Godzoner to break into this salubrious bastion. Tough nut to crack?"

"I had a wonderful opening as member of the Sydney Squadron. Found some people prepared to say I wasn't a total asshole—"

"As Aussies go—"

"Kiwis, actually. Proved not to be impossible."

"Great place for contacts?"

"That's what it's all about. They call it a yacht club, but in fact they've no marina, no yachts, and no sea. But meeting prospects in this kind of setting's a huge help. They assume I'm a member of the establishment." They share smiles. "Same with the Rockefeller address. Subleased a tiny suite to control costs. Luckily it's just off the elevator with a drop-dead view. Then Jill and a local designer created the illusion of luxury and space."

"You always understood these things, Chancey."

"Image is everything in Manhattan. I was dead lucky in persuading Jim McCracken to join Haste and Company as chairman of directors."

"*Doctor* Jim McCracken? The business guru? He must be an old man by now. I imagine he commanded a fat fee."

"Doc's age is a real plus. He's not looking to run the marathon. Just wants to help, and to be in the game. He was very reasonable about money. His name and contacts have been enormously helpful, and his advice even more so. He's always got some special, piercing insight. Calls things as they really are. He can also be very funny, in a deadly kind of way. He's earned his retainer a hundred times over."

After all these years Henry's still in uniform: same suit, regimental tie, white shirt, and black boarding-school shoes.

"Well, you certainly haven't changed, Henry."

"When people say I look the same I know they think I'm looking older." He laughs. "Fact is, I turned sixty last week. But if I've aged, then so have you, dear boy. Not that you're showing it."

"I joined a health club. Work out on a bike and pump some iron. Jill's doing calisthenics—she's really fit. And great with clients, too. Some of these senior men have taken a real shine to her. In fact, she attracted a plum assignment I'm working on right now."

"So you don't take that lovely girl for granted." He laughs. "It's still okay to call her a girl, isn't it?" Polite pause. "I mean she must getting be close to—"

"Whatever. She still looks like a girl to me."

"Fitness is great, Chancey." Haverford's suddenly serious. "You just have to bear in mind that it's only a physical achievement."

"As distinct from—"

"Moral integrity. No good being physically fit if we lose the higher realms. You'll discover this soon enough. Quickly, perhaps, at your age."

"Jill's working on that side of things, too. She got involved with some group that helps autistic kids. She's been off to a couple of weekend conferences, in fact."

"Good for her. How're your own kids, by the way?"

"At private schools and doing well. Blake's always been a maverick. He's had some run-ins. But that's sorted out, now that he's sixteen and in his final year. Angie gets lost in her studies. She's desperate to excel. Too desperate for a fourteen-year-old. Driven by my same demons I guess."

"I imagine." Backgammon pieces clatter behind them. "How old are *you* now, Chancey?"

"Forty next birthday."

"Forty, goodness me. Got to fill the unforgiving minute, Chancey. Eliot completed 'Prufrock' by twenty-eight. Keats and Shelley died in their twenties. Mozart at thirty-four. Wilde at forty-four."

"They say Wilde lied about his age. But what's been going on in your life, Henry?"

"Well I finally inherited my seat in Lords. We went to London for the investiture. As you can imagine it all entailed a heady blend of pomp and circumstance. So much so that for a little while Mildred and I were thinking of retiring there." Long pause. "In the end we decided against it."

"You'd have been set for life with a peerage."

"An angel in heaven is nobody in particular, Chancey. A little glory but no money, that all got used up long ago. And England's not what it was." He sets his mug on the bar. "It was a Rip Van Winkle experience. They've been asleep there these past thirty years. The Empire's gone, but they don't know it. They kid themselves with images and memories." He smiles. "Only the class system remains in bloom. So Mildred and I are on our way back to Sydney."

"Sydney? The dumping ground for convicts and warrant officers?"

The barman's eye is cocked. Another round? Yes.

"Maybe it was, Chancey. But at least they're alive. It's a vibrant city. As well you know. Our kids've mostly settled there. It's a fluke I'm in Manhattan. Little bit of business with my newest son-in-law."

"You let one of your daughters marry an American?"

"Not at all. Grisham Pryce is from a fine old English family. Landowners, too. Coldridge Manor in Dorset. Been in the family for centuries."

"Well bred! Well done!" A mock salute with the fresh mug of beer. "But who'd have expected less from a daughter of yours? What's this son-in-law doing in New York?"

"Investing. Talking to a money manager. And acquiring a painting that's up for auction."

"Sounds like a go-getter."

"Not so much a go-getter as a minder." Henry smiles, then sips the fresh beer. "I told him about you—explained that you're the Kiwi nibbling at the Big Apple. I said I'd try to set us all up for dinner or something. He was delighted by the idea. Insisted that I ask you to choose a first-rate restaurant and bring your Jilly along. "

"I thought you were out of here tomorrow."

"I was until things changed. Now I'm hanging on for a few days. Grisham suddenly has some fellow back in the Village that he wants us to meet. We'll catch up with him at the manor end of the week, take a last look over Mother England's lovely April countryside, then depart for good." He pauses. "So, can I introduce you to Grisham over some haute cuisine?"

"Sure. Let's all meet at my place at for a drink, then grab a bite. Maybe take in a jazz club later."

"That would be lovely."

"Jill'll be delighted. When can Grisham do it?"

"Thursday—that's the only day Elan can join us."

"Elan?"

"You remember Elan. You met her at the Queens Ferry. Must be a whole other life for you, now. Well, they married two months ago at Saint Bartholomew's in Coldridge. The wedding coincided with my investiture—"

"Sunny's your father now, Chancey." His mother's only thirty but she still looks like Garbo. How could she ever've married that grotesque pederast? "You like Sunny, don't you?"

"You okay there, Chancey?"

"Yeah, sure. Did you check out any of this out with Elan?"

"She's in a country cottage that doesn't have a phone. But Grisham's gung-ho, so Elan will be, too." He glances at his watch. "Hey—*tempus fugit*. Got to run." He downs the half-filled mug, drops it to the bar, then offers his hand. "I'll leave you to finish up in peace. He strolls to the door, then looks back. "See you Thursday at seven, then."

One gulp will drain that glass. And there it goes. He sets the empty glass back on the bar. The mirror's suddenly staring at him. That's not her face, either. She's just a fragment of fading memory. An illusion. Did he ever really know her? Not really. They just had a good time. They never had to deal with real-world stuff. Nitty-gritty. Bills. Kids. Things going wrong. Just a lot of running around. And copulating. *Fuckeen.*

"It's just a mirror, sir." The brogue belongs to the bartender.

"I guess."

Forget that lilting voice of hers. Don't start with any of that again. She's in the past. She's out of your life. It took time, but you moved on. You've carved out something a million times better with Jill. So turn the mind to that red-hot candidate that Horst is going to be aching to hire. What's the name, again. Ah, yes—Jesse Green. He's the fuckeen future.

HE CATCHES THE SCENT OF FREESIAS, glances to the vase beneath the gilt-framed mirror, and looks for Jill. "Lovely arrangement, Jilly—you have a real knack with flowers."

Her image appears in the mirror and smiles.

"So—how'd it go with Everness?"

He holds her glance in the mercury.

"Got the assignment! I just have to deliver the goods."

Jill's face is not Elan's face. Elan's five years older now for sure. Is Jill? He focuses on her. She doesn't look like it: same weight, same big blue eyes, and same bright, lively smile. Touch of silver in the hair now, though. She likes it that way. More sophisticated, she says. Sensuous as ever in a red silk blouse above a shapely, knee-length black skirt. Some people shrivel in New York, and others thrive. Jill's a thriver. He grabs her hand and pecks her cheek.

"Hey, that's great, Chancey." She embraces him warmly. "That might take a little pressure off the budget. The school fees are due next week, you know."

He steps back. "Yeah, I know."

"I'm sure I don't need to remind you that this is Blake's big year. He's at the library doing his homework, right now."

"Just sixteen years old and already a slave to the system—Angie, too, I guess. Well, the Everness assignment is a happy omen, so don't worry about the fees. Horst said to send you his best wishes, by the way."

She smiles. "It's nice to be remembered."

"Oh, it's not a matter of guys like Horst remembering you." He laughs. "They love you."

She glances into the foyer mirror. "Can't imagine why." She pats her shining hair. "I'm forty now. I'm losing my looks, and I'm struggling like buggery to keep my figure." They smile at the Antipodeanism. "And for what?" Her expression is quizzical. "Flattery from silver-headed, paunchy old men in striped boxer shorts who likely couldn't get it up if they tried."

"How do you know what they wear under their suits?" She drops the hand. "Speaking of older men, I told Henry to come here on Thursday at seven. He's arranged to treat us to dinner."

"I thought he'd be gone tomorrow."

"So did I. Now he's here for the week with his son-in-law—Grisham. Grisham Pryce. The Honorable Grisham Pryce, I imagine. He's the one who's paying, and he wants to go somewhere classy. I said we could do it on Thursday."

"The four of us?"

"Five, actually. Grisham's bringing his wife. They just got married. She'll be flying in from London."

"Not Elan? The pretty one that you fancied." She looks to catch his eye. "She'll be jet-lagged, that's for sure."

"As it happens, the daughter-in-law is Elan. And, yes, I guess she might still be pretty. And I can admire that without necessarily fancying her."

"I guess you'd have run off with her if you had—"

"Assuming she in turn fancied an old man like me." He laughs and turns. "No such luck."

He glances into the mirror to catch a glimpse of her unguarded face. If she's suspicious it'll show. Their eyes meet in that ever-curious dimension. So, she's checking him out, too.

In the dream he's making love to a corpse on the sands of a cliff-backed beach. It's on top, naked, leaning backward. He closes his eyes and thrusts. An engine roars. He glances over his shoulder. Elan, on a motorcycle, her unbuttoned army tunic flying, races toward them. A British officer on the pillion, his hands cupped to her breasts, is fucking her from behind.

15

Tuesday Forecasts

"HEY, DOC—WE SAW GREEN AGAIN early this morning. Crawley got a transcript of his interview typed up. We're faxing it to you along with the psych-test materials. See what you make of it all, and I'll call you in an hour."

FAX TO DR. JAMES McCRACKEN
FROM CHANDLER HASTE & COMPANY

Search for SCL Cruise Line President
Edited transcript of taped interview
Candidate: Jesse Green MBA
Interviewer: Ungerford Crawley

Crawley: I'm glad you could come in so quickly, Jesse. Our discussion will be informal and everything will be held confidential, of course. I'd also rather listen than make notes, so Miss Timely here is sitting in to catch your pearls. So, now, tell me about yourself, from day one.

Green: It really is wonderful to talk to you again, Ungerford. I just love the way you Brits speak. Since you've asked me to detail my life—from day one, you say—I figure you need a warts and all picture, so I'm going to err on the side of candor. I was born forty years ago, an only child, and I was raised in Queens, New York, where my father was a hard-driving entrepreneur—and a something of a role model.

Crawley: And his specialty was . . .

Green: Retail services, which is to say that he, uh,

owned several, uh, dry-cleaning businesses, actually. We didn't always get along—he was a hard taskmaster, full of piss and vinegar—somewhat tyrannical, actually. But my mother was an angel, an absolute angel, a gorgeous woman. She was ambitious, too. She inspired me to do a whole lot more with my life than clean other people's dirty clothes.

Crawley: What were the schools like in Queens?

Green: Well, I'm very proud of the fact that I attended the local high school. I have to admit that I didn't realize the importance of hard work back then, so my grades failed to reflect my true ability, but I got into New York University anyway, and paid my own way selling encyclopedias. I made a lot of money doing that. Well, it certainly seemed like a lot of money to me back then. I graduated with a bachelor's in business. Then, of course, I went back and did my MBA there, too. By that time I was savvy enough to realize that a person with my level of ambition needed that kind of credential.

Crawley: And your career took off immediately?

Green: Kind of. I fell into the hospitality business. Casinos Incorporated offered me my first real job. I began as a management trainee. Effectively I was just a sales clerk. Just the same, I learned all about the business and soon got advanced to salesman. I promoted their string of hotels and did a wonderful job, even if I say so myself, exceeding every target. Unfortunately, as I guess you know, Ungerford, they went belly-up. So I moved to Golden Casinos where I was number one salesman five years in a row. My boss, a savvy if sometimes difficult guy, died of a heart attack. They brought in some know-nothing from outside the company to replace him and the chemistry between us was all wrong. When a headhunter tapped me to become sales manager for the Harold Crumpet chain, I jumped immediately. I did a wonderful job for him. Before I knew it, I was divisional president of his most profitable casino. I have full P&L responsibility. I recruit and manage the salesmen. Harry Crumpet has the reputation of being an assh—a difficult man to work for.

Crawley: As self-made entrepreneurs so often are, of course.

Green: Right, that's reality, Ungerford. I mean, Crumpet's a wonderful person, don't get me wrong. I personally love the guy. And he's been good to me. Given me some real breaks. But there's just no pleasing him. He's also running in the red. I guess you know all about that. Trouble is he can't really afford me. My salary is peanuts.

Crawley: It's so unfair of him to stint an achiever like yourself—can you share the actual figure?

Green: I'm getting a hundred grand a year, plus commission, but he chisels on that, too. That's why, when you mentioned you were looking for a cruise line president, I knew immediately that the job had my name written all over it. The key to that job is selling and nobody can do a better job of that than me. I say that in all modesty. I could bring your client a ton of business—fast.

Crawley: As your track record surely confirms. Now, off the job, what kinds of interests do you have?

Green: I'm glad you asked. I'm a round-table member of the Sales and Marketing Institute. I'm active in the Young Chief Executive Organization, YCEO. They're the greatest bunch of movers and shakers in the world.

Crawley: I trust your focus on professional interests hasn't hampered your private life.

Green: You must be clairvoyant, Ungerford. In fact, my drive for success was part of the reason for the failure of my first marriage, which I got into straight out of college, by the way.

Crawley: And did your wife work outside the home?

Green: She was a casino receptionist, actually. The marriage was a big mistake. We were just wrong for each other. She was a nice girl, but had no ambition. She could never have kept up with me. We divorced almost immediately. I've been remarried for five years now. Janice and I have one kid, an adorable four-year-old girl. We'll send her to Spence—Janice is a Whitshaw, you know.

Crawley: Of course, a very fine family name, though I do seem to remember something about them having their ups and downs . . .

Green: Well, yes, they've had some publicity. They used to be old money but then they lost it—much of it, anyway. But the name is still gold. And Janice and I really are in love, you know. She's wonderful. It was a blessed day when I met her. We have an apartment on Fifth Avenue—with no mortgage, the building won't allow that, as I'm sure you realize.

Crawley: How wonderful for you both to be in that position. Was Janice in a position to help with the acquisition?

Green: If I'm being utterly candid then I suppose I should confess that she cleaned out her savings to make the deal. We got it before prices went up, though, and it's turned out to be a great investment.

Crawley: Do you do anything to stay fit?

Green: I'm in terrific shape. I'd like to shed a few pounds, of course, but wouldn't we all? I have a weakness for food. Fortunately I seldom drink. I smoke a cigar once or twice a week—but not at home, Janice doesn't like that.

Crawley: You sound like a great fit for the job, Jesse. Now, I just need you to fill out a couple of questionnaires, and provide a list of references—then we'll press your candidacy very hard.

Green: No problem with the references, Ungerford, but if you're talking about psychological questionnaires then at my level I'd have thought that was redundant. Still, what do I care? I'll complete them at home and bring them back tomorrow. I have to do them here? Well, what's a couple more hours in the grand scheme of things? And you'll provide me with a copy of any report, right? I'll take that nod as a yes, okay?

"THE DOCTOR SAYS ANGIE'S got an eating disorder!" Jill sounds distressed.

"An eating disorder?"

"She binges, then sticks her fingers down her throat and vomits. She's lost a lot of weight. He says it's not uncommon among Manhattan teenagers. He also said that it's not just an attention-getting syndrome. He says it's serious."

"She certainly drives herself hard. What does the doctor recommend?"

"Serious help."

"Like what?"

"Private hospitalization."

"Shit—what does that cost?"

"She's starving herself to death—and you're talking money?"

"Look, I'm in the middle of the Everness thing. Can I call you back?"

"Where's your head, Chancey?"

Can you believe that? She just hung up.

Must be time to call Doc.

LONDON

DE-FUCKING-PRESSING, even by the standards of Fuller Fyfe—make that *Mr.* Fuller Fyfe—the official high-flying Rainmaker of London. The city has its charms, that's for sure, but dealing with these fucking Poms isn't one of them. He struts the wispy-mustached employment officer to the mahogany door. The little prick offers a fishy hand. He smiles into the seedy eyes.

"It was a delight to meet you, Mister Hurd." Big beam and the bonus of an accent that might just pass for standard Oxford. "I'm sure when I find you a job we'll be doing some really fine business together."

That *will* be the fucking day. When they get to be clients, these fawning Brits show neither gratitude nor loyalty. He watches Hurd—rhymes with turd—ooze across the soft, traditional carpet of the neat, paneled reception. There he goes. Out into the varnished corridor. Now he's looking back. Little wave! Oh, yes. Cock the hand in a mock salute. Strutting those fancy tan Church wing tips into the elevator cage. Oh, these fucking class-and-status-obsessed Poms: antecedents and schools, clubs and ties, shoes and overcoats, words and accents, U and Non-U, brands and labels, suburbs and vehicles, town and country. Shit—it never fucking ends. The cool put-downs they imagine to be so subtle. The look-down-the-nose distancing. The Aussies were rough diamonds. And of course most of the successful ones were out-and-out criminals. But at least you knew where you stood with them. Just about every one of these eccentric Limeys is a puzzlement. But only to begin with. Behind their oh-so-clever facades there's no one home. No one you'd enjoy sharing a drink with, anyway.

There, by the way, hanging on the farthest wall from the reproduction antique desk, is the degree certificate—*his* degree certificate. Just a shame he had to stick it up too far away for the fuckers to read the fine print. They *grovel* for Oxford or Cambridge and smirk at just about anything else. A *colonial* degree, Mr. Fyfe? Isn't that a bit, uh, oxymoronic? Big joke. Ha fucking ha.

And there, over the Strand, above that row of converted town houses opposite, is the terminally gray horizon that passes for sky. *Where's the fucking sun?* Really. Where *is* the fucking sun? And what about the filthy fumes from those thundering diesel buses? And the oversized black beetles they call cabs.

And, oh, shit, what's that? Time to play doctor and press two fingers of each hand into his stomach. Is it an ulcer? It's certainly a nasty pain. Woke him this morning. Woke him every day last week.

Goes away with food. Then comes back. Shit—it *is* a fucking ulcer. Busted my fucking guts for Bigfoot. Really. Busted my fucking guts for him. He has no idea. Absolutely no fucking idea of the effort that's gone in to making this place work. Just asks about the figures; the bottom fucking line. Well, the figures are great. All things considered. Well, *great* might not be the actual word. But they're very good. If only the certainties had stayed good they'd be very good. Okay, quite good. But, Christ, wouldn't you know it, they fell through. *Fell fucking through! After* being written into the book. In ink. After getting into the *accounts.* What *rotten* luck. Who could *ever* have guessed?

So, let's wander back and shut the door on that icky Hurd. But be fair to the fucker for he really is a certainty. The little turd's as good as placed already. Fuck it—he *is* a placement. The time to observe proper protocol is at hand, surely, so just snatch up the Mont Blanc and enter *Mr.* Hurd's fine family moniker into the book. With a little maneuvering, some of the other certainties'll come good, too. That'll take care of the cash crunch. Then he'll just make the appropriate adjustments. Nobody'll be any the wiser.

Christ—just look at the time! Nearly five already. Well, nearly. Best not to leave yet, though. Chancey might call. A celebratory drink's in order, though. Get rid of the taste of those flat Pommie beers they made him knock back at lunch. Now, where did he put that lovely silver flask?

MANHATTAN

"I READ THE TEA LEAVES, CHANCEY." Even on the phone from Chicago, Doc's voice sounds upbeat, mischievous, onstage.

"So what's the lowdown on this Jesse Green, Doc?" He seats himself on the edge of his marble desk. "To be or not to be? Can he do it? Or not?"

"Well, that's some question. More of a question than you might realize." Doc's excited. He's going to give a performance. He's going to reveal the dark, underlying truth. He's going to let the chips fly all over the place. "Well, my reading of these tea leaves is that this would-be chief-executive candidate of yours is a—*mean—ruthless— sonavabitch.*"

"Mean? Ruthless? A sonavabitch?" If this black phone wasn't jammed so hard into his ear he might not believe that he's actually hearing these words.

"Yeah—a smooth-talking, status-hungry, social-climbing money grubber." Doc pauses, then plows right on. "If it'd help him get ahead he'd take a razor to his grandmother's trachea. He'd do it in a minute."

"How're you drawing your inferences, Doc?" He gazes through the window toward Central Park's emerging dogwood blossoms. "I mean, the bio and psych-test results looked pretty good to me. And he certainly comes across as an achiever."

"Yeah, well, I'm sure he puts on a wonderful presentation." He pauses. "He'd be real good at that. He's a twenty-two-carat wooer."

"A wooer?"

"A compulsive salesman. Straight out of Oedipus. All this stuff about how he just *loves* his mother. He has an underlying wish to bed her. And those disparaging remarks about his father. He's clearly very resentful of authority. Most of these interpretations are pretty self-evident in his career, actually." He pauses. "And, of course, he cheated on the psych testing."

"He did? How can you tell?"

"Well, just too perfect, nothing more than a facade."

"What else?"

"The bio's the giveaway."

"I'm sure he was putting his best foot forward—"

"Sure he was. Put a high gloss on *everything*. He's in an industry that attracts shady characters, of course, so that's more or less par for the course."

"The way he tells it he's an upwardly mobile achiever—"

"Sure—but very little's checkable."

"We've confirmed dates of employment—where we could."

"And that's the point—too many firms and bosses have gone kaput. You can't talk to his present boss, Harry Crumpet, either, I imagine. Too tricky. But even if you could, who'd believe that self-promoter, anyway?"

"You see anything else there, Doc?"

"Yeah, these memberships of his. Gold circle member of the Sales and Marketing Institute. Now, there's a band of sharks for you. Also belongs to YCEO. Little boys playing bigshot. Sucking business from each other. Says he's got an MBA. Now, that just *might* be true. I'm sure he'd love to be claiming a Ph.D. But he might just be too smart to tell you an outright lie. Nothing checkable, anyway."

"None of this sounds too bad, Doc. How do you figure he's a totally ruthless cutthroat?"

"Well, bear in mind that he's a Jew-boy from Queens living in a Fifth Avenue co-op."

"He's Jewish?"

"The names give it away."

"Jesse Green? *Jesse Green?* That's Jewish?"

"I imagine he switched them from Joshua Greenberg. Or some such. You'll find that out when you check his degree."

"He's changed his name? He cares if people know he's Jewish? And, I mean, would it matter, anyway?"

"Well, a lot of people change their names. So that's not entirely related to being Jewish. But graspers like Jesse Green mostly do it to obscure their humble origins. And maybe get some kind of jump start into the ruling classes."

"What's wrong with that?"

"Well, nothing. But from a psychological perspective, what we're talking about here is clues to underlying motivation." He pauses. "Keep in mind that past oppression's the manure that makes the luxuriant rose."

"So overachievers are most likely to come from people who've been deprived?"

"Yeah. But bear in mind, too, that overachievers come in all stripes, colors, and creeds. I've met a lot of Irishmen who were pretty damned sensitive about their origins—and Italians and Asians, too. As I guess are a lot of those convicts from your neck of the woods. It's not about *being* inferior. It's about *feeling* inferior. About feeling deprived on account of one's roots—and of being neurotically driven to prove the opposite. Then, of course, for self-hating social climbers like Jesse Green—or Joe Lampton, or Sammy Glick—of feeling compelled to hide the very blemishes

that spur you on. Kind of *poetic* when you think about it. Not that
Jesse Green would think so. People like him get very antsy about
these things. Especially when sneaking past a supposedly silver-tailed
co-op board."

"Don't the best people live on Fifth Avenue?"

"Well, some might. But Jesse Green's an angle boy who's gone
out on a limb to authenticate himself with a status address. And, I
imagine, some very ostentatious furniture. The apartment itself might
just be small and viewless. The actual entry might even be from a
side street."

"An angle boy?"

"An operator who knows all the angles. A schemer who lies
awake at night working out which buttons to press. He probably
knows every dirty trick in the book. And a lot more besides."

"His wife's a Whitshaw."

"His second wife, according to the transcript. And I bet he
did a sales number on that little princess. She's every boot-strapper's
fantasy. And Jesse Green's ultimate certificate of merit. Might've
knocked her up to marry her." He pauses. "Well, it's not all bad. She
might just keep him on the straight and narrow."

"What I need to know, Doc, is, can Jesse Green lead a major
cruise line?"

"Well, that's the sixty-four-dollar question." Doc pauses. "If
he can it'll be in his own fashion. And that mightn't be what your
client really wants."

"It's a takeover. They need to crank it up real fast. They're
looking for a sales genius. Everness has a touch of Sammy Glick
himself. I think he'll fall totally in love with Jesse Green."

"Green's a dangerous charmer. He might just do a great sales
job. Both on them and for them. He's certainly got the motivation.
And the smarts. This'll be his chance to make good on his big-shot
dreams—maybe his only chance. Just make sure Everness knows
he's making a pact with the devil."

16

Midweek Decisions

WEDNESDAY ALREADY. Elan arrives tomorrow. But put that out of mind. Here comes Crawley, strutting, bouncing, beaming, eyes fixed on the horizon.

"NYU says the degree's good, chief." Light from the art deco chandelier glistens in his bald spot. "Just so long, of course, as Jesse Green's original name really was Jeremiah Greenbaum."

"Thank God for that. Everness is seeing Green right now. So we can put our feet up for a couple of moments, which is exactly what you're going to see me do." He cups his hands behind his head, tilts the swivel chair, and rests his wing tips on the polished surface. "How'd you coax the name out of him?"

"I simply told him we needed to verify that degree." Crawley smiles at his own candor. "He was a touch embarrassed but came clean immediately."

"The birthdate tallied with his age?"

"Indeed."

"What about his references?"

"A bit cagey but not a problem. Said he was a star salesman. Ambitious. Aggressive. Smart. Upwardly mobile."

"But?"

"Rebellious—looks out for number one—"

"Big surprise. Did you verify his dates of employment?"

"As best I could. All seemed okay. A couple of people have to check the files and get back."

"What about income? Did he show you a W-two?"

"He produced copies of salary checks instead." He shrugs. "Everything looks kosher, Chancey."

"We've got to be certain. It'll all be too late after he's got the job."

"I think you're worrying needlessly, Chancey." He pauses. "I think you're mistakenly trying to second-guess your own brilliant original intuition."

"I don't know, maybe—"

"I mean your concern with a client's well-being is always inspiring. But what I see is that you've found SCL a great chief. Everness'll love him. And for good reason. Whatever his warts might be—and I think we know them all by now—he's a first-rate operator who really will perform. So let's just wrap it up and collect the balance of the—" The intercom suddenly buzzes and flashes. Crawley stares at the phone. "If I'm any judge, Chancey, that's going to be Everness on the phone, right now!"

Crawley's right, of course.

"We surely have our man in Jesse Green!" Everness is panting.

Crawley slides into the guest chair where his ears twitch like the antennae they really are.

"I fancied him a lot!" Flash the thumbs-up for Crawley. "He's a real go-getter."

"Glad to hear it, Horst. We pulled out all the stops. He's an authentic sales star. No doubt about that." He draws the phone closer to his mouth. "We just need to discuss, ah, a couple of things about his, ah, personality."

"What sort of things?"

"We'll, he might be, how shall I say, overmotivated."

"*Over*motivated?"

"Driven to the point of ruthlessness, Horst. Our testing said Green'd do pretty much anything to achieve his goals."

"Ambition is a strength—just so long as he's pursuing *my* goals and making *my* cruise line a big success. Then his success will be my success."

"The other thing, Horst, is that motivation always springs from somewhere. So it just might help you to know that Jesse Green's, uh, momentum, seems to spring from, ah, an underlying sense of, ah, ethnic inferiority."

"Are you saying that he's—*Jewish?*"

"Well, I don't know that I was saying that, Horst. Because, you know, overachievers come in all stripes, colors, and creeds—"

"But?"

"But, ah, well, yes. Now that you mention it, Jesse Green does just happen to be Jewish."

"And you think this could be a problem given SCL's history of, shall we say, ethnic purity."

"That's your call, Horst. I just wanted you to have all the information."

"We *need* a sales star. We need someone driven. And we need him now. We must overlook Jesse Green's origins."

"And his motivation?"

"We'll structure a remuneration package to *harness* his neurotic ambitions. We'll use them to *focus* him. We'll fight fire with fire—his fire."

"You're sure you want to go that way? We've got a couple of other strong backups you might just like to look at before you decide—"

"But none with the charm and chutzpah of a Jesse Green. I've hired a lot of people. I know a good thing when I see it. Speaking of which, he doesn't actually look too Jewish. I personally liked him a lot. He'll make us highly profitable. Then everyone will forget all this nonsense about his overmotivation. Why, we might even confer him the honor of making him an honorary Swede."

"So you want to go ahead with him, Horst." Crawley's ears are on high beam.

"I want you to come to my office tomorrow morning. Ten o'clock. And I want you to bring Jesse Green. I'll make him an offer and bring him on board immediately." He's intoxicated by his own decisiveness. "And, by the way, Chancey"—the voice softens—"do pass along my best wishes to Jillian."

"CAST YOUR EYE OVER THIS!" He floats the missive under Crawley's beak. "Came in the midday mail."

Crawley glances upward and momentarily fixes upon the silver anchor embroidered into the New York Yacht Club tie. He squares the ruler on his immaculately clean desk, then pulls a pair of black-rimmed spectacles from a battered leather case and aligns them on his nose. He pores over the perfectly typed pages on crisp bond Haste and Company stationery and commences to read it aloud:

From the Desk of Richard Brittle

To Chandler Haste
New York Office

One of the things I took to heart when I
topped the MBA class was the value of proper
feedback. I'm the leader down here, of course.
But ultimate hierarchical responsibility rests
with you as founder and chief, Chancey. Hence
this "Upward Glance."

He glances into Crawley's lenses. "The little prig's going to
pass the buck."

I just want you to know that my leadership
stance is totally proactive. I am both
results-oriented and action-driven.

"He's frightened witless."

And I need to make some serious points.

"Here comes the baloney—"

There has been a radical change in the Pacific
Rim business environment. It is nowhere near
as easy to make a profit as when you were
operating down here.

"Oh, yes, of course, it was *so* easy way back then. Don't *we*
know all about that."

It's a whole new ball game. Hence the need for
new vision. Mine is to handle only top-drawer
work. We must never make "quickie" placements
to pay the bills.

"He doesn't want to get his hands dirty, he wants big-ticket
business to fall into his lap."

We must put on our thinking caps and craft
clear, inspiring, customer-inclusive,

```
ethically sound, mission and values statements
together with a viable game plan. Only then
will the bottom line come properly into focus.
```

"He wants der Führer to mastermind a plan."

```
We recently lost some consultants by
attrition. (And, of course, when you
transferred Fuller Fyfe to London.)
```

"The rats are fleeing the sinking ship, and he's floundering without a Fyfe to prop him up."

```
In seeking replacements, I have emphasized
building "the right chemistry."
```

"He's going to clone himself."

```
My new-generation subordinates are principled
team players not "hard-sell misfits."
```

"He's hiring hopeless Boy Scouts—"

```
I'm running exhaustive strategizing sessions
for my people and I provide detailed personal
feedback.
```

"And pontificating to those hapless waifs for hours—"

```
I personally handle existing clients and
assignments that come in "over the transom."
```

"He's creaming the business to make his personal figures look good."

```
This doesn't leave time for "smiling and
dialing," or "burning the shoe leather."
```

"The idea of actually doing something to bring in new clients terrifies him."

```
Finally, I'm enclosing a cash-flow statement.
```

"The bungler's going to ask us to send him money."

You'll see we need a capital injection. Bear
in mind that we've kept our shoulders to the
wheel and done the spadework. The soil is
tilled, the seeds planted, and the pipeline
full. If you'll just spray some water on the
beans, the tide will turn.

Best regards,

Richard

P.S. Bronwyn sends her regards.

Crawley drops the dispatch to the marble, tilts back in the
crimson upholstered chromium swivel chair, peers over the top of
his glasses, and strokes the clump of whisker his electric razor missed.
"You're right, Chief. He's certainly spreading his own brand of
manure on those beans."

"Just needs us to come up with the life-giving water."

Crawley tweaks his paisley tie. The colors are better these
days, but the knots are still enormous. "Just as well *we're* doing
okay."

"I guess I should never've put him in charge."

"You didn't have much choice, Chief. He might yet hold it
together. And you can trust him, at least on a personal level."

"The ninny can't hire—his clones'll never sell anything to
anyone. They'll bore people's pants off. Or twiddle their thumbs
while we pay."

Crawley steeples his mandarin fingers. "Mightn't have been
wise to move Fuller to London."

"Maybe not. I guess I should've tried to recruit a local Pom.
Trouble was, Brittle wanted Fuller out of it."

"Maybe you could move Fuller back, Chief."

"He's a piece of garbage as far as Brittle's concerned. Brittle
won't have anything to do with him. Made it very clear. Said he'd
never allow him back."

"So now you might have to let Fuller go, Chief. I mean, he's
got his own set of problems, too."

"The booze? He said he was off it."

"I don't think so."

"The London figures look okay. Better than Fuller himself, actually. But what're we going do about Brittle?"

"Somebody suggested he might crack up."

"What might that actually mean for someone like Brittle? He doesn't drink. He's pussy-whipped. Teaches Sunday school."

"Ever discuss him with Doc?"

"Yes. He says the hyper-rationality's just Brittle's way of coping. Says it could even signal mental illness." Crawley watches him stand and stroll to the window. "Like hair on the palms of the hands. But I'm sure *he'd* never do that."

The sun's bouncing from the canyon of co-ops and mansions. A line of blue-and-white buses crawl down the street like so many snails. One stops. Passengers alight. But, no, Elan wouldn't be among them. Not yet. Not ever. He turns back to Crawley.

"I can't believe he's still going on about defining a goddamned mission. Fuller was very precise about the mission. Putting bums on chairs. Upmarket bums where possible. But, where necessary, downmarket bums to pay the rent. We made our best money when we had none of this MBA baloney."

"We had you, Chancey." Crawley tosses back his head and peers down his nose. "But now you're devoting all your creative genius to New York."

"I guess you're right. Maybe I could wing over there for some of that so-called strategizing. But not right now. We've got too many things going on, on too many fronts."

JILL PROPS HERSELF ON A FLORAL pillow and breaks into his head in a measured voice. "I said they're going to *expel* him, Chancey."

He glances at the spinning balls within the antique bedside clock. "I heard you the first time."

"I wasn't sure you were paying attention."

"You can talk them out of it. Say it's just his Grateful Dead phase."

"It's all catching up with us, Chancey." She pauses. "There's a why to all this, you know."

"We'll get him to a shrink. Maybe a pro will talk them out of it—"

"Oh, for Christ's sake, Chancey."

"I suppose *I'm* to blame."

"Maybe."

"These private schools are riddled with drugs. Best schools, best drugs."

"Maybe we should've stayed—"

"Drugs're everywhere."

"We're here, Chancey. *I'm* here, anyway."

"What does that mean?"

She snaps out the light.

Big day at the Twin Towers tomorrow . . .

MAYBE THOSE REVOLVING DOORS swished too swiftly for Crawley's comfort, or maybe the phalange of security guards spooked him, or maybe he's awed to be pacing the marble floor of such a capitalist shrine. They enter the hissing elevator, hit the sixty-sixth button, and feel their stomachs turn as the floor presses into the balls of their feet.

> Whenever you enter
> The World Trade Center
> You're an A-league player on a quest
> And the throbbing escalation
> Confirms the contemplation
> That dreams pursued
>   are soon made manifest.

They step into Everness's honeyed-marble sanctum.

"Ten A.M. Thursday, that's what he said, Crawley, and here we are, right on the button."

The receptionist smiles politely. "Mister Everness will see you right away."

Faint cigar scent tinges the otherwise antiseptic environ. Everness shows his gleaming teeth, then stabs a sweaty forefinger in the direction of the drop-dead view from his floor-to-ceiling window.

"There she is, gentlemen."

Their eyes follow the digit over Battery Park and thence across the bright but murky waters all the way to Ellis Island and the impassive green-bronze Statue of Liberty. They step to the window.

"The lady's great, Horst."

"The message might seem a touch insensitive these days," says Crawley.

Everness seems perplexed. "Send me your tired, your poor, your huddled masses yearning to breathe free? What's wrong with that?"

Crawley's voice is soft. "Send me the wretched refuse from your teeming shore?"

"Well, you're right, Mr. Crawley, of course." He flashes the Evernessent teeth. "Jesse Green mightn't like to be called trash." He smirks conspiratorially. "But, from what you say, Chancey, it's the wish to escape the garbage pile that drives achievers."

Crawley's eye falls to the scurrying Lilliputians in the plaza so steeply beneath their feet. "Do you ever feel anxious to be so far up in the world, Mister Everness?"

"I can feel a little apprehensive in the streets, Mister Crawley, but never up here." Everness's forefinger raps the double-glazed armor-glass window. "The world's finest architects designed these towers to be more enduring than the pyramids. They're fortresses, really"—he smiles—"but infinitely more habitable." He turns and escorts them to the guest area upon the rich Afghan rug. Crawley's ambivalent of the goodies: black leather and steel Mies couch, matching set of chairs and coffee table, huge art deco oil painting of the SCL line's Princess Vista within a collection of ancient stone heads imprisoned upon the spotlight glass wall.

A metallic voice emanates from the intercom. "Mister Green is in reception."

"Send him in."

Aftershave suffuses the air as Jesse Green bounces through the mahogany-paneled door. His presentation's intriguing. Monogrammed, leather briefcase. tan off-the-rack suit, customized to cover the paunch, black-and-gold vest-pocket handkerchief, presumably to complement the stripes on the wide silk tie. The cream French-cuffed shirt sports jade cuff links. A bit showy but at least he's not wearing a bracelet. The brass-buckled tan shoes are freshly polished. The getup, overall, wouldn't get him past the door of a white-shoe law firm, yet it might just be perfect for a New World cruise line president.

Everness extends his hand. "Welcome."

Green sets his briefcase on the floor, locks the banker's eyes with an admiring gaze, grasps Everness's paw, and latches on to the arm with his left hand.

"Thank *you*, Horst—yes, indeed, thank you."

The pair of grinning sharks, no doubt from related species and knowing it, each smiling a little too widely, circle each other.

The banker pirouettes and points. "And you know everybody, of course."

"Yes, of course." Green beams. "Chancey and I are old friends now." His hand is a little too firm and a little too moist. "As is Mister Crawley, too." He crushes Crawley's limp fish. "Hi there, Ungerford."

Crawley fixes his eyes upon Green's pocket handkerchief and sniffs.

Everness hunkers into a brown leather chair and motions Green to take the other. Green sets his briefcase upon the coffee table, then perches politely. His trousers cut into his ample crotch, and his cuffs expose buff, ankle-length nylon hose. Haste and Company take the sofa. Crawley produces a yellow legal pad and a Parker pen.

The banker casts an almost loving look at Green. "As you know, we are here to settle on an employment contract we can all live with."

"To formalize the understanding already reached," says Green, his head bobbing.

"Since Mister Haste has already discussed the offer in broad terms, we need only sort out the details." The teeth appear. "Wherein, as they say, the devil lies." Everness pulls a file from his desk and extracts a page of penciled notes. "Now let me see. Base salary to be one-hundred twenty-five thousand dollars. Performance incentive to cap at four times that amount."

Green's response is surprisingly clear and resonant. "A total of five hundred thousand—yes, that's what we agreed."

"Providing the results are there, of course," says the banker. "And two and a half percent of stock options."

"To vest at my discretion."

"Yes, of course. We will also pay your private phone, legal, and accounting bills to a maximum of twenty-five thousand a year. All domestic and international entertaining and travel business and personal. That will primarily go onto an Amex card. *Gold*, of course."

Green continues to nod. "Legal and accounting expenses. Right. Entertaining and travel. Right. Gold Amex card. Right. What about private clubs?"

"We want you to belong to a first-rate private club. So, naturally, we'll pick up all club expenses." The voice falls. "We might get you into the University Club."

"The University Club!" Green beams. Then pauses. "And my car? My Cadillac?"

"We prefer our chief executive to arrive in a Mercedes. I trust that will be suitable. You'll choose the model and color, of course."

"You'll lease me the latest-model Mercedes. Right. And I'll choose the model and color. Yes, fine, of course."

"We'd need two other things, Mister Green." The banker's voice becomes somber. "First, a severance clause. If things do not work out, for any reason—and we both know that ventures sometimes go awry—we'd need to be able to sever the relationship at our pleasure. But with a settlement of a year's income."

Green's undulates in his chair. "Well, at this level, finding a new job might not be easy. *Three* years income is the norm."

"That is what you Americans call a deal-breaker, Jesse. We could maybe—just maybe—stretch to two years."

"Including expenses as outlined above?"

"We would have to cap the annual expenses at one hundred thousand. Now, my second point. We would need a restraint-of-trade clause. Should you leave us for any reason, you'll not work for another cruise line for five years."

"I can't imagine that will be a problem," says Green. "But I think just one year would be fair."

Everness is being more generous than he realizes. Time to jump into the act. "If Horst's offering two years severance, Jesse, then a two-year restraint-of-trade clause might be appropriate."

Green nods his approval.

"And, last, of course, Horst, you and Jesse need to agree upon a starting date."

"Now that you and I have a gentleman's agreement, Horst"— Green's nod to Everness shows a perfect blend of gratitude and respect—"I could begin immediately."

Best slow this down a touch. "It might be wiser to wait, Horst. At least until we have the formal contract."

"Chancey's right," says Crawley. "I'll draft something tonight."

Everness rises slowly to his feet.

"We need to move quickly. SCL needs to get into the black. Summer cruises must be sold." They're all standing, now. "Yes, indeed, we have a gentleman's agreement." Everness offers his hand to Green. "Today is Wednesday. So why don't you drop by the office on Monday at seven A.M. for breakfast with your executive team? They'll all be anxious to meet you."

Green's teeth and eyes flash simultaneously. "It's all settled, then." He smothers Everness's outstretched hand. "We have our gentleman's agreement." He wraps his left arm about the banker's shoulder. "And, believe me, you'll be thrilled with the killer job I'm going to do for you, Horst."

He releases the banker, grabs his briefcase, and strides to the door. Then he beams backward and, clutching the attaché to his bosom, addresses the threesome. "It's going to be a whole new era for SCL, you mark my words."

He disappears in a swirl of aftershave and deodorant.

"YOU LOOK A LITTLE WORRIED, CHANCEY."

They're perched upon chromium and leather barstools in a green-and-white-tiled Financial District coffee shop. Two steaming thick white mugs sit before them on a polished white Formica counter.

"I do? Well, yeah. Something about that Jesse Green left me uneasy."

"The meeting went perfectly, Chancey." Crawley plops three sugar cubes into the thick black brew. "Jesse Green's exactly the sales genius Everness called for. As I said yesterday, you should be patting yourself on the back." Crawley clasps the mug with both hands and savors the rich aroma. "Then again, of course your instincts are usually pretty infallible, too. So can you put your finger on anything?"

Crawley's eyes remain on him as he gazes out of the sparkling window to a seething montage of yellow cabs, bicycled black couriers, glazed-eyed stockbrokers, and tight-skirted secretaries.

"Something about the way he comported himself there. I don't know. He just made me feel, well, queasy."

A young woman jumps out into the traffic and flags a cab. Crawley sits stock-still and watches as he rises slowly to his feet, strides to the door, and gazes up the street.

"See someone you know, Chancey?"

"No. Just a passenger hailing a cab." He glances back to Crawley and grins. "Or maybe an illusion."

Infatuation, more likely. He'll know for sure in a matter of mere moments, now. And, whichever way it goes, Elan and her freshly-minted husband are in for a surprise.

17

Thursday Blue Notes

"LOVELY BROWNSTONE!" The accent's unmistakably Henry. "And who'd *ever* have suspected a garden in the middle of Manhattan?" He's peering from an open bay window into the forty-by-twenty-foot patio garden. "And, hey, there you are, Chancey—picture-perfect amid the spring tulips."

Henry's caught him adjusting a cluster of wrought-iron chairs around a tiny waterfalled pool.

Jill appeared alongside. Now she's waving.

"Your guests are here, lover-boy."

Two other figures are hovering in the background.

Henry strides from the French doors onto the cobbled patio. The outstretched soldierly hand rocks enthusiastically. And, yes, there's Elan, just beyond his shoulder.

"I see you've brought us some guests, Henry."

"One old friend, and one new friend." Henry beams, delighted to be effecting the introduction. "Now, of course, you remember Elan—"

He strains for a touch of nonchalance and holds her slate-gray eyes for the fleetingest of moments. The pupils are dilated. She's excited. Slightly out of it. A touch of jet lag has rendered her more vulnerably georgeous than ever. The light's flattering, of course. She must be twenty-five, or so. A few lines around the eyes, and a touch slimmer. She's wearing more makeup and higher heels—perhaps just for this evening. That's a very expensive tortoiseshell clip in the silken cinnamon hair that flows, as ever it did, to the small of her back. She's wearing a simple, just-above-the-knee, black silk dress with matching tunic. Christ—what's under that? A mystery still. She offers her hand. It's whiter than he remembers. Sunless England.

And he touches it. She's not an illusion at all. The fingers are as soft, supple, sensuous as ever.

"Yes, of course. Elan. From Auckland. Jill and I took you out on the boat in Sydney, too, as I recall."

"It was something very special." Her lower lip quivers. She brushes an imagined wisp of hair from her face with the other hand. Rings. A big diamond engagement. Money. And a plain, antique gold wedding band. Old money. She glances behind her. Henry jumps in.

"And, Chancey, this's Elan's husband, Grisham Pryce."

The hand is fleshy and signet-ringed. So this's Grisham. Medium height. Not paunchy but getting close. The bulk makes him seem shorter and fills out the lines in his face. He's fifty-something, all right. And nearly bald. The missing hair used to be black. The absence is artfully compensated with lush, well-barbered, silver-flecked temple growths that reach to just above his collar. He's clean-shaven with thick, sensuous lips in the shadow of a prominent, cavernously nostriled nose. The deep blue pin-striped, double-breasted suit is Saville Row. And, of course, there's a club tie, a white silk handkerchief, and custom shoes to grace a pair of incongruously tiny feet. A gentleman investor. Or a highly pedigreed pig.

"*Wonderful* to meet you, Chancey." Oozey accent and a matching mouthful of porcelain-capped teeth. "Henry often mentions your name. Says you put the lie to the notion that headhunters come to recruiting after failing at all else." He half smiles. "Says you overcame many difficulties to become a trailblazing Antipodean entrepreneur." Now, there's a couple of swift put-downs. Grisham glances solicitously to Elan. "And I understand you and your Jilly—may I call you Jilly?—took Elan sailing on Sydney harbor."

Indeed, I did, my roly-poly friend. Showed her the ins and the outs of the glorious harbor, then frolicked on the squadron guns—did she ever tell you that?

"Indeed. It was a wonderful Antipodean day. Great sailing."

The strains of opera waft into the garden. Jill appears wearing her tailored red suit with the matching shoes. Gray highlights sparkle in her hair.

"Puccini?" says Grisham.

"*Bohème*," replies Jill. A tenor sounds. Grisham cocks an attentive ear.

"Ah, yes! Rodolfo tells Mimi that as long as she's in his life he'll always feel like a millionaire."

"You're an opera fan, Grisham?" asks Jill.

"Of course. *Bohème*'s a lovely story. Idealistic, but lovely."

"Jilly got us season tickets to the New York City Opera."

"A nice introduction, and at bargain prices, I'm told. I'm acquainting Elan with my own favorites at Covent Garden. Then we'll fly to Italy to catch the Milan season at La Scala. She likes *Traviata*."

But naturally, go to Italy to catch the opera.

"Jilly likes *Traviata*, too. The music's wonderful."

"So's the story," says Jill.

"Pity that the heroine has to die," says Henry.

"They all die in the best operas," says Grisham. "Tragedy's ultimately uplifting."

Jill, her face warm and empathetic, reaches toward Elan. Perhaps Elan's newfound state of matrimonial grace has conferred a kind of sisterhood.

"I love your onyx earrings," says Elan.

Jill touches a hand to her ear. "Thanks. An anniversary gift from Chancey." She reflexively touches her outstretched hand to Elan's face. "Is that a tiny rash?"

Elan blushes. "It might be nerves. Maybe I'm still getting over the pressure of the wedding. And then the running around"—she smiles—"and jet-setting."

Jet-seteen—nothing's changed with that lovely lilt, anyway.

"Oh, I'm sorry, I didn't mean to—"

"Of course not," says Elan. "But you're a mother. Comes naturally, I guess."

"I am a mother—and, yes, my children are always on my mind. Tonight, however, they're staying with friends, so I'm on holiday, as it were."

The faintest flurry of spring air ruffles the overhanging maples. Elan leans forward in her chair, as if suddenly aware of being surrounded by the gardens of half a dozen other brownstones. She gazes over the roofs to the skyscrapers. That sun's fading fast. Garden lights glisten on the waterfall and frond'd pool.

"I imagine that not everyone has a garden," says Henry, "even here on the upmarket Upper East Side."

"No—we were lucky to find it."

"Do you rent or own?" asks Grisham.

Such a thick-skinned question from someone so well bred.

"Renting for the moment, Grisham. We'd very much like to buy. Business's going well. We'll invest in something soon."

"Meantime, this's just wonderful," says Jill.

"Oh, it really is," says Henry.

"Creates a decent impression with your business clients, I'm sure," says Grisham. "But I'm not sure *we* could live without a doorman. How's the security? Ever been robbed?"

"Never. But safety-conscious New Yorkers lock themselves into co-op apartments."

"Only to be robbed by their own security guards," says Jill.

"*Quis custodiet ipsos*," says Henry.

"Indeed—who actually will guard the guards themselves?" says Grisham. They all laugh.

"I guess Fifth Avenue's where you'd like to be," says Grisham.

"I used to think so. But someone like your good self mightn't want to be there, Grisham. Most of the savvy, old-moneyed WASPs hive out on Lexington. Some of them even buzz over to the West Side."

"What about brownstoners?" says Henry.

"Mavericks who can't get past a co-op board. And elitists, including some like Richard Nixon, who lives just round the corner."

"Ex-President Nixon"—Grisham sniffs—"the infamous liar?"

"Henry Kissinger's just a few blocks away, too."

"Nixon and *Herr* Doctor Kissinger—such an infamous pair. But I suppose they have to live somewhere." The toothy smile is sardonic. "But sooner in your backyard than mine."

"Let's not leave guests empty-handed, Chancey." Jill's back with a tray bearing red wine and crystal glasses, along with a platter of patè, Brie, and Melba toast, garnished with tomato and parsley. He'd know that bottle anywhere. He reaches for it and pours.

"Grange!" Henry's impressed. "My word, Chancey, you've really done us proud."

Jill's watching closely as he passes the glasses. Elan's staring into the crystal.

"To our hosts," says Henry, hoisting his rubied crystal.

"To the newlyweds," says Jill.

"To loving friends and fond memories." A chancey remark, but he can get away with it. They laugh and sip. He produces two small blue Tiffany boxes from his pocket. Jill shoots him a quizzical look. He passes one box to Elan and one to Grisham.

"Don't be fooled by the upmarket packaging; they're just a couple of very simple gifts for the newlyweds."

Elan looks at him semihelplessly. Then at Grisham.

"Goodness me, this is a big surprise," says Grisham.

"Indeed," says Jill.

Grisham raises the lid and peers inside. "Well, well, well. Silver cuff links with polished green stones. How rather elegant."

He sets the box on the table. Elan extracts the silver brooch and holds it up.

"An artist's palette," says Henry, "with tiny green stones."

"Oh, Chancey!" She's dazed. "And Jill, of course. You shouldn't have. You really shouldn't."

Oh, Chancey, indeed. Time for a bold move. No one will notice—except her.

"Here, let me help you, Elan." He takes the brooch from her hands and fastens it to the tunic top. Her skin's against his wrist. She seems almost frightened. She draws a deep breath. Oh, Christ—that skimpy black silk dress, so flimsy against her skin. Does she feel what he feels? She must, surely—he'd not be feeling this way, otherwise. Or would he? No, this isn't mere imagination. Their paths are not crossing by accident. In the past he failed to act. That was a mistake. There'll be no such error this time.

THE DISHEVELED STREET BEGGAR beside the restaurant door widens his baleful eyes and extends an empty indigo hand. He may be one of the truly needy, or he may just be a phony, but the heart goes out to him either way. Give him something more than charity.

"Maybe we can work a deal, my friend. Maybe you can sell me a dollar's worth of advice."

The beggar glances at him mischievously. Then at Grisham, then Henry. Then back. He smiles broadly. Two front teeth are missing, but the voice is melodic. "Those same people who denies others everything are famous for denying themselves nothing."

"Hey, that's great." He presses the money into the callused hand. "That's worth a dollar of anybody's money."

"I got a five-dollar word for you, too, sir."

"You've got *one* word that's worth *five* dollars—wow!" He extracts a bill and holds it up. "If I think this word of yours really is worth five dollars, the money's yours."

The beggar smiles broadly, then reaches out politely. "The word is *thanks*." He plucks the bill, opens the restaurant door, and waves them in. Jill and Henry go first. Elan wavers in the doorway. The beggar's eyes show authentic gratitude. "God's gonna bless you for this, man."

"I'm not sure I believe in God."

"No matter. 'Cause *he* believe in *you*. He got his eye on you. He gonna surprise you, one day. He gonna make a believer of you."

"Do I have to do anything to deserve all this attention?"

"Just give him room to work." The toothless smile again. "Then get outta the way!" The darkness swallows him.

"From what I hear," says Grisham, "most of these people— I believe *panhandlers* is the correct expression—are professional hucksters."

"Maybe, but who cares? Six bucks for a good line, a great word, and the guaranteed blessing of God, even for an unbeliever." He turns to Elan. "I'd call that a fair deal, wouldn't you?"

The winsome, laughing smile—so warm, so magnetic. "Maybe the Lord really does live in New York City, Chancey."

"As a vagrant? God's a vagrant!" She's still smiling. "So, I've been courting the wrong people—wouldn't you just know it. How am I ever going to get to heaven now?"

Angelo himself leads them through a bevy of glitzy Manhattanites to a round, pink, candlelit corner table within a commodious dining room whose subtly spotlit walls bear murals of sunny, French seaside villages. The room is abuzz with conversation. A couple of the diners, out-of-towners, surely, are sneaking peeks around the room.

Time for a little stage management.

"Jilly, let's seat you between Henry and Grisham, leaving Elan to be flanked by her illustrious husband on one side and my humble self on the other."

"I might have heard of Angelo's," says Grisham, casting a deadpan eye over the room. "Do you come here to spot celebrities?" he asks.

"They might spot us," says Jill. "They're here, of course, but most of them are locals. They like to be seen, but mostly they come for the fine food. I made the reservation because Chancey said you're something of a gastronome."

"That is indeed my one outstanding sin." He smiles. "And I pride myself upon it."

"So perhaps we could let you order for the table," says Jill, "assuming everyone agrees, of course."

Elan's removing her tunic. Best show a little gallantry by helping her lay the garment over the back of her chair. Her shoulders are bare—Franz Joseph, the mirror, the warmth, the fragrance, and still those lips, sensuous as ever, the tongue as pink, the mouth as inviting. So can this really be some kind of fated second coming? Yes, surely. Or is he merely setting himself up for a second dose of infatuation? That's possible, too, of course—and if so, the mind being the trickster that it is, he'd be the last to know. So back up a little, Chancey. Go slowly, if at all. Don't fall for the same ruse of nature twice. Block your ears with Ulyssean wax and strap yourself to the mast. Yes, yes, yes. And no, no, no. Maybe the brain concocts a secret elixir that dispels good intentions. Or perhaps some potent potion—distilled from limbecks foul as hell within, no doubt—arises to arrest the earnest voice of conscience. Adrenaline pours into his gut, and his hand, propelled by some apparently uncontrollable force, drops below the table to stroke a suspender on her garter-belted thigh, and then to seize her soft, slim fingers.

While he's been lost in reverie, Grisham has indeed ordered for everyone—rather extravagantly, too. It must be great to be able to afford whatever one wants. Grisham's gone through his whole life doing just that, no doubt. Elan's fingers draw away, but her warm thigh continues to press. It isn't hard to imagine that Grisham simply sighted Elan and decided to have her. He took a fancy to her—that's for sure what happened—and he simply *acquired* her. He devoured her, just as he's ingesting his fresh and piquant lobster appetizer, right now. Just as he ordered up this finest of white Burgundies.

"This is all very lovely, Chancey." That's Henry talking. "This farm-raised veal chop is perfection itself. But we still don't quite know why you'd want to live in New York and not, say, London, Sydney, or even Auckland."

"Where the people are British?"

"Well, yes," says Grisham, jumping in. "I mean, what can you possibly have in common with all these strangers? Or they you?"

"Well, I have to say I miss the British restraint, the pervasive politeness, and the shared heritage. But we don't live in Sydney or Auckland, or even Wellington, because those cities aren't London. And I don't live in London because I'd always be 'that colonial.' As far as the Brits are concerned, you can never rise above your origins."

"And if you do, they say it's because you don't know your place," says Henry. "It's a catch-twenty-two, Chancey."

"Right—and here it's the opposite. If your parents arrived in steerage and you somehow rose above that ignominy, then, by definition, you're wonderful."

"Britain's as majestic as ever," says Grisham. "An Englishman knows what it is to be part of an authentic nation. We value tradition and integrity ahead of materialism."

Don't let him get away with that.

"My own take is that when it comes to money everybody's of the same religion. I mean, I thought the purpose of your visit to these shores was to make a little money."

Grisham sniffs. "I merely dabble at investing to preserve my heritage."

To preserve his heritage. Of course.

"That's probably a good idea. I seem to remember reading that if all the rich men in England divided up their money amongst themselves there wouldn't be enough to go around."

Grisham's smile is cool. "For me, investing is no more than a duty and a fringe interest. No true English gentleman would stoop to make money the chief object of his thoughts."

There he goes again. Born with money and disdainful of those who have to earn it. The only reason for failing to pounce upon that hypocrisy is the silent message—*Don't go there, Chancey*—in Jill's restraining glance. She's always polite, always the lady—in company, anyway.

"I'm on Grisham's side," says Elan, smiling. "But sometimes a dose of money can be better for a headache than an aspirin."

"And sometimes one of the hardest things to teach children about money matters," says Jill, smiling sweetly, "is that it does."

The waiter appears, and, with a dramatic flourish, seizes the cover from the lemon soufflé.

"Bravo," says Jill. "Our compliments to the chef."

"And while you're at it," says Henry, smiling as he savors the spicy aroma, "tell him that I fear that his soufflé, like the British Empire itself, might all too soon be gone."

"In fact, Henry, the Empire is already gone—that's part of the reason New York has become such a magnet for achievers."

"Magnets attract many things," says Grisham, "many of them undesirable."

The wine waiter's at Grisham's elbow with the dessert wine. Grisham's clearly fonder of wine than of upward strivers. He sips the costly nectar very carefully, rolls it around his highly educated palate, swallows it slowly, and nods approvingly.

"I don't want to talk for Jilly, but as a resident of New York, I have to say that Manhattan sometimes seems to be a microcosm of the world. Sometimes it's good to sight poverty. Need is just a concept in London, Sydney, or Auckland. Here, it's an inescapable reality. You're forced to withhold or dispense charity to people your own eyes tell you are desperately needy."

"Even as you step over them to enter a fine restaurant," says Grisham. He wipes the delicate soufflé cream from his mouth. "But these aren't our problems. The Yanks should put their house in order."

The garter belt—can any other garment seem so sensuous?

"How do you feel about all this, Henry?" Jill asks.

"Chancey's in a New York state of mind. It might pall a little farther down the line."

Grisham's oily face and tony tongue turn to Jill. "Anything *you* miss here?"

"The British sensitivity, I suppose. The manners, the civility, the humor. I might feel isolated and alone if it weren't for my volunteer work."

"Chancey mentioned you'd been to a couple of local conferences on autism—well done!" says Henry.

"Did he tell you it's an international effort?"

"That he did not," says Henry.

"Chancey gets too involved in his own affairs to follow mine." She smiles. "The group began in Manchester, actually."

"Manchester, England? Not the cheeriest place in the world to wake up in," says Henry.

The soufflé's gone and time's slipping away. If a move is to be made it should come soon. A discreet nod to the waiter will have him scurrying for the check. And the second move will take the form of an invitation.

"A friend of ours, jazz guitarist Jimmy Rivers, is playing at the Blue Note in the Village. Anyone want to come along?"

"I'd be up for that!" says Jill.

Grisham turns to Elan. "Are you recovered enough for that, sweetheart?" Sweetheart—emotion from the upper classes, how decidedly Non-U. She gazes distractedly over his shoulder into a mirror. He lifts the voice a touch. "Would *you* like to go to the Blue Note, *darling?*"

"And let the sounds of music creep in our ears?" She tucks a wisp of hair into her tortoiseshell clip. "I would do that, yes."

The waiter hovers with the bill.

Grisham pats his vest pocket. "I indicated to Henry that this would be my treat, Chancey."

Indicated—he *indicated?*

"But I'm afraid I've left my credit cards back at the hotel."

Jill's eyes are beginning to smolder.

"Let me get it," says Henry.

"No, no, Henry," says Grisham. "We can't have that—not on Chancey's home territory. Let's follow protocol. I'll allow Chancey to get it this time, but I'll be sure to treat both of the Hastes to the finest meal that London has to offer the next time they're in town." He pulls a tiny silver box from his breast pocket and extracts an engraved card. "Here's our Coldridge Manor calling card, Chancey. The phone number's unlisted, so don't lose it. Be sure to call us the next time you're coming."

The gesture's okay, but the tone's condescending and the smile vacuous. He shows no insight into what he's done. Maybe aristocrats expect the commercial classes to *want* to pick up the bill. Maybe, to his way of thinking, it's some weird kind of compliment.

The lords and ladies head for the door leaving the colonials to check the computations on the extravagant tab.

Jill peeks over his shoulder. "Did you learn anything, lover-boy?" she whispers.

"What was the lesson?"

"For openers, that gentlemen are apt to take a gentlemanly slice."

"Anything else?"

"I'll leave that to you for the moment. Just promise not to go on being a slow learner."

Britain is waiting outside on the avenue. A slow learner? What's she talking about? He hails a cab and shepherds Jill and Henry into the backseat.

"Oh, damnit! Can't take more than four in a cab. Can't trust these cabbies, either. None of them speaks English. Only Jill and I know how to get there. We'll split and travel separately." He opens the front passenger door. "Here, Grisham, jump in next to the driver." He slams the door on Grisham and leans into the open window. "Hey, driver—take my friends to the Blue Note in Greenwich Village. My wife knows the way, right, Jilly?" Henry and Jill look a little discombobulated in the back. Best reassure them. "Elan and I'll be right on your tail."

Now, slam the door on them—Yes! And savor the smell of burning rubber as their cab pulls wildly into the traffic and careens off down the potholed avenue.

He springs two paces to the curb. Elan's backlit by headlights from oncoming traffic. The draft of a passing bus puffs her hair and presses her skirt against those gartered thighs. Warm air hits his face. She seems to sway. A streetlight falls across her face and breasts. She looks for all the world like an exotic animal at bay.

He reaches for her hand and draws her to him. Cars rush past. Another bus thunders down the avenue. He folds her in his arms. She's warm, lithe, sultry, mysterious as ever. The scent of wine is on her breath. "Lost your husband so soon?" he whispers. A distant siren shrieks. Streetlights dance in her face. She's studying him anxiously.

"Whatever's happening, Chancey?"

Her mouth is sweet as ever, her body just as supple.

He steps back into the avenue and hails a Checker cab. He glances into the cabin. A solid partition separates the driver from the passenger. That refinement shields the cabby from unsavory passengers, but tonight it will serve to obscure the driver's vision of the passengers. They slide into the cab. "To the Blue Note in Greenwich Village—and take the FDR."

Elan's wide-eyed and worried. "Whatever are we doing, Chancey?"

"I was desperate to talk to you."

"Grisham doesn't know. We should never've come to your house." She heaves a sigh and stretches back into the cabin corner. The flash of passing streetlights disappears into her black dress but bounces off her face. Her flickering image, and the shimmering brooch beneath it, seems almost to float within the cab. "And the *brooch*, Chancey! How could you?" Her laughter's distressed.

"He got even, I guess."

"You mean the confusion with the bill. No, that was nothing. He's terribly generous. He's just a little impractical in everyday money matters."

"He seemed incredibly deft to me. I was thinking that maybe I should've kept the cuff links for myself."

"Everything—you should've kept everything."

"I have. 'Tis all locked safely in my memory.'"

" 'And I myself shall keep the key of it'? Is there really such a key?"

"I could have one made. Maybe by the jeweler who fashioned your brooch."

"From slivers of an empty bottle—the Grange you so lustily consumed."

"How's the marriage working out?"

The sigh might be decipherable. " 'How should I, your true love, know from another one.' " She smiles wanly. " 'By his cockle hat and staff?' " That was Ophelia's answer, Chancey." She seems distracted. "Oh, shit—what do I care about Ophelia? I love him, Chancey. Not as I loved you." She puts her hand in his. "You and I started as a whimsy. I was happy to play mistress just to be with you. You liked me. And I loved being with you. It became much more, I know—we both know—yet I never quite realized that you cared so deeply. Then I got your letter. It arrived late. Altogether too late."

"And now?"

"And now? Hell, Chancey—this's more than I bargained for. I didn't know what to expect. I wanted to see you again, of course. I maybe even wanted Grisham to meet you. And wanted him not to meet you, too, of course."

She's as beautiful as ever. More sophisticated and confident, yet more vulnerable, too. Fragile even. The cab glides like a gondola down the FDR. The moonlit East River slides by on their left. A giant tower wall of brightly lit buildings flickers past on the right. The cab sways, tires screech, and thunder hits his ears. He glances over the driver's shoulder. They've entered a tunnel-like underpass. And, again, oncoming, double white stripes hurtle toward them, flash past the window, and disappear into posterity. An optical illusion, of course, for those serpentine lines are always lifeless and stationary. It's he and Elan who are on the move. Or perhaps those double lines portend eternally parallel lives. Maybe he and Elan are destined to race in tandem but never meet. Maybe they'll race toward some unattainable point of infinity forever. But not, surely, if he seizes the moment, takes her in his arms, and stretches her across the seat right now.

The pupils are wide, the neck scarlet, the lips parted, the skirt has ridden above her knees, exposing a black silk slip. And, now, garters. The French panties are black silk, too. The urge to rip that pulsating silk aside is almost overwhelming.

She knows what he's thinking, surely. Will he unfasten that front hook and tumble those silken breasts? She says nothing. Will he slip inside those slim limbs, brush aside the loose silk, and press himself into that other rosy-petaled parallel world? Her face betrays her. The answer is yes and no and both. He wraps her in his arms and kisses her lightly on the mouth. "You'd do it if I would, Elan. Perhaps that was always the way. And now this cabin speeds through all the moments of our lives—"

"Tomorrow, Chancey. Tomorrow. I'll slip away. We'll meet. We need to talk, we really do."

"At Rockefeller Center. Noon. I'll book a hotel for, uh, lunch. Do you want to do it?"

"I'll be there, Chancey." She puts her tongue to his. Her breasts heave—

Light. The tunnel's gone. The cab rolls into the Village, then draws to a halt.

The others are waiting on the sidewalk. She pushes her skirt below her knees and composes herself. The dark eyes are as deep as the night itself. She smiles wanly and touches his hand. The voice's a whisper. "Tomorrow, Chancey."

THE BLUE NOTE'S JAMMED with a hundred or more fun seekers, most of whom seem to be sucking upon fireflies. The tiny stage is lit with a spot for each of four musicians. All the walls are black. Red candles glow upon even tinier red Formica tables. Jill spots the only white man on the stage.

"There he is!"

She waves gaily. He strides toward them. A young forty with chestnut hair, nice features, a happy laugh, big brown eyes, and bright white teeth. He reaches for Jill's outstretched hand.

"Hey! Jilly! Great you could make it." His voice is surprisingly soft and mellifluous. He pulls Jill to him and kisses her softly on the cheek. He draws back. "You too, man." His hand is strong. His jacket smells of smoke. "Hey—what a surprise." The breath is nicotined. "And you've got guests." He drops his voice to a whisper. "Whose cat is *that?*" Best not to introduce Jimmy to Elan. He'll just charm her. Quoting poetry is one way to win a girl's heart. But Jimmy and his guitar would likely prevail any midnight of the week.

"The wife of a friend."

"You don't say." He chuckles quietly. "Well, lose the friend." They share a buddy laugh. Jimmy waves to the manager, and another tiny table is suddenly squeezed into the front row and bedecked with a bottle of champagne and six glasses. "There'll be no charge, Chancey—you're my guests." Jimmy glances at his watch. "No booze for me, man. Gotta swing."

Grisham, for once, seems genuinely impressed. The murmur of the crowd fades. The stage is adorned with a set of six silver drums, giant double bass, golden, gleaming saxophone—and Jimmy, his dark mahogany Gibson slung across his torso, trapped in a pale blue spotlight. He seems to smile in Jill's direction. He hits a chord, then, shaking the guitar to wring out the music, plucks four notes of the moody melody and sounds a satiny voice. *It's the wrong time.* Elan's eyes are bright. *And the wrong place.* She's focused on Jimmy. *Though your face is lovely.* As is Jill, too. *It's the wrong face.* Jimmy closes his eyes. *It's not her face.* And opens his soul. *But such a lovely face.* He carries the band along with him. *That if one night you're free.* He weaves it all into a spell—*Well, it's all right*—and takes them into another world. *Yes it's all right, It's all right, with me.*

Great jazz, like an engrossing book, always seems to end too early. The difference with a Manhattan jazz evening, however, is that there's seldom time to savor the experience. Suddenly the muse is over and you're back out on the street. Suddenly the buildings and the buzz are crowding the music out of the brain.

This time Grisham hails a cab and holds the door for Elan and Henry. And now the valediction. "Thank you *so* much for a *wonderful* evening, Chancey. A real treat for us both. Perhaps one day you and your good Jilly will sojourn across the Atlantic to Coldridge Manor."

"Now, that really would be a treat."

"But for the moment we must go our separate ways."

"Indeed, we must. And, hey, Henry—how great it was to catch up with you again." They shake hands warmly. The threesome bundles into the cab. Elan's between them. He catches her eye.

"I'm sure we'll meet again, somewhere, Elan."

She seems about to reply when the cab kicks back a burst of fumes and pulls away.

Jill's right on his heel. "So *they* were going to treat *us*, right, Chancey?" She's pissed.

"Well, yes, that was the idea."

"But it's all okay because Grisham's going to cough up next time, right?"

"If it ever happens. Listen, Jilly, I really don't know what to make of it. I'm sure Grisham's well heeled."

"Well heeled? He's filthy rich. The mere look of him says that. We're doing okay, too, of course, Chancey. But we're hustling for business and worrying about school fees. And then some condescending Englishman cons us into paying for an extravagant Manhattan night out for him and his trophy wife."

"Or he might merely have forgotten to bring his credit card."

"He might've suffered a lapse of memory, Chancey. But, you know what?" She pauses. "I think he was delighted to stick us with that bill."

"Why would he bother?" A cabbie sights them, makes eye contact, and swerves across the road to pick them up.

"I don't know, Chancey. Did you ever do anything to cross him?"

"Of course not." He cracks the cab door and holds it for her. "I only just met him."

"Well, steer clear of him." She slides into the cab and he follows her. "He's not going to be advancing your best interests, you can be sure of that."

Feminine intuition—suspicion, actually.

"Put him out of mind, Jilly. We'll write it off to experience."

Now the moonlight streams onto Jill's face. The cab weaves along the FDR. Does she really suspect? Something? Sometime? Somewhere? He takes her hand and draws her to him. He kisses her on the lips. She's not as quick as usual to respond. But he's sure she doesn't know anything. How could she? He slides his hand inside her dress, unfastens the front hook on her brassiere, and tumbles her breasts into his fingers. The last time they did this she unzipped him. This time he does it himself, then slips inside her legs, pushes aside her rich, silk panties and presses himself into that other world.

He fumbles for the fare. By the time the cabby's paid, Jill's already inside the house. He follows her and catches the scent of freesias along with his reflection in the hall mirror. He looks a little frazzled. What a week. Does the past ever disappear? He steps to the bedroom. She's doused the light and is already in bed, asleep even, maybe. He props himself gently on his side of the bed. Tomorrow and tomorrow. Do all our yesterdays conspire to steal tomorrow? Are we governed by voices from the past?

Voices—

"Great leaders must be great liars, Mister President."

Those guttural words are coming from the street. He slips to the window. Two patricians are deep in conversation. They look familiar. Could they possibly be who they seem?

"You're right, Henry, deception is the currency of public service."

Yes! That ski-nosed fellow in charcoal flannels and red cashmere jacket is Richard Nixon. But why's the notorious former United States President on the loose at two in the morning? He strides to the door and heads out onto the street.

The cool, misty April air tastes of stale exhaust fumes. The president and his gray-suited sidekick, the robotic Dr. Henry Kissinger, are standing under a streetlamp, beside a chauffeured limousine. The light is surreal, the shadows dark.

"I mean, consider the life of the ordinary citizen, Henry." The president glances over his shoulder. The eyes are deep, the lids heavy, the complexion sallow. "Candor would destroy it."

This is Manhattan, right? Opportunities must be seized.

"Excuse me, gentlemen." The duo halts. "I'm Chancey Haste. I couldn't help but overhear your conversation, and I have a question;"—the president's bony fingers accept his hand— "are you *really* in favor of lying?"

"What Mister President is saying"—Henry presses his black-framed spectacles into the square forehead beneath his homburg hat—"is that lying is vital to making the world tolerable."

"How does that work, exactly?"

Henry pushes a middle finger to his pudgy nose. "The vulgar masses are unfit for truth or liberty, Mister Haste. Their natural human condition is subordination. So those in power must make the rules in their own interests and call it justice."

"That's why wise leaders appreciate the necessity of secrets and lies, Chancey." There's an engaging cello timbre to the presidential voice. The chauffeur cracks the passenger door and the president cocks an eye. "Can we tempt you to a spin around the block, Chancey?"

Why not?

They hunker into soft velvet seats, facing one another. Henry fails to remove the homburg. The air-conditioned vehicle glides as if on a cloud, and a glass shield ascends to shut out the chauffeur.

"So, do I have it right? A culture of lies is the justice of the wise?"

"Plato himself gave us the concept of the noble lie, Chancey."

"The noble lie?"

"A falsehood that justifies a laudable goal, Mister Haste."

"Such as?"

"Well, Chancey, political leaders must inevitably invent false reasons for unpalatable but worthy wars."

"Right. The unwashed masses have numbers on their side." Henry spits his consonants. A burst of breath freshener might not go amiss. "So whatever we do to gull and guide them is legitimate."

"Think of it this way, Chancey: using democracy to turn the masses against their own liberty, then lead them to a laudable goal represents a philosopical, intellectual, and moral triumph."

"Really? But what, exactly, would be the laudable goal?"

"To overthrow the vulgar, Mister Haste."

"It's a terrible thing, Chancey, but right now the vulgar masses have triumphed—"

"They have everything their misguided hearts desire, Mister Haste."

"They do?"

"Wealth, pleasure, endless, mindless entertainment—everything they think they want, but nothing that truly matters."

"But how bad is money, fun and amusement?"

"They're reducing America to embecility."

"Europe, too. England has become a nation of napping nitwits, Chancey. The global reach of American culture threatens to trivialize all of humankind."

"So, what's the cure?"

"The glory of global war in the pursuit of the illusion of democracy."

"Nobody'll buy into yet another war, surely?"

"That's why we need noble lies, Chancey."

"Virtuous deceits to portray imminent catastrophe and the urgent need to secure ourselves against evil external enemies."

"Only panic inspires people to forgo contentment, Chancey."

"Only war motivates the masses to rise above self-indulgence."

"But will a couple of noble lies persuade authentically vulgar people to send their kids to war? I mean, how will that work, actually?"

"We'll enroll the media—fear and frenzy sell papers, so they'll be delighted to play along—and we'll spike the cocktail with religion and patriotism."

"Fear, faith, and jingoism,"—a stubby doctoral forefinger pokes the air—"that's the elixir that transforms hedonists into patriots prepared to fight and die for God and country."

"But doen't it all seem kind of, well, uh, immoral?"

"Not at all, Chancey. Remember, we use noble lies precisely because our values are sacred."

"All other cultures and values pale by comparison, Mister Haste. Supply-side economics and the illusions of liberty and democracy are grand, galactic, universal conceptions."

"So our goals must extend beyond myopic, so-called national security—we are *world* powers, Chancey."

"That is our destiny." Henry's tone is simultaneously somber and exultant. "We are the Zion that will light up the planet."

"But we must act quickly—"

"A new order is unfolding. A newer and more cunning breed of enemy is emerging. A clash of civilizations is inevitable."

"We'll need to strike decisively—"

"And preemptively! If we fail the trivialization of life will proceed unchecked, the animalization of man will become complete, and the night of the world will be at hand."

"That's why we need a brave new breed of noble liars, Chancey."

"Wow! You gentlemen have given me lot to think about. Do noble lies have a place in personal life, too?"

"Of course, Chancey. A man who won't lie to his wife has very little consideration for her feelings." The smile's conspiratorial. "And, anyway, women intuitively understand the need to sprinkle extra sugar where the tart is burned."

"The best liars are the best human beings, Mister Haste."

"As a corporate headhunter I empathize with the sentiment. But how does it all work, actually?"

"Well, to begin with, since he couldn't even tell a lie, George Washington was a failure as a boy." The president offers a half grin. "Most kids understand that"—he pauses—"and good lying calls for empathy and judgment, so the skilled liar is less likely to fall prey to the lies of others."

"And never forget, Mister Haste"—Henry's forefinger attempts to erase a fog from the inside of the left lens—"that lying is just another way of presenting the truth."

"But don't liars pay a price? Don't they finally feel rotten?"

"Well, the knowledge that he is prepared to lie isolates him from the oxymoronic moral majority"—the president grins at his own linguistic coinage—"but it also renders him a winner and ameliorates his loneliness."

"When the battle is won, Mister Haste, the victor will never be asked if he told the truth."

The cabin's suddenly still.

"We're back at your door, Chancey."

"So there's no downside to lying?"

"Let me put it this way, Chancey,"—the chauffeur cracks the door—"some say a liar's punishment, like the boy who cried wolf, is loss of credibility." A film of perspiration covers Mr. President's upper lip. "But an effective liar never gets caught, so that's a nonissue."

The pavement's firm beneath his feet. The limousine door's still ajar. He leans his head back into the cabin. Mr. President and Henry have spread themselves across the velvet like huge spiders.

"So there's absolutely no downside at all?"

"Well, you're asking me to be honest, right, Chancey?"

"Yes."

"Then I shall confess." The cello-voice drops a quaver. "The punishment for the outstanding liar is that he ultimately can't believe anyone."

Henry cranes forward, catching his lenses in the overhead streetlight. "But that's a nonissue, too, Mister President."

The chauffeur snaps the door shut and repairs to the driver's seat. The president's tinted side window descends.

"Henry's right, Chancey." The smoldering Nixonian eyes remain in shadow but the teeth and index finger flash. This time the tone's pugnacious. "For the truth of the matter is that every last one of the cocksuckers that you and I are going to meet around a conference table"—the limousine pulls away from the curb and the window slowly ascends—"is going to be a goddamned fucking liar anyway."

Was he awake or merely aching in a troubled sleep? Doesn't matter. There's a message either way.

But was that deceitful duo delivering an admonition or a warning? An omen or a prophesy? A heartfelt wish or a noble lie?

The morning light will tell. Oh, yes—it'll be a day of deceit and revelation, surely.

18

Friday Kisses

“HEY, HORST, IT'S ME, CHANCEY.” He eyes the gold hands on his art deco desk clock: 8 A.M. precisely. “You must be an early riser yourself to be calling so soon in the day.”

Friday's going to be a great day. On several fronts, too. He winks across the desk to Crawley. But, hey, something's wrong. Horst's tone is all too somber. He slips his hand across the mouthpiece. “Horst's unhappy, Crawley.”

Crawley folds the *Journal*, leans back in his chair, raises his eyebrows, and says nothing.

“What's the problem, Horst?”

“I thought I'd hurry along my proposal of Jesse Green for the University Club. As it happens a friend on the admissions committee knew him.”

“What'd he say?”

“He said that Jesse Green's a total *shit!*”

“A total shit?”

“A total shit! Mean. Ruthless. A real sonavabitch.”

“What else is new?”

“He'll do anything to get ahead. Anything at all.”

“You said you'd harness that drive, Horst. And focus it.”

“Chancey.” The banker pauses. “The very good friend who told me all this is, uh, Jewish.”

“So?”

“He says Jesse Green is the kind of person who gives people like him a bad name. He says he could never propose Jesse Green to any kind of club.”

“Not even the Harmonie Club? I mean that's a perfectly lovely club.”

“He said Jesse Green would be especially unacceptable among his own people. They know him altogether too well.” He pauses.

"I'm having second thoughts. It's not just this thing either. I had a bad feeling after you left yesterday."

"Something he said?"

"Something else. Something subliminal. I don't know what. But I want to rescind the offer."

"That might be difficult. There's no contract signed yet, of course. But you do have a gentleman's agreement."

"*He* said that. Jesse Green said that. He can distinguish between his word and the word of a gentleman."

"And he wants to hold you to the higher standard. Maybe that's what made you uneasy."

"Maybe. Maybe. Well, *fuck* him, Mister Haste—fuck him from here to fucking kingdom come. I look to you now—"

"To rid you of this meddlesome chief? Not a problem, Horst. I'll call him right away."

"The Lord giveth, and the Lord taketh away?"

"Somebody's playing tricks, that's for sure."

"ON HOLD?! ON *HOLD?* He's put the announcement of my appointment on *hold?*" Jesse Green tightens his grasp on the leather briefcase that lies across his knees.

"Let's be frank, Jesse. You've not yet been appointed. Horst still has to look over the formal agreement. And you both have to sign it."

"We have a gentleman's agreement."

"That's not quite the same thing as a contract, Jesse."

"Is he looking at anyone else?"

"We did conduct a search, of course. We have several candidates. It all comes down to chemistry. I'm sure you know that better than anyone."

"There's fantastic chemistry between Horst and me. I love the guy. He loves me, too. He knows I can do a fantastic job for him."

"Sure. He just needs to be sure he's seriously considered all the other options. It's a vital decision."

A cloud of anger crosses Green's face—and is immediately supplanted by a bright-eyed, beaming smile. "Look, Chancey—I really want that job. It's got my name written all over it. And I'll bring credit to everyone. You know my record. I'll bring him business he could only dream of. I'll also make you look like the world's smartest headhunter. And as chief of SCL I'll make sure you get *every* search assignment. I could also plug you into YCEO. There're big fees to be picked up there, Chancey."

"Your competence isn't at issue, Jesse. Horst just needs time to reflect."

The eyes narrow. "Does he?" The bright grin becomes a tight slit. "Does he, indeed? Well, business is business, of course, so I can understand a change of mind. Your client wants to change his mind. Happens all the time. Tell him that just so long as he meets his legal obligations I'll not make waves—"

"His legal obligations?"

"Sure. Tell him to exercise his severance option. Right now. That's one million dollars, in case you've forgotten. And, of course, since he reneged there'll be another five million in damages. Just tell him to pay up and I won't let the cat out of the bag about him being a welcher. Once that gets out, his name on Wall Street won't be worth a damn." He smirks. "Or, of course, we could go through with the deal." The smirk broadens to a smile. "And there'd be absolutely *no* hard feelings."

"There's no contract, Jesse. Details had to be finalized. The incentive formula wasn't fixed. An agreement to agree is nothing. No one signed anything. Nothing's enforceable."

"That's not what my attorney says." He's remarkably composed.

"Your lawyer wasn't present, Jesse."

"Don't try to con me. We both know what was said. You're a *fixer*. So go back to your client and fix things. Tell him precisely which end is up."

"No agreement was reached and your attorney wasn't there, so he's just relying on your word."

"No kidding—well, chew on this: I have a record of the entire conversation. I have all of it—every sentence, every word, every nuance—on tape."

On *tape*—so *that* was it. So that explains the clear-voiced parrotting of the key terms. So that explains the queasy something-else-is-going-on feeling. So that explains the omnipresent briefcase that even now this disgruntled candidate is clutching to his thick thighs. Yes, indeed. For there, artfully studded into the elaborate monogramming of the penultimate *e* in Jesse Green's name, listening to every word, sits a tiny microphone.

"THAT'S INCREDIBLE, CHANCEY."

"Not totally. Not given Green's personality."

"It's dishonest."

"It's devious—might even be unlawful." He pauses. "We'll just have to deal with it."

"What'll you do, Chancey?"

"Think about it over lunch. Actually, I'm *not* going to think about it over lunch. I'm going to push it into the subconscious. Then I'll call Doc. He'll have an angle, that's for sure." He blows a stream of air and puts a hand to a slightly receding temple. "You going to put all this in your novel, Crawley?"

"No. Life can be off the wall, but fiction has to be credible. Anyway, this Everness saga is too offensive."

"Doc says the truth's routinely offensive."

"Of course, that's why art is a lie that reveals the truth without displaying it."

The time. The time. "Hey—it's already twelve! I'm out the door."

SO, THIS, HERE, CARVED IN GRANITE, and strategically placed at the top of the patio steps for every Rockfeller Plaza visitor to read, is the Ozymandian creed of John D. Rockefeller. He shifts to his good foot and cups a hand to mask the sun. Just two months ago that courtyard was a skating rink. Now it's an outdoor restaurant, replete with bright white tables and chairs, and flowery sun umbrellas. The seasons pass so quickly here. So swiftly they can churn your gut. What *is* he feeling? A touch of melancholy. A tinge of guilt. And a burst of euphoria in the face of yet another secret tryst. He's booked a room overlooking the park. They'll send for a bottle of wine. Maybe there'll be some Grange. Then other noble treasures and delights. Later, they'll lunch in bed. Call Doc from there, too, maybe.

" 'Tis a tale told by an idiot,' Chancey"—her hand's on his shoulder—" 'full of sound and fury, signifying nothing.' " The quote is appropriate, but her voice is somber—lifeless, even. How can that be? He turns. Simple, elegant gray pantsuit, low-heeled, gray suede shoes, no earrings or jewelry, minimal makeup. And those eyes. But she's glanced away.

"Can we get a cup of coffee here?" she asks.

Is this Elan?

"I booked lunch at the Plaza. Privately, you know—"

"Coffee, Chancey. You know a place or not?" She glances at a gold, diamond-inlaid watch, then catches him studying her. She's abashed. "Grisham insisted on buying it for me. Across the street."

Tiffany's. And Grisham. That toffy-nosed affluent effluent. The fucker found his credit cards and bought her off.

Ten dollars to the maître dì wins them the secluded corner booth. She stirs her cappuccino, then fixes him with a calculated look.

"We can't meet again, Chancey."

The spinning head. She's been to goddamned confession. Down the street at St. Patrick's. That's likely where the snooties go. Some mindless priest has told her to exorcise the devil. The rush of shame. He's been rammed in the chest. But show her nothing. Nothing. Show her nothing.

"Sure, Elan, whatever you want. I understand."

"It's not what I want, Chancey. Don't you see? There's no yellow brick road for us and there never will be." The voice is pained but crystal clear. "We were selfish, self-absorbed, immature. It's not fair to anyone. Nobody. Least of all what used to be us."

"Used to be?"

"Elan is no more, Chancey. Lay her in the earth." Her eyes sparkle. "Let violets spring from her polluted flesh."

The little cock-teaser. Show her nothing. She led him on. Nothing at all. And now she's giving him the shaft. All for a pedigreed pig. End it. Put her out of mind. Now and forever.

"Okay, Chancey?"

"Well, sure, Elan." He feels his face harden. "Whatever's best for you."

"It's what is right for both of us, Chancey. It's what's right."

"Maybe it is. I just didn't expect you—of all people—to suddenly try to claim the high moral ground. Not after everything you've done." His fury rises. "And I despise this middle-class do-the-right-thing stuff. I liked you better as a mistress. Whatever happened to Khayyam? 'Drink, for once dead, you never shall return.'"

"He was an alcoholic, Chancey. If he'd ever gotten himself sober, he'd have said we squander life when we get drunk on it."

"And if he hadn't been a lush he could never've written the Rubaiyat. So I don't think he'd advocate throwing life away on the rubble of convention."

She's studying him. Can she read his thoughts? Does she know he'd like to take her to a room right now and tupple her from here to kingdom come. But, no. Let her go to her wretched pervert priest. Let her say that Chancey was very understanding, that he only wanted what was best for her. Let her go. To her rich, new, hoity-voiced hog.

"You're right. We've both grown. I see things now that I never could then. I'm sure you'll enjoy a wonderful life with Grisham-fuckeen-Pryce. He'll prize you. You're his trophy. You're the daughter of a peer. I personally preferred you as a cock-teaser and free-spirited whore. Now you're just a pious slut. You used to be beautiful. Now you've lost your spirit. You've become weak-kneed—and scrawny. And all these pretensions have given you a nervous pox."

He tosses his head back, distancing himself from her.

"Why're you saying these things, Chancey? Does Grisham make you feel bad? He's a fine person, Chancey. He's a gentleman."

"A gentleman—my, my—a gentleman." And Chancey never was? No, of course not. Upstart Chancey never could be. Stare her down. "You've sold out to a nobody, Elan. Just because he happens to be a so-called aristocrat." Her face's ashen. "Or is it because he inherited money?"

She grips the table and stands shakily. She touches her face. She's distracted, vacant, stunned. He stares into the deathly cappuccino dregs.

"Why don't you just head off into the sunset? I'll catch another coffee here. Then I'll wander back to the office. I have a life to lead, you know."

"It is finished, Chancey." Tears brim in her eyes. "I've a plane to catch." They flood onto her cheeks. She's looking for assurance. "Grisham's waiting in a limo, now." She chokes. "I never said I love you before—because I never thought I had to. So why would I choose this dreadful moment to tell you now? But I will. So think about it later, Chancey. I've always loved you and I always will." The tears have reached the corners of her mouth. "And I just know, that wherever he is right now"—she raises a hand to her face— "Chandler Haste will always have loved me."

She streaks the tears with trembling fingers. He stares into the deathly cappuccino. She reels out the door and is gone.

He studies the patio anew. This time he's oblivious to the bright umbrellas and chatting diners. His fingers trace the magnate's carved and gilded granite creed but feel nothing. A plane to catch and a limo to take her to it. How could she have pissed him so? Maybe it was deliberate. Maybe she and Grisham were in cahoots, laughing at him all the time. What wretched triggers from his past did she tug on? And why in God's name would she ever care for that dope? But who cares? Does it matter that she married for the wrong reasons? She's not the first slut to do that. She shouldn't have changed things. She should've gone on loving him, unconditionally—isn't that the expression?

He drags the deformity past the massive murals in the oversized foyer of Thirty Rockefeller Plaza. People are glancing at the impediment. He sets his eyes on the gleaming granite floor, stumbles to the elevator, and runs the lines in his head:

> Quit, quit for shame!
> This will not move;
> This cannot take her.
> If, of herself she will not love,
> Nothing can make her:
> The devil take her!

May the devil do that indeed.

QUARTER AFTER TWO—that's midday in Chicago—and the wizard's on the phone.

"I'm feeling bright-eyed and bushy-tailed, Chancey."

"Wish I could say the same. But I'm worried, mostly about this Jesse Green."

"You *sound* worried."

"I've got a few other things on my mind, too."

"Anything I can help with?"

"I don't know. Marriage. Relationships. Love. Any of that stuff your forte?"

"I know a little. I was married twice. It was like living in two different countries, each with its own rules and languages—I remember that. Of course, for a male and a female to live continuously together is, biologically speaking, an extremely unnatural condition. It's also exacerbated by childhood traumas. In reality, we're just children seeking the perfect playmate—and perfection, of course, does not exist."

"How does this play out?"

"Well, marital friction is based not so much upon minor contemporary provocations as upon the earlier frustrations and resentments of childhood. We have to get real. We have to realize that marriage isn't a matter of lovestruck kids gazing into each other's eyes. It's about adults, looking outward, in the same direction, going after goals, raising well-adjusted children." He pauses. "Of course, psychologically speaking many people feel attracted to a person who offers the least possibility of a harmonious union." He chuckles. "This means there's just one woman whom fate has destined for each of us, and if we miss her, well, then we're saved." He laughs again.

"How do we know which one that is?"

"If we don't watch out, we waste a lifetime ensnared in a false enchantment."

"A false enchantment? An illusion?"

"Yeah, I'd say they're pretty similar."

"How does a person break that spell?"

"Reluctantly." He pauses. "But when we really want love, we find it waiting for us—so long as we can spot the clues."

Like what?"

"Well, love's an exchange of psychic energy. The woman who anxiously scans her lover's face when he's disturbed, who reaches out with a soothing hand to comfort him, is actually transmitting a healing force from within her own nature. She's obeying the same kind of impulse that directs the heart to pump more blood to a wounded limb." He pauses. "Of course, there's at least one consolation of marriage—when you look around you can always see someone who did worse." There's that chuckle again. "So now, tell me, what's goin' on with your Jesse Green?"

"I just had a bad feeling about him after the client closed the deal."

"Trust that feeling."

"It's too late for that."

"Check it out, somehow. See where it leads."

"You think I should?"

"Well, yeah. Jesse Green's one of these guys who thinks he can turn the mythological ring of Gyges. It'll backfire on him."

"The ring of Gyges?"

"The wearer of the ring could turn it on his finger and become invisible. Could do anything he wanted. His secret would never be discovered."

"And?"

"In the original story the ring was used to commit murder. All to do with another man's wife. Not a happy outcome. Plato used the idea of such a ring to pose another question: Can the certainty of nondiscovery really make it possible for us to get away with an unethical act?"

"He felt there'd be consequences?"

"There are always consequences. Secrets inevitably result in failures or tragedies. I personally never met a dishonest person who was ever successful."

"I can think of a few."

"You think you can. I personally never met one who held on to his ill-gotten candy. Trouble is, it doesn't taste right. In fact, it poisons life. Not just a career, either. It's all pretty clear, really. Freud got it right. We have to learn to delay gratification in order to grow up. Have to control our impulses. Feelings become thoughts.

Thoughts become actions. Actions become habits. Habits become character. And, of course, character's destiny."

"You think Jesse Green cares?"

"I think if you dig into his life you'll find something to make him care."

An incoming call.

"Chandler Haste."

"Hi, there, Chancey, this's Beryl, Elan's friend—remember?"

Yes, his stomach sinks. That Kirribilli tryst with Elan, and instant coffee with bubbly Beryl. He checks his watch—half past three—cups his hand across the microphone, and nods to Crawley. "I'll let you know when I'm off."

Crawley evaporates.

"How nice to hear your voice, Beryl. And what a coincidence that you should call, for Elan's only just left town." His heart races. Beryl wants something. "But I guess you know that."

"Yeah. But I have some news. For your ears alone. I'm downstairs. Got time for a coffee?"

"Sure. Meet you at O'Neill's."

BERYL'S TOO-RED LIPS DISCHARGE a stream of smoke toward the ceiling. She douses the half-spent cylinder into her saucer. A ring of lipstick circles the upturned Virginia Slims. She seems more worldly than Elan, but her hunt for affection remains unsubtle. The black leather skirt's too short and too tight. The red blouse shows too much cleavage. She's overdone the makeup—and the hair spray, and the perfume.

"Elan loved you, Chancey." Should he even respond? Should he reveal anything? She probably knows just about everything, anyway. "Elan never told me much." She's also a mind-reader. He says nothing. "But she did tell me she loved you."

"That was back then. Things happen. People fall in and out of love. I'm sure you know that."

"Elan never changed. Not down deep. Look, Chancey, I don't know how to say this—"

"To say what?"

"I'm not even sure I should say anything." She reaches for another cigarette.

"Like what?"

"She never told you. I'm not surprised. I only found out by accident myself. She never intended for anyone to know . . ." She knocks a cigarette from the pack and slides it between her lips.

"To know *what?*" Now he's agitated.

"You knocked her up, Chancey."

Beryl scrapes a match and holds a flame between their faces.

"I beg your pardon?"

"You got her pregnant."

She applies the flame to the cigarette and sucks. Nicotine lines appear above her too-red lips.

"I did?"

"Yes, you did. You can believe it, Chancey. It happened in Sydney. I know that for a fact. She'd had her period ten days earlier. When she arrived in London, she missed. She was out of her mind with worry."

"She wrote me a Dear John letter. She never mentioned anything. Anyway, I thought she got onto the pill somewhere along the line."

"She did. But she got off it when last you left Godzone. It never sat too well with her Catholic programming, you know. She somehow figured that she'd be safe for a couple of days in Sydney— what a laugh. And she didn't expect to need anything in London. Look, Chancey, she really loved you. She'd never've messed up your life. She'd never've involved you in anything like that."

She sets the cigarette into the ashtray.

"Like what?"

"Like the abortion."

"She had an *abortion?*"

"She didn't want to. She pretends she's a free spirit, but deep down she's very Catholic. She took it all very hard."

"What does that mean, exactly?"

"Messy hemorrhaging, that kind of thing. She got depressed, too. Very depressed. In the end, however, she got out okay."

"Who paid?"

Cigarette fumes assail his nose.

"She did." She pauses. "I chipped in." Her beady eyes fix on him. "Don't worry, I don't want anything."

"I never heard from her again. Not until just this week."

"I got a three-day excursion fare and came over from England with her, Chancey. I make the trek from Godzone to visit her there from time to time. You met Grisham, right?" She leans forward in her chair. "Yeah, well, I guess he's her kind."

"Him? He's her kind?"

"She went wild after the abortion. Laid a lot of old men. When she got done with them she turned to the younger set. But she was looking for you, Chancey."

She reclaims the cigarette stub.

"Looking for me?"

"Yeah. She was obsessed with you. I tried to tell you that back in Sydney, remember."

"Playing with fire?"

"Yeah, I said you were playing with fire. And you were. You never knew of Elan's capacity to fall into a dark mood. That's because it vanished whenever you showed up." She pauses, then sighs. "Then Grisham came along. I never much cared for him, personally. One of those dopey upper-crust Brits with a class hang-up."

"How unusual is that?"

She sucks on the stub, then emits a sideward puff.

"He was worse than most."

"She must've liked him."

"Not really. He was just all over her. Fancied marrying the daughter of a peer. He liked her looks, too, of course. But only as an add-on. Oh, he wanted a kid, of course. Well, not so much a kid as an heir. Elan looked picture perfect."

"But if she didn't love him—"

"That's pretty naive, Chancey. She was broke. He was a rich aristo. There were family pressures." She drops the burning stub into the saucer moat. "And you'd never be there." He's momentarily lost. So many thoughts clamoring for attention. "She still loves you, Chancey."

"That's not the impression I got."

"She wouldn't want to lead you on. She believed down deep that it had to end. But you were nice to her, right? I'm sure you were. I mean you've had problems of your own." She leans forward. "Chancey—"

She pauses.

"Yes?"

"She's not, uh, well."

"She's sick?"

"They gave you the story about the cottage without a phone?"

He nods and she smiles knowingly.

"I never thought about it—"

"She had some, uh, problems. She went away to get, uh, well."

"Problems?"

"Stress. Broke out in hives. She's okay now. Only giveaway's the trace of a nervous rash. I just worry about what's going on in her head."

Beryl's reaching for the cigarette pack again.

"She's highly intelligent."

"She might be a genius for all I know, Chancey. Trouble is she's also been living on the edge for years. It all got worse after she moved in with Grisham. Something's wrong there. Talk to her, Chancey. You can make a difference." She stuffs the battered pack back into her purse. "But you must get her alone. And do it in person. Believe me, on that, please."

"I can't just drop everything and go to England. Not right now."

"You'll find a way. You always did." She stands, glances into a mirror, and smooths her skirt. She pats her hair, runs her tongue around her lips, and glances at him. "Got to run, Chancey. I hope I did the right thing. I had it all sitting on my conscience for too long."

She swivels her narrow hips in the direction of the door. "Oh—one last thing"—she plucks a cream Sherry Netherland envelope from her purse—"Elan asked me to deliver you this."

If her high heels clack upon the timber floor he doesn't hear them. He doesn't feel the rush of air from the brass-railed oaken door that swings closed behind her, either. The envelope contains one page with fourteen bronze-blue lines.

The village I dwell in, Thinkingofyou,
Is a maddeningly melancholy town
Where the clocks are locked in a strange snafu
And the forget-me-nots are hand-me-downs

A second-class citizen trapped in time—that's how she saw
herself?

Clandestine lovers crave sweet rendezvous
But I chance the night streets, alas, in vain
For lanes are manias in Thinkingofyou
That sunbolt beams are inept to unreign

Sunbolt beams! Shock therapy?

Folks never slumber in Thinkingofyou,
In the mornings we do not wake either,
We lie in a state we dare not adieu,
Valedictions merely fan our fever.

Is she playing on the word *lie*? Was she really catatonic, or is
the reference simply to love?

Thinkingofyou is the sweetest of jails
But I pray reprieve lest sanity fails.

Yes, longing for the impossible can create a prison. Maybe
some errant Catholic girls hope to earn liberation by falling pregnant.
But if so, abortion must seem like the gateway to hell. How she
must've suffered to buck all that guilty programming. The courage
it must've taken. The remorse that must've followed. And all for
his sake. Is that really so? How could he doubt it? Even for a
moment. Yet she could've maybe kept it. Jill might've come round.
She's always loved kids. She might've come to love this one too,
given the chance. So, is it all too late? Has he missed the boat with
Elan? Completely? Is it irrecoverable? Not yet, surely. So track her
down and talk to her. Explain, at the very least, your rotten behavior.
And your words. Oh, shit, how could you ever've said all those

rotten things? But she'll understand. She knows you. Talk to her.
Go to her. *Help* her. Show her some real love for a change.

So she, the daughter of a peer, was carrying his child in Mother
England. Would it've been an aristo or a colonial? Would it've gone
to St. Cyprian's? Eton? Oxford? Would it've claimed a title? The
honorable Mr. Haste. The duke of Chancey. The duchess of
Chancey. *Prince* Chancey. What would it do with its life? Would it be
a gentleman investor? A rag-and-bone merchant? A rocket scientist?
A rock star? A plumber? Or maybe an artist, writer, or poet? Yes,
of course—a poet. But that'll never happen now. What were those
lines again—Whittier, remember? Yes. And no. "For all sad words
of tongue or pen, the saddest are surely these, it might have been."

"SOMETHING'S AWRY with Mister Fyfe's figures, Mister Haste."
The auditor's pained English accent wavers on the line.

"Awry?" He stares into the phone. His stomach turns. And
turns again.

"Something's not right."

More British understatement. The voice's steady, calm,
measured.

"With the *figures*?"

"I fear he's cooking the books, Mister Haste."

"Fuller's not always a man for detail—"

"It's more than that. Debtors are way too high, and he's hiding
things. He won't submit to our routine audit. He balks, obfuscates,
and delays. I fear that many of his so-called placements are nothing
more than, shall we say, phantoms."

"Phantoms?"

"He's made them up. He's jiggling them. Perhaps he hopes to
tide over poor performance till things get better. You'd best do
something."

"Do something?"

"What you do is up to you, of course." He sniffs. "But waste
no time."

THE WORDS THEMSELVES ARE OKAY—

"I've got to go to England. I've got to get there quickly. I've got to check up on Fuller."

It's the tone, the pitch, the cadence that's all so totally wrong. It sounds phony to them both. Jill glances very coolly in his direction, then looks away.

"Of *course* you do, Chancey."

Her voice drips with sarcasm. She puffs a sofa pillow. Her face is drawn, stressed.

"You okay?"

"*I'm* okay, Chancey. *I'm* fine. I'm just fucking great. *You're* the one who needs help."

"I need help?"

"Oh, Christ, Chancey! Do you think I'm *stupid?* Do you think I'm *blind?*" She throws down the pillow and matches his gaze. "You think I don't know about you? And that mucky little tramp? Is that what you think? Christ, Chancey, I've known for years. For fucking years! Don't give me the gaslight stare. I always knew in my heart that something was wrong. But then I had to hear about it. You and your dirty weekend. One of God knows how many, I imagine. A friend of my brother's saw you. With *her.* He didn't get it wrong, Chancey. How many clubfooted philanderers prance around Franz Joseph?" She stares at him. "I mean what sort of charade do you think you've been strutting there, Chancey?"

He reaches out to her. "I was . . . I did . . . It's all in—"

"*The past?*" She draws away angrily, and sets her hands on her hips. "All in the *past.* You want *me* to believe *that?*" Her face is white with fury. "You bring that little bitch into *my* house. *This* week. *This fucking week!* You sit *me* down at the same table with *her.* You tuck yourself into a cab with *her.* I imagine you even get off thinking about *her* when you're fucking *me.* Oh, shit, Chancey. You look so sleazy. Your mind must be as calloused as your foot." She glares at him. "As callous, as deformed, and as ugly. You're a fucking sicko, Chancey. I *had* to put up with it before. The kids were too young. And I was in another country. I had no intimate friend to confide in—you were all I had. I also believed that given time it would end. So I simply looked the other way. And you know what? My wedding vows meant something to me. I *wanted* to believe in you, Chancey.

I wanted one man for the rest of my life, a man I could love, and
trust. I didn't want to see the clues you left lying around. I blocked
them out. For as long as I could." She chokes. "All that puerile
moping about and thinking of her . . . oh, shit—you make me sick.
You, make—me—*sick*."

Her face collapses. Tears stream down her cheeks. She sobs.
He dare not touch her.

"I don't—I'm sorry—I won't—"

She composes herself. But the face remains livid.

"And now you're suddenly off to *London*. And you won't see
her again? You're going there to see *Fyfe?* Don't make me laugh."
She emits a scornful sigh and springs to her feet. "Look, Chancey.
Our marriage is over. Got it? *Over!* I want you to know right up
front. I'll be seeing someone else now. And a lawyer, too. So you
just get on your plane and slide off to London. Make a big hero of
yourself there with Elan. And all your high-falutin clients. These
full-of-themselves nobodies you jump on planes to impress. Go to
London, Chancey. *Please.* Go right away. Now! Tomorrow! *Who*
cares?"

She glares at him and continues, "Just don't come back. Not
this time. I'm still young, Chancey. Men still look. They look at me,
Chancey. *Me!* Somebody could still love me. Not relegate me to
second best. I've just wasted too many years with you. A fucking
lifetime! *My* lifetime. Not *yours*, of course, because you were never
there. And even when you were there you weren't there. And if
you don't believe me just ask your kids. Always looking over your
shoulder for her, that's where *you* were. But not anymore, Chancey.
Not anymore. Go to her. See what it's like to live with a fantasy. Let
her see what you're really like, too—a real-world Walter Mitty. She'll
love it, I'm sure."

The voice is suddenly icily contemptuous. "And, if it's not too
much trouble, perhaps you'd convey her a message for me, Chancey.
Tell her I couldn't give two shits about her shacking up with my
husband—I mean that's something I can get my mind around. But
do please be so kind as to tell her I'm pissed with her for other
reasons. Tell her she denied a father from children who just also
happened to be *mine*. Tell her she fucked with *their* minds. Tell her
she stole the precious, irrecoverable days and nights of *their*

childhoods. Tell her I don't think my kids will ever recover. Maybe, since this slut of yours comes from such wonderful family and is so incredibly intelligent, she might just understand all that. Yeah, Chancey. Pull on your platform mukluks and hop off to London right now and tell her all that for me, would you? Then wallow in your undying love for each other till the twelfth-of-fucking-never. And, before you go, just make me one more of those worthless promises you specialize in." She pauses. Then her eyes flash. "Never come back. *Never* come back, you hear me, Chancey? Not *ever.*"

Part Three

Empirical Judgments

"I shall tell you a great secret my friend.
Do not wait for the last judgment.
It takes place every day."

—Albert Camus

19

Silver Bullets

THEY'RE MAKING LOVE on the silver sands of a cliff-backed moonlit beach. Elan's on top, naked, save for an unbuttoned army tunic. Blood runs from her mouth. He glances down; it's oozing from her cunt, too. She falls to the sand. His cock's a cobra with a double-sided, razor-sharp knife for a tongue. She staggers, trailing crimson, toward a nurse in a landing boat. The nurse, naked but sporting a Red Cross cap, is astride a British army officer, fucking him. The nurse is Jill, and she's bobbing and throbbing and loving it.

The 747 cabin's pulsing, probing, pressing forward. His eyes decide to open. Bright clouds hover in the deep blue sky beyond the window. He flips the aluminum widget that shoots the so-called air. It hits his face. No oxygen in that. He glances up the aisle and then into his conscience . . . Has he treated Jill appallingly, or what? And now it's all caught up with him. She's talking about seeing someone. Read between the lines. She's *got* someone. Very coy about who. Should that be whom? Maybe it's optional. Who Down Under, whom in London. She's not seeing anyone in London, anyway. But Down Under? Is she seeing anyone Down Under? No, no—she'd only ever do *that* with him.

"Paa-perr, sir?"

The tone is arch and the ferret face beneath the incongruous British Airways bowler hat is two parts Mother Teresa and three parts mother-in-law. What was he expecting? The Virgin Queen? Not really. Just hoping for a fun-loving kindred spirit. A sweet-faced, light-fingered lassie who'd cheerfully slip her soft hands under the gray blanket resting across his knees and . . . Travel does that, of course. Researchers say that airline travelers constantly obsess about getting laid.

"Paa-perr!" Now she just sounds bitchy. *"Sir."*

He smiles and glances at the magazine cart. "I was deprived as a child, so I'll take one of everything."

She shows her teeth and dumps a bunch of papers onto his tray. Not amused. Perhaps she caught the traces of a colonial accent. Or maybe she thought he was an Aussie—now that, for any kind of uppity British lass, might definitely put the kibosh on any budding hanky-panky. She hoity-toits off down the aisle. What we're really looking for in a hostie, of course, is a mother. Maybe we want that from just about every woman. Especially a wife—

One way or another
every man marries his mother.

Who was it who said that? No matter. What's this? He glances to the *Telegraph* headlines. Oh, yes, of course—what else would you ever expect to find on the front page of a British paper? "The Happy Family." The happy *new* family. All this incredible concern with the undying love of Prince Charles and Diana. And now they've got a bonny heir. And the paper's still going on about the mammoth wedding rite. The putative princess nixed dowdy Westminster Abbey, where such couplings are routinely consecrated, for light-and-airy St. Paul's Cathedral. An uncalled-for trammeling of tradition that'll offend the gods and break the royal spell, says some snooty soothsayer. Not at all, says the archbishop of Canterbury, for the match originated in heaven and was merely solemnized in the cathedral. He knows this to be so because in the moment of blowing the blessing he felt the breath of God surge through his lungs.

Hey, what a guy to have on your team. If only that archbishop had consecrated Chancey and Jill's nuptials in some such illustrious edifice they'd have been assured of God's blessing, too. Then God'd have ensured that Chancey never even laid eyes on Elan. Or, at the very least, that he'd kept his hands to himself. Oh, to be a prince and to be able to command not just authority, but, in fact, the forces of the spirit to one's undertakings. And not just a prince but a gentleman, too. An English gentleman with no hideous deformity needing to be kept under wraps. How much simpler life would be. And just feast the peepers upon this princess, will you? With the armies of the aristocracy and clergy on one's side one could wish up precisely this kind of well-bred, long-legged, milky-skinned, big-titted, sweet-faced, bug-eyed, neat-lipped, butter-mouthed piece of crumpet—and settle into it very happily. And forever after, too, that's for sure. And in a *palace*. Not just living there, either. Fornicating in a palace. Now, there's a bit of one-upmanship for you. Fucking 'em Palace. No need for bonny Prince Charley to be chasing stray pussy. Not with that delicacy to breakfast upon. Not that *he'd* ever even think about such things as pussy and straying. Aristocrats like Charley—feel free to call me Highness, please—are cast from finer clay. This glacial princess, too, no doubt—so pure, so innocent, so radiantly without guile. So, how to compete with the wiles and the arsenals of a prince? The fact is that it can't be done. Not by Chandler Haste, anyway. No, unlike Prince Charles, he's traveling economy on just about every level of his life. Pimping for Everness. Struggling to hold a business together. Watching his kids screw up and his marriage go down the gurgler. And completely missing the boat with Elan. Till now, anyway. But marriage? What is marriage really? Does anybody ever take those vows—those noble lies—seriously? Are there not chords in us that need to be struck by other people? Who said that? Elan. The other half of that idea, of course, is that full many a flower's born to blush unseen and waste its sweetness on the desert air. So marriage is akin to dying. Or is it? Jill never thought so. Their first meeting—her azure eyes, high cheekbones, sweet smile—nothing seemed merely accidental. Was fate the force that delivered Jill into his life? Crawley, McCracken, and Fuller, too. And Elan, of course. Someone said life has to be lived forward but can only be understood backward. Looking backward, all those meetings really did seem kind of preordained. Willie knew it—there's a divinity that shapes our ends, rough-hew them how we will. Hamlet. No prizes for guessing that. But what about . . .

> The ancient saying is no heresy
> Hanging and wiving go by destiny

Now, who said that? Elan'll know. He gazes out the window. Where is Jill, anyway. The "seeing someone" thing was probably just a come-on. God only knows what she's up to. God . . .

> Does God get a share of the action?
> Is he on the board and the team?
> Or does he merely mastermind
> The compensation scheme?

"You seem distracted." That voice in his ear is both guttural and gravelly. He glances into the face. It's a behatted rabbi sporting ringlets, straggly beard, a big belly, and a puffy face. No restriction on dining, anyway. Oh, Christ, this's precisely the trouble with travel. You never know who or what'll be sitting next to you. These fellows have always been a bit of a mystery but this one seems empathetic. Indeed, those dark-ringed saucer eyes seem almost to be twinkling.

"Yeah, I guess I'm a little spaced."

"You're admiring the princess?"

"Admiring her? Well, yes, I suppose I was admiring her. And no, too. I mean those royals can drive me crazy."

The rabbi chuckles. "Is it the prince or the princess who drives you crazy?"

"It might be the princess. Not that I need another princess. Three would be altogether too many."

"Already you have *two* princesses?" He gives his head a little shake. "So much to think about."

"Is it okay for a man to have two princesses, Rabbi?"

"In his mind or—"

"In every way."

"Some people might think it okay." The lips pucker. "Yet to you it seems to be bringing grief."

"It's causing me to examine my soul."

"Your soul?" He smiles. "This is good, then."

"I guess I'm just a little confused."

"To be confused is easy." His fortune-teller eyes are suddenly hunting for facial clues. "At your age, especially." He pauses. "Solomon got confused, too, you know."

"Solomon?"

"In the book of Ecclesiastes."

"I loved that stuff."

"It's beautifully written." He pauses, as if to deliver a warning. "But with great care we must contemplate that most dangerous book in the Bible."

"Dangerous? I must've missed that. I liked it. Especially where he says everything's vanity."

"That is indeed what Solomon found. He pursued everything. And won everything. Success, money, power, women, and knowledge. Yet he concluded that all is vanity and vexation of spirit."

"Well, yes, but he worked a few things out—right?"

"Solomon said he who increaseth knowledge increaseth sorrow."

"Didn't he also say there's a time and a place for everything?"

"Mmm, yes and no. He said we should enjoy our youth. He said that everything has its season, that there's a time to every purpose under heaven."

"I thought he also came up with some conclusions."

"He did." The head shakes forlornly. "But wrong." The eyes roll. "His conclusions, they were wrong."

"Solomon—King Solomon of Solomonic judgment fame— he got it wrong?"

"*Wrong* might not be right. But for sure he missed the mark on work and love."

"I liked what he said about work."

" 'Whatsoever thy hand findeth to do, do it with all thy might; for there is no work, nor device, nor knowledge, nor wisdom, in the grave, whither thou goest.' "

"Yeah, I mean that's good stuff, Rabbi. And didn't he also say to live joyfully with the wife whom thou lovest all the days of thy life?"

"He did indeed."

"And these are the wrong conclusions?"

The voice drops. "Solomon was the original man in the midlife crisis."

"You mean he got everything he could've wanted from life and it still wasn't enough?"

"Right. And, in the end, he could really only suggest more— or less—*of the same.*"

"What'd he miss?"

"You'd really like to know?"

"Would it help me?"

"Mmm. For most people yes. For you maybe so, maybe not. You see, what Solomon failed to take into account was God." He leans forward in his seat. "God!" He raises his right index finger. "God is the answer. He should have turned his life over to God."

"Why couldn't Solomon run his own life?"

"He tried that, with enormous success but no real happiness. For fulfillment we must come to God."

"I was kind of hoping, Rabbi, that that wasn't the answer. I mean, as of right now, it won't do the trick for me." The fellow seems a little miffed. "Unless, of course, you can be a tad more specific."

"About a decision concerning these two princesses?"

"Exactly, Rabbi."

That world-weary sigh could be a model for spiritual advisers of every ilk.

"So many people only come to God to attain the impossible." He pauses. "You truly love both these princesses?"

"That's the heart of the problem, Rabbi. I mean that's what my dreams tell me."

"Then examine your heart and your soul—and answer a question?

"Uh-huh."

"Do you love either one of them enough to let her go?"

MANHATTAN

CRAWLEY DO THIS, AND CRAWLEY DO THAT. Well, it's no trouble really—but authenticating the existence of a degree can call for the patience of Job, and infinitely more delicacy than Chancey might just realize. Merely attempting to decipher this faded transcript spread out before him on the registrar's desk calls for no little amount of skill, especially with this thin, horn-rimmed, black-skirted clerk hovering over him. He pokes his own falling glasses back onto his nose. He really should have the optician make another adjustment to the frame. But no matter. The grades were inferior, all right, but, no doubt about it, Jeremiah Greenbaum did indeed complete a bachelor's degree in business. He slides the paper back to the clerk and strolls to the door. But wait. And back we go. The clerk seems a little confused. He motions to her.

"You didn't have any other Greenbaums enrolled around that time, did you?"

"Might have. It's a common enough name. Let me check the files again."

Let us pray that she finds something in that back room.

It's a bad time for Chancey to head for London. Is it to see Fuller Fyfe? Or might that well-bred piece of fluff just be back in the picture?

The clerk's back, and she's clutching two faded manila files. "*Two* other Greenbaums enrolled, sir. *Rachel* Greenbaum. She completed her degree." She continues. "And *Joshua* Greenbaum"— she shakes her head disapprovingly—"who's showing unpaid tuition fees."

Joshua Greenbaum? Did she say, Joshua Greenbaum?

"Did you say, Joshua Greenbaum?"

"*Joshua* Greenbaum was enrolled in business studies for two years. He failed to complete any degree."

A dispeptic knot is forming in his stomach. *Joshua* Greenbaum! He checks the date of birth. One year's difference. A year younger. God in heaven! He checks the clock behind the clerk's left ear. Chancey's plane should be arriving in London about now. Wait'll he hears about this.

HEATHROW AIRPORT

Half-past four in the afternoon by that Heathrow clock. He grabs the extended handle on his carry-on suitcase and rolls it toward the exit. The automatic door opens to a maze. He glances into the mirror directly in front of him. Be careful not to smile or stare or scamper. The spying eyes of some officious official likely lurk behind that shadowy glass. He raises a hand, smooths his features into a bland mask, then turns. The mirror's gone. He's out. He's through the looking glass and into England. He's the rabbit running out of time.

He strides to the yellow phone, leans his carry-on against a wall, extracts the vaunted Pryce calling card from his wallet, fumbles for a coin, grabs the handset, and dials. The line clicks, very slowly, in his ear. Is it reaching into the future? Or backward through the days and nights of his life? Maybe both. And now it's ringing.

"Coldridge Manor." That snooty voice is not Elan's. But don't hang up. "May I speak with Mrs. Pryce?"

"The Honorable Elan Pryce is unavailable. Can I take a message?"

"I'm a friend of the family. Passing through town."

"You might try Mister Pryce. He's in London at the moment. Staying at the Saint James Club."

"When will Mrs. Pryce be available?"

"If you'd care to leave a name, sir, I'll try to get a message to her."

"Tell her Chandler Haste called."

"Let me just write that down sir. One moment—"

Silence. And a swirl of air as a gaggle of giggling bejeaned, T-shirted, backpacked female students rush past. His eye follows them out the door. Overcast sky. Murky air. Oh, to be in England.

"Chancey? Is that really you? Calling me in England?"

Oh, that beguiling, lilting, dulcet voice.

"How many Chanceys do you know?"

"I used to think there was only one."

"I'm in London. At Heathrow. We must talk. We must meet."

"We can't, Chancey—you know we can't."

"And I know that I know that. But you also know, I think, that there are things I must say to you. And I need to say them in person."

Long, long silence.

"Grisham's in the city."

"I could drive down tonight."

"In the morning, Chancey. Eleven o'clock at Crystal Pond. It's actually a park just outside the village, and a pretty jaunt past the country graveyard where locals say Gray wrote his elegy."

"Sounds quaint. But how're you? How do you, uh, feel?"

"I'm fine. I'm great." She pauses. "I'm lying. Lying's an art. I do it exceptionally well." Another pause. "Tomorrow, Chancey."

"I'll rent a car. I'll arrive in Coldridge tonight."

"So stay at the local inn—the Hero and Leander."

"Hero and Leander? Why does that stick in my mind?"

"Because you're fond of a line from Marlowe's poem of the same name."

"Ah, yes. 'Whoever loved—'"

" '—that loved not at first sight?' We came in on that line, Chancey."

"Yeah, a Godzone lifetime ago. So tomorrow at eleven then?

" 'Hope's a lover's staff. Walk hence with that. Manage it against despairing thoughts.' " She pauses. "And, Chancey—"

"Yes."

"I'll be there."

He cradles the phone and closes his eyes. A lover's staff. Despaireen thoughts. Ah, Elan.

Hey! Who's that? He's the focus of piercing eyes within a seventy-something, silver-maned, weathered face. The head itself is poking from a full-length, double-sided sandwich-board replete with a spidery, hand-formed message:

WITH

SOAP

BAPTISM

IS A

GOOD

THING

The message and the head above it are suddenly in his face. A little levity might be in order.

"Are you representing God or the devil?"

The huge emerald eyes, glistening like pools, are mesmerizing. Is this crank the Ancient Mariner, or what? But here's a surprise: the voice's soft and silky, almost BBC quality.

"No fundamental difference, sir. God and the devil merely represent specialization and the division of labor."

Maybe the fellow's a bargain-basement Bertrand Russell. Or an upmarket Quentin Crisp. Or some unholy amalgam of both.

"You sure about that?"

"I'm a devil myself, sir, I should know."

So the guy really is a nut. Not surprising in such an eccentric culture.

"The devil himself—wow! Well, I don't know why I'm surprised, I mean it's a dirty job, but I guess somebody's got to do it."

"I'm not *the* devil." His head swings gently. "Just an associate devil." He smiles a touch reprovingly. "And Lucifer himself's a real gentleman, you know, never goes anywhere uninvited." The smile widens to reveal curiously pointed, corn-yellow teeth. Crisp words continue to trip from a pastel-pink tongue. "Lucifer's currently working on some very big accounts. He's tempting emperors and kings, princes and princesses, prime ministers and potentates, bigwigs of all kinds."

"He likes to hang out with movers and shakers?"

"Lucifer doesn't necessarily *like* these people. In fact, he mostly despises them. He merely mixes with them to leverage his capacity for evil." The voices drops to a sincere whisper. "He's dedicated his whole life to evil, you know."

"Quite a sacrifice, I imagine."

"Of course. But that's the kind of being he is. Always thinking of others."

"What's a devil's special skill set? I mean, what do you guys actually do better than other people?"

"I told you, we tempt."

"I might be in much the same business. I'm a headhunter you know. We're always being called upon to tempt people."

"Of course. You deal with money, minds, and hearts. You entice with limousines and corner offices, expense accounts and stock options, platinum plastic and plutocratic perks. It might sometimes seem a touch tawdry, a little like the minor leagues, perhaps, but never forget"—he beams—"you're doing a devil of a job. And you're making a very real difference in people's lives." He pauses. "So congratulations." He pauses again. "Don't get smug, though. You might graduate to lower things one day, but for the moment you're only a temporal tempter. Whereas, of course"—a note of pride infiltrates his words— "Lucifer and I are playing for eternal souls."

"I suppose tempting at that level's terribly complex?"

"It's surprisingly easy, actually. I mean the church goes out of its way to help."

"I kind of thought so."

"Oh, there're a million idiotic examples. Pregnancy, for instance, may be avoided by mathematics but not physics or chemistry."

"You're not a fan of the Pope?"

The pointy head swivels sadly. "Pope's not too bright, I'm afraid. And, of course, celibacy's one of the basic perversions. Makes tempting a cakewalk." The pink tongue flicks at the corner of thin, bloodless lips and the eyebrows arch quizzically. "And people wonder why seminarians and their altar boys so quickly become familiar with the back passage."

"Well, I can see that pederasty's a no-no. But what about sex generally? I mean I have to confess I've fallen prey to sexual temptation."

"Sex is a very real problem for most people. Orgasm's the most obvious lie yet designed to thwart man, you know."

"I know from personal experience that a standing cock has no conscience."

White lids slowly descend, stage-curtain-like, upon the gleaming eyes. The fellow really does look like a devil when he does that. The lids lift again. The piercing green gaze fixes upon him.

"I'm saying something much deeper, sir. I'm saying that orgasm defeats logic."

"How does that work, exactly?"

"Orgasm convinces man of something unreal. He mistakenly believes the power of his excitement lies outside his own physical apparatus. He then compounds that error by ascribing the power to God."

"Are you saying that I don't have to go looking for God? That I can find Shangri-la within my own genitalia?"

"Ab-so-lutely." The head nods enthusiastically. "Sex is not only one of life's greatest pleasures, but also the most illuminating. Heaven has nothing finer to offer. A properly handled phallus becomes a multifaceted instrument, a periscope by which to observe mysteries, a divining stick to tap energy, a lightning rod to tame the universe."

"So you're telling me to get in touch with the feelings in the head of my cock?"

"Exactly. I'm saying to trust the wisdom of the pudendum. I'm saying that the phallus is the axis upon which the entire cosmos revolves. I'm saying that all the angels in the universe can be found dancing upon the head of a penis."

"Do you have any thoughts on monogamy?"

"It's not as self-destructive as celibacy, but it's also a kind of perversion. Fortunately, we devils have moved society to serial monogamy."

"That's a step in the right direction?"

"In many ways it's not as good as run-of-the-mill adultery."

"From your perspective, of course."

He's a little miffed. "We devils have everyone else's interests at heart, you know."

"Well, that's sex. Do you have a quick take on religion?"

"It's morally useful but not intellectually sustainable. Sets up a wonderful bridge to hypocrisy."

The arrival doors suddenly hiss open, and a mélange of tourists exits into the arrival area. "I find these philosophies very tempting." This admission evokes a decidedly devilish sparkle within the gleaming green eyes. "So, hey, you've been tempting *me*. So you really *are* an old devil. Trouble is, I've got to rent a car before these gypsies grab them all." Time to pay the devil his due, and one of these heavy coins in your pocket might just do the trick. "Here's a couple of quid for your trouble, buddy."

A withered, scaly, long-nailed claw appears from behind the placard and grasps the gleaming disc. The gray head shakes. The glistening eyes fix Chancey's. The teeth flash.

"If you're really seeking Satan, sir"— the throng of travelers begins to encompass the devil—"you might try looking in the mirror."

The world's turning, slowly but dizzyingly. "Hey! What?"

The head's rapidly disappearing, but there's a glimpse of the reverse side of that weird sandwich board:

SHAME
CAN
LEAD
TO
DECENCY

He hears himself cry out: "Hey, Lucifer! What the hell does *that* mean?" The impediment seems to take on a life of its own, strutting him into the midst of the crowd. "Did you intend that slur for *me?*" But the devil and the board are gone. "Hey, you hoary Beelzebub, where'd you go?"

People are shrinking from him. He blinks. He's standing alone within a circle of bemused observers. A black-uniformed security guard emerges, glances at the wing tips, and then up, solicitously.

"Are you all right, sir?"

The bright-buttoned scarecrow's concerned. He thinks *Chancey's* the eccentric. And, maybe, he's got that right.

"I guess it was, maybe, uh"—flash the sincerely apologetic smile—"just a touch of, uh, jet lag, officer. I got a bit strung out, actually. Then I guess I just sort of, uh, nodded off and got to daydreaming."

The voice is professionally considerate. "You do look a little, shall we say, hyped, sir." He pauses. "But I presume you know where you're going, now?"

The words come out much too quickly. "Oh, absolutely, yes. *I* know where *I'm* going." Pull back. Grab a deep breath. That's better. Now the words'll sound calm and reasoned. "I mean why in the world would I not know what I'm doing with my life?"

But the crowd's moved on. Nobody's listening. The guard's strolling away, in search of other troubled human cargo, no doubt.

The overbright fluorescent lights in this antiseptic Hertz booth aren't helping to soothe your jangled nerves, Chancey. This squishy Styrofoam cup of lukewarm tea isn't doing much good, either. Maybe a quick scribble on this airline notepad will help:

> I've been flying
> on a plane
> Slowly turning
> quite insane
> For the journey's
> been inane
> all my life

I've been buzzing
on a jet
And I'm really
quite upset
And only God knows
what I'll get
in the afterlife

So, shame can lead to decency. But how does that actually work? Or does it at all? Dreams, hallucinations, do any of these things ever make sense, really?

"We have a choice of two cars for you, sir."

He glances to the counter. No one's there.

"We've got a compact Ford." The voice is coming from behind a murky mirror. "Or, if you'd like to invest in something special, something that'll make people sit up and take notice, then perhaps we could tempt you with the latest, forest-green, eight-cylinder, leather-trim, luxury Rover."

What the hell, a few extra dollars for a graceful, comfortable ride—where's the downside, really?

M3 TO COLDRIDGE

SO, IT'S A GAS GUZZLER—that's why no one wanted to rent this handsome vehicle. The nozzle of the gas pump jerks in his hand, his eye flicks to the spinning meter, and the invasive smell of petrol boards the escalator into his lungs. Costly business, fueling a car in England. What percentage of the tax on that outrageous total goes to funding the Royal White Elephants? Not to mention their wretched retinue of hangers-on. But, hey, if the people of England don't care, then why should he? Maybe Doc could offer some insight on why these drones irk him so. Maybe Chandler Haste suffers an underlying antipathy to authority. Go on—really? Might be more fun to pillow-talk the issue with that lovely princess, actually. He snaps the fuel cap back onto the tank. Maybe a cake of creamy English chocolate might sweeten his petrol-fumed nasal passages.

He wanders inside to the franchise shop. Ah, yes, it's all here—
first-aid kits, travel-sickness remedies, confectionary, chocolate, travel
guides, paperback books, magazines, even a volume of horoscopes.
Does anybody actually believe in horoscopes? No, but they're
intriguing. Not really, but it's hard to resist peeking. Some people
apply the Jungian notion of synchronicity to horoscopes. According
to this line of thinking, the prognostication is meaningless until the
very moment one chooses to read it. This flimsy tome he's holding
in his hand, for example, contains predictions for this very week
that virtually no one in the world will ever read—which is just as
well, because, since they never bothered to stop and inquire, the
prognostication is lifeless. But just as a stopped clock tells the right
time twice a day, the prescribed destiny, according to this theory,
anyway, comes to life with deadly accuracy for the stargazer whom
curiosity induces to crack the pages, locate his particular star—
Capricorn in this case—and contemplate the prophecy for the week.
So let's see what the fates have in store for Chancey:

> An advantageous week for conflict resolution but a
> solemn time for crossroads and reversals. Travel raises
> the prospect of adventure. There will be vexation at
> the beginning, but enlightenment in the end.
> Business affairs call for a sharp mind, a steady hand
> and resilience. Heed good advice but beware of
> treachery or false counsel. Follow your heart and not
> temptation. Romantic interests are resolved to your
> bliss if not your delight. The eyes are not always
> reliable, so watch the mouth. The way is clear, but the
> road proves hard.

Clichés and old saws dressed up with cagey equivocations. Let the
unconscious try to turn and twist all that into something sensible.
Do the scribblers who pen this stuff laugh up their sleeves or might
they pride themselves for providing an authentic service? As a
detached, rational observer, perhaps he has a duty to track the
prognosticator down and make a couple of points. Like, for openers,
ambiguity has rendered the predictions pointless. What, really, is the
difference, in this context anyway, between a conflict and a crossroad?
Precious little, yet the former is forecast to turn out better than the
latter. And who, other than a befuddled fortune-teller, would care

to make a distinction between bliss and delight? The erstwhile seer might also be a plagiarist. That line about the eyes and the mouth looks suspiciously like a paraphrasing from the infamous Dr. Freud. Ego—discerning adult conscious control—is to be observed in the eyes, he said, whereas the unconscious secret desires of the id reveal themselves in the lips, be they stiff-upper, lower-trembling, or whatever. The only prediction that might apply, the treachery of Jesse Green and Fuller Fyfe, is already in the past. But, okay then, score the shadowy sage one out of ten for getting at least something right. All things considered, however, a bar of local chocolate will likely represent a wiser investment.

The cashier returns his credit card. Mmm, the chocolate really is a mouth-melter. He steps to the Rover, turns the key, and ignites the engine. Perhaps the universe is running in sync, after all. He checks his watch. He'll arrive in Coldridge in time to grab a good night's sleep, which is just as well, for both head and heart are humming.

He sets the Rover to reenter the throbbing motorway. Life's a journey. So, the way is clear but the road is hard. Frankly, the sky is overcast and the way is hardly ever clear—but here goes. With a powerful engine, a burst of acceleration, and decent set of wheels, it doesn't much matter how hard the road might be. He's cruising at seventy miles per hour, which is just as well, because so are most of those ugly, oversized, back-winding semi trailers.

"Romantic interests are resolved to your bliss if not your delight." Really? A blissful solution would entail having his cake and eating it, too. A blissful solution would be for the whole thing to resolve itself to the satisfaction of all parties. But how could that happen? And, if it did, why might he not be delighted?

> If love is the name of a question,
> Then romance is a place in the sky,
> Delight is a wicked, wayward glance,
> And bliss a mote in the eye.

COLDRIDGE

THREE THIRTY-SEVEN A.M. AND WIDE AWAKE. Jet travel corrupts the circadian rhythms. A glass of milk and couple of cookies might set them right, but there's no room service, of course.

In consideration of which it will be perfectly acceptable, surely, to steal downstairs and check out the kitchen. The used-to-be-white bathrobe's torn and tatty, but better than traipsing naked.

The carpet's soft upon the balls of his feet, and—surprise, surprise—the stairs fail to creak. He pushes back the heavy oaken door and creeps onto the polished, wide-plank floor of the country kitchen. And here's a delectable astonishment—

A lovely kindred spirit, blond and twenty, is already raiding the ancient, oversized refrigerator. She's caught him in her peripheral vision. A long, slim index finger reflexively crosses the full red lips— make no sound. The face is warm, innocent, and beautiful. By the look of the getup—full evening makeup, white taffeta gown with a flowing train, and a diamond tiara—she's returning from some kind of beauty-queen ball. Or maybe she's a goddess. She plucks a wide-lipped white china jug of milk from the refrigerator, seals the door, and grabs a clear confectioner's jar of yummy biscuits from the battered butcher's table. She radiates a winning smile that seems almost to emanate from her soul, tosses the train of her gown over her arm, and silently motions him to follow the subtle scent of her perfume as she tiptoes out of the kitchen, up the stairs, and into— can this really be so?—her room.

The rich pile of white woolen carpet presses up between his toes. This softly lit, white-chiffon-curtained chamber is surely the bridal suite. The furniture may be antique, but some poncey decorator has burnished it white. A commodious crystal chandelier, gently dimmed, hangs from the ceiling. The guest table bears an abundant, sweetly scented bouquet of gardenias, lilies-of-the-valley, white freesias, golden roses, white orchids, and stephanotis. There's a full-length silver-framed mirror on the wall opposite the neat heart-shaped bed, but no husband in sight. And, judging by the goddess's relaxed demeanor, nowhere in the vicinity, either.

She sets the milk jug onto the bedside table and produces two sparkling tumblers.

The voice is dulcet. "You can't sleep?" The deep blue eyes are wide. She pours the thick country milk into the tumblers.

"I just arrived from New York—I'm jet-lagged."

"New York—wow!" She passes him his glass and salutes him with the other hand. Now she pushes her rim to his and smiles over the top. "Here's to the New World, then."

Mother's milk could not taste better. There's something familiar about that doe-eyed smile.

"Haven't I seen you somewhere before?"

"That's a very old line."

"I seem to remember seeing your photo—"

"It's possible, my husband is something of a celebrity—on this side of the Atlantic, anyway."

"A celebrity. That must be nice."

"On a good day it's like having an extra lump of sugar in your coffee"—her smile's engaging, and she seems entirely oblivious to the impediment—"and on a bad day, it's like walking around in your underwear." She pauses. "Well, I guess he's more of an icon than a celebrity, actually."

"An icon! Say, now—aren't you connected to the, uh—"

"Royal family? Sort of. My role is to deliver eggs and provide surrogate services." She smiles wanly. "Other than that they give me the feeling that I'm not good enough for them to treat me as an equal."

"They give that feeling to *you?*"

"They do it very artfully. There's no group so uncongenial as an uncongenial family, you know."

There's an authentic empathy here. He sets the tumbler back onto the bedside table.

"Really? Well, I'm not surprised. I used to pick up on that not-good-enough sentiment when I was a kid in the colonies. A barrage of royal-family books and magazine articles lauded the supposedly superior virtues of those so-called nobles. I could never quite figure why the man in the street was prepared to foot the bill."

She sets her glass beside his. Her voice is confiding. "Well, you have to realize that a key royal role is to generate tourism and hard currency—which is, in fact, exactly what happens."

"Ah, yes, Windsor World. My hunch, however, is that the citizens of England would make more money, and employ better-quality people—present company excluded, of course—if they fired all the kings and queens and lords and ladies and incorporated their property and paraphernalia into theme parks operated by a public company."

She reaches out to him with both hands. Her fingers are soft, but her grip strong. Her eyes are intense. She's applied that makeup with a rather heavy hand. The effect is almost surreal.

Her voice, however, is soft and sincere. "Royalty's more than a theme park. I mean, the British people need someone in public life to give affection, to make them feel important, to support them, to lighten their dark tunnels."

"I guess we all do. But you're talking about ceremonial roles that pay a fortune. A lot of highly qualified commoner candidates— funeral directors spring to mind—would love that job. So I have a problem with the selection process. If I tried to assess competence on a lucky-sperm-club basis, I'd be laughed out of business." She remains unfazed, softly attentive. "To be quite honest, I don't know why the taxpayers don't rebel."

She beams patiently. "That's because they need someone to look up to." Her breath is sweet. "In America you make idols of pop stars and politicians. But British aristocrats are obliged to observe a higher moral code." Those wide blue eyes are disarming. "Noblesse oblige, and all that, you know."

"My hunch is that noblesse oblige is a child of the noble lie. Doing the right thing's surely a function of maturity, not genetics. And pop stars are as likely to evidence that sensibility as so-called nobles. But, anyway, pop stars and politicians come and go, whereas aristocrats feed at the public trough forever."

Maybe went a bit far, there. No. She's still in a warm-and-lovely mood.

She turns on her heel and flashes that doelike glance back over her shoulder. Hey—does she really want him to unslip those taffeta-clad buttons?

"Would you mind, terribly?"

Should he succumb? Not really. He's in town to resolve romantic issues, not to complicate them. Yet she's clearly sensitive to rejection, so how can he possibly decline?

The fasteners seem almost to melt in his fingers. The gown cascades to the floor. She steps out of it like a nymphet rising from a bath of cream. She spins, a high-heeled, six-foot-something blaze of white—silk bra, panties, garter belt, stockings, everything. The rubied cross in the center of that sparkling tiara is a delightful finishing touch.

Her legs are long and slim and every bit as silken as her gown. Her breasts are full, blue-veined, and milky. The stomach's firm. She strikes a Varga pose, one hand to her hip, the other to her head. Oh, yes, this is her, all right. How could that nincompoop prince ever hope to satisfy such a full-blooded creature?

She kicks off the satin high heels and grins. "Contrary to popular belief, not all Englishwomen wear tweed nightgowns."

"So I noticed—very, uh, sexy. But where, if I may ask, is your handsome prince?"

"Sex appeal is forty percent what you've got and seventy percent what people think you've got." She pauses. "My husband? Well, to tell you truth, he's off with his mistress."

"Just married and already he has a mistress?"

She perches, very gently, on the edge of the bed. "She came with the package." She reclines, ever so casually. "There's always been three in the relationship." The smile's decidedly inviting. "It makes for a crowded marriage."

"Came with the package? Are you telling me that even as he swore his marriage vows before the world—God, too, presumably—that this purported prince was already intending to continue to bite from an apple he'd already been nibbling on the side? I mean I know that kind of thing happens among commoners, but what about all that noblesse oblige?"

"People aren't perfect." She pats the satin bedspread.

Best not offend her. He draws alongside. "Three in a marriage, how does that actually work?"

"He keeps her for companionship and me for breeding."

"Why can't you be his companion, too?"

She sighs. "I might be as thick as a plank, but my guess is that men are children who need more than one playmate." Deep breath. God, that heave is sensuous. "The other reason is that in his mind

I'm still just the eighteen-year-old girl he got engaged to. I get no credit for growth. And, of course, he never really wanted to marry me, either."

She seems so vulnerable.

"It was a shotgun wedding?"

"Kind of. He had to marry a virgin, and time was running out. Now I have to produce an heir. Otherwise, we lose rank."

"And money?"

"Of course. Wealth—money, power, status—all of that."

"Do you ever feel as if you're being used?"

"I can feel taken for granted."

"I guess your prince would argue that a really royal marriage rests upon his capacity to command one of those delightful noble lies."

She's studying him playfully. "So maybe that should be a two-way street." She flashes an intimate grin. "And if so where's the harm? I mean husbands and wives probably make the best lovers when they're betraying each other."

Now, *that* is a definite come-on.

"Are you saying we should tolerate betrayal for the good of the marriage?"

She pauses. "We should turn a blind eye because that's ultimately the best way to hold the one you love."

"But what if the see-no-evil strategy doesn't work?"

"Well, maybe nothing would've. Perhaps a great love is never returned. Anyway, it's a better strategy than trying to confine someone in a cage—that only provokes frustration and resentment."

"I seem to recall someone saying that a man should be friends with a nun and a whore and while talking with them forget which is which. Of the two, whom would you rather be?"

She takes both his hands in hers and pulls herself into a cross-legged elflike pose.

"I'd rather be the queen of people's hearts." She pauses, then tosses him an impish glance. "Do you have a wife?"

"I'm not sure. We had an argument. She's disappeared."

Her smile is caring. "Married people are always arguing. It's a sign that things are going right. It's silence that's the killer." A soft glow refracts in her shimmering blond hair. She leans forward.

Those breasts could not be more tempting. But follow the heart and not temptation.

This time the voice's a whisper. "Hey, listen—do you like to try new things?"

"I've sometimes been too curious for my own good."

She reaches under the pillow and produces not one but two glistening pairs of silver handcuffs. Ah, English girls, they look so innocent yet know every trick. A burst of adrenaline floods his groin.

The intimate grin again. "Try these on for size."

"Can I trust you?"

That smile's an open invitation. "Of course, you can trust me. Now, just lie facedown and close your eyes."

"I shall remain your obedient servant."

She applies a cuff to each of his wrists. And does it rather too expertly for comfort, actually. And then, in the twinkling of an eye, she's fixed the other end of each set of cuffs to the bed legs. Hey! She's done the same with his ankles, too. There's a little bit of slack. At least he can elevate his head. God, look at that—

She's standing, feet set wide apart, with a fearsome black bullwhip in her hand. The grim expression on her face is something altogether new.

"Hey, what's with the whip? I put my trust in you, remember."

She struts to the dressing table and seizes a lipstick. Her butt shakes as she scrawls a message upon the mirror. She steps aside and points the whip to the blood-red words. The voice is stern. "Lesson number one, Mister Haste." She spits the line:

Fidelity

is a virtue

peculiar to those

about to be

betrayed

His voice cracks. "How do you know my name?"

"I know your name, and I know my role, and I see my duty. But there's no need for alarm. Every strong woman has to walk a similar path. It's feminine strength that's causing your confusion and fear."

"Your role?"

"I already told you—the British people need someone to lighten their dark tunnels."

"But I live in America."

"The biggest disease this world suffers from in this day and age is the disease of people feeling unloved. My job is to give a special brand of love."

"Where's it written that you have authority over nonresidents of the British Empire?"

She snorts like a wild mare. "I do things differently. I don't go by a rulebook. I lead from the heart, not the head. Someone's got to go out there and love people and show it."

The full-length mirror behind her continues to reflect her magnificent Amazon back, her tight butt, her blonde tresses. She turns, wipes away the lipstick—then scrawls anew. The breasts jiggle as she spins. He studies the words:

The family
you come from
isn't as important
as the family
you create

She strides toward the bed. God, she's beautiful. She tilts and writhes before him. Those breasts are gorgeous. He's losing control of his male member. But what's that second leathery object she's extracting from the bedside table? Oh, God, no—a dildo! She straps it on and tests it with a wicked thrust. The head is huge—who could possibly need so much light in their tunnel? The whip's back in her hand, and the air hisses as she flicks the malevolent leather toward his butt. A very near miss. But what's she doing now? Just look at that incredible image in the mirror. She's mounting him. She's raised his tatty bathrobe, and her silken thighs are straddling his naked butt. The dildo's pressing rudely at the valiantly tight-lipped portal. Her eyes are blazing. She leans back on her haunches like a jockey controlling an unruly steed. This time the grin's pure schadenfreude.

"Feel free to address me as Your Royal Highness."

She unslips a front hook on the bra. Her breasts tumble and dance. The inflamed nipples contrast sharply with the milkiness of all else. He closes his eyes. How could he have been so foolish as to trust her? Oh, Christ, the pain—how long must he endure this false enchantment? He hoists his head and casts an imploring look into the mirror . . .

But she's gone.

This time the snorting jockey—sporting a coronet, an ermine cape, and nothing else—is Grisham Pryce. He's sweating, panting, heaving, wheezing. "There is sex after death," he cries. His eyes are blazing, his mouth exultant. "*You* just won't be able to feel it."

20

Velvet Shoes

TREACHERY AND TEMPTATION. So the horoscope crept into his dreams. Fidelity is a virtue peculiar to those about to be betrayed. Or perhaps this rather nice line was referring to his own treacherous behavior. Perhaps the princess was Jill. Perhaps she wanted him to experience the kind of shame he'd inflicted upon her. Perhaps the subconscious was saying that Grisham's peeved, too. Or maybe all of the above. Or none. Maybe the mind was merely playing pat-a-cake with that hazy horoscope. Right. So put it all out of mind.

His eyes seem almost locked shut. That's jet lag, too. Pry those peepers open, Chancey. Oh, God—ten already by the bedside clock. That's three in the morning in New York. More sleep, he needs more sleep. He rolls onto his back. That couldn't really be Elan's face. Not up there in those Elizabethan rafters. Could it? And the face within the face—the bright eyes, the smile.

He drags himself to the bathroom. That other set of eyes, the green pair in the mirror, is strained. Both the right and the left. The lips are weak and facile. He splashes his face with cold, purifying water. "But if you really want to know what you look like asleep simply stand in front of a mirror with your eyes closed." Who said that? That wino. In Sydney. By the Gap. That tramp knew something. And what else did he say? Oh, yes—the curtain that conceals the future is knitted by the hands of mercy. That hobo was sharper than he seemed. Maybe Father Time was cruising Sydney.

The phone rings. He grabs it.

"You awake?" The voice is Elan's, but edgy.

"That's a deep philosophical question. I think I'm awake. But I thought so in Rockefeller Plaza, too. In fact, I might've been sleepwalking all my life." He spreads the bedroom curtains. A pale sun peeps from a bed of light gray clouds onto a camellia bush within a garden of azaleas. "But, today, for you, right now, anyway, I'm pretty sure I'm awake."

"I dreamed about you, Chancey."

Dreams must be the order of the day. She sounds fearful. Listen carefully.

"You did?"

"I was in a torture chamber. I was strapped into an iron maiden. My head was locked in place and two rapierlike blades in the lid pointed directly at my eyes. Others, in the middle, pointed into my torso. My inquisitor was threatening to close the cover. I'd be blinded and disemboweled." She pauses. "You were a giant bird flying overhead. You were looking for me, but I was hidden from your view. I was trying to cry out to you, but I was gagged."

"Who was the inquisitor?"

"I don't know. He wore a black robe and a mask."

He reaches for a joke. "At least it wasn't one of those Maori gods dancing a haka." She fails to laugh. Try again. "And an inquisitor wouldn't gag you, anyway. They get off on the screams of the victim."

Her voice is contemplative. "Right. They don't want you to die quickly, either." She sounds a little distraught, actually. "They want you to suffer. They want to hear you plead."

"Come *onnnn*—it was only a dream. You're still breathing the sweet countryside air. And the bird of your dreams is just about on the wing to meet you right now. I mean, we're still on for eleven, right?"

"Sergeant Pepper will play for you, Chancey."

THE AIR'S SWEET, AND THE ONE-MILE WALK to Crystal Pond is better therapy for jet lag than that wayward princess's jug of milk. Or so one hopes. Faint midmorning sun warms the air. Now, there's something you don't see every day. Metal-and-glass cat's-eyes studded into the center of the road at twenty-yard intervals. A navigational aid, no doubt much needed for night driving on these lonely roads. A meandering lane runs off to the left. Headstones in the distance catch his eye. Did Gray really write his Elegy there? Probably not, but who knows for sure. He presses on, and, as predicted, there they are, two huge wrought-iron gates alongside a cluster of overhanging oaks. And, within those trees, mostly hidden from view, a white vehicle.

Acorns pop beneath his feet. A shaft of filtered sunlight strikes a sunglassed face momentarily framed in the open driver's window. It's Elan, all right. But something's radically different. The hair! The silken, cinnamon hair that fell to her shoulders. It's gone. And in its place a half-inch ragged-urchin cut, dyed to ruby red. She spreads the fingers of her right hand upon the window lip and pushes the horn-rimmed sunglasses to her forehead. The face's thinner, slightly lined, lightly made up. The eyes and aspect seem strained. But that smile. Hey, she's suddenly the very stunning teenager whose image he could never erase. No wonder he's hustling and breathless.

"I walked, see?"

"From breakfast to madness, Chancey? Maybe not. You look okay. Just like the same blue-jacketed, gray-trousered, white-shirted, velvet-shoed, soft-spoken, sandy-haired Chancey."

"Velvet-shoed?"

"We shall walk in velvet shoes wherever we go, Chancey." Her voice is a mixture of pleasure, humor, irony, and distress. "Elinor Wylie said that back in the twenties."

"I never realized these shoes were velvet, till now."

"Do you like my time machine, Chancey?" Her long-sleeved black silk blouse contrasts nicely with the gleaming vehicle. The original paint is as-new and buffed to a high luster.

"I like it very much. I think I always did."

"You're right, of course. It's a classic Jag, exactly the same as yours. I looked all over England to find it." She waggles the leather-clad steering wheel. "Plus power steering, see."

He steps back and studies the sedan. "It looks like magic."

"It *is* magic, Chancey. And it runs like a dream." She pauses. "A very pleasing dream—a reverie." She smiles. "Care to share a lifetime's reflections in Crystal Pond?"

He strolls to the passenger side, opens the door, and eases himself into the seat. A neat black leather skirt rides on her knees.

She smiles. "Same red trim, see." The voice is bright yet strained. "Same leather smell. Same mahogany dash. Same everything." She hits the ignition and the engine purrs. "Grisham has a great mechanic in the village. He keeps it hyped to the hilt, no expense spared."

She eases into gear, and the time machine rolls onto a soft, narrow, crackling gravel road flanked by sun-filled trees. Kaleidoscopic patterns of shadow and light reflect in her silent face. She brings the car to rest upon wispy grass beside an empty, rustic timber bench overlooking Crystal Pond. In fact, the pond's a tiny, perfect spring-fed lake, maybe half a mile in diameter.

She cuts the engine and turns to him. He reaches for her hand. The fingers are soft, tentative.

"What can I say, Elan? I'm ashamed. Of my behavior. Of the terrible things I—"

Her fingers touch his cheek. "Say nothing, Chancey."

"I owe you— "

"You don't owe me anything, Chancey. You never owed me. We were in love. It's not a tender thing. It's rough, rude, boisterous. It pricks like a thorn. It's not an ideal condition. It can fuck up your life, Chancey. It can raise you to heaven and cast you to hell."

"Were?"

"We moved on, Chancey. You can't keep love in a bottle."

"I still love you, Elan. I've always loved you. You were the one who went away. You were the one who called it off."

She gazes at the pond as he continues.

"But I always believed I'd see you again. Then I did. And messed it all up, made a complete fool of myself. I spoke to Beryl. She called me just last week. She said that you—that we—" She turns her head and meets his eye, but says nothing. "You never told me . . ."

She sighs. "I loved you, Chancey." She bites her lip. "I shared all secrets and revealed all mysteries—in my fashion, of course. Okay, so we spent a lot of time fucking. Maybe too much time. So people got hurt. You got hurt and Jill got hurt and I got hurt—and God only knows who else got hurt." She studies his face. "Got a question, Chancey? I'll be your Delphic Oracle. I'll be your Sergeant Pepper. I'll be your Pied Piper. I'll be your Wizard of Oz."

He squeezes her hand. "If only I'd known."

"I was your mistress, Chancey. That was the deal. A mistress is not an ethicist. A mistress accepts you on your own terms. Her job is merely to sate and satisfy you. Love just throws the relationship into jeopardy. That's why we never spoke about love. If we'd talked about that, we'd have had to acknowledge Jill—and we didn't want that. We'd have had to answer the question of what the hell we were really up to. No, the thrill lay in the triangular nature and clandestine content—and the intensity of the necessarily fleeting moments we had together. We fucked as if our lives depended on it precisely because our life together did. Did you ever really work out who you were making love to, Chancey? Don't try to answer right now. Let me offer my perspective. When I was with you, I didn't really think of you and me. I thought of us—and less. When we were around each other, we were one person. It was all so effortless. You were a drug to me. And I guess I was like a drug to you, too. We got high on each other. We filled a void in each other's lives. For me, anyway, the void was both emotional and intellectual. You were something like the high to be had from literature: it mirrors our deepest thoughts and hopes and dreams; we merge with the writer; we enter his mind, his soul even. That was us, Chancey. We were on the same page. If I were more precious than I am, and that is the way I am, I know, I'd have said we were soul mates. But I try not to kid myself. I realize that for you, initially, anyway, it was mostly about fucking. No need to deny it, Chancey. But don't get me wrong. I loved making love to you. But what I really got off on was sharing ideas and lines and poems. They were irresistible intellectual bonbons. We tasted them and became one person. All that copulating was merely the orgasmic center." She smiles. "Or maybe it was the other way around." She pauses. "But what the hell, at the end of the day, I was your mistress, and that was that."

"You were more than—"

"I was more, I was less, I was whatever I was, and I'm still the same. And, yes, okay, I'm entirely different, too." His eyes follow hers to the utterly still lake. Reflections of sun, sky, and cloud. He reaches out to touch her face. She takes his fingers and pushes them through her stubbled, silky hair. "I got a haircut last week, Chancey. I needed to be different, needed to rid myself of all the tension. It was eating me away. Literally. I was losing weight." She strokes her cheek. "I needed to be someone else. The old Elan had to be put to rest, once and for all. So now she's gone. 'At her heels a grass-green turf, at her head a stone.' But I told you that, already, right?"

"Hamlet?"

"Ophelia, actually. I'd made up my mind not to see you again, Chancey. I'd plucked the nerve of love. I'd become the respectable wife of my second covenant."

"But—"

"I should never've taken your call. The old Elan was suddenly back in my brain."

"What'd she say?"

"Terrible things. She said the essence of love is uncertainty. That nothing is serious except passion. That they do not sin who sin for love. She was always saying that." She reaches into the glove box, produces a slim, beaten, leather-bound book and a tired envelope. She smiles. "Homework, Chancey." She holds the book aloft like a priest with a communion host. "Willie's sonnets. Nothing we don't already know, of course. Summer's lease has all too short a date, and so on and so forth." She drops the slim volume to her knees. The pages fall open to a pressed flower. "A bookmark's a place in time, Chancey. This one used to be an impatiens. And it used to be red, too." She snaps the covers shut and pushes the book back into the glove-box. "Care to breathe some authentic country air?"

She flings open her door, springs from the car, and stretches. Her back is arched, her palms are pointing to the sun. The leather skirt has ridden high above her knees. Her skin's paler than he remembers. The door falls back and snaps closed. She strolls to a bench. He follows, trailing uneven footprints in the moist grass. They lean back upon the bench, fill their lungs with sweetly scented air, and gaze over the pond. A line of ducks paddles around the edge. A distant pair of geese settle to rest.

"It's deep out there, Chancey. It falls away quickly. Maybe you're like that, too." She smiles. "I brought your letter." She passes him the envelope. "Clairvoyants say you don't need to open a letter to know what's inside, that you can feel the message through the sheath."

He weighs the missive in his hand. She takes it back, removes the letter, and passes up the pages.

"Your reply to my good-bye, Chancey."

He glances to the epistle from his past. The paper used to be white. Not now. The folds are deep and worn, and the faded blue script's uneven. But that's definitely his handwriting. Used to be, anyway . . .

> Dear Elan,
> Scobie's mistake lay in putting pen to paper. I thought about your letter. I thought about it for a long time. I'd been thinking about it before it arrived. But it arrived anyway. I never thought I'd get in this deep. But how could I not? With you singing, bump-bumping and choo-chooing, and reciting Xanadu, and fucking. Someone smarter than me would let you have the last word. I'm not so clever. So let me ask a question: how can this be the end of the yellow brick road when I never met the wizard? Was it all a dream? Maybe. A silhouette framed by green hills. Sunshine on a window. Light upon a face. Oysters in a shell. Prawns in a buttered roll. A mud-and-sulfured moon. Cabernet against sin. Tell you this then, honey-mouthed sunshine girl, pixie demon, olive-skinned lover—I never met anyone like you. Something happened and we floated in the sky. How will I ever get back up there? Where do I go now? I wish I could run and not look back. I wish I could. Got your note. Read it and reread it. Then took my time and studied it again. After all, it exists and we don't. So now you're gone. Or maybe you were always just an illusion. Maybe love's a jewel on a beach that we can marvel at but never own. If we do it just becomes an empty shell. Maybe all the shells are jewels in disguise. So many things to regret. But I'd do them all again. And I'll always love you.
>
> Chancey

"I got the poem, too, Chancey. Everything arrived just after my, uh, operation." She bites that lip again. "My excision. My closure. My termination. My remedy." She half smiles. "The remedy to do me good. To do us both good. To do the world good." She studies the pond. "I thought I'd feel some kind of relief. I thought I was putting it, something—you, me, the devil, maybe—behind me. I thought I'd feel like an autonomous, New Age, adult woman, an honest-to-God, self-reliant grown-up. Instead, I just felt disemboweled, lobotomized, and depressed. I went to church, but the hymnal lyrics merely haunted me." Her grip on his hand tightens. " 'Wake, wake, for night is flying; the watchmen on the heights are crying.' " Tears swell in her eyes. He draws her to him, holds her tightly. "I knew why, Chancey. Because I'd killed someone. I just didn't know who. Then your letter came." Her tears are on his neck. "Oh, Chancey." Her perfume is sweet. Her stubbled, silky hair is soft on his lips. "I knew I'd always loved you, Chancey. I just hadn't realized that you cared so deeply. I felt to blame for that." She looks squarely into his eyes. Her face is streaked with tears. Her lip trembles. "Your life was settled. You had a wife and children. You had dreams and ambitions. I could never've told you. I'd have ruined everything for you. I saw no alternative, just dead ends."

"You could've—"

"Kept it? Yeah, maybe. I'd always wanted children, especially a child of yours. And I got my wish. But should I keep it? To be or not to be? I worried the question to death. Trouble was you'd never be there with me. With us. Never. I prayed, Chancey, that somehow we'd be back together. But I knew, deep down, it could never happen. So the prayers didn't work, my ancient incantations were too weak."

"Beryl said life got tough—"

"My life? I'm not sure I had what people call a life. I went off the rails, Chancey." She laughs. "I did drugs. A lot of drugs. A lot of other things, too. Nothing you want to hear about. I was fucked up, Chancey. Fucked up and fucked over." She pauses. "I tried to write about it. Nothing good appeared. It was all terribly depressing. I got desperate."

"And?"

"And Grisham came along."

"He changed things?"

"He picked me up. He was wealthy and well connected. He was decent. He paid for me to get help."

"Treatment?"

"Yeah. Fucking treatment. They sent me to the funny farm. Yeah, well, I guess I was pretty funny. It all got a bit much. I just lost it for a while, there. But I'm okay now. They put me back together again. As much of me as they could find. I'm just not sure everything quite fits the way it used to."

"You fell in love with Grisham?"

"He fell in love with me. Or what he thought was me. He wanted to take care of me, protect me. He was kind and caring. And he asked me to marry—"

"And you said?"

"I said, my girl, it's your last resort—will you marry it?" She tries to laugh.

"Did you love him?"

"Oscar said a man can be happy with any woman as long as he doesn't love her. I thought I might pull off the same act."

He begins to speak. And she to answer. Their lips brush. Her skin is soft. She nestles into him. A bird sounds in the background. His mouth is at the nape of her neck.

"Elan." Her eyes are wide, innocent. "So here we are then, girl."

"What to do, Chancey?"

He straightens, gazes over the pond, then turns his eyes back to her. "If we sit quietly the world will go away."

She springs to her feet and speaks to the lake. "No, the world won't go away, Chancey. You'll go away. Just like after Anzac Day."

"Anzac Day?"

"You haven't forgotten, have you, Chancey?" Her eyes are wide. "The sun'll be rising on yet another twenty-fifth-of-April Godzone Anzac Day tomorrow. I'll catch it here a day later."

"Ah, yes, I remember. Lost youth. Scarlet sands. And crimson linen."

"I always remember, Chancey. Even in England. Because that turned out to be our whole story. A lifetime of exciting, fleeting, but ultimately depressing Anzac Days with never enough time." Distant geese break the surface of the water and flap into flight. "You were always flying somewhere, Chancey." The distressed laughter's back in her voice. "Hey—the world's come back! See, boy! No more bump-bumping and choo-chooing. And now you'll fly away, again. And I'll go back to the new Elan's entirely new, entirely gratifying, entirely fulfilling, entirely exciting life. No shit."

She saunters to the car and cracks open the door. He follows and reaches into his jacket pocket.

"I wrote you a poem." He hands her a yellow sheet of paper. "Wrote it in the plane on the way over. I had to say something. It's just words."

She leans back upon the gleaming white time machine and smiles.

"Life's just words, Chancey." She drops her eyes to the lines:

> I loved you then
> > and do now
> > and always will
> I loved you deeply,
> > darkly,
> > desperately,
> > and blindly,
> > and do now,
> > and always will
> Virgin,
> Lover,
> Mistress,
> Friend,
> > You were all these things to me
> > > and more
> > > **And will be**
> > > > evermore
> > > For I love you still

She reaches for his hand. Her eyes find his. She smiles.

"Not bad—for a wild colonial boy."

She's warm and soft against his torso. Her mouth's sweet, her tongue gentle. She pulls his fingers to her unrestrained breast, then gently pushes them back.

"Any more of that and you just might have to marry me."

"Marry—"

"But you couldn't do that. I mean, could you?"

"Maybe if you could I could."

"No kidding." She squeezes his hand. "I mean, no fucking kidding. So maybe we should leap into the time machine and fly." A burst of sunlight bounces off the pond and into her eyes. She gazes into the shimmering water. "There's another world beneath that looking-glass lake, Chancey." She pauses. "The trouble is, I'm trapped in a bad dream. I'm drowning in a ghastly aquarium. I'm incapable of breaking the glass that separates our lives." She heaves a deep breath, then turns her eyes to him. "No one's rich enough to buy back the past, Chancey. We can't go back and force it to work out. You have your life, and now I have mine. We've been selfish and self-absorbed. When I met Jill in New York, I felt utterly ashamed. She loves you, Chancey. You're a mere male, so I guess you just don't see it. You see so many other things but not that. I'm a woman, so I saw it in her every movement around you. I knew we had to end it. I knew if I repented, if I made what the nuns used to call a sincere act of contrition, I could turn it all around." She holds his gaze and smiles. "Like the rider who falls from the horse and within that twinkling moment of crashing to his death, repents—and is forgiven." She glances to the horizon. " 'Twixt the stirrup and the ground' "—she turns her eyes back to him and smiles softly—" 'mercy I sought, and mercy I found.' "

"But you saw me again."

"Yeah. I saw you again." She slips into the driver's seat and hits the ignition. "Buckle up, Chancey. I'll drop you back to the Hero and Leander. After that you're on your own."

On his own? So that was it? Maybe not, for she's driving so slowly that something tells him she's got something else to say, and is contemplating how best to say it.

Thick, thatch hedges pass on both sides. Emerald meadows stretch beyond them.

Her glance is tentative. "I'm going to ditch the time machine, Chancey, and trade down to something less stylish. It'll be a symbolic gesture. I have to grow up and face reality." She pauses. "I'm glad you came. I'd been keeping a secret from you, Chancey. I sensed you'd found out. I had to put the past to rest; I needed to talk about it. When you called from the airport, I knew that you did, too. We needed to break the spell, set each other free. 'Golden lads and girls all must, like chimney sweepers come to dust'—don't you just love that line, Chancey? A golden lad is a dandelion, you know. Then, at the end of its life, when its seeds are ready to blow to the wind, they call it a chimney sweep because that's what it looks like. Lovely imagery, right?" She's stalling, but why? "Hey listen, Chancey, you'll still love me. And I'll still love you. It'll just be different."

"Different?"

She eases the car to the side of the road and draws to a gentle halt. The engine continues to purr.

"I have to tell you, Chancey." This time she's going to say it. "I'm pregnant."

The adrenaline rush, the spinning head.

"You okay, Chancey?"

"I just somehow didn't—"

"Expect it? Neither did I. Grisham's not exactly a stud. I wanted a child, but I didn't really want to be pregnant. Only with you." She smiles and eases the car back onto the road. She catches his eye in the rearview mirror. "I might have succumbed right there in that Manhattan cab otherwise. Really. But I was pregnant, so I just didn't want to risk anything. It's Grisham's, so maybe it's going to be something of an aristocrat. And it's mine—so this time I'm going to clutch it to my bosom with hoops of steel. I'm kind of half pretending it's yours, too, of course. Nothing'll take it from me. Hey, Chancey, you're all choked up."

She cuts the engine, then props forward on the red leather. She's suddenly so calm, so mature, so poised. She suddenly knows what she really wants to say. Her eyes hold his.

"For years I felt guilty and confused about us. I couldn't balance that something that felt so good—such a powerful expression of love—could be considered by so many to be so wrong." She drops an elbow to a hand and cups her chin. "When I got back from New York last week, I talked it over with a friend. Well, she's more than a friend, actually. She's a nun who moved out of the church." She smiles. "You might call her a guru. She's kind of New Age. But, anyway, she listened to all my guilt and confusion. And then she set me back on my heels. You know what she said, Chancey? She said it was a lucky day when you came into my life—"

"Lucky?"

"Yeah. She said that as a wild, young, naive girl, which is what I was—"

"I seem to remember—"

"That I was lucky to meet someone who really loved me." She smiles. "Or came to, anyway. And who showed me how to love. In every way." She pauses. "Until that conversation, I'd seen only the negative side of, uh, us. The pain we'd brought to ourselves, to our families, maybe even to God. Now, suddenly, I began to see us in a free, unencumbered, exhilarating way. Always before the good'd been tainted by the guilt. But now the guilt's evaporating, Chancey." She reaches for his hand. "We shared something special. Okay, so it wasn't purely good. But it wasn't all bad, either. And, even after all this time, it's still part of us. And I'm going to carry that special thing to my child, Chancey. And that child's going to take it all—the best of you, the best of me, the best of us—to the world. You'll see, Chancey, you'll be proud, you'll know it wasn't all for nothing." Her cheek's on his neck.

He catches a shadow in his peripheral vision and glances up. A uniformed figure floats by.

She glances into the rear window. "It's just a local copper on a bike, Chancey." She smiles. "A gliding bobby in blue."

She reaches into the mahogany glove box. "I wrote you a poem, too, Chancey." She produces a folded sheet of rich gray paper. "I mean, this time, we really do have to end all our clandestine capering." Conscious of her gray eyes, he accepts the missive and studies the bronze-blue ink—

> I never lamented nor even sighed
> For you; I never whined, whimpered, or wailed;
> No tear was shed, no incipient tide
> Of melancholy brine was ever bailed.

"You felt nothing?"

"Nothing, Chancey, nothing."

> So tender no nauseous, giddy good-byes,
> Bear no mawkish sentiment on your sleeve,
> Feign no fervor in those fine feckless eyes,
> Neither delay, nor distrust, nor reconceive.

"Feckless?"
"Feckless—"

> Run from me, chancelessly, hastily, leave
> Spring from me, speedily, ever so quick,
> Swiftly, remorselessly, end this upheave,
> Flee from me, fly from me, smoothly and slick.

"Quitting time?"
"It surely is—as well you know."

> But as you retreat down the trail of time,
> Promise you'll ever and always be mine.

"A paradox. I like it."

"Irony, mockery, paradox—it's all part of the mask we well-bred Pommie girls use to protect our feelings." That half grin could crumble in a moment. "Well, I kind of hoped you'd like it." She stretches forward, ignites the engine, and eases the car back onto the road. "Sets us both free, right?"

"And makes me a lifetime captive, too."

"What could be nicer? Well, it's just words, Chancey, you know—"

"Oh, yeah, sure, life's something else again."

She spins the time machine into the Hero & Leander roundabout driveway and brings it to rest at the polished-oak front door. She pecks his temple.

"I can't stay." She draws back. "I couldn't live through any more good-byes." He puts his hand to her cheek, rustles her hair, catches her perfume. "Don't say anything—just go."

He steps from the car, closes the door, and leans back in through the passenger window. "I know I'll be seeing you again, Elan . . ."

"Yeah, we'll meet again. On the other side of the looking glass, maybe." Her eyes brim and her lip quivers. "And, if not, why then—"

She swallows the words. He steps back, and she eases the time machine onto the country road. He catches her glance in the rearview mirror. Those eyes—ever-deep, ever-dark, ever-haunting. She waves. How many memories can swirl in a tear? An acorn spits from the back wheel. He glances down, then up again. But the time machine's gone. And she with it.

"Enjoyed your stay, Mr. Haste?" The pudgy Hero & Leander proprietrix seems genuinely interested.

"It's a lovely village. I was delighted to take it in."

But, frankly, since there's something spooky about the whole place, happier to be checking out.

THE ROVER HUMS ALONG the M3 to London. The rigid, paved highway resounds with the sound of pounding rubber. The blue-fumed back wind of speeding semitrailers rocks the car and whistles past the narrow slit in his window.

So what's he feeling? Sadness. Melancholy. Loss. Yes, all of the above. And a touch of—is that feeling relief? So it is. Yes, indeed. And what's that running in behind it—guilt? Can it be? Elan's found a guru to absolve her of all such shame. If only he could conjure such a sage. A confessor to commend him for leading that good, sweet, Roman Catholic girl down the primrose path. Ah, for such absolution. Oh, for such a noble liar.

And, while we're thinking about that, let's put a little more on the table. His treatment of Jill has been tacky and tawdry, shabby and low, puerile and shameful. Maybe he really was lost in a blur, the victim of a false enchantment, an illusion. Maybe he really was a dehydrated soul thirsting after the mirage of a quenching spring. And maybe he's just rationalizing. The fact is, he chose to work that mental gremlin overtime. He can try to argue that he didn't give Jill—or Blake or Angie—even a moment's thought. But it's a lie. The terrible truth is that he did give them a moment's thought— and nothing more. He fled from contemplation, scuttled off and left them fending for themselves at every turn. The nuns would've seen right through his ruses. So maybe that devil will yet jump up to give him a whipping. Or maybe he already did. Maybe that clever, all-seeing serpent rendered him lost, obsessed, asleep, an honest-to-God zombie. Until it all caught up with him. Until Doc dropped a couple of his ultimately spell-dispelling lines. Until Elan pointed to

Jill's affection. And what about that princess? "The family you come from isn't as important as the family you create." His own unconscious retrieved that message and posted it in bright red letters. The princess was Jill, surely—with a cry from the heart. There've always been three in the relationship, and it makes for a crowded, stifling, suffocating, doomed marriage comprising a distraught wife, two troubled kids, and an emotional quadriplegic.

But in the dream Jill was also more than willing to accept another man into her life. Chew on that for a moment. So is it too late to make amends? To win her back? To create a real life together? Hope springs eternal. But where is she, anyway? With another man, according to the dream—but he can't imagine that. Just the same, she did drop that decidedly ambiguous phrase, *seeing someone*. So perhaps she really has excised him from her life. And Everness is definitely lurking in the background. Oh, shit. Jill. Jill. Jill.

Maybe he'll wire her some flowers. That wouldn't be clumsy, would it? Or precious? But what the hell, do it anyway. He checks the mirror. He looks okay—in this light anyway.

Darkness suddenly extinguishes the faint sun. He lowers the window, inclines his head out, and glances back. Thick, black, moist, rolling nimbus clouds threaten to envelop the speeding Rover. And, look, there's a giant, grotesque face in the racing mist. Maybe it's another of his Rorschachian fantasies. But maybe it really is a serpent, too. Maybe it's chasing him. Maybe it's pissed he's getting away. Well, screw you, serpent!

He jams the window closed and hits the accelerator. Face it, viper, you've missed the boat. He mouths the lines as they come to him:

> You'll never catch Chancey here today,
> He's fled your fangs I'm pleased to say,
> He'll heal his soul and mend his way,
> And laugh at you on judgment day.

The Rover gains speed and momentum, and the lush brown leather seems almost to clench him in a viselike grip. Why, it's almost as if that serpent might just be in the process of crushing the Rover in order to ingest Mr. Chandler Haste. But that's just free-floating anxiety—or maybe guilt—right?

LONDON

HE CHECKS HIMSELF AS HIS BAD FOOT slides on
something—a hotel envelope beneath his heel. He snatches it up
and rips it open. It's a message from reception: Crawley's called,
three times. No wonder that amber message light on the bedside
phone's blinking so urgently. And now the phone has burst to life.

"Whoso diggeth a pit shall fall therein."

"You got the dirt on Green?"

"Jeremiah's his *cousin*—he's the one with the degree."

"Jesse's not Jeremiah?"

"A jinx but not a Jeremiah. Jesse's original name is Joshua. He
took business studies for two years but failed to complete anything
and still owes on his tuition. Seems that when he changed his name
to Jesse he also gave himself a false degree."

"Holy shit!"

"It's a holy mess."

"Did you call him on it?"

"I phoned him at home and left a message with his wife. I
said we'd struck an administrative glitch and needed to confirm
that his name didn't used to be Joshua."

"That'll shake him up."

"The wife sounded shaken herself. I haven't heard back from
Jesse, though. I rather doubt we ever will."

"Did you mention anything to Everness?"

"I'll leave that to you, Chancey."

"Yeah, I'll handle him."

IN THE DREAM, AN OPERA CURTAIN HAS RISEN to reveal
Doc in the costume of a medieval executioner. He's carrying an ax
and standing on a jury-rigged gallows. There's a blood-drenched
chopping block at knee level before him. He winks, then sings.
Who'd have guessed he'd produce such a lovely baritone? And, hey,
there's a nice touch, his lyrics are appearing in lights above the stage:

> Until you wrest the outcome that you need,
> Termination is a problematic deed
> So summon all facts before you wield the axe
> Or you're the one who'll ultimately bleed

Now Doc's sashayed into a dance, using the ax as a mock partner.

> The termination tango heats the pips
> So hold your tongue real tight behind your lips
> Keep it on a latchet as you ratchet up the hatchet
> And leave no fatal trail of Freudian slips

While Doc's been singing, a enuch has bundled a rickety cage up the gallows steps. But that's not a cage. It's treadmill with a giant white rat trapped inside. And that's not a white rat at all—that's Fuller, wearing an operating gown. He's grabbed the bars of the treadmill and cracked a bizarre grin. Now he's swung the cage door open and he's stepping out. The eunuch's attached a surgeon's headlight to Doc's forehead. They're all linking hands for a big-time finale. And here it comes:

> The termination theater's full of strife
> So mind how you thrust the knife
> For the very punctuation intended for the patient
> May redound to claim a clumsy surgeon's life

Hey! Since when did Doc have a clubbed foot?

21

Steel-Toed Slippers

"WELL! CHANCEY!" Fuller proffers a moist, fleshy palm and a comradely grin. On the bright side, his two-piece, gray-flannel suit is well pressed, his shoes shined, his matching tie and handkerchief perked, and his hair recently barbered. On the downside, his face is adrenaline-puffed, his waistline bulging, his eyes bloodshot, and his breath sour.

"Well, Fuller, it's good to see you, too."

Perhaps he's caught wind of what might be coming.

"Long way to come just for that"— Fullerian wink— "I imagine you'll be looking up old friends, too . . ."

A dig?—probably. A threat?—maybe. They face off awkwardly.

"Strictly business, Fuller." Best play it deadpan. "Time to restructure."

"Restructure?"

Fuller knows the meaning of the word. "Yeah, well. I guess we both have to face facts. Things just aren't working out here."

"Things mightn't look as bright as you'd like, Chancey, but I have a ton of prospects in the pipeline."

A sweaty film breaks on Fuller's brow, and a whiff of Old Spice emanates from his underarms as he slithers into his swivel chair and fails in his attempt to strike a pose of hands-behind-the-head nonchalance. Best take mercy on this squirming creature. First by slipping into the guest chair and second by assembling some tactful words. "Yes, ah, well, look, I've given this a lot of thought, Fuller. Your great strength is dealing with people one on one. Administration's not only a waste of your gifts, it's exhausting, too. People get burned out. Good people, wonderful people—"

"You think *I'm* burned out?"

"I think it's time we made some changes. Maybe it's time to look out for the inner child."

Fuller stands, strolls to the window, and pats his groin. A red bus thunders past. A bilious web of carbon monoxide rises. Fuller produces a clean white linen handkerchief and blows his nose.

"The inner child. The inner fucking child." He returns the handkerchief to his pocket and stares off into space. "Sounds like hokey California bullshit to me, Chancey." He pauses. "I relax. I look after myself. I wind down with the occasional drink."

"People say you've a drinking problem."

"People say." He spits the words. "Who cares what people say? What I do out of the office is my business." He snorts. *"In* the office, now, that's another matter. And I've achieved incredible things inside the office, Chancey. I've contacted more prospects than you'll ever know. I've busted my guts bringing in work. And I've done it for you, Chancey. Not just here, either."

"And I'm appreciative. It's just a pity you've not built repeat business."

"I have clients! I have a personal following. I have people who'll deal only with me."

"You have?"

"Sure I have. Big-time clients. Quasi-government agencies, too. You look as if you don't believe me, Chancey. So let me just show you something." He grabs his Gucci briefcase from beneath the desk, snaps it open, and peers inside. He pulls out a copy of a letter, passes it over, snaps the briefcase closed, and stows it back under the desk. "Get an eyeful of that!" Rotten quality, the Xerox of a fax. "Hang on to it, Chancey. I have a copy."

He fingers the paper.

AUSIMPAIR
THE AUSTRALIAN INSTITUTE for the
MANUFACTURE of PROSTHETIC
APPARATUS and IMPAIRMENT REMEDIES
chartered by government decree
2305 Government Drive, Canberra
Australian Capital Territory

Mr. Richard Brittle
New South Wales Manager
Haste & Company
Golden Ring House, Sydney

Dear Mr. Brittle,

I am writing to confirm our recent discussions that::

· Fuller Fyfe will lead recruitment assignments to result in the appointment of a chief operating officer, a marketing officer, and a production manager for AUSIMPAIR.

· The successful appointees will likely come from Australia, but we will be prepared to search abroad.

Fees will be solely on a retainer basis and at the rates and arrangements discussed elsewhere.

Yours faithfully,

Robert E. Ballast

Managing Director

"Well it looks like nice business for Brittle in Sydney, Fuller. I'm surprised he hasn't mentioned it. But where do you fit it? I mean how could you possibly handle it from London? And, who the hell is AUSIMPAIR? And why're they nominating you to handle the work, anyway?"

Fuller perks semicockily but still looks shifty. "I once went out of my way to place the managing director and he never forgot the service I gave him."

Who's he talking about? Revisit that signature: Robert E. Ballast. "Not *Bob* Ballast! Not the quadriplegic."

"Yeah, Bob Ballast. He used to be a DeadBeat Quadriplegic. Our only DBQ in fact." He grins. "But then he recently fell on his feet." He steeples his pudgy fingertips. "The government advertised for a chief for AUSIMPAIR. Had to be significantly impaired. There weren't too many replies. And, as you can imagine, Bob had fewer limbs and more business experience than anyone."

"A lot more experience, I imagine. Got fired from a whole string of jobs. No one picked up on that?"

Fuller smiles proudly. "Well, of course, I wrote a very nice reference for him, too. I mentioned how well I knew him as a result of my earlier in-depth interviews and reference checking."

"Not on Haste and Company stationery, I hope?"

"Only good can come of it, Chancey. I thought he might just come back as a client." He smiles wanly. "I mean what goes around comes around. Anyway, it's all water under the bridge now." Fuller's almost got a Jesus-thing going with those outstretched, upward-facing pink palms. "I mean, Bob's got the job!" His eyes twinkle. "So he's in charge of all AUSIMPAIR recruitment." He's suddenly misting. "And Bob remembered me." He points to his heart, and his lower lip quivers. "He wants to work with me." Triumphant smile. "Exclusively." The handkerchief again. A rather forceful honk this time. "I called him. Said I'd get back to Sydney in time to handle this." He tucks the gooey linen back into his pocket, glances to the window, then looks back, coyly. "He might also want me to do some discreet poking around in the market here." Now he's beaming proudly. "They're also going to need maybe a couple of hundred physically challenged factory operatives"

"Shop-floor stuff? And they all have to be impaired?"

Fuller's smile disappears. "Physically challenged. Impaired. Maimed. That's what the charter calls for."

"Oh, shit, Fuller—do we even want to touch that work?"

Fuller's moved to hurt-and-miffed mode. "I'd have thought that you of all people, Chancey, would show a little more empathy and understanding." He pauses, then smiles impishly. "Anyway, they don't need to be total fuck-ups. Just a limb or two missing. Or eyes. Blindness and deafness are also acceptable. Maybe even stuttering if it's severe enough."

"Oh, shit."

"Legally we have to look in Aussie first. But I'm gonna try to talk them into fishing in the UK. I could nick back over here and close it out real fast." He beams. "There're a ton of them here, Chancey. All those thalidomide fuck-ups—"

"That's the sort of work Brittle wants?"

"It's fast money."

"Let me get this straight now: you want to go back to Sydney? And what about Brittle? Is he happy about that?"

"It's only for a stint. A month or two. And Richard's delighted. It'll be like old times."

"Oh, hell, Fuller. You say you're not going to address your drinking problem. Instead, you'll fly back to Sydney to help Brittle place a raft of shop-floor impedimentias with Bob Ballast?"

Fuller blanches. "I don't know, Chancey. Don't you think, really, when you get right down to it"—the tone's earnest, inquiring—"that every candidate we ever see is some kind of quadriplegic? Not just Bob Ballast. I mean the moment you clap eyes on him everything's out in the open. Not so with the others. They can walk and run and tap dance. But when it comes time for us to place them in jobs, well, then, if you ask me, they're all some kind of quadriplegic. I mean, they're all helpless and hopeless and hiding their problems.

"I look across my desk, and all I ever seem to see is some unhappy fucker who can't get a job because his thinking's all screwed up. I know you say that we're making a difference in people's lives, but, honestly, Chancey, is all the effort really worth it? Really? I mean, in this business you're only as good as your last placement. Nothing leads anywhere. You have to find some other DBQ to stuff into some other job somewhere else—probably working for some *other* DBQ. I mean, really, who's to say that Hank Van Epenheusen was less of a DBQ than Bob Ballast? I bet, if you think about it, you're probably working with some kind of DBQ in New York right now. Trouble is, Chancey, we're in a job where it's impossible to be truthful. If we ever told the truth we'd never make a placement. Not ever. It might be better, if you ask me, only to deal with the real Bob Ballasts. That way you're not kidding yourself. I mean, the walking DBQs are infinitely worse. Don't you think, Chancey? I mean, really, don't you?"

That's pure Fuller. Crass on one level, caring on another. So what's the answer? Can there be one? Maybe.

"What I think, Fuller, is that what we see is a function of who we are." Fuller's eyes are wide. "What we see are fallible human beings. We kid about them being DB this or that, but only to mask the pain, theirs and ours. But if we do our jobs right and place them into roles that match their talents and dreams, then we really do make a difference, both in their lives and in our own. We're going to fail along the way, too, of course. And, yeah, telling the truth's a luxury. Ask Crawley. He says he can't even tell the truth in his novel. But if we get our thinking straight, if we really understand what we're trying to do, then we become better people, too. I think, with any luck, that's where it's all leading, Fuller." He's crossed his arms—doesn't want to listen.

"I also happen to think that you're depressed, Fuller." Best take a quick stroll to ensure there's no one in reception. No—and the secretary's leaving now, too, a touch earlier than usual, as instructed. Fuller's eyes are waiting as he turns. "And so am I." Fuller's trying to stare him down. "Because I've got to deal with this mess you've created here." Fuller's eyes tighten. "What you do outside the office *is* your business, Fuller. But you simply must get a handle on your drinking problem, it's affecting everything."

"I *don't* have a problem."

"Then why not take the pledge?"

"You want me to swear off?"

"You need professional help—"

"You're talking *AA*—all that shit?"

"Only if you want to stay working here. Or anywhere."

"Is that an ultimatum, Chancey?" Fuller glares angrily. "You're giving an ultimatum to me. Me? I can't believe I'm hearing this. Look"—Fuller's face's florid, but the enunciation's paced—"*I don't have a fucking drinking problem.* I can take it or leave it."

"But you just don't want to stop—"

"That's right! And that's *my* decision. It's got absolutely nothing to do with you or this firm!"

"That's not quite true, Fuller, the auditor says things aren't right." Silence. "So unless you can explain the phantom placements"—let that sink in—"or get on the wagon, then we're at the end of the line."

"Phantom placements?" Fuller blinks. And now he's hyperventilating. "Well—I— let me say right away, that, ah, the, ah, *prospects* were there. And I was focusing on the Sydney thing with Bob and Richard."

"Prospects aren't reality, Fuller—and screw Bob and Richard. Why Brittle didn't mention AUSIMPAIR is beyond me, but that's all a red herring, anyway. I'd like you to finish up, Fuller."

"But, Chancey, I—"

"Right now"—show him the severance check—"this'll pay off your creditors and buy you some time to think. Meantime, I'll need the office keys."

Fuller sullenly extracts a key ring from his trouser pocket. He unfastens two keys, passes them across with one hand, and clamps onto the check with the other. Now he grabs his coat. "Can I keep my BMW?"

"Since you're no longer insured that won't be possible."

Out they go, through the empty reception area and into the tiny empty hallway foyer opposite the ornate, polished-brass, cage-elevator shaft. Fuller sneaks a peek at the check before folding it into his wallet. Then he hits the elevator call button. The machinery grinds into gear. As the cage ascends, an oblong counterweight slithers down the elevator shaft like a giant, black beetle. Fuller glares.

"You think you're so smart, Chancey. Well, you'll get yours one day." The cage creaks slowly upward. "You say *I* have an alcohol problem. How hypocritical can you get? Are your distractions any different?" He gasps for air. "You're a DBQ, Chancey. You just run that bastard foot of yours all over the world trying to prove you're not a withered cretin."

The cage shudders to a halt. Fuller releases the lattice-iron door then turns. His backside's to the cage, and his eyes are blazing. "Do you think people don't know what you're doing? Do you think they don't know that you'd die without the oxygen of publicity, praise, and pussy?" Foam's in the corners of his mouth. "You think they don't know you've been desperately fucking that little piece of Limey pussy you think you're hiding? The one you sailed to Cockatoo Island. Oh, yes, she's seen a cock-or-two, no worries." He strides into the cage, turns, crashes the gates closed, stares back through the iron lattice, then smirks. "Well, ha fucking ha. Because no amount of neurotic globe-trotting's gonna change a goddamned thing."

He whacks the DOWN button. His head rocks as the cage jerks into a slow-motion, whirring descent. He's suddenly gazing upward. "You'll always be a little man attached to the business end of a repulsive stump." Spittle flies from his mouth. A couple of blobs clear the latticework and settle on the impediment.

"Oh, *sheeee—-iiii—ttttt!*" Fuller hits the PANIC button. Brakes screech, the black beetle clamps onto its oily track, and the cage lurches, then abruptly stops, aligning Fuller's eyes with the spittled impediment. "My *briefcase!* My *things*! I left *everything!*"

The bloodshot eyes are upturned. *"Everything!"* He sounds incredibly distressed. "I'll have to go back, Chancey!" And whiny. Very whiny. Altogether too whiny. Even for all this. Why would that be? Trap him and find out. Suspend him in no-man's-land by grabbing the outer cage door handle and sliding the cage door open an inch or so, thereby abruptly aborting his descent.

"Oh, Christ, Chancey, now you've fucked up the elevator!" He's utterly pissed. "Now it's *stuck!*"

"Just hang on a minute, Fuller. I'll go back and get your briefcase."

"No! No! *I'll* get it." He rattles the cage. "*I'll* get it! *I'll* get it!"

But he'll never slip that steel cocoon.

The voice fades to a whimper. He strides back into the offices, reaches under Fuller's desk, grabs the briefcase, dumps it on the desk, snaps it open, and peers inside. The *Times* and *Telegraph*. He lays them on the desk. A faded hardcover copy of *How I Raised Myself from Failure to Success in Selling*. A subscription copy of *Penthouse*. A bundle of expense vouchers. Fuller's still whining in the distance. He riffles through the vouchers. Outrageously expensive but nothing out of order. The stub of a theater ticket. A bunch of unused Concorde luggage tags. A sleek, sterling-silver hip flask. He holds the vessel to his ear and shakes it. Empty. And a manila file. He opens the file. There's a fax of Ballast's letter. And, what's this? Even more faxes. This time from Brittle. And a handwritten note:

> Dear Fuller:
>
> I'm enclosing the note from Bob. I spoke to him. As long as we pay him the one-third commission he'll push all the work to Brittle, Fyfe & Co.—

including, if all goes well, the UK thalidomide roundup. I've arranged accommodation offices for us at the MLC center. I'm enclosing a business plan. We'll shoot for the MBA market. Keep the riffraff out of the office. Some initial assignments will likely be beneath our talents, but, as you perceptively say, let's stick a few downmarket bums on seats to pay the rent.

       I'm also enclosing a draft letter that I'll immediately send to the Haste & Co. client list. We should pick up some other clients from this. I'll tell Rumpelstiltskin I'm quitting in a couple of weeks and be gone the same day. He won't realize what's happened till we're up and running.

       Best, Dick

P.S. I can't begin to say how much I'm looking forward to working with you again. It was a bad day, indeed, when Bigfoot split our winning team.

The hypocrite! No ethical problem with kickbacks. Still on the payroll and no problem with the clandestine poaching of Bigfoot's clients, either. Well, at least he'll screw Fuller too. And what's this?

> Dear [Prospect]:
> DRAFT
>   I am writing to advise you that Fuller Fyfe and I will shortly be establishing our own exclusive executive search firm.
>   As you know, I have been manager of Haste & Co for the past three years, a role in which I oversaw local operations and personally handled the most senior assignments. Fuller Fyfe will be returning from London to join me. Fuller and I were the senior Australian team members before his temporary posting to London, where he established the Haste & Co. office.
>   Our decision to establish our own firm is in recognition that we can provide a more effective service, working to the highest ethical standards at a significantly lower cost when operating on our own account.

```
        My leaving is entirely amicable, so until
the end of the month, I can be contacted at
Haste & Co. offices.
        We welcome the opportunity to work with
you and your organization in the future, and
I'm planning to call you over the coming days
to discuss any upcoming needs. Meantime,
please don't hesitate to contact us if we can
be of assistance.
        Yours sincerely,
        Richard Brittle
        Senior Partner / Brittle, Fyfe & Co.
```

"Help! Help!"

Fuller's whines are sounding weaker. The bulk of the other papers is the Haste and Company client and prospect list. The nerve of this ninny. The sheer, unmitigated gall! Talk about putting in the slipper. The Janus-faced fool is maligning Haste & Co quality, ethics, and fees even though it's he who's been responsible for all of the above. And what gross stupidity—the dimwit's put it all in writing. He'll never be able to explain this in court. He'll be a laughing stock.

He slips the papers through Fuller's copier, slides the originals back into the file, and the file back into the briefcase. Such an elegant attaché for such graceless documents.

"Help! Help!"

Still going. He grabs the phone and dials.

The voice's bleary and peeved. "It's two in the morning, mate." But it is, indeed, the distinctive Down Under voice of the local Haste and Company lawyer. "I mean, fair go, mate, a man needs to sleep sometime."

"Fire Brittle for me, would you?"

"Oh, Christ—is that you, Chancey?"

"Get him out of the office. Right away."

"Got it loud and clear, Chancey. What'd he do, steal the company secrets?"

"Something like that. Walk him to the door and change the locks. Tell him it's for cause. He won't argue. Tell him the check's in the mail. You're in charge till I call—oh, shit! What the hell! I'm hearing alarm bells! They're shaking the whole building. Fuller must've hit the emergency button. I've got to run. I'm in London if you need me."

He drops the phone, grabs the satchel, rips Fuller's degree certificate from the wall, and strides to the elevator.

By the sound of those voices a gaggle of rubberneckers has gathered on the ground floor. He slides the outer cage door wide open. Fuller's bloodshot eyes peer up through a four-inch slit. Don Giovanni on the way to hell? Orpheus heading for the underworld?

The scent of fury, sweat, halitosis, and deodorant assails his nostrils as he kneels to proffer the attaché. Fuller releases the alarm. Silence at last.

Let both Fuller and Brittle find out tomorrow. Innocent smile. "I found it, Fuller." The briefcase navigates the narrow gap and falls into Fuller's stubby, outstretched fingers. The degree certificate, too.

"If there's anything else, we'll send it on." Fuller's eyes catch his as he closes the cage door. "And good luck."

Fuller stabs the DOWN button. The elevator lurches back into life. The beetle slithers up the oily track. Then the entire mechanism grinds to a reverberating halt.

Fuller rattles the cage, rips open the doors, and clumps angrily out of the building.

Silence once more. Oh, how pleasant it is.

He produces a linen handkerchief from his vest pocket and removes Fuller's spittle from the customized black wing tip so skillfully crafted to disguise the deformity. Why is everybody suddenly so anxious to link their woes to the Chancian impediment. Is his foot really a bringer of grief? To Jill? Fuller? Brittle? Elan? To himself? Has his foot made the world an unhappier place?

Motivation has to come from somewhere, surely. Does it matter if it comes from a foot? Where do people get off blaming his foot—his enfeebled foot, for Chrissakes—for their screwups? The foot's *his* problem. Does a foot make him want to fall in love? Does his foot—his *foot*—make him yearn to fulfill his potential? Educate his kids? Experience the richness of life? Does a foot inspire awe at the ineffable beauty of a word, a line, a thought, a poem, a song, a smile, a person—whatever? Does a foot make people want to steal his clients and ideas, and set out secretly to sabotage him?

Maybe if other people had such a foot, they wouldn't do that. Maybe everyone should have such a foot . . .

The spittle's gone from the shoe, anyway. And the shine's burning brighter. He could see his face in that leather if he tried. There's a moral there somewhere.

Hey, there's the nagging beep of the fax machine. He strides back into the reception area, rips off the curling paper, and studies Crawley's neatnik handwriting.

> Chancey! Barabbas walks! The guilty go free. See what you make of this—a cat among the pigeons, a spanner in the works, a fox in the henhouse. Whatever! I'll call or fax you just as soon as I find out what's really going on—

His eye falls to the circle around the faxed "What's News" item from the *Wall Street Journal* front page.

> Harold Crumpet, chairman of the Crumpet Conglomerate, today announced acquisition of the controlling interest in Swedish Cruise Lines from prominent international investor Horst Everness. "I am proud to divulge assembly of this stupendous deal," said Mr. Crumpet: "It's a natural. SCL is a jewel that will fit right into the Crumpet crown. The synergy will be incredible. Horst Everness will remain as minority shareholder. Everybody's a winner. I will be appointing Jesse E. Green as chief executive. Jesse's a hospitality-industry dynamo. He'll do a terrific job. The new investors are all very excited."

And again, in Crawley's hand:

> Chancey:
> Just in! Rumor has it that Green slipped damaging confidential figures to Crumpet. Effectively set him up to steal control of SCL. Couldn't track down Everness. Secretary says he might be on his yacht, entertaining guests. Of the feline variety, apparently.

Of the feline variety. So, Everness's entertaining pussy. On his yacht. And where's Jill? But she wouldn't. Or would she? No, never. Then again what about that crack about silver-headed men in boxer shorts. And seeing someone. *Fidelity is a virtue peculiar to those about to be betrayed.* So she's about to betray him, if she hasn't already. And who could blame her? Everness fancies her, too, no doubt about that. So Everness is also about to betray him. And if Jackie Kennedy could go from a Greek god to a goddamned Greek, might Jill be any less choosy? And, let's be fair, compared to Onassis, Everness is Robert Redford. So call her. Call her now.

Her voice, as ever, is pure and bell-like: "We're away from the phone at the moment, but if you leave your name and your number we'll call you back. *Beeeeeep.*"

Spit it out, Chancey. Now.

"Hi, Jill, it's me, Chancey. I called to, uh, apologize. Yeah, you were right. I was going to see, uh, Elan. And then I, uh, did. And it's, uh, over. Yes, over. Really. You'll know it when I tell you why. You'll know I've always loved you. Not always as I should've. But I always did and I always will. I had to fire Fuller, so I'm picking up the pieces. Everything'll turn out right. I'll be back in a day or so. I'll call again. Soon. And I love you. And I know that you know that. I know that's why you didn't give me the, uh, shaft—a long, long time ago." *Beeeeep. Beeeeep.*

He's talking to the air. Vocalizing to space. Speaking to a spinning tapeworm. Communicating with no one.

He cradles the phone, rests one thigh on the edge of the desk, and gazes back over the murky Strand, just four floors below. The brakes of a bus sound in his ears. The street's alive with scurrying people. Everyone's in search of something. A meeting. A fortune. An assignation. Couples bob within the passing parade. Executives and sidekicks. Bosses and secretaries. Husbands and wives. Friends and lovers. A news vendor proffers a paper and finds a taker. A purchaser pockets his change and studies a story . . .

The phone bursts to life. Who'd be calling at the close of day? He grabs the handset.

"Chancey?"

Oh, no, it's Beryl. But what's she doing calling him in London? A jolt of adrenaline hits his stomach. But mask all apprehension.

"Beryl, how nice to hear from you. What's the good word?"

"You didn't hear?" She sounds distraught.

"Didn't hear what?"

"And you don't know anything, right?"

"You're talking in riddles, Beryl. What should I know that I don't?"

"A couple of things. Look, where's your office?"

"Palace end of the Strand."

"I'm fifteen minutes by tube. Can we meet? Somewhere private."

"There's a coffee shop downstairs, the Golden Bean."

"I know it, I'll see you in twenty minutes. Meantime, check out today's *Telegraph*—small item. Page eight, bottom left." She clicks off.

He cradles the phone, reaches for Fuller's *Telegraph*, and rips it open at page eight.

> GAY-BASHING IN EARLS COURT
> Two men were badly beaten in what appears to have been a "gay-bashing" incident outside Jackie's Place, a well-known Earls Court homosexual hangout. Police say a group of unidentified "skin-heads" attacked two males: a local twenty-year-old window-dresser and his companion, a fifty-year-old investor. Both victims were hospitalized. Their condition has not been advised, and their names have been withheld.

So? Gay bashing—such terrible, mindless violence, but why would Beryl want him to read about it? Maybe she's trying to say that he's been an emotional pugilist himself. And that perhaps he should grow up before he gets beaten up. She might have a point. He's certainly treated Jill cruelly and mindlessly. He can't fix everything at once, but he could at least send her that message right now. There's a florist downstairs, too. She'll have it all tomorrow. And he'll call her again, too. He tosses the paper onto the desk, reaches for a sheet of blank paper, and takes the pen in his hand.

You were just eighteen,
We rode upon the pike
A two-backed beast
On a leather-seated,
    750 cc
    chromium-plated
    bike

She'll remember that.

We vowed we'd love
Till eternity's swoon
And made gold-plated oaths
Beneath a crazy-round
    ever-smiling
    luminescent
    moon

She'll remember those promises, too.

But I descended to hell
Jumped in the fire
Ran off with the devil
And became a tinsel-tongued
    two-timing
    fast-talking
    liar

She'll agree. What else can he say?

Will you ever forgive,
Will your heart convalesce,
Now that I'm out of
This brain-clouding
    heart-breaking
    soul-numbing
    mess?

And, of course—

Hey, Jill,
Love you still,
Then and now
And always will

BERYL FAILS TO REMOVE THE KNOCKOFF Burberry
raincoat. "I can't stay for long, Chancey." Her heels are still too
high, her makeup too thick.
"The coffee's terrible, I've ordered tea." He grasps the plastic
handle on the chromiumed teapot. "Here, let me pour."
She produces a pack of Virginia Slims. "Mind if I smoke?"
She lights up and draws heavily. The tip glows. "You read the piece?"
She directs the used fumes to the side of his ear.
"Yeah—gay bashing, right? So depressing." He pauses. "But I
imagine you must've asked me to read it for a reason."
She nods. "You didn't recognize anyone, did you, Chancey?"
"Should I have?"
She leans forward. "The investor who got beaten up was
Grisham Pryce."
"Grisham?"
"And his boyfriend, too, of course. One of them, anyway."
"Grisham's gay?"
"He was usually very discreet."
"Does Elan know?"
"She knew about Grisham. Kind of, anyway. She didn't much
seem to care." She sips from her gilt-rimmed, pastel-blue teacup—
then shoots him a hard look. "Elan's missing!"
"Missing?" His stomach churns. "She's missing?"
"She got some bad news yesterday, Chancey." She pauses.
"After she left you."
"She told you about that?"
"Not till afterward. She wouldn't have, but—"
"But?"
"She went to the doctor." She sets her cup down. "He told
her."
"That Grisham got beaten up?"

"No, he didn't know that. Nobody knew that it was Grisham. It was all hushed up."

"What'd he tell her?"

"He should've told her when Grisham was on hand. Someone should've been there. She wasn't well. She was sick. You know?"

"Should've told her *what?*"

"That she was sick."

"She indicated that she was a little on edge, a touch rundown maybe."

"She didn't know how unwell she was, Chancey. Look, Chancey. She's really sick."

"How bad is it?"

"It's very bad, Chancey. Apparently she's had it for some time. Nobody knew what it was."

"It?"

"Apparently she's picked up some nasty new, sexually transmitted bug. Nobody quite knows what it is. They say it mostly affects poofs. It's really nasty."

"How nasty?"

She pauses, inhales, slowly puffs, then locks on squarely. "They die, Chancey."

"Elan'll die?" His head swims. "She was only just getting it all together."

"She might not die. Nobody knows for sure. I'm not really supposed to talk to anybody about it." She tilts her head and releases a cloud of smoke upward. "The doctor didn't tell her she'd die. Not for sure, anyway. But he might as well've."

"What do you mean?"

"He told her she'd have to, ah, terminate."

"The pregnancy? The doctor told her she'd have to *abort?*"

"Yeah. Said the kid'd likely never live, or come out funny, you know. Said pregnancy'd put her at risk, too." The smoke settles into her veil of hair spray. "Can you believe it? Someone should've been on hand for her. I mean she was sick. Not just physically. She wasn't right. You know?"

They're both breathing deeply. "How'd she take it?"

"She called me, Chancey. Sounded very calm. I was surprised actually."

"Where'd she call from?"

"Doctor's office. Apparently he'd sedated her. Something light. Intended for her to go straight to the hospital. Someone was going to drive her. The doctor left the room and got on the phone to hunt down Grisham. He didn't know about Grisham. Or his most recent problem. No one could find him. That was when she phoned me."

"What'd she say?"

"She was very calm. She said she'd never abort. Not again. She told me she met with you, Chancey, that you talked. She didn't say what about, though."

"Then—"

"I got the impression she was going back to Coldridge Manor and get her head together."

"What did she actually say?"

"She muttered something about going back to check her reflection in the mirror."

"In the mirror?"

"Yeah. In the looking glass, actually—same thing but more poetic. She was always going in for that sort of thing."

"Then—"

"Then she just hung up the phone." Beryl raises her eyebrows and turns her palms to the air. "And then she vanished."

"Vanished?"

"The doctor came back and she was gone. She apparently strolled out the back door, got into what she calls her time machine"—she looks at him knowingly—"and blazed off into the sunset. She had some credit cards. She could be anywhere."

"But nobody's seen her?"

"As far as I know. That was yesterday. As of now, her whereabouts are a mystery, to me, anyway. And inquiries are being made. You might get a call yourself. You might want to beat them to it."

"Beat them to it?"

"The doc got spooked and notified the police." She stands, and extracts a final puff from the remains of her cigarette. "They might just call you"—she stubs the butt—"I don't know." She smiles briefly, waves a hurried good-bye, and heads for the door.

A residue of smoke and nicotine rises into his nostrils.

Vanished? Nobody just vanishes. People in crisis return to a safe place. Or regress to a happier state. Maybe she's cocooned in that so-called country cottage sans phone. Perhaps Grisham knows more than he's telling. But if the police ever need a statement from Mr. Chandler Haste, he'll tell the truth. Yes, Elan was a friend, and, no, he has absolutely no idea of her whereabouts. Yes, a close friend. Intimate? Well, if you really must know, yes, way, way back in the past, we were briefly lovers. Well, it seemed brief. Yes, I met her a couple of times recently. I needed to get her out of my heart and my brain. Look, here's the problem, Officer, she was an illusion. I imagined her to be the perfect woman. Yes, I realize that Grisham Pryce probably felt the same way . . .

In fact, there'll be no such interrogation. Elan'll simply reappear from some kind of sanctuary, and everyone'll shuffle onward. Isn't that what always happens? So put it to rest. It's been a traumatic day, and what he really needs right now is a light supper in his room, and a good stiff nightcap.

THREE IN THE MORNING, YET AGAIN. To sleep or not to sleep?—that's the question. The plane home isn't leaving till afternoon, so why not pop the pill?

> Bring me slumber
> Golden biscuit
> Rest my aching eyes
> Steal my mind
> For your sweet pleasure
> This I thee entice

But, oh, Christ, who the hell can suddenly be knocking so insistently? He slips from the bed, cracks the door, and peers out into to the corridor. But there is no corridor, only the iron gates to Crystal Pond—and a throng of surly Coldridge Villagers behind a black-robed judge.

"You're under arrest," barks the judge.

A villager steps forward with a set of leg irons. They'll not shackle the impediment, surely. But, yes, the insensitive bastards have done just that. They lead him to a giant timber seesaw at the lake's edge. Three burly locals fasten him onto one end of the ugly contraption, then, using a thick hemp rope attached to the other, spin him out over the moonlit water, hoisting him high into the air in the process.

The judge steps forward, holding a prayer missal in one hand and a red flag in the other. "Where is the Honorable Elan Haverford?" he demands.

"I do not know, Your Honor."

"And you swear that upon your oath as member of the British Empire?"

"I do."

The judicial pause is brief. "Then I hereby find you guilty of lying"—the crowd murmurs approvingly—"and order you immersed in the waters of Crystal Pond to refresh your memory." He raises the flag above his head. "You have five seconds to revise your answer."

From this height the water looks colder and deeper than the judge's eyes. It's so unfair, how can he enlighten anyone when he knows nothing? Enlightenment—that's the effect the emerging moon is having on the lake. Crystal Pond suddenly seems like a huge looking glass—*another world, a peace-filled place where deepest longings are fulfilled.*

He knows! An embryonic cry forms in this throat. He knows! He tries to shout but nothing comes. He knows! He shakes his head wildly and rattles his shackles. He knows! A terrible knot forms in his stomach.

The judge peers upward, seeming to realize that the called-for revision is imminent. The magisterial lip curls into a sneer. "Too late, Mister Haste." He drops the flag, thereby signaling the villagers to release the ugly cord and plunge their hapless victim toward the cold and cruel waters of Crystal Pond. "Once a liar, always a liar."

22

Angels and Insects

H E KNEW HE'D BE TOO LATE. He brings the Rover to rest just inside the gates to Crystal Pond. The dream was clear—clear as crystal—but he simply had to see it for himself. He glances at the Rover clock. Quarter to three in the afternoon already. That yellow pill proved an all-too-diligent jailer. He cracks the door and steps out into light mist. The rain's holding off, but only just. The wing tips trail peg-leg impressions in the damp dirt path. He strides the two hundred or so yards to the lake. The leafy trees that filtered yesterday's morning light are damp and lifeless.

A battered black bicycle leans against the bench overlooking the lake. The grassy mound in front is deeply tire-marked. He approaches a youthful wispy-mustached, blue-shirted bobby reading the local paper.

"Something happened here?"

The bobby peers over the top of the paper.

"I guess the whole village knows by now. It was a local lassie. Grisham Pryce's wife—attractive but quirky. She drove into the lake. Didn't have a chance." He pauses. "I didn't quite catch your name, sir."

"Chandler Haste—a friend of, uh, Henry Haverford."

"Yes, of course, sir, Lord Haverford." He folds the paper neatly, tucks it like a baton under his arm, and turns his eyes to a muddy swath of tire marks. "The water falls off very quickly. She drowned in fifteen feet. It happened yesterday, at dusk, apparently. They got her body out very late in the evening."

The murky water refuses to reveal anything or to reflect anything. He feels incredibly sick. He might throw up. Perhaps it's just another of his nightmares. Perhaps he'll wake up.

"Nothing to see there, sir. They towed the car, as you can see from the terrible mess they made of this grass."

The bobby glances over his shoulder, then half turns. "She started from back there." He points to a weeping willow upon a slight incline, fifty yards or so back from the lake. "Picked up quite a head of speed, I gather. I was there when the vehicle came up. And when they, ah, pulled her out. Lovely lassie. Still was, despite the cold and all. They wrapped her in blankets and rushed her off in an ambulance. But too late, of course." He pauses. "Nice vehicle, a classic Jag, actually. She was always gadding about the village in it. They say she called it her time machine." He spots a line of ducks paddling across the water. "Very apt, if you ask me."

"It was, uh—"

"An accident? People say so, sir." The voice drops. "Nobody wants to suggest—"

"Suicide?" The word steals reverently from his tongue. He tries to hear her voice—the lilt—but only silence . . . He runs her words inside his brain: *Yeah, we'll meet again. On the other side of the looking glass, maybe.*

The bobby nods "Looks a bit like that, I suppose. Car was going pretty fast, apparently. Some people say she was, well, ah, the word they use is *unhappy.*"

No geese are hovering over that lake today. None. Maybe the bobby's just a figment of his imagination. Maybe the fellow will vanish. Maybe Elan'll come strolling down the path, skipping in her black skirt and leather jacket, tilting a headful of silky, cinnamon hair. She'll grin the widest of grins and put her long, slim fingers to a lithe, cocked hip. Then she'll bump-bump and choo-choo, and sing. He glances in that direction. Nothing. No one. Dusk is falling. No birds are singing. *The world won't go away. You'll go away.* But the bobby's not gone.

"The surmise, sir, is that it took some time. Quarter of an hour or so, maybe longer. Diver said there was an air bubble in the car, you know. I hope she didn't change her mind."

Twixt the stirrup and the ground—

Drizzle hits the trees. Rain specks pock the lake surface. The damp earth sends up a musky scent. A puff of air ruffles the leaves. He feels it on his cheek. Raindrops tap the shoulders of his cashmere jacket. Perhaps she'll be waiting just outside the gate. In the time machine.

"Drizzle's getting pretty heavy, sir. Might as well pack it in. Nothing to see here now." He glances down at the impediment, then produces a faded black umbrella. "I'll walk you to your car, sir."

The bobby shelters him with the umbrella as he slips into the Rover and winds down the window.

"Thanks for the briefing, officer."

The mustache is suddenly at the level of the window. "Funeral's at eleven tomorrow morning, sir. Not wasting any time. It's already in the afternoon paper." He produces the newspaper and taps his forefinger to a circled item within the births, marriages and death's column:

> PRYCE—Elan. 1 August 1955—25 April 1980. Beloved
> wife of the Hon Grisham Pryce of London and Coldridge
> Village. Survived by her parents, Lord and Lady Haverford
> of Corfe and Sydney, Australia; and her siblings, Elizabeth,
> Anne, and James. She wore the rose of youth upon
> her. Private Service. Coldridge Village.

"Hey, thanks again. I see no mention of the venue."

"Saint Barts, of course, sir, where else?"

The engine purrs and the bobby fades into posterity as the Rover rolls out onto the road.

So, what to do? He feels too rotten to drive, and, anyway, there's no way to catch a plane to New York tonight, so stay right here and make a couple of calls. And, though the funeral's private, it might just be okay to hover quietly in the back of the church, so think about that, too.

The Hero & Leander proprietrix assigns him the same room. He grabs the phone. Jill's not there, again, just that wretched answering machine.

"I'm in Coldridge, England, Jilly, staying at the Hero and Leander. There was, uh, a tragic accident here while I was in London. Elan died." Hold the voice steady. "The funeral's tomorrow. I can't make a connection back to New York today so I might attend. I can understand you might not want to join me, but if you feel up to it, call me here. I love you, Jilly."

He feels washed out, but life must go on. He dials again.

"I fired Fuller, Crawley."

"There was no alternative. Where are you now."

"In Coldridge Village. The Haverford girl suffered a tragedy."

"A tragedy?"

"She died in her car. It happened last night, apparently. I drove down today. I'm at the Hero and Leander Inn. I might attend the funeral."

"The funeral." Crawley pauses. "They say we can survive everything except death, Chancey."

"I'll fill you in on the details when I get back. Any further news on Green or Everness?"

"Not yet. But I'm watching closely. I'll keep you posted."

He cradles the clunky phone. Dusk seems to be falling on the other side of that window. He checks his watch: 6 P.M. already. He feels both drained and restless. It would a relief to weep but the tears seem locked en route to his eyes. He needs some air and some exercise. He tucks the complimentary Hero & Leander notepad into his vest pocket and heads out the door.

He's traversed this road before, but this'll be the first time he's turned down the meandering country lane that leads toward those beckoning headstones. There'll be no better place to collect his thoughts.

Or so one would think. In fact, a rhythmic scraping seems to be emanating from the earth itself. He treads softly between the graves in the direction of the offending resonance.

"Looking for anyone in particular, sir?"

The voice, laden with the local accent, is coming from the level of his feet. It's the local gravedigger, apparently, hard at work within a five-foot trench. A neat mound of clay has been amassed on one side of the pit, and a rickety ladder lies alongside the other. The fellow's sweaty, weathered face is peering upward, seeking an appropriate answer, no doubt.

"I was looking for a place to sit and write a poem, actually."

"Something to immortalize someone, sir?" The breathing's heavy, the tone genial.

"Myself, maybe."

"That might present an immediate problem, sir"—he leans on his battered shovel—"for the first requirement of immortality is death"—he smiles, wearily—"and since dying is a very dull, dreary affair, my advice to you is to have nothing whatever to do with it."

"I'm not sure that option's open to me."

"Oh, don't say that, sir. You're a young man, and every young person is immortal for a limited time."

"That's a lovely thought—and more apt than you might appreciate. Maybe I'll quote you."

"No point immortalizing me, sir"—he tosses his shovel up out of the pit, pulls down the ladder, and proceeds to climb out— "I don't believe in an afterlife."

"So what's it all about, then?"

The fellow steps off the ladder, kicks each foot against the grass in a vain attempt to dislodge the dank clay that's clinging to his boots, then clasps his hands behind his back and stretches his shoulders backward. "I say there's no cure for birth and death, sir, save to enjoy the interval."

"And the prospect of dying doesn't bother you?"

"I wouldn't mind dying—it's having to stay dead that could be bothersome."

"Yet some people say they welcome death."

"Those who say that have typically only tried it from the ears up." He casts his eye over the trench. The dark shadow within the neat but muddy walls contrasts sharply with the lush green grass around it. "Though that remark might not apply to the poor soul they'll be consigning to this particular trench tomorrow."

"Tomorrow?"

"I'm afraid so. Grisham Pryce's young lady, don't you know. God only knows what her philosophy might have been." The voice softens. "I suppose if all else fails, immortality can always be assured by spectacular error." He recovers the ladder, hoists it to his shoulder, then tucks the shovel under his arm. "But let me leave you to pen your rhyme in peace, sir." He disappears into the dusk.

Solitude at last. And, so, this quaint garden of souls is to be her resting place. He'd suspected as much. The air is fresh, and laden with the scent of wildflowers. He seats himself on a stone bench, feels his eyes return to the open wound within the grass, and reflexively extracts pen and pad from his pocket. Words, words, words—poets are merely their slaves. So what will the words say then? The trick is to hold the pen above the paper and watch, for the best kinds of words, like elves, appear in their own good time.

This be the verse where you grieve for me . . .

A beautiful line, but plagiarism will be unacceptable, Mr. Elf. Well, to be fair, that was not such a gnome, but merely a feeble effort to tempt one into peeping forth, which might just be happening . . .

The moon with silver-sandaled feet . . .

Pretty good, but Wilde holds the patent.

So what kind of undying sentiment might *you* like to share, Chancey? What's the message? Oh, please, no messages. Feelings will suffice. But what *is* he feeling? Nothing. He's benumbed and mute. And nothing comes from nothing. And there's surely yet another reason why the elves are refusing to come out and play. This surreal cemetery is altogether too precious: the pastel moon is too prescient, the flowers too dainty, the scene too self-consciously coquettish. No wonder that even the sullen pit itself is refusing to yield a single secret. No wonder he can't tempt even the image of Elan into his own consciousness. So there'll be neither a caprice, nor a conceit, nor a poem, nor even a tear, tonight. Just about the only thing he can feel right now is a leaden weight in the cavity that formerly harbored his heart. And, now, all of a sudden, there's a chill in the air—

"You're Mister Chandler Haste, right?" That brusque, startling voice belongs to a bulky figure that seems to have stepped straight out of the dusk.

"Yes"—he returns the pad and pen to his pocket and stands— "and you're . . ."

"Boyle Pryce, Grisham's brother."

Of course—the fellow's heavier than Grisham, the abundant crop of hair is jet black, the complexion and the features are coarser, but the resemblance is plain.

The extended palm is tough, the grip strong, the voice unrefined. "I gather you heard about the accident." The eyes're beady and bloodshot.

"Yes—so very tragic. A friend of Elan's left the news with my London office. I happened to be there, so I took it on myself to drive down. It seemed the right thing."

"I'm sure it was, Mister Haste."

"Call me Chancey, please."

Boyle extracts a cigar stub—the better part of half a cigar, actually—from his handkerchief pocket. "News travels fast in a small village, Chancey." He rolls the stub with thick, well-practiced fingers. "When Grisham heard that a Mister Chandler Haste had visited the scene of the accident, he sent me to say that he'd like you to come to the funeral."

"How'd you find me?"

"Like I said, it's a tiny village. The woman who runs the Hero and Leander used to work at the manor, so I checked with her." He pushes the saliva-stained end of the cigar into his mouth. "When she said you'd gone for a stroll I suspected you might come here." He sets a match to the ashen tip and puffs, raising a reluctant glow. "I mean you know about the funeral, right?"

"Someone mentioned eleven tomorrow at Saint Bartholomew's—but I wouldn't want to intrude."

"Oh, you won't be imposing"—fumes waft from his coarse lips—"Grisham was very clear about that." He pauses. "I gather you and Elan were good friends."

Good friends? Ah, yes, my comrade, we were very good friends, loving friends—intimate friends. We maintained a blissful, clandestine relationship for years.

"I'm probably better described as a friend of the family." Now there's a lovely noble lie. "Henry brought her along to a couple of meetings. When she later passed through Sydney my wife and I took her sailing. And, then, of course, we all caught up again in New York, last week." He pauses. "I imagine Henry and Mildred will be attending the funeral."

"Yes—the news came on the eve of their departure for Sydney. They took it badly, as you might expect. The rest of the family is flying in, too." He tosses the cigar butt to the grass—not quite tasty enough, apparently—and crushes it with his heavy shoe. "I have my car, can I offer you a ride back to the inn?"

"Thanks, but I'm still getting over a touch of jet lag so I need the walk."

"Enjoy the country air, then, Chancey." Boyle steps away, then halts. "You'll come to the reception after the funeral, too, of course. Since you're a longtime friend of the family everyone will be looking forward to catching up with you, I'm sure." The dusk reclaims him.

So that was Grisham's brother, not exactly Mr. Charm. And his presence seems to have chased the moon from the sky. Maybe this trek to Coldridge was a touch inappropriate. It kind of feels that way. Or is this queasiness mere guilt? If so, a good night's rest at the Hero & Leander might ease it. So quit this lonely place right now—without looking back, please.

ELAN'S SINKING INTO BLOODY quicksand on a cliff-backed beach. He races to her in a landing boat. He jumps ashore and dashes up the beach. He arrives too late, the mud has already closed over her head. A burst of gunfire sounds in the distance. A firing squad's on the cliff. Bullets plow into his army tunic. He turns to run, but his legs become bayonets.

He wakens to the sound of footsteps in the corridor. Eight in the morning says the bedside clock. Someone's sliding something under the bedroom door. He slips from the bed, grabs an envelope from the floor, and rips it open. It's a fax from Crawley—came in late last night, apparently:

> Jesse Green called. Vital, he says, that he talk to you. Insists you call him on the enclosed Manhattan number anytime after eight in the morning, New York time.

Doesn't sound like good news, but in a couple of hours he'll know for sure. He'll call Jill then, too—but, hey, who's that ringing on the phone, right now?

"I heard you came down, Chancey." It's Henry Haverford, and his voice is strained. "I'm so very glad."

"I don't know what to say, Henry."

"Say nothing—words are useless. But you must come to the funeral."

"Grisham's brother already asked me, but I'm still a touch unsure."

"Come, please—and to the reception after. You really must." The voice cracks. "I'll see you at Saint Bartholomew's Church, then. It's on the main road in the village, just across the bridge, a short and pretty stroll—assuming you feel up to that, of course."

"I'll be there, Henry."

COBBLESTONE STREETS ARE QUAINT but intrinsically treacherous, especially for anyone with a gammy foot. He paces gingerly down the mostly deserted street leading to the bridge. A stray brown, shorthaired mutt briefly pads beside him, then meanders up a side street. He stops midway and sights, in the distance, the white spire of a church, presumably St. Bart's. Pastel single-story storefronts, a couple of them thatched, line the way. A sparkling black car with a cargo of somber passengers—mourners, maybe—eases past him.

He suddenly catches, in his peripheral vision— the image of— Elan! How can that be? He turns. Fading gilt letters above a musty store window proclaim B-O-O-K-S.

He crosses the street and stares into the window, the centerpiece of which is a black-ribboned, silver-framed, monochrome head-shot. Elan's face, sunglasses hoisted above her head, looks out at him. Natural smile. Wide, clear, bright eyes. Innocent, vulnerable mouth. Perfect teeth. The image is outlined by a car window. The time machine. Maybe Elan's been studying his reflection, too. Now he's on one side of a window. And she, doubly trapped within a second sheet of glass, is on the other. An exotic fish within an aquarium? A lifeless butterfly pinned within a box?

A sixty-something black-frocked figure steps out of a shadow, startling him. The voice is thin, reedy. "Lovely likeness." She spins a pair of horn-rimmed, pince-nez spectacles in her red-nailed, bony hand.

"You knew her?" he asks.

"She was a customer and quickly became a friend. She often browsed."

"What'd she read?"

"A bit of everything. She collected some minor poets. Recently took to Sylvia Plath and Anne Sexton." She raises her eyebrows. "But her favorite was Shakespeare. Old editions." They study the image. "I took the photo myself. She was parked right out here. It's a tragedy about the accident."

He nods, sorrowfully.

She studies him closely. "You here for the funeral?" She glances downward for the briefest of moments.

"As it happens."

"You're Chandler Haste?"

"I guess I'm kind of, ah, conspicuous."

"No, but, well—" She's abashed. "Elan was here just before the, ah, accident. Left a wee package. She said she was off to keep a rendezvous but that you'd likely drop by to pick it up and that if you didn't come by, to mail it on to London. She left an address, and I taped it to the package. Just a minute." She disappears inside the store, then returns. She produces a carefully folded manila envelope. "There it is, see."

He takes the envelope and weighs it in his hand. His name's penciled on the front. Beryl's name and address are taped to the back. The handwriting's Elan's.

She glances over his head. "Village clock says eight to eleven. You'd best hurry. Go ahead. I'll close up and see you there."

He stands on the tiny, wisteria-wrapped and purple-budded stone bridge that straddles the inlet. He breaks the envelope with his thumb, then glances inside. There's a battered book and a letter. He withdraws the disintegrating tome. Willie's sonnets. It falls open to the pressed, dry, pale, Gap-plucked impatiens. He touches the wiry stem. His eyes fall to the poem beneath.

No longer mourn for me when I am dead
Than you shall hear the surly sullen bell
Give warning to the world that I am fled
From this vile world, with vilest worms to dwell.

Behind him, the bell in the spire tolls. He cranes his neck to sight the clock. Three minutes to eleven.

> Oh, if, I say, you look upon this verse
> When I perhaps compounded am with clay,
> Do not so much as my poor name rehearse,
> But let your love even with my life decay

He closes the book and slides it back into the envelope. He leans across the rail and tosses a coin onto his own murky reflection. It splashes and disappears into the dark water. Ripples reach for the daffodil-lined bank. He runs the kicker in his head.

> Lest the wide world should look into your moan,
> And mock you with me after I am gone.

He tucks the envelope under his arm, turns, and hustles across the cobblestone path to the church.

The worn stone steps to the ancient oaken door are empty. Everyone's inside. Everyone but Chancey. He steps up and reaches for the polished brass handle. A black-suited usher parts the door and beckons him inside. An organ sounds "Jesu, Joy of Man's Desiring." The scent of incense and burning candle wax suffuses an air already thick with funeral flowers. He stands beside a timber confessional box. The thirty or so souls now gathered in golden-pine pews seem sufficiently to fill the tiny church.

A commodious, gleaming silver-handled oaken coffin overpowers all else. It sits in the center aisle, directly in front of a becandled, white-linened altar, beside which sits an assembly of wreaths. Some are simple; many seem fulsome, overdone. Roses, gladioli, daffodils, camellias, and on it goes, all so lush. A spotlit, life-sized, carved-oak crucifix hangs from the ceiling. The light from a dozen or so stained-glass windows falls upon the scene. The music stops. Save for the sound of muffled weeping, the congregation is silent.

A second usher beckons him to the second row from the front. The uneven clunking of the wing tips upon the creaking, bare plank floor burns in his ears. A couple of mourners peer. One of them is Grisham. The usher points to an empty space immediately behind Henry, kneeling, his back hunched, lost in his rosary. Mildred's black-clad shoulders, next to his, are shaking. Two veiled young women, Elan's sisters, perhaps, huddle into Mildred's frail form. That's probably the brother, next to them. The mourner to Henry's right reflexively turns and glances up briefly. The face is masked with large horn-rimmed sunglasses. The forehead and left cheek are dressed with fresh white bandages. The features are dark and puffed, the lips swollen and split. Poor Grisham. Nobody deserves so much pain.

It might have been a mistake, on several levels, to join this gathering. Religious rituals, though intended to be uplifting, inevitably depress. But it's too late now, so enter the pew and bend the knees. At least the leather's soft. Should he cross himself? What the hell, when in Rome.

His mind's a dark abyss. He holds his breath and listens for Elan's voice. Nothing. He waits. Still she says nothing. Someone pushes a Xeroxed outline of the service into his hand and a shuffle of leather shoes signals the priest's arrival. His silken white raimants and cap are trimmed with gold. The pews and plank floor creak as the congregation stands. The priest raises a pale, long-fingered hand and blesses the congregation: "May the Father of mercies, the God of all consolations, be with you." The complexion's clear and pinky-white, the voice mellifluous, practiced, and professional. The mourners respond: "And also with you." The congregation kneels. The priest sprinkles the coffin with holy water—they say it's holy, anyway—then turns to the altar, kneels, and kisses it. He stands, wraps the chain of a flask of steaming incense around his fingers, waves the hissing fragance over the altar, and then the coffin. The scent is thick, mysterious, intimidating. "In the waters of baptism Elan died with Christ and rose with him to new life. May she now share with him in eternal glory." The priestly eyes turn heavenward. "Lord God from whom human sadness is never hidden, you know the burden of grief we feel at the loss of Elan Pryce. As we mourn her untimely passing from this life, comfort us with the knowledge that Elan lives now in your loving embrace."

The mourners lean back, and the pews moan. Grisham seems caged within the confines of the primitive wooden bench. The priest ascends to the tiny carved-oak pulpit, inhales deeply, and gazes over the congregation. "We are gathered to mourn the tragic loss of Elan Pryce, beloved wife to the honorable Grisham Pryce, daughter to Lord and Lady Haverford, sister to Elizabeth, Anne, and James, and sister-in-law to Boyle. As you all know, Elan was just twenty-four years old when this most tragic accident took her from us. She was beautiful, vibrant, gregarious, and loving. This most terrible misfortune is distressing for us all, but most especially for Elan's loving husband, the Honorable Grisham Pryce, for Elan was carrying the heir to Coldridge Manor, and that life, too, has been calamitously snatched away." He pauses. "Elan had everything to live for, and was dedicated to fulfilling God's plan." He pauses again. "Lord Haverford will eulogize. The honorable Boyle Pryce, younger brother of Grisham Pryce, will read from Corinthians, and Elan's sisters, Elizabeth and Anne, pay homage with a verse dear to Elan's heart."

Henry rises and marches, infinitely more old-soldier-like than ever, to the altar. His face is racked with pain. He attempts to compose himself, but his gaze locks uneasily upon the coffin. "Elan was the pride of our home. We all loved her. We loved her mind and her spirit. She was curious, carefree, and daring . . ." The voice cracks. "She loved ideas. She loved people. She was gentle. She loved to say gentle things . . ." He chokes then produces a white handkerchief and attempts to wipe away tears. "We will miss her. We will miss her laughter . . . terribly. We always will . . ."

He puts his hand to his eyes and stops. He waits. He tries to start again but crumples and chokes. He staggers unsteadily back to his pew, where he buries his face in his hands. Mildred's bony arms embrace him. The two black-veiled sisters lean as one into Mildred's shaking frame.

Boyle moves awkwardly to the pulpit. Those buttons on his ill-fitting, dark, pin-striped suit might just pop. The shock of black hair falls across his nervous features. His strong fingers clutch a scrap of paper.

"My brother, as you'll appreciate, is shaken to his soul by this terrible loss of the wife he loved so deeply." The voice is clumsy and dissonant. "They were made for each other, as everyone knows.

Grisham has asked me to read Elan's favorite passage." He cracks
a heavy black Bible:

> "Love never fails:
> but whether there be prophecies they shall fail;
> whether there be tongues they shall cease;
> whether there shall be knowledge it shall vanish
>   away—

If only he wouldn't mangle those lovely lines . . .

> "For we know in part and we prophesy in part.
> But when that which is perfect is come,
> that which is in part shall be done away.

Where's the lilt? The meaning? The music?

> "When I was a child, I thought as a child,
> I spake as a child, I understood as a child;
> But when I became a man I put away childish things.
> For now we see through a glass darkly
> But then face to face:
> Now I know in part, but then shall I know
>   even as I am known.
> And now abideth faith, hope, love, these three;
>   but the greatest of these is love."

Boyle bangs the Bible shut and crashes back to the vacant
space beside Grisham. The pew groans. The two sisters, their pallid
faces discernible behind the opaque veils, float as one to the pulpit.
A sweet if shaky voice breaks the dead silence.

"Elan committed this dirge from Shakespeare's *Cymbeline* to
memory. It is spoken by young princes over the supposed corpse
of their playmate, their sister Imogen." She breathes deeply, then
speaks confidently, lyrically.

> "Fear no more the heat o' th' Sun,
> Nor the furious Winter's rages,
> Thou thy worldy task has done,
> Home art thou gone, and ta'en thy wages.

Golden lads and girls all must,
As chimney sweepers come to dust."

He closes his eyes. She's at the gate to Crystal Pond. A second silvery voice sounds in the background . . .

"Fear no more the lightning flash,
Nor all the dreaded thunderstone.
Fear not slander, censure rash,
Thou hast finished joy and moan.
All lovers young, all lovers must,
Consign to thee and come to dust."

Her face is framed by the window of her time machine. The voices alternate musically:

"No Exorciser harm thee—"
"No witch-craft charm thee—"
"Ghost unlaid forbear thee—"
"Nothing ill come near thee—"

The ruby-red, urchin haircut, the raised sunglasses, the ever-impish smile. Grace under pressure. He'd hold that image, but the final couplet breaks in. This time the voices merge:

"Quiet consummation have,
And renowned be thy grave."

The sisters evaporate back to the pew, and the priest sashays to the altar. The congregation kneels, and the priest's voice washes over them. "We make our prayer through our Lord Jesus Christ, your son who lives and reigns with you and the Holy Spirit, one God, for ever and ever. Let us pray for Elan, her family and friends, and for all God's people. We pray that she will be held securely in God's loving embrace now and for all eternity."

The congregation responds, most of them, anyway, "Lord hear our prayer."

"You entrusted Elan to our care and now you embrace her in your love. Comfort us, your sorrowing servants, who seek to do your will and to know your saving peace."

"Lord hear our prayer."

"We ask this through Christ our Lord."

"Amen."

The priest prepares the host and wine, then glides to the front of the altar. Twelve or so mourners trek behind Henry and Mildred to receive holy communion. Grisham falls into the line behind Boyle, who stoops, perhaps to conceal his condition. Some mourners peer, most glance away. One by one the supplicants accept the host. Now it's Grisham's turn. The crucifix seems to hang directly above his stitched, bruised, bandaged head. His split and swollen lips open like a flower for the host. The priest holds the wafer aloft, blesses Grisham, lays the slim, white biscuit upon his thick, moist, mauve tongue . . .

So, yet again, the wafer. Last time it fell to Elan's lips in that sun-filled Franz Joseph chapel. If only someone could lay a healing wafer on Mr. Chandler Haste. If only he could be comforted by all these holy trappings. If only he could believe as they all seem to believe. If only he could be forgiven. If only he could believe she's risen to heaven. If only he could call up the same privilege betwixt the stirrup and the ground by confessing and repenting. So maybe he'll spring to his feet right now, maybe he'll confess his sins before the entire congregation. Before God. And the devil—there has to be a devil in the middle of all this. He'll come clean. He'll say that he, Chandler Haste, is responsible for this whole terrible situation. He'll avow that it was he who perverted the path of Elan's life. He'll admit to all the world that he's a self-indulgent sinner who's abused so many lives, betrayed so many fidelities. Elan and Jill, Henry and Grisham, Blake and Angie, and on it goes—

Grisham's mouth closes on the wafer. The bulbous head drops to the barrel chest.

She said she loved that fellow. And maybe she did—in a fashion. But hang on a minute there. Maybe, just maybe, Grisham's the one who's responsible for this wretched tragedy. Maybe he's the culprit. Maybe he was the carrier. Maybe it all comes down to his bodily fluids. A low blow, Chancey. Give it up.

Perhaps, maybe, who knows, but perhaps anyway, when he opens his eyes, the coffin'll be gone. Maybe, when he opens his eyes, she'll be restored; watching waves roll, tasting salt air, inhaling jacarandas, catching the cackle of swooping seagulls . . .

Leather soles shuffle upon the plank floor. The censer creaks rhythmically upon its metronomic chain. Incense assails his nostrils. He opens his eyes. The gleaming coffin sits like a giant, immobile, Kafkaesque cockroach. Incense soaks into the white-velvet pall. She's not there. She'll never be there. She's gone. Tears blur his vision. He holds them back. Then he tries to swallow but cannot. He peers back over his shoulder to the heavy oaken door. If he doesn't get into some air, and some sunshine, real soon, he'll vomit.

23

Cat's Eyes

E NURSES THE LUMP IN HIS THROAT and tosses the pale, dry impatiens into the pit, and watches it fall. Down, down, down it goes. Down into the slick, mud-walled grave. So, this is the way it all ends. All the smiles, all the laughter, all the good times, all the dreams and lines and quotes and poems, all that sharing of marmalade and tea, all that gulping of wine and oysters, all that planning and scheming and running and flying and pacing and racing and lurking and shirking and skipping and jumping and huffing and puffing and lilting and kilting, and cooing and mooing and honey-dewing, and humping and pumping—and fuckeen—and this is the way it all ends. So Khayyam got it right: "Make the most of what we yet may spend, before we too into the dust descend."

"We'll be tempting you back to Coldridge Manor?" The eyes of Boyle Pryce lock onto his. A cloud of fumes rises from the fresh but decidedly bilious Cuban cigar that commands the corner of his mouth.

"I'm afraid I—"

"Henry insists. Grisham, too, of course. We all do." A tight smile is confined to his nicotine-stained teeth.

"That's very kind. But apart from any other considerations, I have to get back to the Hero and Leander to make a couple of phone calls."

"Make them from the library at the manor. You won't be disturbed. Make as many as you like."

"They're long distance."

"Don't give it a second thought. The manor's just a couple of miles along the country road. It'll be a lovely little run for your sparkling Rover."

HE BRINGS THE ROVER TO REST at the bottom of the long, winding gravel drive. So that, up there, is Coldridge Manor. It's right out of *Town and Country*. A central sandstone-block building plus two wings, one for the master, one for guests—or so one supposes—and quarters for the servants. Is that a Roman statue in front of the huge main door? Probably. The two-story structure is set back into the hill to catch the view over the meadows with their running creek. And oaks, maples, camellias, and weeping willows. Trouble is, that hill blocks the afternoon sun. And there's the giveaway: green moss growing up from the bottom and reaching a couple of feet up the sandstone. No wonder they call it Coldridge. Probably as damp and chilly as a tomb, even in April. One would need a mountain of woolen underwear and tweed to survive a winter. He glides the Rover up the drive, circles the decaying stone figure of a discus-hurling nude male, cuts the engine, and steps out onto the gravel.

An ashen-faced, morning-suited servant cracks the oversized oaken door. Smoky fumes catch in the nostrils as he steps into the foyer. Thank God for a wood-burning fire. Some life at last.

The servant glances at the impediment. "Ah, Mister Haste. I understand you need to use the library." He points a spindly finger. "It's the first door on your right, sir."

The library. Oh, yes, of course, the library. Every home should have one just like this. Two walls of leather-bound classics cocooned in mahogany bookcases. In the opposite corner sits an antique ship's desk with sturdy captain's chair in place at a green-felted, fold-out desktop, bearing a black phone. A brown leather sofa in front of the bookcases faces the desk. An antique timber chandelier, the candleholders of which have been adjusted to accept electric imitations, hangs from the ceiling. The wall behind the desk carries a near life-sized oil of Grisham and Boyle in pheasant-tormenting gear. Grisham's in the foreground, half crouching, his arms cradling a shotgun, a cluster of a dozen or so bloodied birds at his feet. Boyle's right behind him, leaning back onto an ugly, oversized black shillelagh. Coldridge Manor's in the background.

There's a silver-framed photo of Elan on the desk. She's standing beside the time machine, dressed in what seems a trademark black. Black jeans, blouse, and the tailored, three-button leather jacket. Grisham, betweeded, stands stiffly beside her. Boyle, also in tweeds, clutching that surly stick again, seems to hover in the background.

He seats himself gingerly in the captain's chair, grabs the phone, and dials. Jill's not answering and neither is the machine. His stomach turns. Wherever is she? He redials.

"This's Jesse Green." The voice is honey-smooth, confident, silky.

"Hi, Jesse—and congratulations."

"Hey! Chancey! Well! Hi! And *thanks*. I guess you heard the news then. Harry Crumpet appointed me chief executive of SCL."

"I did indeed, congratulations."

"Yeah, well, Harry knows me real well. He needed someone he could trust, someone he could count on—and I'm in your offices for the same reason." He pauses. "I was impressed with the way you worked. I really mean that. You're smart. And I'm going to be needing help. I'm planning to recruit an entire new top team. First-class all the way. Top fees on everything, of course." Another pause. "Farther down the line, I could maybe swing you all the other Crumpet work, too. I'd just have to clear you with Crumpet himself, which shouldn't be hard. I already ran a check on Haste and Company."

"*You* ran a check on *me?*"

"Due diligence, Chancey. The only blot seemed to involve litigation with some Aussie printer." *Burnham!* "We might not need to inquire further, though." He's actually going to talk to that potbellied blockhead? "Not if *I* say everything's kosher." Maybe he already did. "Well, think about it, Chancey. I've got to rush now, but I'll call you in your office on Monday."

So, fortune plays for the long haul. Destiny's impervious to the mocking finger. Fate's messenger cannot, with impunity, be puked upon. What to do? What to do? He redials.

"Well," says Doc, "Jesse Green wants to make real sure you don't say a single word. It's a tempting proposition offering a fortune's worth of business with little to lose—at this point, anyway."

"At this point?"

"As long as you've got something over him you'll likely be okay. Soon enough he'll be looking for finder's fees. Fat finder's fees. Bribes, actually. He might need you to make him a director of Haste and Company to legitimize things."

"What would you do, Doc?"

"I might think about it for a moment or two. But if you're going to sup with the devil, you need a very long spoon, and that may be too high a price. You've got to ask yourself if this is why you went to New York. Life can be real short, you know."

He cradles the phone and reaches for the photo. Follow your heart and not temptation. Why go to New York—or to any Land of Oz? Why fall in love or out of it? Why live and die? And how can a mere image, whether in a silver-framed photo or upon a Grecian vase, seem so ineffably sad? The face, the eyes, the smile, the grace. She's there, yet she's not there. So where is she? She's gone. Gone, gone, gone. Irrevocably and forever. Something's been done that can never be undone.

Bilious fumes catch in his nostrils. And here it is again, the cigar-chomping face of Boyle Pryce.

"Everything okay, Mister Haste?"

"Call me Chancey, please. Yes, everything's okay. I just had to make those phone calls. Got kind of lost in them." The beady eyes fall to the photo. Best set it back immediately. "Picked up the, ah, photo by, ah, accident."

Boyle grabs the silver frame with a grubby thumb and forceful forefinger. His barrel chest's too close for comfort. "Lovely girl." The breath's ripe with smoke and whiskey, and the complexion's beet red. "Such a terrible accident. She was besotted with that car. Called it her time machine. Nobody knew why." He sets the photo back. "I see you drive an impressive car, too."

"The Rover? You noticed it. Yes, well, I guess it's a little out of the ordinary. But just a rental. Well, I imagine we should mingle with the other guests."

They step out of the library and into the babble of the banquet room. A uniformed servant presents a silver tray. Boyle grabs a glass of whiskey and moves away. That red wine looks lovely. The glass in his hand, like the oversized chandelier that hangs from the soaring cathedral ceiling, is the finest crystal. His wing tips sink into the rich, tapestried carpet. A uniformed servant prods the smoldering split maple in the oversized, carved-oak fireplace. The reluctant fire hisses and spits. A ghostlike puff of smoke is sucked up the chimney. The mantel's laden with overpowering funeral flowers. A life-sized portrait of Elan hangs high above. She's standing, her hands upon a pedestal, in a deep blue ball gown. The painting is well done but too perfect. He turns and pushes his tail toward the fireplace. The oversized dining table is set in starched white linen and dressed with funeral flowers, mostly crimson roses. The china's heirloom, and the food goes on forever. Honey-glazed ham, steaming fricassee of chicken, freshly carved leg of roast lamb, steaming vegetables, and, on a separate credenza, trifles, jellies, and dainty pastries.

The thirty or so mourners are an eclectic bunch. But no one else's sporting a clubfoot. Henry and Mildred are probably the oldest. That otherworldly woman from the bookstore isn't much younger. Grisham seems to have a gang of fortyish friends, and a couple of handsome young fellows on the side. Boyle's mumbling something to a couple of coarse-faced country cronies. Elan's friends, presumably, in their twenties and early thirties, along with the brother and the lovely sisters who recited that very appropriate dirge are well and truly out of it, distraught and weepy, comforting one another. Most everyone's besuited. Many are smoking. Alcohol's loosened tongues. The babble's rising.

"This really is a funeral banquet." Beryl, balancing a salad plate on the fingers of one hand, is suddenly in his space.

"So we meet again."

"I was going to be staying with Elan for another three weeks before heading back to Godzone. Now I'll hang around until the end of next week." The black dress is too tight, too flimsy, and too short. The voice drops to a whisper. "Grisham looks a real mess, eh?"

"Indeed."

"All that stuff about them being made for each other"—she glances over her shoulder—"just a crock of shit."

"I think it's called a noble lie."

"Whatever. They must've pulled a few strings to hush a suicide. Accident, indeed." She pokes a dainty forkful of salad between her red lips. "And all this rush to a funeral. These people look harmless,

Chancey. But they're country cunning, really." She sets her plate back on the table and grabs her glass of Burgundy. "They even got the priest to mention the pregnancy." She smiles a mocking smile and gulps the wine. "Now, there's a beard for you."

"It's a pity people need to hide their true selves. I've done it myself, so I know. But it was Grisham's kid, right?"

"Elan said so. And she wouldn't have lied. Not to me." She empties the glass. "Big question isn't whether he knocked her up, Chancey." She leans her nose to his. "Big question is, did he give her the bug?"

"If not him, who?"

"Not you, right? No, of course, not. Forget I said that. No. The fact is, Elan bedded so many men in search of you, Chancey, that God only knows where she picked up that wretched pox." She half glances over her shoulder. "But at least she never got it from Boyle."

"From *Boyle?*"

"He's not a nice guy, Chancey. He might also be bent." She half smiles. "Some people say he might be responsible for Grisham's recent beauty treatment. Indirectly, of course."

"I thought that was a random gay bashing."

"Maybe. Grisham's the pillow-biter, of course. But the whisper is that Boyle gets off on putting in a bit of the slipper. That he might've gotten carried away and hurt somebody's friend."

"Male or female?"

"He mightn't be fussed either way." Her eyes dart away, then back. "The inference, anyway, is that Grisham's beating might've been somebody's idea of revenge."

"A solemn week for crossroads and reversals, right? So this is what they learn on the playing fields of England."

She laughs. "It's probably just a nasty rumor—"

She stops short. That soft touch on the shoulder is surely Henry's fragile hand. "I can't begin to thank you enough for coming, Chancey." The face's puffed, the voice slurred. He's nursing a generous whiskey in a sparkling glass. "It means so much to have an old and trusted Kiwi friend along, a Godzoner." The touch of his hand evolves into the drape of an arm. "God's still thinking about you, Chancey"—his eyelids close—"and now that Elan's up there with the angels, with Jesus and the blessed apostles and saints, looking down on us, and looking after us"—then open again— "well, I'm sure she's looking out for you, too. I mean, you *knew* Elan. She spoke highly of you. She would've cared what happened to your soul."

Don't bite into any of that.

"She was a lovely person, Henry."

"Lovely— love—" Tears brim in his eyes. "Love obeys itself, Chancey." He sips the malt, glances in Grisham's direction, then brings his eyes back. "Love can't be called out like a dog merely because its master wants to see it."

Grisham manifests himself and offers his fleshy hand. "Thanks indeed for attending, Chancey."

Ignore those startling facial injuries. "Well, thanks for asking me. I just don't know what to say. I mean mere words—"

"Are quite useless," says Henry.

"And unnecessary. Just being here's enough," mumbles Grisham. "Elan would've liked that. She might've liked you to look over the manor, too. Should you feel so tempted, be my guest."

Just beyond Grisham's shoulder, Boyle's setting a match to yet another of those oversized cigars. The bloodshot eyes, narrowed to suppress the smoke, capture his. "Stay on as long as you can, Chancey." The voice's husky. "There's plenty to eat." The fulsome tongue runs over the teeth and the lips. "And let's tempt you with another drink." Boyle's nod to a white-waistcoated waiter effects an immediate topping of the Burgundy. The brothers drift away.

Another hand alights upon his shoulder. The owner is the pince-nezed bookshop proprietor. "Do you have a minute, Mister Haste?"

"Why, yes, of course."

"Somewhere a little more private."

"I might know just the place."

He leads her to the library and presses the door closed behind them. They stroll to the leather sofa and perch on the edge. She drops the spectacles to her lap, clasps her hands, and smiles. "I came to know Elan very well."

"She was a lovely person."

The complexion's almost crystalline. The eyes are confident. She knows a thing or two—and might just have a handle on what she doesn't.

"Elan liked to confide in me. She sometimes called me her spiritual adviser."

"And were you?"

"Not really. I gave that up when I left the church. I was a nun, you know."

"She might've mentioned you."

"She talked about you a lot, Mister Haste."

"Call me Chancey, please."

"She had some guilt. She was conflicted in her feelings for you."

"She said you eased those feelings, that you told her she was lucky—"

"To meet you, Mister Haste. Yes, I told her that."

"Maybe you can absolve me, too." She perks. Perhaps she'll rise to the challenge. "But was she lucky? Really? How can that be? For her, for me, or for anybody? I mean how does that actually work?"

Something's going on behind those eyes. "Affinities are rare. They come but few times in a life. It's awful to risk losing one when it arrives."

"We had more than just an affinity. It was very, uh—"

"Physical?"

"It began as a caprice—"

"It's the ability to love capriciously that distinguishes man from the animals."

"I was married."

"Real friendship's just as sacred and eternal as marriage."

"It all became so much more than merely physical."

"She said you loved her—"

"But not enough to let her go."

"She didn't want you to. She needed to effect her own salvation."

"But she took her life. Isn't that the, uh, ultimate sin?"

"It can also be the ultimate act of self-determination."

"You really think so?"

"It takes something like religious valor to follow our own inner consciousness to its last whim and eccentricity. To be free is to be able to do that." She smiles. "You might've been pursuing the same kind of freedom all your life."

"Would God approve?"

"The sin that brings God the most grief is when we fail to be ourselves." She lays her hand on his. "Take yourself as you are, whole. Don't try to live by one part alone and starve the other. You still have a restless searching. Pursue it. It'll lead you to God, the Great Lover, the Bringer of Peace. You and Elan were part of that great plan. Still are, no doubt." She sets the glasses back on her head, then slowly stands. He follows her lead.

"I can see why Elan liked to talk to you. I mean, you've been very, uh, supportive."

They edge to the door. She cracks it and executes a sparkling version of the Crawley nod. "God always forgives, you know." The eyes flash. "That's his business."

He blinks, and she's suddenly gone.

He moseys to the desk, picks up the phone, and dials.

Still no Jill—but leave no message, this time.

A solemn week for crossroads and reversals. Fidelity and betrayal—and bad karma. It's all coming back at him. It's the Everness thing, all right. Or something like it. Oh, God, what to do? And, while he's mulling that, the Oracle might welcome one last call.

"I'm at a funeral reception, Doc."

"So I gathered."

"Everybody seems to believe in God."

"They're wishin' for a cosmic bellboy."

"Do you have any insights into God?"

"Well, God's never been my specialty." The line crackles. "Some people say he educates us through our deceptions and mistakes. But my advice is to steer clear of him—my hunch is that he might just be a terrible sadist."

"What makes more sense than God?"

The answer's both confident and quick, "Repetition-compulsion."

"Huh—repetition-compulsion? How does that work, exactly?"

"It's the neurotic drive to replay an unhappy childhood, over and over and over again, hoping to make it come out right somewhere down the line, which it never does, of course. So it's a special Sisyphusian hell all of its own." He chuckles. "And that Jesse Green of yours, well, he's stuck in it, that's for sure."

"What should we be doing with our lives, Doc?"

"Well, let me see, now." Doc's brain almost seems to be clicking down the line. "For openers, staying out of trouble. And believe me, that's something a lot of people just never manage to do."

"Then what, Doc?"

"Well"—the brain's whirring again—"getting into a job we love. *Supporting* ourselves by making a worthwhile contribution. *Expressing* ourselves. *Creating* some love in our lives."

"Love."

"Yeah. And, since we're back on that subject, I think the bottom line is that we should commit to a partner for life—for the simple reason that even a long life with all its accidents is barely enough for two people to understand each other, and to understand is to love. The man who understands one woman is qualified to understand pretty much everything."

"I should've extracted that nugget from you earlier, Doc. Anything else?"

"Well—" This time the pause goes on forever. "Well—" He's obviously lost in the deepest thought. "Well—" How great to be able to tap into such a fount of wisdom. "Well—" Who's also such a straight shooter. "Well, nothing else comes immediately to mind."

So, there goes the guru. It's time to get out of this musty mausoleum. But maybe, there's something to be said for accepting Grisham's tempting offer to look over the manor? He'll never have this chance again. No one else seems to be making the tour, but that needn't stop him. And there's one room he'd particularly like to see.

He climbs the stair and gazes down the long, cool, musty corridor. Oils of ghastly, stone-faced white males, formidable antecedents no doubt, line the way. And there, at the very end of

the hall, that's bound to be the room. He pads his way down the
floral carpet, turns the polished-brass door handle, and slides inside.

And so it is—the master bedroom. Chilly. Lack of sun or
something. But a giant, foot-warming square of lush, white virgin-
wool carpet on the bare oaken floor.

He steps to the white-linen-curtained, leaded window. Two
panels are slightly ajar. The view's classic England: lush green grass,
thicket hedges, half a dozen huge oaks, several blooming camellias,
at least a couple of wisterias, and scatterings of wild daffodils beside
the edge of a meandering country road. And there's his forest-
green Rover down below, a standout among those other death-
black vehicles.

He turns. And there's the bed—a huge, king-sized, mahogany
four-poster with a mountain of pillows. Just about everything's in
white linen. The floral wallpaper is expensive, handmade, pastel.
The ceiling's a gentle pink, as is the trim. So, this is where she slept.
He's known her all this time but never seen her lair till now, when
all's too late.

He perches on the bed, on the left side she always favored,
and studies the mahogany dresser. Five wide drawers, and some
knickknacks beneath an antique mirror. He stands, and the image
of a decidedly edgy Chandler Haste manifests itself within that
looking glass. And there's the obligatory wedding photo. Grisham
in his morning suit—very aristocratic. Elan in white silk. Long,
tapered sleeves cover those lovely, downed, willowy arms. High-
neck collar—and a cluster of dainty flowers in her hair. Very Ophelia.
They're trying so hard to look natural that they seem like caricatures.
He and Jill have a photo like that. Maybe everybody does.

Hey, a *door*. To the bathroom, no doubt. Indeed. All in white.
Grisham's splashed money on this: two basins, a Jacuzzi, a bidet.
Given the typical British plumbing, he might just be the most hygienic
aristocrat in all of England.

And yet another door, to yet another bedroom. This one's
done altogether differently, in blues and reds and thick dark oak.
Grisham's bedroom. His Honor had his own bedroom. Wouldn't
you know it? With yet another king-sized bed. Christ—Grisham's
eyes! But, fortunately, only from within a gloomy head-and-shoulders
oil portrait on the wall above the cold, black, marble mantel of the

stopped-up fireplace. A fireless grate, pretty apt. And here's a Louis-the-Umpteenth desk. He's into the *Times, Town and Country, An Investor's Guide to Bond Issues, Burke's Peerages,* and, of course, *Exclusive Sotheby's Auctions.* That's probably where he procured this very same escritoire, the drawers of which glide like new. And, hey, what's this nestling in the corner of the drawer? A blue Tiffany box with a letter poking out of the corner. The cuff links, and the brooch, too, are all wrapped in tissue. He opens the letter and studies the engraved red lettering on the rich cream parchment:

Fondling Jewels of Bond Street
by appointment to HM the Queen

25 April 1983
The Honorable Grisham Pryce

We have studied, for insurance purposes, the cuff links and brooch so kindly forwarded and are returning the same herewith. The workmanship is indeed by Tiffany's. I have to report, however, that the "stones" in question are in fact nothing more than the cheapest of colored glass, all, apparently, from the same source, to whit, as far as we can tell, one deep-green wine bottle. Overall, as I'm sure you'll immediately appreciate, we can assign no value to these items other than sentiment.
As ever, we welcome the favor of your instruction in this or any other matter.

Yours respectfully,

Percival Fondling

So, Grisham's uncovered the Grange-bottle caper. But when? Some wretched intuition—or ingrained routine—impelled him to send it out upon their return from New York. But this letter apparently only surfaced after the so-called accident. So she never saw this tacky missive. Thank God for that. And Grisham mightn't know much, anyway. Or so one hopes. Such a revelation would undoubtedly irk him: family honor impugned by upstart, clubfooted colonial and all that. He should never've pulled that sophomoric prank. But it's all water under the bridge, now.

He carefully replaces the box and slides the drawer closed. This dark, damp room doesn't have a good feeling. It's more than just creepy, too. There's a sense of—of what? Of rage? Of menace? No, that's mere projection.

He steps back into the bathroom. Is this the way Grisham came? No doubt. But how often did he come? Indeed. And did he stop in the doorway and sight her naked in her bed and pleasuring herself? Did she close her eyes and go to heaven for you? With you? Not likely. No, Grisham's just got a drafty, sunless house, a hand-me-down trophy wife, a photo of a funny, false moment, and a pair of mocking cuff links. Oh, Elan probably did love that aristo, in a fashion. Perhaps Jill'll experience the same kind of thing with Everness. Adrenaline pricks his gut. More guilt or just run-of-the-mill distress? Is Jill distressed? She was in pain. Real pain. He tried to block it, but it surfaced in his dreams. He carried that grief across the Atlantic. So he's infinitely more distressed than he'd realized. But no wonder, for the week's been frantic. The past two weeks. The past forty years. No chance to think, nor prospect of so doing . . .

And here, beside her bed, is a hope chest. What lies within? Something, perhaps, to distract a young mind from the damp emptiness of this glorified Pinchgut. There's no lock, so just raise the lid. Just books. But they might have done the trick. So many leather-bound books. Mostly poetry. And a worn, used-to-be-red-ribboned prayer missal. The very same one, in fact, that she smuggled along to Franz Joseph. The gold-leaf embossing on the battered cover's just about all gone. A gift, no doubt. Indeed, for here's the inside cover inscription:

> To our beloved daughter, Elan,
> in celebration of the blessed sacrament
> of her first communion,
> with all our love,
> Mother and Father.

And, hey, the missal's fallen open to a ragged, red-edged bookmark:

> They
> Do
> Not
> Sin
> Who
> Sin
> For
> Love

That's her handwriting, of course, and the ink's long faded. So all these years she prayed to ease her guilt. And Oscar helped. Oscar in a prayer missal, best leave him there and pry no further. But, hang on, what's this? A folded sheet of worn cream paper falls from the book to the bed. He replaces the missal, sits on the bed, sinks back into the feather pillows, and carefully opens that sonnet from the past—

> My paramour belongs in other places,
> And trims his words to suit a distant peal,
> And marks the dipping sun beyond my graces,
> And flees from me as shadows prick his heel.

Yes, that was him, always running, always glancing over her shoulder, always mindful of Jill, always pressed by time.

> Imprisoned time flees fastest when I'm doting
> Upon the vision of my love before my lips
> Aboard a haunted craft so wanly floating
> Upon a doldrummed sea of empty ships.

She felt trapped in those moments that went so fast?

> If he were mine, and mine alone forever,
> Intensity of love might subtly waive,
> So bind these blinding moments to me ever,
> To shimmer from within a mirrored grave.

Would he really've lost interest? The mirrored grave and all her other fantasy worlds. So will she shimmer from that lake?

Superior then, I say, is lust in Haste
To sanctioned love and ever-lost embrace.

And that was the kicker. So, she had him figured out. Some time ago, too, by the look of this fading ink. But she loved him anyway. Women, they need so much yet ask for so little—or is it the other way around? Can she sense his presence? It would nice to be able to believe that. But what about that other missive burning in his pocket? That's real.

He sits bolt upright—careful with those wing tips on the white linen bedspread—and slips the poem into his breast pocket. But, hey, what's that aroma? A cigar—Boyle's. And receding footsteps. So, that thick-pawed, beady-eyed, barrel-chested buffoon's been creeping about. Cool air rustles a curtain and catches the hair on the back of his neck.

Go Chancey! Go!
Go now!
Dance away in velvet shoes!
Dance! Dance! Dance!
Dance away now!
Go! Chancey, go!
Go now!

HE CHECKS THE REARVIEW MIRROR. Coldridge Manor's passing into posterity. Will it disappear to the left or to the right? No matter. Just so long as it vanishes, once and for all. He hits the accelerator.

Not that whip again. The old man's not dead at all. He's coming in the front door, grim-faced. Chancey runs just as fast as the deformity permits. Out the back door, up the street, up a hill, down a hill, around a corner, another corner, another hill, panting, aching, never looking back. He hears his racing heels upon the hot pavement—ta clock, ta clock, ta clockety clock—

And, there, it's gone, obliterated, out of his life forever. The Rover door jams his right hip as he takes the corner more quickly than anticipated, kicking up billows of dust behind. Stay on this gravel for a hundred yards or so, then point these bounding wheels to Crystal Pond.

Acorns pop as the forest-green Rover rolls to near-invisible rest beneath that weeping willow on the incline overlooking the lake. So, the sun's about to set, and here we are again then, girl. And from this very spot you glimpsed your destiny, your timeless realm. That lake's dead still—on this side, anyway. But what's on the other side of that enigmatic looking glass? That's what you were wondering, girl, right? Might there really be another world of souls and dreams and unlived lives? A peace-filled place where our deepest wishes are all fulfilled? And if so are you down there, now? Waiting for Godot. And Chancey. Maybe. Or are you up here, looking out, again?

Those two geese are back. And so's he. But where are you, girl? Maybe you'll say. He plucks the envelope from his pocket and extracts two sheets of fresh cream paper. The ink's the same bronze-blue, the hand is hers.

25 April 1983, Anzac Day

Dear Chancey:

We talked about destiny. Mine wasn't looking like anything I fancied. I'd hoped that getting something down on paper might help me, might point me in the right direction. I mean—

Consider the equation of my life:
The formula's abjectly all awry,
Fortune's fast falling, apprehension's rife,
What'ere I do I diabolify.

Yes, things are bad, and, yes, I keep making them worse. Nothing others haven't faced, of course. I mean what about Cleopatra's big query: is it a sin to rush into the secret house of death ere death come to us? In fact, the Queen of the Nile was caught on the horns of a false dilemma. She didn't realize—how could she have?—that all the days are Anzac Days.

She didn't know that life, love, death—everything—
begins and ends in the same moment. That's the
insight that sets us free—

> The trickster on the stage is vaulted time,
> Who casts a trance of momentary daze,
> So exit from his pointless pantomime,
> And gather in the next world all bouquets.

Yes, well, sorry about the ending, but only for others.
Best to go out in a bit of a burn, and, anyway, one
must be prepared to start life anew every once in a
while. You once said something like that yourself
way back in Godzone. I tried to put that precept into
action many times but until now could never make it
stick. Don't think I just finally snapped, Ophelia-
like. I've tried to make my maxim, My life, My rules,
so I'm merely extending that adage to the closing
scene. I'm the Fiddler of Dooney heading for the
other theater. I'll take the time machine through the
looking glass into that bourn from whence et cetera
and so on.

> Roll the fickle dice and seize the chances,
> Ride on to colliding parallel worlds,
> Disdain all pain of darkling nuances,
> Impasses implode as valor unfurls.

That's what came back to me, Chancey. It seems
churlish to quibble and futile to confect further
rhymes or reasons. There really are other worlds, and
I truly can see my way out of this one. Say a prayer for
me—and I'll do the same for you from wherever I
land. Shall I tell you I love you and always will? Yes,
now and forever—

> My spirit to another globe has flown
> Yet rests within your palm to claim your own

Elan

Within his palm. Words. Bronze-blue ink. Words evaporate if
not trapped in ink. Spirit. Is the spirit ink? No. But can the spirit
find sanctuary in ink? Yes, of course. And it has. And thanks. Thanks,

Elan. Thanks for the life and the spirit. Thanks for catching the melancholy mood. And thanks for pinning it to paper with a nibful of bronze-blue ink. And thanks, so many, many thanks, for placing that parchment into this undeserving palm. But look. It's fluttering, fluttering in his fingers. See faster, and faster, and faster. And that's not rain upon the window. No. That's an uncheckable vale of bursting tears. So let them go. Let them go. You'll never stop them now, so just put your hands to your head and let them go. Let it all go. Just let it go . . .

See, he can weep, too. He's not just a witness to this event, this spectacle, this maudlin melodrama that's burned so many lives. He can feel it, too. He has a heart. And it's telling him something. It's telling him that it's time to let it all go. See? Those tear-drenched hands are saying that he can feel, and not just laugh. He can feel the pain of loss. And you know what else? He can even apprehend the beginnings of remorse. More of it, perhaps, than he could ever've known, or guessed—or feared—might ever come his way. So let it go. Let it go. Let it all go.

So, there it was, there it was. And now it's time to raise your red-rimmed eyes.

This time the lake's in focus but rapidly disappearing into the darkness. What's it really all about? What forces have brought him to this godforsaken pond? Old Testament gods? Can he really believe, for one minute, that this whole thing with Elan, from the beginning of it right through to this moment, was ordained by any kind of god? Surely God's more than just a cruel and capricious tyrant waiting to trick us in a one-chance game of snakes and ladders. Or, maybe, perhaps, is it possible, that, in fact, there really is a God? Perhaps there actually is a master of the universe who really does want the best for us and who has no choice but to educate us through our deceptions and mistakes, so that shame really can lead to decency. Isn't that what his own unconscious has been trying to say? Maybe so and maybe not. But what about Doc's advice? Repetition-compulsion. Maybe there's actually, absolutely, no God at all in any way, shape, manner, or form. Only good old psychological common sense. And if so, then, according to that line of thought, if he's got it right, he's just been struggling inside a terrible mental Pinchgut.

Maybe Chandler Haste is just another Jesse Green, the victim of an unhappy childhood, desperately seeking a mother's love, in Elan's arms. But why Elan? Why not Jill? Because. Because, because—*of course*—because Elan was *off-limits*. Always was and always would be. He'd always be safe with her. He could replay all their liaisons and trysts a million times over—and hasn't he already?—and they'd always come out the exactly the same. As they always did. Leaving him free to fly off back to Jill. Strong, steady, loyal, dedicated, beautiful Jill, the perfect wife, friend, lover. The Madonna-Whore syndrome? Kind of, yet not really, for either princess could fill either billing in a moment.

Yet he thought he'd figured a way to have his psychological cake and eat it, too. Jill was his North Star in one life. Elan was his false enchantment—his boot-strapper fantasy—in another. Elan was everything that he was not, an exotic flower in a backwater garden, literate, lovely, graceful, aristocratic—yet fun-loving and unaffected, too. No wonder she pushed his buttons. No wonder he fell so deeply, darkly, desperately, and blindly. Her own interest in him might have to remain a mystery. Maybe Doc'll sort that out, too, one day.

But Elan's not to blame for anything, really. No, Jill got that wrong. The culprit was always himself, the person they call Chandler Haste. And, of course, the old man inside that person's brain who stoked the fires of repetition-compulsion, so that Chandler Haste overlooked the needs of his kids, just as his old man had ignored him. "The family you come from isn't as important as the family you create." Right, Chancey, but instead of creating a family, you let that mindless Mr. Chandler Haste pursue the ghosts of childhood down Byzantine corridors within the mind. Repetition-compulsion—unconscious, fulfillment-killing behavior that passes from generation to generation. Repetition-compulsion—God and the devil rolled into one. So Oscar had it right:

> Strange I was not told
> The brain could hold
> In one tiny, ivory cell
> God's heaven and hell.

That insight came too late for Oscar—but, with luck, in time for Chancey. He might yet make amends by committing to understand and to love—to truly love, without illusions. But none of this heaven and helling. Shield Jill from the machinations of Everness—if not too late—then apply that same concern to Blake and Angie before they become as dysfunctional as Chandler Haste and his old man.

Fuller was right, he's been a mental quadriplegic. With a little understanding, he might even have helped Fuller, who was always searching for something, create a decent life. Brittle, too, maybe. If Chandler Haste had been paying attention Brittle mightn't have cracked. People can't let you down unless you're leaning on them. No. Chandler Haste really was a mental quadriplegic. But now he can bound from the chair, now he can kick off all that rotten programming, now he can tell all those silly gods and devils to go jump. Because now, what he can clearly see, what he can acknowledge, what he now knows for sure, is that it's up to him. And most crucially, of course, to Jill.

Fidelity—must it always precede betrayal? No. Fidelity can also be forged in the fire of betrayal. And this time must be. He's suffered vexation and attained enlightenment. Or something that passes for it, anyway. So now, finally, he'll show real love—adult love, authentic commitment—to the woman who has, until now anyway, unstintingly given just that to him, every day of their relationship. What a fool he's been. And what bliss it would be to be reunited. Bliss and delight, both. The way is clear, Chancey. So make it happen.

He glances to the lake. Dusk's given way to darkness, and two full moons are out, one in the sky, one in the lake. That couldn't be her face, not within that watery moon, could it? Unlikely. But maybe she's up here, behind this misting windshield, lilting into Chancey's ear. Maybe she's still his Delphic Oracle, his Sergeant Pepper, his Wizard of Oz. Would she be his guardian angel, too? God knows we all need one. She accepts? Okay then. So that faintest of still, small voices might actually be hers:

> Go Chancey, go
> Dance away in velvet shoes
> Go now!

Also unlikely. No, that urgent whisper's just a zephyr breeze rustling the leaves of the weeping willow, then shaking other husks inside this guilty head. And now the moon's gone. In fact, both moons are gone. And the lake, too. Only the flickering hands of the luminous dashboard clock defy the night. Eight minutes past eight. He tucks the papers back into the manila envelope and presses it into his coat pocket. He hits the ignition, savors the salvo of the purring pistons, then flicks up the searing headlights. Gravel crackles as the Rover rolls out of the park. He'll pick up his overnight bag from the Hero & Leander, hightail it out of this depressing little village to the Heathrow Hilton, then take the first plane home in the morning.

The leathered wheel's soft upon his hands, the night air's cool upon his cheek, and the murmuring pistons stir his mind—

> Upon ruminating the mystery
> In my staggering run of rotten luck
> And mulling my puzzling history
> Of shining dreams reduced to sullen muck

Yes, his dreams turned sour, and the puzzle of why seemed no conundrum at all—

> I conjured surly saboteurs corrupt
> Who schemed, alas, to scuttle every goal
> Invoking cunning curses to disrupt
> The stars that held my fortune in control.

Save for the darkling specter of his own face, the rearview mirror's filled with gloom—

> Then a plaintiff entered my reflection
> Whose inverted visage made me shiver
> For the eyeballs that coerced connection
> Condemned the countenance in my mirror.

Yes, the villain in the melodrama was always yourself, Chancey, and the moral's crystal clear—

> Yet if I'm creator of all my strife
> I can surely fashion a whole new life

That was the kicker. If you hadn't lost yourself you'd never have found yourself. And now, these upcoming gleaming metal-and-glass cat's eyes studded into the center of this lonely country road portend a heightened sense of intuition. Maybe these glowing eyes are hinting that the road is never hard when we clearly see the way. Cat's eyes, indeed, for they really do seem like living things as they hurtle to the bonnet, then disappear beneath it. An optical illusion, of course, for those glinting pupils are both lifeless and stationary. He's the one on the move. It's he who's rolling over them to a fresh life. Maybe even to that Great Lover and Bringer of Peace.

Now here's a real crossroad—and perhaps a solemn one, too. He eases up on the accelerator. There's possibly been an accident, for a car and a pickup completely block the mouth of the intersection. The brake and tires lament their failure to hold traction, but finally do, bringing him to a skewed halt on the side of the road. Three thick-set, shadowy figures—he can barely make them out—are kneeling with flashlights, inspecting a bad tire, apparently. He yanks on the hand brake, leaves the lights on full, the engine running, and cracks the door. Harsh roadside gravel crackles beneath his heel. The moon momentarily appears, then, as he steps toward them, is reclaimed. "Anything I can do to help?" Searing beams from three powerful flashlights blind him. *Fidelity.* Three pairs of boots stride into his space. *Is a virtue.* A whiskey breath's upon his face. *Peculiar to those . . .*

"Not at all, mate!" The voice's rough. *About to be betrayed.* "In fact, *we* owe *you.*"

A flashing fist sears his solar plexus. He gasps and buckles. A knee crashes into his face. He tastes blood. The ground rises to meet him. He's gasping desperately for air. His nose is surely broken. A heavy boot crushes his kidneys, and another rips into his ribs. Are his cheek and temple fractured? Is that a club against the sky? It's something—and that something's crashing down into the knee of his good leg.

"And one for the road, to haste you on your way!"

Bootlaces tear into his groin. That feels bad. More like a deep, deep, sickening ache than a pain as such. Heavy footsteps rush to vehicles. Engines roar. Bilious fumes envelop him. The racing whine fades into the distance. Burning Rover headlights catch in the cat's-eyes and sear his broken frame. The moon emerges. His eyelids fall.

> *Jill and Chancey hang by their hands from the fuselage of a tiny single-engine plane passing over a sea of Manhattan lights. A 747 dips beneath them. The back wind will surely send them toppling to the Hudson below. He clutches her tightly. They'll be safe together. They jump, pull their parachute ripcords, and fall softly to Forty-second Street. Hand in hand, they enter a Broadway theater and take the limelight. A top hat falls from the rafters and lands rakishly on his head. The shoe flies from his clubfoot and becomes a silver-topped cane. The deformity's gone! He grabs the cane and twirls it. To the delight of the audience they dance a showstopping Fred Astaire and Ginger Rogers routine.*

His bone-dry tongue explores the wide, jagged gap in the front of his mouth. So what happened to the guardian angel? And what about that prognostician: *The eyes are reliable but not the mouth.* Trouble was, he became so focused on those cats eyes that the mouth of the intersection did him in. He twitches. If it weren't for the pain he might retch again. So, there really is a god. And Doc was right. That God's an almighty sadist. His head's a raw wound. A pool of blood's beneath his mouth . . . and might just be reflecting the darkest of moons . . . and a face. But that couldn't be her face, not in his own congealing hemoglobin—could it? In heaven so soon, girl? So send a message, a sign, a symbol—a courier would be nice. Stillness . . . silence. So, the reflection's just another illusion. He tilts his head. No—not wise at all. His good eye closes again.

> *He saunters up a silvery beach. Elan, in a white linen frock, and Grisham, in a pinstriped suit, are helping their baby twins, a boy and a girl, build sand castles. He catches her eye. "Whatever went wrong?" he asks. She squeezes Grisham's hand and smiles her winsomest smile. "In life we move from right to left," she says, "whereas in dreams we move from left to right."*

An urgent whine sounds in the distance. It's homing in on him, closer and closer it comes. And now there are vibrations beneath his throbbing temples, searing white lights invading his pupils, wheels rolling toward his burning eyes, the scent of rubber fusing with carbon monoxide in his nostrils, and heat from roaring engines. Flashing blue beams refract from a chromium hubcap, and doors are thrust open. "Over here! Over here!" exclaims a male voice.

It's followed by the urgent click of heels. He knows that sound—it's Jill. He sights her image in a hubcap. She stops in her tracks. "No—no!" she cries. She's spinning like a broken marionette in a mirror box. Her anguished voice sears the dark meadows. "What coward?" She gasps. "What fucking coward—did this?" She chokes. "To my husband?" She's on her knees, her perfume's comforting. "Oh, Chancey, Chancey, Chancey . . ." Her soft hands cradle his face . . . "Oh, Christ, Chancey—are you going to be okay?" He'd nod if he could. Instead he widens his eyes, questioningly. She understands. "I went to a retreat in Manchester, then got your message—about the funeral—this morning." She smiles through her tears. "Got your flowers and your poem from New York—all your guilty love-offerings." Her breath's warm. "The Hero and Leander said you'd not checked out. I said to tell you I'd drive down and meet you there for dinner." Her voice cracks. "But you didn't show, Chancey . . . Coldridge Manor said you left hours ago, said there might've been an accident . . ." She draws a deep, aching breath. "Is that what this is, Chancey—an accident?"

Her hot tears fall onto his cheeks. "Oh, Chancey, Chancey." Her voice's a whisper. "You've been a bastard, Chancey, a proper bastard. I gave you license, but you're a slower learner than I'd reckoned, a wayward kid . . . Don't think this sudden conversion of yours has won me over. Or that some divinely implanted nurturing instinct has you off the hook. I'm with you because I made a promise. I said for better or worse . . ." Her lips are soft on his cheek "Oh, shit, Chancey, and yes, maybe I love you, too— God knows I sometimes wish I didn't."

He reaches for her fingers. An agonizing stilettolike pang pierces his ribs, yet still he reaches, right through that paroxysm, to wrap her hand in his. Elan's given him Jill, has given him bliss if not, in these circumstances anyway, delight. God only knows how it all works . . . Okay, Mr. Deity, so you finally caught Chancey's attention. So the way is clear but the road is indeed hard—very droll. Hope it amuses you, God. Hope it makes everyone else happy, too. He holds on tightly, both to Jill's hand, and to the image of that sweetest and most luminous of troubled, trembling faces. Not to worry, God. The reconstructed Chandler Haste will never let this beautiful and utterly faithful princess ever slip from his life.

"Oh, Chancey, Chancey, Chancey . . ." Something in that voice of hers, something in that tone, something in the way she whispers his name, something in the gentleness of her lips, something in the tips of these healing fingers . . . something says . . . that if he can just, somehow, pick up the pieces . . . everything'll turn out okay.

Codicil

Concerning the Sonnets
of Elan Haverford

The William Hall Literary Agency
The Arches Resolution Way, Deptford, U.K.

25th April, 1993

Professor Brian Sutton-Smith, Ph.D.
University of Pennsylvania
3340 Walnut Street
Philadelphia, PA

Dear Professor Sutton-Smith:

You have been recommended as an eminent psychologist with impressive literary credentials, who might give an opinion on the value of some sonnets submitted to me by an unknown source.

The putative poet, Ms. Elan Haverford, who is reputed to have been a member of English upper classes, apparently resided in several British colonies, completing an undergraduate degree in literature in New Zealand, about which time it seems she also fell into an illicit liaison with a local married man significantly her senior.

Ultimately, if we accept the authenticity of the work, Ms. Haverford committed suicide in 1983, at age twenty-four, drowning herself in a pond in the south of England. The sonnets seem to trace the course of that tragic affair.

Virtually nothing is known of Ms. Haverford's lover except that his name may have been Chauncey or Haste, for the words "chance" and "haste"—sometimes one word, sometimes both—are woven into each poem.

Your insights as to the authenticity of the work, your critique of the sonnets themselves, and your professional opinion concerning the poet's psychological makeup would be much appreciated.

Very truly yours

William Hall

University of Pennsylvania
Professor Brian Sutton-Smith

11 May 1993

Mr. William Hall
The William Hall Literary Agency
The Arches Resolution Way
Deptford, United Kingdom

Dear Mr. Hall:

Many thanks for the commission. Let me immediately say that following careful consideration I accept the authenticity of the work. The sensibility in play seems innately that of a courtly English lass intent upon revealing authentic feelings and insights. The vulnerability suggests a youngest child, one of whose parents, probably the father, instilled a predilection for analysis.

Ms. Haverford's deep insecurities were doubtless exacerbated by removal from England and being rendered, effectively, an alien in an obscure British colony. That she confined her poetic output to Elizabethan sonnets suggests a neurotic longing for the past and an obsession to exert control over at least one aspect of her world, thereby to ameliorate her anxieties. That said, the lively libidinous undertones suggest that she projected the persona of a free spirit.

People who enter illicit relationships are, of course, seeking otherwise unattainable affection, and being precociously intelligent, Ms. Haverford likely needed a mature companion—hence the attraction of the seeming sophisticate, who then evolved into blend of lover and surrogate father, invoking the so-called Electra Complex. The danger inherent in that relationship likely also served to distract Ms. Haverford from her problems, as would a drug.

Overall, Ms. Haverford's sonnets reflect a psychological journey from innocence to sophistication, and from hope to despair. They are elegant and complex, modeled, doubtless, after those of William Shakespeare, but quintessentially feminine. Like her literary role model, Ms. Haverford possesses the knack of saying one thing while indicating many others. The layering of meaning is mostly intentional, but the lines often flow with an almost stream-of-consciousness ease, and she consequently communicates more than she realizes. Let me turn to specific sonnets.

1. Suitors

My suitor sounds a truly tempting tongue
And teases me with tantalizing lies.
I merely smile and let myself succumb,
Thus feigning innocence of subtleties.
But subtle ties will bind his heart to mine,
And truths untold will overpower my woes,
His chancing eyes for me alone will shine;
I'll have no need of otherworldly beaux.
He'll never flinch or leave me in disgrace,
Nor come to me without a tender show,
He'll always know he won by perspicace,
Seducing me with derring-dainty prose.
In love then, poets are constantly gracious,
Yet all their stratagems quite mendacious.

Overtly, the poet ironically observes that whereas her suitor believes himself a would-be seducer, in reality she is leading the chase. The subtext reveals darker and more complex intuitions. She has sensed the dangerous nature of her so-called suitor. She notes that his eyes suggest a potential for deceit, and that he will chance a lie to win whatever he wants. Line nine—*He'll never flinch or leave me in disgrace*— in fact indicates a masked fear of ultimate shame. The suitor, a man of apparent charm, also possesses strong linguistic skills, hence the references to his capacity to engage in *tender shows* and use *derring-dainty prose*. Her strong identification with him is revealed in her unwise dismissal of all other suitors, or *otherworldly beaux*. Again, however, Ms. Haverford recognizes the swain's potential for deceit, a quality that she unwisely chooses to emulate.

The sonnet itself neatly blends metonymy and alliteration, especially the sexually charged opening quatrain with its images

of a *truly tempting tongue* that *tantalizes* and *teases*. The use of language from a bygone era—*perspicace, mendacious*, et cetera—enhances
the suggestion of sexuality and deception. While this is a strong
opening sonnet, those that follow are perhaps more elegant and
complex.

2. Paramours

My paramour belongs in other places,
And trims his words to suit a distant peal,
And marks the dipping sun beyond my graces,
And flees from me as shadows prick his heel.
Imprisoned time flees fastest when I'm doting
Upon the vision of my love before my lips
Aboard a haunted craft so wanly floating
Upon a doldrummed sea of empty ships.
If he were mine, and mine alone forever,
Intensity of love might subtly waive,
So bind these blinding moments to me ever,
To shimmer from within a mirrored grave.
Superior then, I say, is lust in Haste
To sanctioned love and ever-lost embrace.

Superficially, the poet makes the case that gratified lust is
preferable to long-term commitment. It is better, she says, to
lust hastily than to take the risk that *intensity of love might subtly
waive*. A close reading, however, reveals that she in fact believes
the opposite. The feelings of shame foreshadowed in the first
sonnet are being realized. Now, the lover hides his true feelings
from her, circumscribes his words, and recoils from displays of
affection. The ninth line—*If he were mine and mine alone forever*—in
fact suggests the yearning to make precisely such a binding claim
upon the lover. The apprehension that this will never be the case
is presaged in line twelve—*To shimmer from within a mirrored grave*—
which reveals underlying depression along with perhaps
unconscious suicidal tendencies. The heroic couplet is, again, a
rationalization, which not even the poet herself believes.

As a poem, I find the sonnet wan and graceful, especially
the opening quatrain with its images of distant peals, dipping
suns, and shadows pricking the lover's heels, presumably as he

runs off to the third corner of the love triangle. Puns on the words *heel* and *prick* suggest the scoundrel nature of the lover, and his flight to the sexual attractions of another. The image of the *doldrummed sea* is reminiscent of the hopelessness inherent in Coleridge's tale of the Ancient Mariner.

3. Sanctuaries

The village I dwell in, Thinkingofyou,
Is a maddeningly melancholy town,
Where the clocks are locked in a strange snafu
And the forget-me-nots are hand-me-downs.
Clandestine lovers crave sweet rendezvous
But I chance the night streets, alas, in vain
For lanes are manias in Thinkingofyou
That sun-bolt beams are inept to unreign.
Folks never slumber in Thinkingofyou,
In the mornings we do not wake either,
We lie in a state we dare not adieu,
Valedictions merely fan our fever.
Thinkingofyou is the sweetest of jails
But I pray reprieve lest sanity fails.

This time the overt and covert messages are in harmony as the poet unfolds her neurotic obsession with the unattainable lover. The first quatrain reveals a so-called *maddening melancholy* or depression. The allusion to *forget-me-nots* and *hand-me-downs* indicates abject humiliation and shame. The second quatrain describes aching longings and desperate searches. These yearnings may have been transferred to other inappropriate lovers, perhaps even strangers she has chanced upon in the course of solitary nocturnal sojourns. The seventh line—*lanes are manias in Thinkingofyou*—might even seem to acknowledge dementia. The entire third stanza suggests that the poet has in fact been institutionalized and is receiving treatment for a fever of the mind. The final line is clearly a prophetic cry for help.

This poem successfully leads the reader on a tour through a surreal village of secret aches and desires. The notion of such longings as a village is original; the images of stopped clocks, hand-me-down affections, moonlit lanes, and sunbolt beams that cannot break the spell of dementia are haunting. The eleventh line—*We lie in a state we dare not adieu*—invites at least three interpretations: sickness, deceit, and sepulture. Once again, the poet selects apt words from an earlier era. The tone is consistent, the quatrains seamless, and the overall effect indelible and surreal.

4. Paradoxes

I never lamented nor even sighed
For you; I never whined, whimpered or wailed;
No tear was shed, no incipient tide
Of melancholy brine was ever bailed.
So tender no nauseous, giddy good-byes,
Bear no mawkish sentiment on your sleeve,
Feign no fervor in those fine feckless eyes,
Neither delay, nor distrust, nor reconceive.
Run from me, chancelessly, hastily, leave,
Spring from me, speedily, ever so quick,
Swiftly, remorselessly, end this upheave,
Flee from me, fly from me, smoothly and slick.
But as you retreat down the trail of time,
Promise you'll ever and always be mine.

This fourth sonnet is an ironic lie rather than merely a paradox—yet the poet's assertions of equability upon the breakup of the relationship are not intended to be credible. Indeed, the heroic couplet clarifies Ms. Haverford's yearning for the chance to command a permanent place in the lover's heart. More intriguing are the veiled but deep ambivalences toward the unattainable lover. She has apparently seen through his deceitful mask—*feign no fervor in those fine feckless eyes*—and tellingly characterizes his unuttered apologies, remonstrances and farewells as *nauseous, giddy,* and *mawkish.* The phrase *smoothly and slick* carries overtones of sexuality and slyness. The poet has clearly been badly hurt, infinitely more so than she pretends, more so too, perhaps, than she realizes. She seems, nonetheless, finally prepared—perhaps even anxious—to introduce some realism into her life.

While this poem is a work of the mind rather than the heart—in fact, using the mind to salve and mask emotional wounds—it makes appropriate use of poetic devices and apt

348

images. The alliteration seems effortless, and the metonymy—
neither delay, nor distrust, nor reconceive—effective yet not contrived.
The image of tears as a *tide of melancholy brine* is affecting. In all,
this is an ingenious poem.

5. Valedictions

Consider the equation of my life:
The formula's abjectly all awry,
Fortune's fast falling, apprehension's rife,
What'ere I do I diabolify.
The trickster on the stage is vaulted time,
Who casts a trance of momentary daze,
So exit from his pointless pantomime
And gather in the next world all bouquets.
Roll the fickle dice and seize the chances,
Ride on to colliding parallel worlds,
Disdain all pain of darkling nuances,
Impasses implode as valor unfurls.
My spirit to another Globe has flown,
Yet rests within your palm to claim your own.

Having tragically regressed, the poet finally expounds a
philosophy of fateful delusion: to survive she must die. The first
quatrain rationalizes her depression. The second says that life is
meaningless, so go somewhere else. The third asserts boldness in
the face of death. In fact, however, these latter lines indicate
deep anxiety, guilt, and fear. The final decision to commit suicide
was apparently not made hastily. The heroic couplet rationalizes
the poet's ultimate self-delusion; she clings to this world, aching
in the moment of taking her own life to live on.

William Shakespeare's seventy-first sonnet has a lover
speaking from the grave, but Ms. Haverford's must be the only
suicide note to ever take this form. Again she favors apt but
arcane words—*abjectly, diabolify, vaulted, bouquets, fickle, unfurl*. Again
the allusions, while cerebral, catch the emotions, too. Time is
personified as a trickster who casts *a trance of momentary daze*. The
word *daze* is less a pun on *days*, than an allusion to earthly time
compressed to nothingness. The real trickster in this ultimate
sonnet, however, would seem to be the sonneteer herself—

especially in the heroic couplet—for, in the best Elizabethan tradition, in the moment of her death—which, by subtly capitalizing the word *Globe,* she indicates merely to be another theater— she lays a compelling claim to immortality.

I have enjoyed immersing myself in these poems, and reflecting upon the tale they tell. Each stands well on its own— perhaps most especially the third—but given their narrative nature it will doubtless be best to present them in their entirety. I gather you have enjoyed success with similar literary discoveries, which might tend to confirm my conclusion that Ms. Haverford's small body of work indicates a unique and quite brilliant talent, and that she may well have transmuted her reckless life and anguished, ambivalent emotions into poetic gold. With publication, there seems a real chance for her valiant spirit to live on. Given that the sonnet form is out of favor, however, finding the right vehicle will be both difficult and crucial. I wish you luck, and trust you will advise your progress.

Very truly yours

Brian Sutton-Smith

University of Pennsylvania